The Time Master

a novel
by Dmitry Bilik

Life is meant for good friends and great adventures! Happy reading.

S. Bilik

Interworld Network I

Magic Dome Books

The Time Master
Interworld Network Book #1
Copyright © Dmitry Bilik 2019
Cover Art © Vladimir Manyukhin 2019
English Translation Copyright ©
Elizabeth S. Yellen, Irene and Neil P. Woodhead 2019
Editors: Irene and Neil P. Woodhead
Published by Magic Dome Books, 2019
All Rights Reserved
ISBN: 978-80-7619-065-8

Table of Contents:

Chapter 1

MY LEAST FAVORITE things in the world were chicken liver, heartburn, and helping people. No, my parents hadn't spawned a heartless scumbag. It's just that I'd rather help someone of my own free will, and not because I'm being manipulated into doing it.

"Sergei, it won't take you long. He's probably gone to the foundation pit," my neighbor's words added boiling oil to the cup of my already-heated patience.

Lydia was only three years older than me, but somehow she made me feel like I was a kid and she was an adult graciously talking down to me. At twenty-eight, she had two kids, a docile husband and her own apartment albeit not in the best of neighborhoods. In contrast, besides nine pairs of oddly colored socks, I owned nothing in particular.

But that mischief maker known as fate had brought us together on the same floor of an apartment building after my father's grandmother died. I'd inherited her apartment, breaking free of the parental nest but falling directly into Lydia's well-organized web. Apparently, the universe was doing its best to maintain equilibrium.

You'd be hard pressed to call me a pushover. At no time would I have a girl order me around. I always made that much perfectly clear. Yet I'd somehow missed that opportunity with Lydia. I once helped her carry her stroller downstairs — you know, as a neighborly thing to do. Then one time when I went to the store, I picked up some yogurt while I was there. After that, there was no stopping her.

I should probably mention that Lydia was smart. She never crossed the line with her many errands, but she could occasionally knock you off balance, like today. Her quests came with the label "legendary" and forced you to work up a major sweat.

"The foundation pit? OK, I'll check if he's there," I said with a nod, reaching for my cigarettes.

Her window immediately banged shut. I couldn't blame her: she didn't want her newborn baby to catch a cold. I heaved a heavy sigh and threw on my hood.

"I see that our young man is helping out the needier families?" an old man in a ski cap inscribed "Sport" observed snidely from his perch on the bench by the entrance.

I smiled. I liked Mr. Petrov. The old fellow was a local institution. He was a professor who'd once taught the history of the Communist Party[1], but who'd failed to change his ideas in time. When the country had gone through perestroika, Mr. Petrov was left behind. Eventually he developed a taste for the demon drink and lost the battle for good. He was supported by his wife, a hardy, permanently angry woman for whom her hubby had become something like a suitcase that had lost its handle: it was hard to drag around, but it would still be a shame to discard it.

"Something like that," I replied. "Her husband is away overnight and her little Boris went for a walk. He was supposed to be home a half hour ago. Apparently, he's gone to the foundation pit. I'm on my way to the store anyway, so I volunteered to go see where he's hiding."

"The road to hell is paved with good intentions," Mr. Petrov said sagely.

"Oh, I know that. What are you doing hanging around here? You're gonna catch your death of cold."

"Waiting for a buddy. We've decided to hold a symposium[2], the two of us. Give me a cigarette, will you? It's not for me — my friend is the one who smokes. I always tell him it's bad for him, but he'll hear nothing of it."

I smirked and gave him a cigarette, then walked away from the entrance and lit up myself. I took a couple of drags and fell to thinking, listening to the crackling of cigarette paper and dry tobacco.

The foundation pit, huh?

It was right across the street from the local supermarket where I was heading. At one point, an ambitious development company had decided to build a modern, attractive multistory building in our backwater. It had bought out a bunch of private homes, surveyed the land and began to excavate a foundation pit. But something hadn't panned out on their end. More precisely, something literally flamed out: one night, their office downtown caught fire. Perhaps competitors were to blame, or a short-circuit, or maybe a combination of the two. So the company had vanished into oblivion, leaving behind nothing but a foundation pit.

You can guess who immediately took a liking to this local monument. It's true that every man is a former kid — but the kids from our neighborhood did everything they could in order to stay at that tender age forever. And any half-destroyed or half-built property in the vicinity seemed to help their cause.

Very well, I'd have to stop by the foundation pit on the way home from the store. Boris was a good kid, if somewhat mischievous. God forbid something happen to him.

The supermarket was on the first floor of a five-story building, well off the beaten path. Next to it was the ring road, followed by lane after lane of dilapidated log huts echoing with guard dogs' indistinct, sad barking and filling the air with the woody scent of heated bathhouses.

I had time to smoke two cigarettes before I reached the shop entrance. Inside, some kids were jostling each other by the vending machine.

"Hey, guys, have you seen Boris from number 8?"

One of the kids raised his head in obvious resentment. "Boris? Boris Korshunov?"

"Yes, Korshunov. His mom's looking for him."

"No, haven't seen him."

Shit. Now I'd need to cross that street and get myself over to the foundation pit. There was only one streetlight there, and it only illuminated part of the pit. At least I had a flashlight on my phone.

I wandered through the aisles tossing simple

food into my basket: some sausages, three bottles of beer, a packet of macaroni and a bottle of mayo. As I approached the register, I stopped by the stand holding the deodorant. I did need some; I was almost out. That took care of it.

It had gotten cold outside. I raised my hood and shifted the flimsy plastic grocery bag so it was more comfortable to hold, then set off for the edge of our world.

Before crossing the street heaving with heavy-duty traffic, I looked both ways a few times. This was a place where you needed to teach kids the rules of the road, under conditions that were, shall we say, reminiscent of war. I managed to get across without any mishaps and heaved a sigh.

The streetlight flickered hostilely in unison with my thoughts and blew out. Great.

I turned on the flashlight on my phone but predictably, I couldn't see more than five yards in front of me. I tried to peer through the dark for a while, but nothing useful came of that.

I swore and put away my useless phone. "Boris! Boris!"

The last thing I wanted to do was climb down into the pit on the slippery frozen ground. I was tempted to give the whole mission a miss and head off home. I mean, really, was I ultimately responsible for other people's brats? Just do a better job raising your kids and don't hassle your helpful neighbors.

It was warm and cozy at home right now. I could go home, cook some macaroni and sausage, turn on a TV show, and enjoy it all with a beer.

"I'm over here!"

Damn it. I'd planned it all out so nicely in my head. "Boris, where are you?"

As if! Now the kid was silent. I had a feeling that today I'd need to personally take care of his upbringing and give him a good taste of paternal tough love.

With a technique that would have put Cirque du Soleil to shame, I started to lower myself into the pit, scattering hard pieces of frozen clay with my feet. In one outstretched hand I held my lighter, and in the other, the bag with the clinking bottles. All I needed was a tightrope and an audience.

Which I apparently had. Someone was watching my clumsy descent — that became clear when I was halfway down. That's when I finally made out two figures on the bottom of the foundation pit: Boris and a guy I didn't know standing next to him.

Oh great. A Pedobear was the last thing I needed. Considering that at no time was I a fighter, and my adversary had more girth on his side, things could turn unpleasant.

"Hey, what's going on, man?" I shouted, trying not to betray my anxiety.

No answer. The kiddo was silent, too. They just stood there looking at each other without moving a muscle.

I kind of wanted someone to jump out and yell, "Surprise!" No such luck.

So I took a few steps forward. "Dude, don't make me do something I'll regret."

I stumbled but managed to stay on my feet. The bottles jangled plaintively, but even that didn't provoke a reaction.

I guess I was going to have to sort him out, after

all. I squeezed the lighter, placed the grocery bag on the ground, and strode toward the stranger who apparently enjoyed chatting up kids at night.

Only then did I notice the guy's odd clothing. He was wearing a long cloak devoid of any labels or designs. The hood was over his head.

Well, terrific. Good job, Sergei, now you're going to meet a cult follower. And the night had started off so well...

"Man, get away from the kid," I uttered an idle threat, my arm already drawn back to punch him.

My father had never taught me to fight — his thinking was that a smart man could always reach an agreement. But his best friend, Uncle Denis, disagreed. He'd made sure I threw a decent punch, and his opinions on the matter were far more straightforward. As in: if there's a fight in the air, go for it, and then afterward you can sort out who was right and wrong. That's not to say that I often made use of this maxim, but it was much more in line with my own philosophy.

Somehow, it looked like the man in the cloak must have had his own Uncle Denis because he turned sharply and thrust out his hand.

He didn't hit me but I could feel some sort of force coursing through his fingers. My body flew several yards like a defenseless rag doll. I landed on my back on my ill-fated grocery bag. Judging by the sound, the packet of macaroni had split. The bottles clanked but at least they didn't break. The stick of deodorant bumped up against my side.

I grunted. What was that? All I knew was that I was in pain. My spine wasn't the strongest part of my body: because of my line of work, I constantly needed to massage the small of my back so it wouldn't ache.

It took my angst-ridden brain a couple of seconds to realize that I'd gone flying even though no one had touched me.

It was unlikely that the approaching stranger was a Jedi. I didn't see a light saber. Well, maybe not yet. In any case, he was obviously a master of telekinesis.

I would have liked to know what the hell was going on, but I now acted on the most ancient instinct, putting everything else on the back burner.

I tried to use my free right arm to lean on the ground so I could get up. That didn't work: first I slipped over a bottle, then over the scattered macaroni, and then bumped up against the stick of deodorant.

Then I had an idea. I wouldn't say it was a bright one, but it wasn't bad. The stick of deodorant was in my right hand with its cap flown off; the lighter was in my left hand, and the approaching adversary was only a couple yards away.

I held the deodorant in front of me, catching a whiff of its rank scent (I'd missed the mark this time — I made a mental note to buy something else next time), and struck the lighter in front of it. I may not be a master of telekinesis, but we all have our fireballs.

For a moment, the place was flooded with light. I managed to discern the garbage-strewn foundation pit, Boris' frightened face, and the stranger's cloak which was being licked by the flames. Biting my lip and trying to ignore the pain, I hurled my improvised lifesavers aside and leaned my arms on the ground.

I stood up with the speed of a pregnant

Seychelles tortoise and threw myself at the assailant. He was still swatting his smoking hood, so he couldn't respond adequately. He swung his arms wildly and punched, attempting what's called a one-shot.

Never in my life had I been known for my heroic strength, but I managed to land a hook that was a work of art. I heard an unpleasant cracking sound as the stranger fell to the ground. Or maybe the opposite: first he fell, and then I heard a loud crack.

I stood for a few seconds with my fists raised, ready to punch some more if needed, but the Satanist guy lay there motionless showing no intention of standing up.

"Is he OK?" Boris spoke up.

I shrugged. "Probably."

I took my time going over to him, and carefully checked his pulse. I felt pretty arrogant as I did this because I'd breezed through all the health and safety training classes in school. I touched his wrist and then his neck. I thought I felt something, but it could have also been my own heartbeat.

I touched his head, and my fingers came away bloody.

Fantastic. I'd just smashed his head.

"Is he alive?" Boris asked.

"Yeah, yeah," I answered, starting to believe my own words less and less.

I straightened up, trying to get hold of myself. All right then, another one bites the dust. Now you've become a murderer, Sergei. Damn, how did that happen? Now what? Who was I supposed to call first? The police or an ambulance?

First of all, I still had to take Boris home.

"Let's go," I said. "Your mom's beside herself."

In a stupor I picked up the remains of the food I'd bought. To my surprise, not a single bottle of beer had broken. I tied up the bag — its handle had been torn off — and started to plod along. Boris trudged behind me, wheezing and scattering clumps of earth underneath him.

"Uncle Sergei!"

"What now?"

"Um, he's gone."

I turned around. Boris was right — there was no sign of the body. Either this mysterious telekinetic had passed himself off as a zombie and buried himself in the ground, or he'd turned on escape velocity and sped off.

Well, no body, no problem. Except that what happened next really frightened me.

You've killed a Player who was neutral to you.
-100 karma points. You gravitate to the Dark Side.

The main development branch has been determined: Time Master

You've gained a Divine Avatar: Savior.
You've gained the Insight ability.
You've gained the Light spell.

I looked at the message scrolling in front of my eyes. It's all right, I said to myself. You're just in shock. You're not going crazy. Just go home and have a beer. If it doesn't pass, you can go to the hospital tomorrow.

Boris tugged at my arm. "Uncle Sergei, you all right?"

"I'm OK. I just got a little dizzy. I hit my head when I fell. Let's go... Hey, watch out! You shouldn't be running across the road like that! Look both ways — left, then right."

I suddenly realized that I was acting exactly like my father. When they're young, all children probably think, "I'll be different when I grow up." But then it turns out that either deliberately or not, we all subconsciously copy our parents.

"Boris, how on earth did you end up in the foundation pit with that, er, stranger?"

"He said he was a wizard. A real one. He said he knew everything about me: where I lived, Mom and Dad's names, everything."

"What do you mean, everything?"

"Don't tell anyone."

"Mum's the word," I promised.

"Last spring we went rafting. We made the rafts ourselves: you know, foam plastic ones. And I crashed into the water. I got soaked. We lit a bonfire and stayed until all my clothes dried. Mom didn't even find out. That's it."

"What do you mean, 'that's it'?"

"No one besides the kids knew about it. Get it?"

"Ah, Boris. Has it occurred to you that maybe he just saw you guys? Or the other kids spread the word? Think about it. Figuring out where you live and your parents' names doesn't take a whole lot of intelligence, either. And that's why you went to the foundation pit with a strange man at night? Isn't that a stupid thing to do?"

"It was stupid," Boris admitted. "I got scared after. It's just that his... face was familiar. And he's a wizard. He did all sorts of tricks. Like spells, you know?"

"Did he... do anything to you?"

"No. He said we had to wait for something. So we stood there and waited. Then you came."

"What if I hadn't come? Don't ever go anywhere near strangers, especially when you're alone. And if you see him again, run home and call the poli — no, on second thoughts, call me. Is that clear?"

Boris nodded.

I patted him on the shoulder. There was a lot in this story that I didn't understand. What did this Satanist weirdo want to achieve? From what I understood, he hadn't laid a finger on Boris. And yet... Boris let slip that they were waiting for something. Maybe a full moon on Saturn? You couldn't be too sure with lunatics. Plenty of them around.

But what about "he did all sorts of tricks, like spells"? Did telekinesis count? On the other hand, what made me think that that's what it was? There are all sorts of schools of non-contact fighting. Maybe this misfit had practiced one of them. He must have distracted me somehow and I'd just flown a few steps without realizing what had hit me.

Of course this sounded crazy. But my brain was desperately trying to find a logical explanation for what had happened. It wasn't really succeeding.

"Boris, let's not say anything to your mom right now about this guy. OK?"

"Of course we won't," Boris agreed easily. "I might get into huge trouble. I'm already in trouble as it is."

He suddenly looked sad. We made the rest of

the trip across the courtyard in silence. The dimly lit streetlights illuminated the ice-covered asphalt. Harried people loaded with shopping bags were heading home from work. A prickly snow was dropping from the sky. Neither Mr. Petrov nor his symposium buddy were sitting on the bench. They had probably already drunk their fill and drifted away to their separate lairs. All the better — that meant there'd be fewer witnesses. Ugh, I was thinking like a criminal.

I tapped my key fob on the entry system and let Boris walk in before me. The door on the third floor was already open for us. Apparently, someone had been waiting and heard steps in the entrance.

"*Boris*? Where were you?"

Lydia was ready to give Zeus the Thunderbearer God a run for his money. From personal experience I knew that when your parents use this kind of voice, it's unlikely that it's out of respect for you. Instead, you can expect fury to be unleashed. Seeing Boris hunch his head in his shoulders, I felt that my theory was confirmed.

"Thank you so much, Sergei. Where did you find him, in the foundation pit?"

"Yes, he was messing around with the kids," I replied, fixing Boris with a stare. He blinked slowly — he understood.

"How many times have I told you not to go there? Your father will set you straight!"

The threat didn't work on either of us. Everyone knew that Lydia's husband was totally henpecked and that he adored his wife. Boris obviously resembled his mother in nature. His dad might admonish his son, but he wouldn't force him to kneel on dried peas as they'd done to kids in Victorian times, let alone larrup him with a steel-buckled Red Army belt.

"What's with your bag?" Lydia looked suspiciously at the plastic bundle in my hands.

"I slipped and fell. All right then, goodnight."

"Good night. Thanks again."

I opened the door, crept into my own lair and turned on the light. Was this night really ending after all? It felt like enough had happened to fill the next week.

I finally realized that I was sitting on the doormat, still fully clothed. No, I needed to get up, cook something to appease my growling stomach, and gather my thoughts.

I tossed the beer into the fridge and threw the dirty shopping bag into the sink with the sausages still in it. I just needed to rinse them off, and then they'd be fine to cook.

As for the macaroni, it was much worse for wear. Most of it had remained strewn on the bottom of the foundation pit. I looked in the cupboards and found half a pack of rice. That would do.

I hastily put a pot of water on the burner. Now I had to see what I looked like. Despite my fall, my pants were practically clean. My hands, however...

That was the strangest thing. My right palm was covered in dirt even though I remembered clearly the wetness of blood as I'd touched the man's open wound. You don't forget crap like that in a hurry. Talking about which, the bag also should still have had drops of blood on it. But I didn't see anything of the sort.

The evidence of my fall was there — but there was no blood from the dead man left anywhere on me.

What was it that those bizarre messages had said? Apparently, I'd killed some Player. Bullshit. Had I killed him, he wouldn't have disappeared. Rather, he would have lain there nice and quiet like Lenin in his tomb, waiting for the police to arrive. No, if anything, I must have hit my head a little as I fell, resulting in minor hallucinations. I should actually take a closer look at my own stupid head to see if it was injured.

I went into the bathroom, turned on the faucet and started to wash my numb frozen hands. The water stabbed my fingers. But it was no big deal; the most frightening events were behind me now. I just needed to calm down a little and gather my wits.

I smoothed my hair with my wet hands, straightened up and walked over to the tiny mirror above the washing machine.

I nearly screamed. A completely different person was looking back at me.

Chapter 2

AS BULGAKOV ALLEGEDLY wrote, "Fear your wishes, for they have a habit of coming true." I'd add that when they do come true, it's in a twisted way that you could never have fathomed out.

Like anyone with average looks, I'd always wanted to appear a little cuter than I actually was. Nature and my parents hadn't done an excellent job fulfilling their duties. Unlike my gorgeous sisters, I didn't have wild success with the opposite sex. You might call me average: narrow chin, long, straight nose, sharp cheekbones. A typical Hollywood-style villain nerd.

But the guy looking out at me from the mirror actually was quite cute. The jaw was more prominent. Against the backdrop of the jaw, the sculpted cheekbones looked completely natural. The ears were small, unlike the radio detectors I'd grown used to. The eyebrows were blond — actually, silvery — and the skin and hair were noticeably lighter. The only thing that hadn't changed was my brown eyes. That was the only way I knew that the reflection in the mirror was mine.

But there could be no mistake. The light-haired, sturdy guy in the mirror was me. I frowned, scratched my forehead, and adjusted my slightly wet hair. It looked like I was the one who needed first aid, not the stranger in the foundation pit. Calm, I had to stay calm.

I went back to the kitchen as if I'd been hit by a ten-ton truck. The water had begun to boil long ago, but instead of the rice I just threw in the sausages and opened a beer. What a business. No, not quite. *What a business.* And I couldn't really tell anyone about what had happened. I'd be shipped off to the loony bin immediately. To be honest, at this point even I wasn't completely sure that I hadn't gone crazy.

What if the things that happened in all those fantasy books were coming true? Had the apocalypse come, were most people turning into zombies and just a few into Players?

I turned on my small kitchen TV and flipped through the channels. *Vremya*, *Vesti*, *Novosti*, *Comedy Club*,[3] a soccer match — nothing out of the ordinary.

I even looked out the window, just to be sure. Occasional passersby, wrapped in thin jackets that were still too light for winter (it was all the fault of the late cold spell) were bustling home. No one was chasing or devouring anyone. Maybe I'd been hurled into some sort of parallel universe?

I gave my apartment a check. No, it didn't gel with my theory. The same crumbling Soviet-era furniture: the folding couch, Grandma's old table with my laptop on it, the Czech wall unit[4] — the last vestiges of a country that no longer existed. The chipped wooden windows, the wallpaper that had been put up when my grandfather was still alive, the curtains... They obviously didn't match the interior and who knows when they'd last been washed? Other than the computer and TVs — one in the tiny kitchen and the other in the bedroom-living room-only room — nothing had changed since my grandmother was around. I mean, I'm a self-confessed slob and my bachelor's lifestyle does nothing to counter that.

I went back to the kitchen to mull things over, especially because I'd already finished the first bottle of beer and the sausages were cooked. I poured some mayonnaise and ketchup onto a plate and created an absentminded meal to the accompaniment of a sports commentator lamenting about how a soccer striker had missed an empty goal from 10 yards away.

My head was heavy. I couldn't get myself to form even a few intelligent thoughts, all the more so because my body's efforts were focused on digesting the food. In fact, the beer was acting like a sedative. My eyes were sticking together and my nose was trying to get acquainted with the table. Sleep. I needed some sleep. There must be a reason why people say you should sleep on it.

THE ALARM ON MY PHONE had been screaming for nearly a minute before I turned it off. I pattered to the bathroom in the darkness. The things you dream!

I turned on the light and nearly yelped. That sturdy blond guy was still there. He gazed out of the mirror looking a little frightened, but he obviously hadn't gone anywhere.

So I guess it wasn't a dream. I put toothpaste on my toothbrush, sat down on the edge of the tub and started to think about how I'd continue to live.

When I'd nearly finished brushing the right side, I froze in disbelief. How had I never noticed these progress bars before? They hovered in my line of vision in pairs, two on top and two on the bottom, scaring me in the way that I imagined a 16-year-old girl felt when taking a pregnancy test. The two on the top were sort of gold and green, while the ones on the bottom were red and blue.

OK, let's think about this. It all had started yesterday when I'd punched that stranger. Someone in my head had called him a Player. As in, *Ready Player One*?

Maybe I'd somehow taken his place? In that case, everything would be simple. The red bar was health, the blue one was mana, the green one was vigor, but what about the gold one? Who the hell knew? The level of my sex appeal? Considering my new appearance, it was entirely plausible.

I finished brushing my teeth and climbed into the shower. The water was barely warm; the water main in our district had probably burst again, but I was used to it. Ever since I was a kid, I'd never been afraid of the cold.

After I'd dried off, I got dressed and sat down in the kitchen to contemplate. By all accounts, I needed to go to the hospital. To have a brain scan or whatever. Maybe it would simply turn out that there was a tumor in my head, and that tumor was trying to put me at odds with reality. On the other hand, if I skipped work right now, Bones definitely wouldn't be happy. My boss was thin and sinewy, and on top of that he was also grim — obviously you didn't need to look far to think of a nickname for him.

I thought for a bit, then dialed his number.

"Hello," said a disgruntled voice.

"Eh, sir — "

"Sergei, I don't want to hear it. Fyodor and Alexei are kicking back again. No matter what's happened, I'm not giving you the day off. The van of beer is coming today. And who's gonna supply the stores?"

"But — "

"But what, do you have a fever? Did you break your arm? No? Then you have no excuse. Do you expect me to run around the warehouse myself?"

With that he hung up.

As the saying goes, it wasn't in the cards. I guess I'd need to go out. The news that Fyodor and Alexei had gone on a bender was unwelcome, of course. Everyone would need to run around more. On the other hand, the work was such that it attracted a certain crowd. People with college degrees don't typically become warehouse loaders. I mean, normal people.

In my case, it was a conscious choice. I'd spent five years getting an economics degree just to go and work with my hands. You should have seen my father's face. In fact, that was the first and biggest reason I'd done it. They'd already bought me a military card[5] and got a cushy job lined up for me in a fancy company — the job which, according to them, had "a lot of potential". And I just left and got myself a menial job with a bunch of like-minded losers. That was the second reason.

Of course, it was hard to brag to my friends that

I had gotten a job as a loader all on my own without connections, but I really didn't care. When you talk about a grown-up, independent life, the emphasis is on the word "independent." Thirdly, it turned out that the job paid reasonably well for our rather large provincial city. I could afford to eat, drink, buy some clothing, and take my latest crush to the movies.

And to be honest, I didn't have any particular friends. I had a couple of acquaintances from university I could meet once every couple of months to grab a beer and hear about their sexual conquests or failures or commiserate about their workloads. They tactfully avoided bringing up my work.

It's clear that loader isn't a career you dream about when you're a kid. No one ever says, "If you do well in school, you'll be stacking pallets of beer for a living." I understood very well myself that with time I'd need to grow in some direction. But for the time being the question didn't concern me much. What did concern me right now was the fact that I needed to run like hell to get to work on time.

I looked in the fridge. Other than yesterday's sausages and a couple of eggs, it was blissfully empty. Although an omelet with a grade-B meat product isn't bad in itself, you shouldn't eat one every day. It had been drummed into me since childhood that breakfast was supposed to be balanced and contain the right amounts of protein, fat, and carbohydrates.

There was only one dish that fit these criteria, and it was sold close to my house. According to the clock on my wall, they'd already been open for a half hour. That meant that they'd had time to put out the meat and fry enough for a few portions.

The Time Master

In front of the door I felt as worried as Leonov[6] when he was about to step into outer space. The colored shapes before my eyes hadn't disappeared, and my hands were shockingly pale. Apparently, I was supposed to get used to the changing reality and my new body. More precisely, I felt it like the old one, but my eyes didn't lie. OK, I'd talk to Bones, anyway. Not for today maybe, but I'd ask for tomorrow off.

The stairway was silent; even Lydia didn't poke her head out at the sound of my slamming door. On the third floor my nose started to itch as usual from the smell of cat piss coming from the apartment that belonged to a self-sufficient and independent (read: lonely) woman of an indeterminate age who seemed to hate people just as much as she loved cats.

As I skipped the rest of the way, the green bar trembled a little and began creeping downward. I pressed the button on the entry system next to the front door and dashed out into the fresh, frosty air.

"You understand what it's about, my dear sir, don't you? They've b... br... bred a feeling of inferiority in our people. They've drilled it into us that if we want to be great we need to hate someone. We need to have a common enemy that supposedly prevents us, the powerful and awesome, from getting on with our lives... Ah, Sergei, greetings and salutations," Mr. Petrov waved to me.

I stopped for a moment and nodded. His friend — or to be more precise, his listener — was sitting next to him, struggling to stay awake. He had a neglected appearance: a battered sheepskin coat like they wore in the late 1970s, a drooping sweatsuit, and old shoes with scuffed and cracked leather toecaps.

The two were clearly conducting a sophisticated discussion and they'd already had quite a bit to drink. But there were two things that interested me.

First, what time did you have to wake up so you'd be so wasted by 10 a.m.? It's true what they say: desire is the best motivation. But the second thing was the most curious.

There was a text box floating over the Professor's head.

Alexander Petrov
Academic
???
Carpenter
???

This was amusing. It was just like in an advanced online game.

I looked at the man in the sheepskin coat.

???
???
Plumber
???

That was it. There was a little more information about the Professor. Maybe it was because I knew him and I was seeing the other man for the first time?

"Mr. Petrov, you never told me you used to be a carpenter," I said.

"A carpenter!" he waved my remark aside. "My father, God rest his soul, now he was a cabinet maker from God. I'm just a tinkerer. I can only fix things or just potter about."

I nodded, put my hood on, and skirted the building to go out to the street. The most dangerous thought of any madman crept into my head: what if I was normal? Meaning that maybe that guy from yesterday really gave me some sort of superpowers? Maybe it was even by chance, like bad diseases are typically transmitted? No, I wasn't going to start wearing my underpants on the outside. But what if I had also become some sort of Player, and I was now looking at the world through the concave mirror of convention?

The people who were hurrying to work only confirmed these wild ideas for me. They all had question marks floating above their heads. Some of them had only a few lines, while others had nearly ten or so. But they all had a line I could read: pastry chef, coin collector, leader, shoemaker, Tatar, teacher...

So this mysterious system was displaying not just professions, but also nationalities, certain personality traits, and hobbies.

With these thoughts I literally flew past the three buildings until the intersection where the bus stop was. The traffic was a little livelier here. But most important, that's where Uncle Zaur made the most delicious shawarma[7]in his rather filthy-looking snack joint.

"Hello," I said, nodding.

"Good morning," the old shop owner returned my greeting.

A notification appeared over his head:

Zaur
Azerbaijani

Very funny. As if I didn't know it. "One please, to go."

"You should come in. I'll give you some tea with it. You all eat on the go and then you have stomachache and blame it on my shawarma."

Uncle Zaur muttered all of this as he spread sauce on the lavash bread, then began throwing hot meat on it with quick, agile movements. All I knew about the owner of this hole was that he'd come to Russia a long time ago, married a Russian woman and ran his own small but formidable business. He also had two guys working for him making shawarma and shish kebab, but Uncle Zaur himself was always close by. Sometimes he'd drink with the regulars or thoughtfully smoke a cigarette, arms crossed over his small belly.

"Here you go, no change," I said, holding money out to him.

"Enjoy," he said, handing over a bag with the shawarma.

I wolfed down the hot meat in the lavash before I even got to the bus stop, just in time to helplessly watch my departing bus. Now I'd have to wait another ten minutes or so. I stepped to the side, lit a cigarette and took a drag.

If you thought about it, things weren't so bad — provided my head was in order. So if I were of no interest to shrinks, I needed to figure out how to take advantage of what had befallen me. As far as I could understand, the message said something about the Insight ability, the Light spell, and the Savior avatar. It wasn't yet clear how to activate the latter two. As I understood it, Insight was passive and worked all the time.

The Time Master

The bus, which arrived before too long, thwarted all my plans to enslave the world. I had to get on. As I paid the driver, I noticed that in addition to the occasional question mark, a Speeder sign was burning bright above him. I immediately plopped down on a seat and grabbed hold of the handle in front of the standing spot.

I was really starting to like this new ability of mine because after three intersections, with a wild screech of the brake pads, the bus stopped after nearly crashing into some ancient dude driving a cheap sedan. All the passengers lurched forward. Except me. The Speeder tried two more times to hasten my meeting with God, but he didn't succeed. When I got out by the building materials plant, I was a little shaken, but intact.

And there were advantages to the driver's speed. I thought I'd be cutting it close, but I ended up arriving twenty minutes early. So I took my time crossing the street and beelined for our base.

It was made up of five identical warehouses on one side and an office that abutted them on the other. Nothing to write home about — just a small private business owned by a Russified German who rarely made an appearance, usually just when he had to pick up his earnings or give us a major dressing-down. Incidentally, when it came to dressing-downs, he could go toe to toe with Bones. As I'd already mentioned, the workers were a diverse bunch: former convicts, a few drunks down on their luck, a couple of migrants, and the occasional student. And me.

Over the course of the day, trucks came up to the guardrail, filled out requisitions, and then, under the alert supervision of the shipping agents and Bones himself, we loaded their vehicles with goods for small stores. At a different time, usually in the evening, vans with water and beer arrived.

Today, too, a van was scheduled to come. Nothing major, just about 20 tons, but, as I understood it, two of our regular crew had gone on a bender.

"What's up?" Marat said, holding his hand out.

He'd already changed his clothes, laid a few pieces of cardboard on the guardrail in order not to freeze his rear end, and sat down on them. When he saw me, he smiled, flashing the two gold caps on his upper teeth, and extended his hand.

"Hi," I answered him with interest, shaking his hand and examining his stats.

Marat Gubaydullin, age 32
???
Thief
???

Marat had been a young offender when he'd first gone to jail, and he'd left it long after he'd been transferred to the adult division. When he'd finally got out at the ripe age of 23, he got married and even had a little kid. But my secret assistant still designated him a Thief.

I doubted it was referring to Marat's slippery past. He'd been in jail for robbery, not theft. That meant that he was stealing from the warehouse on the sly. Now I understood who Bones had in mind whenever he was swearing to bring everyone into the open.

"The van from Samara is coming today," I said.

"Yes, I heard. I'm sure we'll get a good drink out of it," Marat nodded, flashing the gold-lined "Hollywood smile" that he'd gotten in the slammer.

I nodded. During any delivery there were enough faulty goods, or, more accurately (air quotes) "faulty goods". Sometimes the drivers themselves left a couple of pallets at our mercy so they could finish the trip faster. On days like that the loaders went home tipsy and happy. Even Bones couldn't do anything about that.

"Uncle Alexei and Fyodor are already drunk. They won't be going out today."

Marat cringed. "Shit."

I understood him. We had no equipment. Our workload was measured utterly simply: in human — or if you approached the process with a sense of humor, donkey — power. Two extra pairs of hands unloading the van meant a lot to us — especially because, counting the two shirkers, there were only seven of us altogether.

"So we work overtime," he immediately shared his unhealthy optimism. "A little extra cash won't hurt."

"Right. I'm going to get changed."

As I left the closet, I ran into Bones. To me, despite the insulting nickname, our stock manager was the binding force here. He kept a firm hand on the loaders. If you took him away and put someone else in charge, it was unlikely that anyone here would actually work. You'd need to put together an entire staff again.

"Hi, Sergei," Bones shook my hand like a genius diagnostician trying to determine how sick I was by looking at me. "How are you feeling?"

"My ears are sort of ringing," I lied, scanning his

face.

In addition to his full name, the Insight spat out new information: Model Maker. That was interesting. What kind of models did Bones make in his spare time?

"You'll be sick tomorrow. But today, no way. By the way, the vehicle from store number 9 has arrived. Let's go load it. There's water, beer, energy drinks, and cookies. Marat, you hear?"

"Fifteen minutes until the shift starts," my hardnosed coworker called out lazily.

"I'll let you leave 15 minutes early."

"Yeah, that's if the van doesn't show up when we're closing," Marat retorted, but moved from his spot.

It's probably not worth bragging about, but I was very good at preparing shops' orders. When I first started out, I looked like a complete misfit. But it's like that in any field. You'd get the job, make people smile because you're new, but then you gradually become an expert. In the beginning, I was constantly scurrying around and getting in the way, but now it was a real pleasure to look at me. I didn't make a single extra movement.

"Carbonated water, six pallets, check," Bones counted aloud. "Beer, glass, two, check. Beer, plastic, three crates."

Marat and I danced around each other. He dove into the warehouse while I walked out with my load. Twenty bottles aren't very heavy when they're inserted with heavy cardboard and sealed thoroughly in new polyethylene.

Unfortunately, today we didn't have such a luxury. All the beer was from an old delivery that had been sitting in the warehouse for a long time. The cardboard had fallen apart, and then a radiator had leaked and the packaging had gotten wet. As a result, I had to carefully hold the beer from the bottom. No matter how experienced I thought I was, better safe than sorry.

I wasn't aware exactly at what point the case fell apart. Four bottles fell out through the hole in the bottom at the exact moment when my foot was already lifted onto the body of the truck.

I raised my head and saw Bones' angry face. He opened his mouth and...

Marat and I danced around each other. I couldn't shake off the feeling of déjà vu. This had already happened, just now. I had exited the warehouse and the case of beer had fallen apart in my hands.

More precisely, I was now exiting the warehouse and...

By reflex I shifted the case in my hands, taking a better grip. The glass clinked mournfully.

"Be more careful, Sergei."

"The case has no bottom, sir. We should tape it up."

"Go ahead. Marat, one more case of glass bottles. Then we'll move on to the cookies."

Holding the tape, I crouched down, staring with acute fascination at the intact case of beer.

First of all, now I knew the purpose of that gold bar, which had now lost a third of its length. It was displaying the progress of that most important development branch.

    And secondly, I now had the ability to rewind time.

Chapter 3

IF YOU WANT to keep yourself from having destructive thoughts, you should lose yourself in hard physical labor. Just read the history of any totalitarian regime, and you can see that those governments recognized this simple truth. People under those regimes toiled hard, from morning to night, leaving them no time for any foolish ideas.

I was lucky enough to be able to deal with my mental issues that way. In my line of work, I had to focus on whatever I was carrying, without descending into contemplation. I worked on autopilot — my arms and legs knew exactly what they had to do.

There was no real lunch break. The damned van that was scheduled to come in the evening arrived at 2 p.m. To unload it, we made a human chain, with Marat as the anchor. He adeptly punctured a few 1.5-liter bottles with a rusty nail, flipped them so the beer wouldn't spill out, and set them off to the side. There you go, faulty goods!

By 6:30 p.m., we'd not only managed to finish our work, but had polished off most of the expropriated beer. I declined. My head was so muddled that drinking would be a terrible idea. In any case, beer had little to do with this grotesque beverage in plastic bottles. I preferred to hold off until the evening when I could drink a normal beer — a draft or at least something from a glass bottle.

Bones was a good guy who always kept his word. At 6:45 p.m. I shook Marat's hand and we went our separate ways. He lived nearby, which was probably the main reason he wanted this job. I headed to the bus stop.

A snowy sleet fell on my face. It was dark on the way from the warehouse to the street, but that was typical. I walked slowly so I wouldn't lose my footing. As I shuffled along, I tried to grasp at the thoughts swirling through my head like they were Chinese meditation balls I was trying to manipulate.

The main development branch was Time Master. Now I knew what that involved: rewinding time. That was what the gold bar showed. Apparently, I could rewind three times in a row, going back three or four seconds. I'd need to keep experimenting. The only question was how to do it.

I looked in front of me and gave myself a mental command to move through time. Predictably, nothing happened. The other time, it had been fear that had moved me. I'd had a scare and then I was propelled through time.

I shook my head. This was crazy. The whole incident in the foundation pit, and now the time travel. I touched my forehead. No fever. But this was definitely out of order.

I emerged into a small, illuminated open space

under a streetlight. Now I was within spitting distance of the bus stop. I stepped onto the path dusted with prickly snow and immediately slipped. It happened so suddenly that I didn't even have time to pull my hands out of my pockets. My vertebrae cracked...

I emerged into a small, illuminated open space under a streetlight. Now I was within spitting distance of the bus stop.

Stop!

I carefully skirted the snow-dusted icy patch.

The adrenaline was still racing through my veins. I had just time-traveled — again!

I mechanically took a few steps and looked at my watch.

I looked at my watch again. This time, the rewind ability went back exactly three seconds. The gold bar was only one-third full. But the most important question was, how was I able to do it? This time I had just willed it to happen. So why couldn't I do it before?

I reached the bus shelter and sat down on the bench. My heart was beating wildly; my skin was covered with goosebumps. They weren't from the cold, but from what I had just experienced.

I could now achieve whatever I wanted. What if, for example, I learned some boxing, landed a good hook, and became world champion? Why not? Suppose I knew where to punch my opponent, and I had three chances to duck and knock him out.

But what if he stood his ground? Hm, a punchfest didn't sound like a good option.

What if I were a soccer player? Yeah, that would be cool. On the field, Sergei Dementiev who can dodge any world-class defender with a single movement because he knows where the other guy is headed. But once again, I'd only be able to do that three times. And then what? Substitution, the bench, class demotion. My fantasies of having Cristiano Ronaldo's career ended with me in the second amateur league.

I could become a firefighter and save lives. But three seconds and three chances weren't that much. If only there were some way to extend the rewind or get more of this goodie!

Hold on… If I was indeed a Player, that made it perfectly feasible. There had to be some levels and experience you could collect. All I needed to do was find out how to do it.

I hailed the approaching bus, got on, and went to sit at the back. I caught myself thinking that the little text boxes over my fellow passengers' heads already seemed completely normal. That made sense — you always get used to good things quickly. I perused the passengers' descriptions. There was nothing interesting, except the guy by the front door turned out to be a Lothario.

I gazed out the window at the somber landscape of the dark winter evening. I knew every angle of every building, every bump on the road, and every turn by heart. I didn't even need to look through the mud-spattered glass. When you spend a few years traveling the same route to work, it's impossible not to memorize it. But today it was like everything around me had been transformed.

I didn't recognize the buildings lining the avenues. The stalls in one of the little markets looked old and shabby, and in some places signs had been changed. At the same time, the city was still recognizable by certain scattered fragments - like the stained-glass jigsaw puzzle I had to put together. That said, it appeared completely new to me.

I felt like I'd stepped through Alice's looking glass. Or like this was in fact two worlds merged together: one old and familiar, the other one new and open to discovery. For example, why would someone hang a sign in an incomprehensible language in the middle of the main street? I could swear it hadn't been there yesterday. And why were planes flying so low over the city? Or were they even planes?

I took out my headphones and put on some Rolling Stones, my all-time favs who'd wrongly been shoved aside by the fab four from Liverpool. Ironically, the shuffle mode landed on *Paint It Black*. It perfectly matched the reality unfolding outside the window.

On the other hand, things weren't quite so bleak. True, there was some sort of crap at work here. I didn't understand it and that frightened me. But as everyone knows, when one door closes another one opens. All I needed to do was force myself to see it.

I was about four minutes away from my street when I noticed him. He was an ordinary man, just one of many. But the text box above his head was brighter. I could spot it from thirty yards away. He looked around as though he sensed that he was being watched, and ducked into the closest bar.

"Hey! Please stop! I missed my stop! Please!"

The bus, which had just begun to pull away, braked sharply. Under the disapproving stares of the other passengers, I leaped out and pulled on my hood. I all but ran to the traffic light and waited for it to turn. If only my eyes weren't playing tricks on me...

"Excuse me, where's the stop to Friendship Street?" an ancient voice said behind me.

I looked to see who it belonged to. Just some old lady, wearing a threadbare fur jacket, felt boots and knitted mittens, and wrapped up in two shawls. And of course she had a trolley bag. These ladies can never find a handbag big enough.

"You need to go that way, ma'am. Friendship Street is over there," I pointed.

"But where's the bus stop?" she looked around.

"On the other side. Right in front of the traffic light. I'll take you there, if you wish."

"Oh, good boy, yes, please do."

She grabbed her cart and graciously offered me her arm.

Just then the light changed. As I shuffled across the street with the little old lady in tow among a swarm of passing pedestrians, I kept my eyes on the bar's door through which the man had entered. It looked like no one had come out. Excellent.

We reached the other side just in time when the "don't walk" signal had already started to blink warningly.

"Thank you, young man, thank you."

You've helped a commoner who is neutral to you.

The Time Master

+10 karma points. Current level: -90. You gravitate to the Dark Side.

I looked at the semitransparent notification that was scrolling fast in front of my eyes.

Eureka. So if I helped nine more old ladies cross the street, would I make it to zero?

"Ma'am, do you need to cross back to the other side?"

"Why would I need to do that?"

"Uh... so I can help you. To increase my karma."

"Look at him, he's completely off his face," she snapped, promptly turning into an indignant fury. "They get high on their drugs and then they hassle you. Get away from me right now!"

So much for her gratitude. I shrugged off my ten karma points and headed toward the bar.

What is it they say? Good deeds will never make you famous? Well, up yours! I just needed to think a little about what to do. Anyway, why was I trying so hard to get above zero? First I needed to find out what this "karma" thing was supposed to do.

I ended up in front of a locked steel door sporting a sign that read:

Tavern

That was all. Nothing indicating the business hours nor a colorful menu displaying Russian delicacies. They could have at least painted some appetizing pictures of borscht, meat dumplings, or aspic on the shop window. Otherwise, how would visitors know they could get a good meal here?

What an odd place. Hesitantly I pulled the door toward me.

I stepped into a small lobby. A glazed wooden partition separated it from the main room. Tavern was the last thing you'd call this place. "Restaurant" would be more accurate. And if you wanted to be even more accurate, it actually appeared to be an exclusive club.

The room was decked out in English-style arched leather armchairs, couches, small tables, and a bar in the middle with a television above it. But most important, all the patrons had the same illuminated text boxes over their heads.

Except the information that was displayed kind of put me on my guard. *Vivisectionist, Sorcerer, Wrathful, Mercenary, Guard, Swordsman, Artist_Chick, Runner, Armor-Clad Warrior, Coward, Archalus, Turncoat.*

My eyes paused on the Archalus because this creature looked exactly like the classic image of an angel: light, flowing clothing, long hair, two wings folded over each other. The other beings too would stand out in the crowd because not all of them were human, either.

"So you've decided to drop in on us, Korl?" a tall burly man asked, appearing out of nowhere on my left.

I jumped. The notification above his head said:

Teleporter

I nodded. "So I have."

"You know the rules."

It wasn't a question, but he was obviously expecting an answer. I'd need to improvise.

"Don't break the dishes and don't get into fights?" I offered.

"Something like that," he said with a smile. "Come on in."

The Teleporter dissipated as if the wind had blown him away, only to reappear behind a table on the other side of the partition.

Now I had no choice. If I left now, I'd look like an idiot. You never know, they might even catch up with me and teach me a lesson in manners.

I could rewind time, I suppose. Except that here, three seconds clearly wouldn't get me out of trouble.

To be honest, I'd never been afraid of being onstage, even though I'd never had the chance to perform before. But now, with some twenty-five pairs of eyes staring at me, I felt my palms and neck break out in a sweat. Thankfully, most of the eyes looking at me belonged to humans.

I noticed a stocky blond guy sitting at a far table. He had the same fair complexion as myself — or rather, as the stranger who had recently settled into my mirror. He nodded, obliging me to respond.

I stole over to an empty table by the entrance and sat down. The others soon stopped eyeing me openly; a few of them resumed their chatter. A Sorcerer bartender — if the information provided by my Insight was to be believed — scurried over to me.

"Greetings, Korl. Dust or cash?"

He handed me an open menu. I looked at it. Opposite each dish there was either a number 1 or a 3, and an unusual image of what looked like a small mound of sand.

"Cash," I answered.

The bartender waved the menu in the air. The indecipherable currency disappeared, replaced by familiar price lists. Now I could find my way around it. The prices suggested that this was a second-rate restaurant; I could actually bring a date here without going bankrupt.

"Can I have a couple of minutes? This is my first time here."

"Of course," he said with a nod and went back behind the bar.

Everything here was weird. Weren't there any waiters? Actually, judging by the half-empty tables, people didn't really eat here. It looked to be more of a drinking establishment. Anyway, it was irrelevant. I had more important things to contemplate.

Now I had a chance to take a closer look at the representatives of all the different races or species — whatever they were supposed to be. The guy nearest to me appeared to be human with pitch-black skin and yellow eyes. He had bizarre growths jutting out of his head which looked like a few meager strands of hair that were gathered together and covered with hairspray. They must have been some sort of outgrowth, like small, flexible horns. According to my Insight, this guy was very *Wrathful*.

The Archalus was sitting nearby. He was sipping a beer, shooting the breeze with an ordinary person — as much as the beings sitting here could be called ordinary. A bit farther away, a peculiar creature sat perfectly motionless: it had a human head and torso, but its limbs were clearly made of a dull metal I couldn't identify. *Armor-Clad Warrior.*

There was only one girl here: tall and slim, with

large, expressive eyes and short chestnut hair. She was cute, if you ask me. She gave me a quick glance and then stuck her nose back in the sketchbook, scribbling with a pencil. *Artist_Chick.*

All right, now I needed to act like everything around me was business as usual. I leafed through the menu. This place was anything but a humble tavern. If they had even half the dishes on the menu, they could safely claim a Michelin star.

Still, I wasn't about to experiment. I lifted my hand, beckoning the bartender. "I'd like the mutton dumplings and a pint of the Czech beer."

"One moment."

The bartender took the menu and went back behind the bar, and that's when I saw real magic. He made a mysterious flourish with his hands. A clump of light that looked like a crumpled piece of paper flitted from his fingers. It rocketed up, circled for a moment, then flew toward the kitchen.

The Sorcerer caught my surprised look and winked. All right.

This was obviously not a demonstration of telekinesis with contactless combat. This was what you read about in books. Yet the bartender had done all of this with such a bored and indifferent expression as if it was nothing out of the ordinary. Or maybe it was, for him at least.

I scratched the back of my neck and turned my eyes to the TV screen above the bar.

The news was on. But there was something different about it, too. National reports were interspersed with petty little stories from small-town studios I'd never even heard about. From what I could tell, no one had deliberately changed the channel.

...

Zoologists are sounding the alarm in Voronezh Province. The number of wolves has reached a critical level. The frequency of wolf attacks on people has surged. For retiree Ludmila Sokolova, an encounter with a wolf was nearly her last.

"It was so terrifying! I was heading home, I was almost there, and someone was puttering around next to the doghouse…"

...

The search for a missing eight-year-old girl has been going on for a day. Vicky Novoseltseva left for school yesterday morning. But she didn't make it....

Oh, boy, that was our city. I recognized the presenter. That was definitely our city. I craned my neck to try to see the details, but my view was blocked by the stocky blond guy who had nodded at me earlier.

"*Haisa*, brother," he said, offering me his hand.

"*Haisa*," I said, guessing that this was some kind of greeting.

"Have you been here long?"

"In town?"

He chuckled. "In this world."

"Yes... a long time."

"I've only been here a month," he said. "And I don't like it. It's too hot here, even now. It's snowing out, but there's no point."

Once again he looked at me steadily, evidently considering something, and then he spoke,

"My name's Traug. I'm here for at least three months. I got into trouble in Elysium so I decided to sit it out here. If you need any help, come find me. The second house to the right from the city Gatekeeper. Korls always stick together, even the half-bloods," he added after a short but meaningful pause.

He shook my hand again and left.

I set about trying to untangle all this information. He said that he hadn't been in this world long. And he came from someplace called Elysium. That was the first thing. And he and I were both Korls. That's what the guard at the door and the bartender had called me, too. Since he and I looked quite a bit alike, I figured it was some race.

But it was nonsense. Why Korls? I was a human. My parents were human, and so were my grandparents. Having said that... I couldn't vouch for anything now. As recently as yesterday, I would have never thought of investigating this sort of thing.

OK, I'd figure this out later.

Thirdly, he mentioned some Gatekeeper. Did he mean the one for the local soccer club? In which case his would be the second house from the stadium, right? Only there were no houses next to it. No, by saying "city Gatekeeper" he must have meant something else.

My thoughts faded so fast that I promptly forgot what I'd been thinking about, distracted by a fragrant plate of dumplings and a sweating glass of beer that had appeared out of nowhere in front of me.

No, there was no magic involved. I was just so lost in thought that I hadn't noticed the waitress. She was around fourteen, and she wore her hair in a bun. Most important, she was an ordinary person. She had a dull label over her head which informed me that in addition to whatever else she was supposed to be, she was also a *Musician*.

"Enjoy."

"Thank you."

Like any other Russian, I had a lot of preconceived notions about mutton dumplings. Slaughtering and cooking lamb is an art in itself, and I didn't have the knack for it. Most of us only ever taste this meat when it's cooked poorly and has a sharp, repugnant odor — and then they say that we're unable to appreciate it.

But these dumplings... they were so good that after the first one I was afraid that I'd just choke on gastric acid. Juicy and sprinkled with chopped spring onions, they simply melted in my mouth. I only paused my eating to swill it down with some beer — and then I nearly lost my mind again.

You should never, ever drink quality draft beer. Because after that it's impossible to swallow that foamy, rubbery beverage that passes for beer in this country. I had the impression that on the other side of the door stood Pilsen, the good old Czech city where authentic Czech brewers were making their fabled beer. There's no way ordinary brew could be as delectable as this.

I sat back from my empty plate feeling happy and sated. I finished the beer and took out my wallet. It turned out not to be so cheap — $6 for a portion of dumplings and $3.50 for the pint of their Czech ambrosia. What the hell, it was worth it. I didn't know if it was customary to leave a tip here, but I added one anyway and started for the door.

Still, the moment I'd polished off my dinner, I realized that I felt uncomfortable here. A bit like a farmer in ripped overalls who suddenly ends up at the White House. Every passing minute increased the risk of me being found out. So I did the only thing I could. I left money on the table and quietly exited. Fortunately, everyone, including the bartender, was fixated on the next gruesome story on TV.

I got outside and took a deep breath. The air was warm and pleasant, and even the snow falling on my face felt familiar. And it wasn't hot outside at all — this Traug guy had been talking a lot of BS.

I strode over to the intersection and searched for an old lady to help cross, but had no luck. I crossed the street empty-handed and went to the bus stop. By some sort of miracle, my bus showed up almost immediately. I plopped down in an empty seat, ignoring the messages above people's heads. I'd gotten sick and tired of it all in the last two days.

I must have dozed off because I very nearly missed my stop. I jumped out at the traffic light as the migrant driver swore at me in his own language. It was almost 9 p.m. already. All because of that foolish trip to the bar.

And what had I learned? Apparently, there were these creatures called Players. I wasn't the only pretty face around. If I were to believe Traug, there was also this other world called Elysium. And maybe there were also others like it. The existence of all those different races suggested that that there might also be lots of worlds. The Players had their own currency which they called dust. I doubted that it was the same dust that collected on my shelves. What else?

I was lost in thought when I got to the door of my building. There was no one sitting on the benches. That wasn't surprising — a snowstorm was brewing, gusts of wind blowing handfuls of prickly snow in my face.

I opened the security door and nearly knocked heads with the upstairs neighbors, a married couple.

"Hello," I said mechanically.

"Hello, Sergei," the woman said. "Nicky, why are you stopping? Let's go."

But both I and the fifty-year-old Uncle Nick had stopped dead in our tracks.

Because I was staring at yet another Player.

Chapter 4

ACCORDING TO LEO TOLSTOY, happy families are all alike while every unhappy family is unhappy in its own way. I totally disagreed with this. Just take a look at Lydia who ran her family with the heavy hand of a matriarch. She was both god and emperor for them; her husband gave in to all her whims, and still everyone seemed perfectly happy.

Or take my parents' relationship, where my father always had the last word. Even if it was sometimes incorrect, it was always ironclad and left no room for objection. And that, in my particular household, was normal. Somehow my parents had raised three kids, and the family didn't seem unhappy in any way.

At first glance, it didn't look like anyone had the upper hand in Uncle Nick and Aunt Nina's relationship. They were cordial and respectful toward each other. And as unthinkable as it was, they didn't suffer for it.

So there was no way that Count Tolstoy, who deflowered more than one village girl on his family estate and who near the end of his life ran off into the night, fleeing his own wife, was in a position to talk about family happiness. The guy was full of hot air, if you ask me.

My ruminations on the influence of literary genius on matrimonial stereotypes were interrupted by Uncle Nick's voice.

"You gonna stand like this for long?" he asked. "I don't have much time. I told my wife you needed help."

He set his toolbox down in the hall and took off his boots. I ushered him into the kitchen, where there was hot tea waiting, and observed him intently.

Uncle Nick looked just like he always did — in other words, he hadn't undergone a metamorphosis like I had. The only thing that gave him away as a Player was the brightly illuminated text box over his head.

???, Nick
Shadow
???
???
???
???
???
???

Judging by the number of question marks, he wasn't your ordinary Player. All the better for me. I wanted more information, didn't I? All right, let's begin.

"Nick isn't your real name, is it?" I asked.

"How — " he asked guardedly, but then nodded to himself. "Insight?"

"Yes."

"Tell me everything, from the beginning."

That actually suited me just fine. Right now I desperately needed someone who'd help break everything down for me. But if you're demanding that someone be honest with you, you should be prepared to pay by being honest with them too. This was even more true seeing as I had a good relationship with Uncle Nick — or at least, the Uncle Nick of the past, the one who was my upstairs neighbor and who worked as a lathe operator at the factory, or whatever he was supposed to be doing there.

Now I needed to figure out how I might get on with Nick the Player.

"I see. Well, that's more or less how he said it woul-" Uncle Nick broke off, as if he'd blurted something he shouldn't have. "I meant to say, how on earth did you end up in this mess?"

He wasn't actually demanding an answer; he just drummed his fingers on the table, looking around at my crudely decorated kitchen. For a moment I felt self-conscious on account of the soot-covered air vent and the grease-stained lace curtain on the window. I made a mental note to do a major clean the next time I had a day off. Probably...

"Anyway, listen. For now try to take everything I'm gonna say with a pinch of salt. Because to put it mildly, this sort of information is rather unusual for a Commoner like yourself."

My hackles went up. The Uncle Nick I knew from before used to be rather tongue-tied, but this one expressed himself like an educated person with at least one university behind him.

"Let's suppose that there are many worlds all around us," he said.

"How many?"

"Thousands. No one knows exactly how many. And it's unlikely that we'll ever find out. They seem to be strung on a long, intricately twisted thread; you might call it an interworld network. The worlds located closer to the middle of the thread are more numerous, and they're better developed, too. Each world has its own laws and unspoken rules. That's also logical. The only thing that connects them together is the presence of the Seekers, or the Players, as you called us."

"They are the only ones who can travel between worlds?"

"Exactly. The Gateway is closed to Commoners, that is, the ordinary people."

"The Gateway?"

"The path to the other worlds. It's the most common method of travel, and the simplest one. All you need to do is use the services of a Gatekeeper. The only restriction is, you can only travel between neighboring worlds."

"A Gatekeeper?" I exclaimed, remembering what my new friend Traug had said. "Is there a Gatekeeper in our city too?"

"Of course, as in any large settlement or strategically important place. He can help you travel to the other Gateways of either this world or the next one. It's just a question of cost. As you've already figured out, our currency is a dry magic substance otherwise known as Dust."

"But what if I don't want to use the Gatekeepers' services? Is there a way to travel to another world without their help?"

"Five hundred years ago I would have said absolutely not. But in the last couple of centuries there have been more and more rumors about Players who are using some sorts of *gaps* in the fabric of time and space. Don't ask me how, but as far as I can tell, there are fewer and fewer Gatekeepers. Maybe the day will come when there'll be no need for them at all."

"OK, tell me about the dust. What does it do?"

"The dust is used to make potions, elixirs, maps, spells, and weapons. To put it simply, it's in everything that's somehow connected to the Seekers. By the way, tomorrow morning we're going to the foundation pit to look for some."

"Uncle Nick..."

"Call me Hunter. That's the name the Seekers in this world and a couple of the neighboring ones know me by."

"OK, Hunter. What's the point of all of this? If there are Players, doesn't that mean that there's a Game? And every game has an object."

"What's the meaning of life?"

I shrugged in confusion.

"Everything that has a beginning has an end. But I can't tell you what all of this is for. Just like I can't explain the meaning of life. I spent many years roaming around the worlds searching for an answer to that question. I killed other Seekers; many a time I almost died myself. But I only found meaning in simple human happiness. I got married and stayed here."

"What exactly do you mean by 'many years'?"

"'Many' means many," Hunter said with a sarcastic chuckle. "A lot more than you can imagine."

"How old are you?"

"Let me put it this way: I've already lived a few dozen human lives. Maybe even hundreds. You know, in the past people used to die pretty young."

"Are you immortal?"

"Everyone is mortal. Especially the Seekers. A lot of people want to kill us, both Commoners and Players like ourselves. There are only a few worlds, including the Cesspit" — for some reason he motioned to my kitchen — "where you can feel safe, or relatively safe. But time doesn't have as much power over us as over other people. And Players don't get sick. Anyway, speaking of time" — Uncle Nick looked at his watch — "I'll come by in the morning, after my wife leaves for work. Be ready."

"Hunter," I caught up with him in the hall. "Apparently I'd gained some sort of Light spell. But how am I supposed to use it?"

"Light?" for some reason, the word made Uncle Nick laugh. "You need to calm down, close your eyes, and look inside yourself. Then you'll find out everything. One more thing: Players don't reveal their spells, abilities, and main development branches. Even to friends, if you ever have any. Because indiscretion can attract unwanted attention."

I shut the door behind him and scratched the back of my neck. Was he making fun of me? I'd told him everything just now without a second thought. Couldn't he have clued me in on some of the finer details beforehand?

I went into the living room and slumped onto my sagging couch. What did he mean by 'looking inside oneself'? Meditate? To be honest, I hardly had any experience with that. But there was no harm in trying. I doubted it would make things worse.

I inhaled and exhaled deeply and shut my eyes. Cars were driving by outside the window. A television was blaring on the other side of the wall. The third-floor neighbor's cat was soliciting a partner. How could I possibly engage in spiritual practices under these conditions? I chuckled to myself and already wanted to open my eyes when I suddenly realized that some unfamiliar outlines were taking shape in the darkness.

It was like flying through the universe. I was a tiny speck of dust surrounded by the boundless cosmos. My consciousness was whizzing at a speed that would have amazed all the scientists in this world, and then it returned to the point where it started.

By then, the cat downstairs had apparently switched to summoning Lucifer. Some political TV show continued to drone on beyond the wall.

But none of this mattered anymore. Because something that looked like a stat chart had appeared before my eyes:

Sergei Dementiev
Age: 25 Earth years
Human (15/16), Korl (1/16)
Race characteristics:
Heightened cold resistance
Heightened resistance to Water and Frost spells
Accelerated leveling of the Rhetoric branch.
Karma: -90. You gravitate to the Dark Side.
Strength: 20
Intellect: 15
Resilience: 20

Agility: 10
Stamina: 15
Rhetoric: 8
Speed: 12
Health: 30
Mana: 25
Vigor: 25
Charge: 30
Development branch: Time Master
Abilities: Insight
Spells: Light
Divine Avatar: Savior

But most important of all, I could click on all the information. By hovering over any component, I got an expanded view.

I started off with Resilience.

Affects the ability to withstand magic, and the use of spells from the Transformation, Destruction, Mysticism, Witchcraft, Illusion, and Regeneration schools.

Well then.

Light (Illusion school) is the creation of a small illuminated area. Use: on self. Cost: 10 mana points. Duration: 60 seconds.

Now things were starting to make sense. I understood that the gold bar showed the amount of charges used for rewinding time. I'd need to figure out the rest as I went along.

I opened my eyes and saw my old room in a new way. It's like when you returned to your old stomping grounds after a long absence. But I'd only been gone for a few seconds. Or...

No matter. Logically, I now had enough mana to cast spells. All I needed to do was try to figure out what kind of animal it was and what I could do with it.

An icon popped up on my right. I used my eyes to move it to the farthest edge and activated it.

Now. My arm stretched out like it had a mind of its own, palm facing front, and then it flashed like a 70-watt bulb even though my body temperature didn't change.

Your Illusion skill has increased to level 1.

The spell ended exactly one minute later. I stayed rooted to the spot, readjusting to the semidarkness. Whether a curse or a spell, this was a bomb, no doubt about it. I might use it to walk around dark backstreets shouting "Leave the Twilight![8]" to put the fear of God into local thugs. Or I could get a job at the local power station with a work schedule that was two minutes per hour.

But I still needed to check to see how fast mana was replenished. On the whole, things didn't turn out as awesome as I'd initially thought.

The only plus was that if I leveled up this spell, my overall level will grow too. I didn't know how many points I needed to go up. But I fully intended to try.

I activated Light again, but to no avail: the skill didn't increase. Mana was dangerously close to zero but at least now I knew what to aim for. OK, let's read a little more.

> *Divine Avatar: Savior*
> *Activation requires 1000+ karma points.*

Holy crap! With my -90 I'd better shut up and forget all about it. I really should post an ad on a bidding website for transporting old ladies across busy thoroughfares. Or start thinking about other ways to get above zero. I had a feeling that incentives would be given for any good deed, big or small. I just needed to understand what "big" meant in the context of the Game. What kind of a goody-two-shoes did you need to be to make 1000 points?

I spent the rest of the evening perusing my inner manuals, or whatever this System or Game had issued me. No idea what the actual name of their guide was. While I was at it, I saved money on electricity bill by using Light. I brought the Illusions skill up to level 4, and feeling as satisfied as a bull leaving the proverbial china shop, I finally went to bed.

I had a funny feeling that I was on the right path.

* * *

Sometimes you wake up for no apparent reason a few seconds before your alarm goes off. That's what happened to me today, but it was because of the knocking at the door.

I unstuck my eyes and looked around the familiar room even though I didn't completely understand what had jolted me awake. It was only when I heard the sound of knuckles rapping on the door that I jumped to my feet.

It was 8 a.m.. Even when I had to go to work, I usually didn't wake up until half an hour before I had to leave. But I'd already figured out who it could be.

My gut feeling was correct. Uncle Nick a.k.a. Hunter was standing in the doorway, clean-shaven and full of energy, as though to taunt me. He hadn't come empty-handed, either.

"Are you going to let me in or are we just going to stand here?"

"No, of course not. Please come in."

I dashed into my room to pull on some jeans and a T-shirt. When I came out, Hunter was sitting in the kitchen. The tea kettle was already heating on the stove. A sheathed knife was lying on the table. Next to it was a folding pocket mirror, the kind women walk around with to use when they put on their warpaint.

"Are you a righty?" Uncle Nick asked.

"Yes."

As though conjured up by a magician, a few thin leather straps materialized in Hunter's hands. He threw them over my left shoulder, tightened them, and then fastened the sheath to them handle down.

"Draw it."

I obeyed. The knife was large and heavy, and the blade was nearly ten inches long. It exuded a certain invisible force.

Flesh cleaver
Moon steel
Enchanted to cause harm to physical beings
Restriction: Players only

But where was the information on damage, weight, and every nick on the blade, like in every other RPG? What a mess.

"I recommend that you wear it just like this. Do you know how to use it?"

"Only to chop up French fries," I joked. When I noticed the sober look on Hunter's face, I added, "No, I don't."

"Then don't draw it unless you need to. But hold on to it. A Player without a weapon is like a naked man in a women's bathhouse. He's out of his element, if you know what I mean."

"And what if subway security stop me? Or I run into a police check on the street? How am I gonna explain this?"

"You won't get stopped. The weapon is enchanted. Only Players can see it. It's inaccessible to Commoners. Even if someone frisks you, they won't find anything. All they'll see is a skinny young man. That's why you also need a mirror."

"I have one. It's in the bathroom."

"That's a different kind. This one is old: it's a *true mirror* made of a silver alloy. Look into it."

I obediently pressed a button, opening the miniature mirror. And, as they would have said a hundred years ago, I was rooted to the spot. I was once again looking at the person I'd seen in the mirror my entire life, the one who'd vanished the day before yesterday: Sergei Dementiev, a scrawny but good-natured guy.

It turned out that Hunter was right. I definitely couldn't see the knife strapped to my shoulder in the mirror. I even had to touch myself to be convinced. It was perplexing — I felt it, but I couldn't see it.

"The silver blocks abilities to some degree," Hunter explained, "so in mirrors like this one you can see yourself through commoners' eyes. You can look at things that Players are accustomed to from another perspective."

"Silver," I chuckled, "it's to ward off vampires, isn't it?"

"Silver doesn't kill vampires," Hunter replied in all seriousness. "Those are stupid fairy tales spread by filmmakers. In order to kill a vampire, you need to cut his head off first."

Did that mean there were still vampires around? Oh great. I might have to keep my eyes peeled walking through dark alleys. But there was something else altogether that I was curious about.

I looked at Hunter. "Why are you helping me?"

"Because I have no choice. Two Players in the same building, virtually next door to each other..." he averted his gaze and shook his head. "If you stupidly attract unwanted attention, they'll also notice me. So it's in both our interests to turn you into a typical, ordinary Player as quickly as possible. Someone who isn't surprised by a flying port or magician using sorcery. The only other option is to move house, but I wouldn't be able to explain that to my wife. And I don't think you want to move, either."

"And what if... you simply killed me?"

"That's against the rules of the Cesspit. I wouldn't say that I'm a rule follower deep down, but I'm not excessively bloodthirsty. In the past, I never killed Players just for the sake of my own comfort."

"What's this Cesspit?" I asked, remembering

that I'd heard that word somewhere before.

Hunter ignored my question. "Are you going to have breakfast or are we leaving?"

"I'll have a couple of sandwiches and then I'll be ready."

"I'll wait downstairs."

Ten minutes later, I'd finished my hygiene routine and eaten my poor excuse for breakfast (because my mother wouldn't consider two pieces of bread and butter a bona-fide meal). I dashed outside, worried that Hunter might have given up on me and left.

But no, he was standing there quibbling with the Professor about something. Not quibbling really: our homebred literati was busy showing off his intellect while the working-class-hero a.k.a. Hunter was unenthusiastically countering his highbrow arguments.

"The most important thing in life is the path of spiritual development," Mr. Petrov pontificated. "The attainment of the wholeness of your outlook and endeavors with the desires of the soul. Then and only then can you become Godlike not only in appearance but also in substance."

"Geez, what are you supposed to eat while you're attaining this wholeness? You'll die of hunger, man, and then it's all over."

This last sentence was so typical of Uncle Nick. It was as though Hunter had never existed and I'd dreamed everything. So! We seemed to have an actor here in bad need of an Oscar. No offense, DiCaprio, but we're taking away your statuette to give it to someone more worthy.

"Oh, geez, Sergei, are you going to the store? Let's go, man, I also need to go."

"Good day," the Professor tipped his knitted cap in response to my curt nod.

As soon as we were away from the entrance, the Hunter that I knew promptly returned. I didn't even have a chance to pinpoint when the metamorphosis happened.

"The funniest thing is that that commoner couldn't be more correct," he said. "In just two sentences he described the ideal path for a Player."

"Become Godlike not in appearance but in substance?" I chuckled.

He didn't reply.

"Wait a sec," I said. "Does that mean that Players can become Gods?"

"They are the only ones who can," he answered sharply, "and may you have the good fortune of never crossing their paths. But you've already acquired a divine gadget."

"What's that?"

"Your Divine Avatar. It's a unique image. Each particular Avatar can only belong to a single Seeker. It's a bit like your development branch in that it can also be leveled up. But that's not quite the right way to put it. It's more accurate to say that it will allow you to develop and might even endow you with stronger abilities. I confess that I don't know if there's a limit to those abilities. By the way, your Avatar already showed up in the Cesspit once, albeit a long time ago — like 2,000 years ago. The Player was named Yahweh, but after he acquired his Divine Avatar, he changed his name to Joshua. The things he did! There was no stopping him."

I tried to submit all this information to my

subcortex as fast as I could. When Hunter stopped talking, I didn't open my mouth for a while, hoping to hear another revelation. When I finally realized he wasn't going to say anything else, I ventured another question.

"What's this Cesspit?"

"That's what this world is called. It's hidden at the very edge of the Path in the area free from wars because there's almost nothing valuable here. To the developed worlds, it's like the provinces. Or, as the Seekers named it, the Cesspit."

"That's not a very appealing name."

"But it describes it perfectly. Among the Seekers everything is much more straightforward. Except that in order to become one of them, one needs a colossal amount of luck... or misfortune."

"I don't get it."

"How do you think people become Seekers?"

"If I've understood everything correctly, you need to kill a Player."

"Correct. Most often, one Seeker kills another. That's not a rare occurrence."

"But why?"

"Well..." my simple question seemed to have floored him. "When you kill a Player, you can capture their spells, abilities, occasionally even their Avatar. You can change your development branch. There's also loot... and dust. Last but not least, in a real battle all the skills level up faster."

I regretted not bringing a tape recorder with me. No, I had no intention of going to the local branch of the FSB[9] looking like a city idiot to report a worldwide (or in our case interworld) conspiracy. I was just afraid of missing something important.

"So being a Player isn't very safe."

"That's putting it mildly. Now listen..."

We'd reached the street and were waiting patiently for the light so we could cross. Just to please, our usually godforsaken roundabout was now packed with rush-hour traffic. The sidewalk was crowded with visibly unhappy people sleepwalking to work.

"In many worlds, commoners hunt Seekers. Those are mere mortals who have somehow found out about us. But that's in places where people know about us and where there are no protective pillars — or just protectors, as we call them — to conceal us from their eyes. In Cesspit, it's not like that. But a few of us do get hit with bad luck" — here he looked at me — "and your case is unique in its own way. It's one thing if you hit a Seeker with a car. But in a fight, on equal terms — something like that is almost impossible. Think about that. I doubt that the blood of your ancestor had anything to do with it."

"Meaning?"

"Did you look at yourself in the mirror? You're a Korl. It's clear that you're a half blood. But Korl genes are much more powerful than human ones, and that shows in your appearance. When I saw you for the first time, I was on my guard. But it turned out that you were an ordinary commoner. Interracial relationships are quite normal in all worlds. One of your ancestors must have sinned with a being from another world."

"So one of my grandparents was a Player?"

"Oh, yes. When you get the chance, try to ask your parents if any of their direct relatives ever went missing. Players are forbidden to spend more than one terrestrial life in the same place. That's rule number one of the Guard of the Cesspit. So they fake their own deaths or just go missing."

"What's the ru — "

"Let's hurry," Hunter said, pulling me across the street by the arm. "Come on, show me where it was."

"Over there, I think. Probably. It was dark, you know."

We lowered ourselves to the bottom of the foundation pit. I started to wander past the scattered trash, strewing it with my feet. Looking for yesterday was a fascinating endeavor. Using the sound of the macaroni crackling under my shoes as a guide, I outlined the approximate area where the scuffle must have occurred. But what was the point? The snow had done a good job powdering everything, concealing any traces of blood.

"There's nothing here," I said.

"Over there," Hunter replied.

I looked where he was pointing. Nothing. Without waiting for my answer, he approached a tiny mound and began to dig it up with his fingers, showing no disgust.

Finally, he stopped and pulled out a very small leather bag. He shook off tiny clumps of frozen earth and snow, loosened the cord, sniffed, and nodded in satisfaction.

"Dust. Take it," he said, lobbing the unexpected loot at me.

I caught the purse, then mimicked what Hunter had just done. The dust had a distinctive smell I couldn't quite put my finger on, reminiscent of cinnamon, chocolate and vanilla. It smelled so good I didn't want to tear myself away.

"Make sure you don't start *sniffing* it," Hunter said. "Or shooting it up, God forbid. A junkie next door is the last thing I need."

I hurried to pull the tiny bag away from my nose, drew the strings and weighed the bag in my hand. "How strange. I know exactly how much dust there is in there. Sixty-eight grams."

"Nothing strange about that. It's your loot, your money, which is why you know how much there is," Hunter replied. "Make sure you hide it from prying eyes. There's not a lot here, but people have been robbed for ten grams even. Not here, of course. But money is money."

"So what do you think?"

"What can I say? Here we have a Seeker without weapons or magic scrolls, virtually naked, with nothing but a few specks of dust to his name. Killed by a commoner."

"Maybe he wasn't very strong?"

"He had the same development branch as you have now, but for some reason he didn't rewind time. If push had come to shove, he could have activated his Avatar, only he didn't. I won't even mention the spells that every Player has in spades. He could have killed you with ordinary Telekinesis if he'd just made a little more effort. And despite all that, he's dead and you're still with us. Does it suggest anything to you?"

"It does. That the world has gone crazy. But what difference is that to me? You need to work with what you have."

"Good point. OK, seeing as we're finished here," he looked around the floor of the foundation pit as if he wasn't just examining the snow-dusted trash, but rather trying to convince himself of something, "we need to go."

"Where to?"

"Just to do some shopping. We need to make you look at least a little like a real Seeker. Especially now that you have some dust."

Chapter 5

QUITE A FEW of us must at some point have wished they'd been born to different parents and had nothing to do with their current families whatsoever. For centuries, writers have been bringing up the issue of relationships between fathers and children, describing the parents' narrow-mindedness and the children's lack of empathy for their elders. In this respect, I was no exception.

My entire relationship with my dad rested on an interesting dynamic. I was constantly trying to prove that I could live without anyone else's help, while he was constantly trying to prove that his son was an overgrown dimwit who didn't understand basic things. The list of these things was rather typical. It goes without saying that neither of us wanted to give in to the other, so not surprisingly, this dynamic had distanced us from each other. He had no leverage over me, and since he was a natural autocrat, this drove him crazy. Over time, I came to understand that no matter what I accomplished in life, it would never live up to my father's expectations. So I just learned to live with it.

Nevertheless, we still saw each other occasionally. My mom liked to get the whole family together once a month or so. Under our parents' roof we played the role of happy, contented offspring. And that's how it would be until the next time.

The incoming message I'd just received from my Mom meant that once again the time to "gather the stones" had come.

"OK, Mom. Tonight at 6. I remembered. I can't talk. I'm on the bus.... I'm out doing errands. OK, bye."

As usual, Mom wanted to know everything that was going on in her son's life, preferably in online mode. Hunter appeared curious too, judging by his pricked-up ears.

"Is it far?" I asked him.

"No."

The exact location of the "local community," which was what Uncle Nick had called our destination, was still a mystery. Of course, I'd already pulled up the bus itinerary on my phone. We seem to be traveling either to the center of town or further on, to the old part of the city. The latter possibility seemed much more likely, because the town hall had just flashed by outside the window and Hunter didn't make a move.

As before, our busy million-strong city seemed different somehow. I'd say that it had aged. The century-old stone houses that once used to belong to rich merchants were now decorated with peculiar stuccowork depicting fantastical monsters. I could tell other half-blood commoners like myself in the crowd. Something clearly bigger than an ordinary bird shot across the sky overhead.

But the most amusing metamorphosis of all

were the shop signs. To give you some idea, there was an old, rain-beaten sign on a battered building, reading "Various Ingredients, directly from factory". My magic mirror just showed a standard removable sidewalk sign advertising a pharmacy. I had a funny feeling that the place traded in items that were somewhat more potent than aspirin.

Finally, Hunter stood up and headed for the door. We got off at the next stop. Just as I'd guessed, we'd come to the old part of the city. I could never remember the name of the street we were on. I didn't have any special veneration for dilapidated legacies — I'd much rather stroll through a shopping mall with my latest crush.

"Keep your eyes open," Hunter warned.

We walked for a while along the main street, then turned into a courtyard which seemed arrested in time. Ramshackle roofs gave us a disapproving look; an old, rusty motorbike squinted at us with a broken headlight. A one-eared alley cat stopped and gazed curiously after us. Time may have frozen here, but we had to keep walking.

We crossed courtyard after courtyard. That made no sense: at some point one of them had to lead to the street. But the low buildings suddenly parted, revealing a broad square that was swarming with Players. I felt lost at the sight of all the bright text boxes above their heads.

"The entry and this whole place are enchanted, just like all the communities in large cities. Your average commoner won't wander in here."

I looked around. Alchemy Shop; Swordsmith; Thrift Store; The Best Secondhand Items from

Purgator; Top Brands from the Lower Swamps; Kalinin Brothers War Trophies; Protection by Smith; Arsenal; and so on.

I looked at the reflection in the true mirror. Just a bunch of abandoned buildings with boarded-up windows. Lots of fun indeed.

"Hunter," a man with skin the color of a cooked carrot broke off from the scurrying crowd and stepped in front of us. He must have been bingeing on vitamin A. "I didn't think you'd show your face here. I guess you've completely lost your memory, huh?"

"I don't want to talk to you," Hunter said as he tried to edge past him.

"Well, I really want to talk to you. I've been looking for you. It's your fault my buddy was killed. Meanwhile, I'm forced to rot here and I can't go home."

"Don't you have enough dust to pay the Gatekeeper? Or are they only letting people with positive karma into Purgator and Elysium now?"

"Don't you dare mock me," a pistol materialized in the orange man's hands. If I wasn't mistaken, it was a Beretta. "You know very well what I mean. The moment I set foot there, I'm dead meat."

"Whatever. It's your call. Nothing to do with me."

The orange man waved the pistol. "You owe me 300 grams of dust for my inconvenience."

"I don't owe you anything. Get your ass back to Firoll, you idiot."

"Three hundred grams or..."

"Are you threatening me?"

Apparently, that word meant something here because a few people — or creatures, rather — immediately peeled off from the throng. Despite the difference in their age, build and hair color, they all looked like they could be brothers. It was probably because they were all dressed alike, in long robes and black masks that covered their faces.

"So you're threatening me, Eriol?" Hunter said. "You're threatening me in front of the Guards?"

He appeared surprised rather than concerned. His commanding voice grew louder; his gaze hardened. His inner calm and self-confidence — infallibility even — had a powerful effect on the orange-skinned man who nervously looked around and tried to smile, then holstered his gun.

"Just making conversation. Why would I do something stupid like that in the city? In public. I know the rules."

His words didn't seem to have appeased the Guards. The guys in the black masks kept approaching, their tunics rustling. One of them, who appeared to be their leader, addressed neither Hunter nor Eriol but me.

"Greetings, Player."

I nodded. "Hi."

"This is your first time visiting our community. May I ask you if you're from this world?"

"Yes, I am."

"How long have you been a Player?"

"Since the day before yesterday."

"In that case, you need to come visit the sachem so he can explain a few rules of conduct in this world."

I turned to Hunter. He nodded calmly as if he did nothing else but escorted newbies to see guys with funny nicknames.

I had no choice. I was willing to bet that these

guys too were wearing firearms under their robes.

To my surprise, the building they led me to wasn't the grandest one of all. Instead, they took me to a much more modest one that stood beyond a larger one. But the security detail posted at the door made it clear that this was the residence of some local bigwig. I could tell they weren't the local guards but some hired mercenaries: two guys built like brick shithouses dressed in camouflage fatigues, with some sort of compact assault rifles slung over their shoulders. They were both Players. The one on the right sported the moniker Bulldozer, while the one on the left was called Champion, whatever that was supposed to mean. The two looked like they meant business.

They sized me up so intently that I felt like they were strip-searching me. The taller one pointed at my knife and authoritatively reached his hand out. Maybe when you're at the airport you can play hard to get and have a bit of fun acting up in front of the customs agents, but I sensed that I'd better not fool around with these guys. So I handed over my knife without protest.

"You'll get it back when you leave."

I nodded. What else could I do? I wondered if I could use my time rewind ability to knock them down, then laughed at my own stupidity. Of course I couldn't. I shouldn't even bother trying.

It was rather dingy inside the house. The light hardly penetrated the murky splotches on the windows. The place smelled of dust with some perspiration mixed in.

I made out an expensive leather recliner that seemed out of place in the old, abandoned house. The man I had come to see was ensconced in the chair.

??? city sachem
???
???
???
Leader
???

"Hello," I said, trying to be polite.

"Hi." The sachem's face was lifeless and jaundiced. Was he ill or something? "So you're the new Player?"

Although I felt somewhat anxious — scared even, — I struggled to keep myself from blurting something sarcastic. You see, to put it mildly, I have a complicated personality. When I was in school, my big mouth often earned me a slap across the face. As they say, you can't teach an old dog new tricks. But in this case I really did restrain myself — it's usually a bad idea to try to be too witty when you meet someone new.

So I just nodded, using the opportunity to examine the *sachem* more closely. Oddly, his neck was a different color from his face. It was the same carrot color as Eriol, Hunter's enemy.

Damn! He was wearing a mask! But unlike the Guards' mask, his was made of gold.

"I'm guessing you have a lot of questions," the sachem said. "I'll answer some of them. Then, when you've heard everything I can tell you, you'll need to make a choice. You can either remain in the Cesspit and accept its rules or you'll have to leave and make your home in some other world of your choice."

I what? He had a cheek, really! I hadn't taken so much as my toothbrush with me, I hadn't even turned off the water supply at home, and he was about to extradite me? Where to? Most importantly, what for?

Still, there was nothing I could do; I wasn't the one making the rules here. Did he say 'questions'?

"How long has this Game existed?" I asked.

"For at least as long as the Universe. Some of the Gods claim that they came across the very first Gatekeepers. But there are people who think that's all bullshit. I think the Game came into being when man erected the first city. The Game created paths to new worlds and transformed and destroyed the old ones. It morphed on its own as it adapted to the Players' perceptions. Now it's in its current form."

"Can you tell me a little more about these Gods? I was told that some of them travel between worlds, like regular Players."

"We call them the Wandering Gods. They're dangerous and unpredictable. Ordinary Seekers who achieve the Absolute — the highest point of enlightenment — become Gods. A Player like that generally departs for one of the worlds forever. There he either lives as an ascetic recluse or he creates a cult around himself."

For some reason that made me think of my own Divine Avatar and the person it used to belong to two thousand years ago. A cold chill ran down my spine.

"Wandering Gods are Gods that haven't found themselves after the ascension," the sachem said. "An encounter with them doesn't bode well."

"How do you travel between worlds?"

"With help from the Gatekeepers. That's the most powerful and ancient Order, and its job is to transport Players. But there are specific rules. A

Seeker can only carry with him things that either he or other Seekers have created. Everything else scatters in transition like dust on a hot wind. A Gatekeeper can send you to any world, but your ability to access some of them is limited by your karma."

"What does that mean?"

"Elysium, the residence of the Archali, is accessible to Players who gravitate to the Light. It's the opposite with Firoll."

"But can't a Player use... what's it called... the *gap*?"

The sachem nodded. "Nothing is impossible for a strong Player who has gained particular knowledge and strength, and acquired certain artifacts. Still, I haven't heard any reliable accounts of any such feats. I don't want to talk about hypotheses. There are too many."

"Well then, what worlds can I get to from here?"

"It's not for nothing that Earth is called the Cesspit. We're off the beaten path, so the only place you can get to from here is the world where I come from, Purgator. To be honest, it's not a good place. There are no protective pillars there. The local commoners know about Seekers. But Purgator opens several more routes to Elysium, Firoll, Mekilos, and Atrain. Any of those worlds can take you further to your own home world, which is Noggle. Except for Atrain. I recommend that you avoid that one."

"My home wo... oh, you mean the place where the Korls live?"

"Exactly."

"OK, I think that's it. One last question: how is it that a Player might not leave anything but dust after he dies?"

"It just means that he only had dust on him."

"No, that doesn't make sense. He must have at least had clothes. I've seen them myself. But they weren't there when he died."

"It means that the clothes were only conjured up by a spell that must have dissipated after the conjurer died. The Player must have been a good wizard if he could conjure up warm protective clothing. Pure and simple."

"But why would he want to do that?"

"The only one who can answer that is the Player who did it. All right, I think I've answered enough questions. Now listen to what I'm about to tell you."

I wanted to protest that strictly speaking, I hadn't asked that many questions. Anyway, the way I looked at it, this was just a pleasant chat between a neophyte and a hard-nosed Player. We'd just been making small talk, nothing more. But I doubted that the sachem would listen to the objections of a common Seeker. So I bit my tongue and gave him my undivided attention.

"Every world has its own laws. These are rules that help maintain order. In some places they're strict and in others they're lenient. But one way or another, they're what holds everything together."

"Let me guess. You have rules for planet Earth, too."

"Yes. There are only three, and they're all connected. If you break one of them, that might make you break another one. So it's important to follow all of them. Are you ready to hear what they are?"

I gave a quick nod. The sachem certainly knew how to arouse interest. Also, three rules sounded like a no-brainer compared to the 100+ articles of Russia's Constitution. At least you could remember them.

"A Player may not stay any longer than one human life in the same country governed by commoners. Is that clear?"

I pondered on his words for a bit. What this gold-masked dude had just said seemed to make sense. Anyone who has been alive for more than 100 years is bound to attract attention. Even if his or her next-door neighbors failed to notice it, the Pension Fund certainly would — and that particular governmental structure was infinitely more lethal than any Player. So, all kidding aside, you needed to live quietly and inconspicuously, and when the time came, you just disappeared. You had to be on the go all the time, moving country... or world.

"I got it. What else?"

"A Player may not attack another Player within the boundaries of local settlements without an apparent reason. He also may not rob them or cause any other harm."

Is that why Eriol had just backpedaled? He couldn't attack Hunter here, otherwise he'd be declared an outlaw. Those burly dudes in robes and black masks were anything but lenient.

"So for example, if I kill a Player in a place where there are no people around, there won't be any claims against me?"

"That's right."

How interesting. I'd never been a nature lover, but now there was no way you'd catch me backpacking now. It looked like feral bears would be the least of my problems.

"It's important to understand that a Player can't feel safe anywhere, not even in a quiet, calm place like the Cesspit. It attracts a lot of strangers from other worlds who just don't bother following the local rules. So keep your eyes peeled. The Guards may be strong but they're not omnipotent."

Well, that sure put me at ease. In other words, I couldn't do anything at all just to make sure I stayed out of hot water. But even if I did, abiding by the laws wouldn't get me out of trouble.

I was suddenly a lot less interested in becoming a Player. When you're a human being, at least you know the lay of the land. True, you can get attacked or even mugged. But when someone does that to you, it's to take your valuables, not just because you exist.

"So what's the last rule?"

"It's simple, but at the same time it's the most complicated one. At least, it's the most complicated for a Player who has fallen in love with a mortal," he continued, building suspense and making me almost dance with impatience. "A Player may not reveal his true identity to a commoner."

Hm. Indeed, the rule was both simple and complicated. What could be easier: just keep your mouth shut, no big deal. If you want to talk, go find other Players. But what do you do in case of intermarriage, which, as I gathered, weren't that rare? It looked like Hunter managed it admirably. Whenever his wife was around, he promptly transformed into a tongue-tied factory worker.

And one of my ancestors must have also kept his or her mouth shut. But could I live a fake life alongside a person who would grow old and eventually die?

"Do you understand the rules?" the sachem asked.

"Totally."

"Then you need to make a choice right now: either accept the rules of the Cesspit or leave this world."

"One last question, just to be sure. Do these rules only apply in this country or everywhere else on Earth?"

The sachem hesitated. After a pause, he nodded. "The other sachems, my brothers, monitor order in the local settlements. They're the eyes. The antenors, the most virtuous of the sachems, keep watch over the vast branches of this world's many cities. They're the arms. The Kaheed, who is chosen from among the antenors, watches over the entire Cesspit. He's the head. Does that answer your question?"

"Plenty."

"Then make your choice."

"What the heck, I accept. Do I need to sign somewhere in blood or something?"

"Your word is enough."

Before he could finish speaking, a brilliant gold mist emanated from my lips. It floated to the sachem in his chair and was absorbed by his mask, illuminating it for a moment. Then once again everything was submerged in the soft gloom.

"You are now initiated as a Seeker of this world. If it's more convenient for you, in the language of the commoners, you are now a citizen of the Cesspit. No matter what happens in other worlds, you can always come back to this one. Provided. . ."

"Provided I don't break the laws of the Cesspit."

"Exactly." You're now a full-fledged Player. Dismissed."

A "full-fledged Player"! That didn't sound like something to be proud of. I sure wouldn't be bragging about it in decent company. But the sachem had spoken and I'd heard him. I bowed just in case and hurried outside, wiping away the sweat that had broken out on my face.

One of the guards stopped me outside. I tucked my head into my shoulders and was just about to rewind time when he handed me my knife. Whew. I'd forgotten all about it.

Other Players didn't seem to notice me. They ignored me entirely; a few eyed me with contempt. Well, so much the better. I didn't have to worry about fitting in.

This was just like the regular human world. No one gave a damn about anyone else.

I spotted Hunter next to Thrift Store. Showing no interest in the second-hand apparel, my accidental mentor was talking to a man who looked completely ordinary despite his unusual tattered clothes. The text box above him read Spy.

I caught a snippet of the conversation.

"The Seers are nervous," Spy said. "According to them, a Chorul died in the Cesspit the other day."

Hunter snorted. "You know very well that's impossible,"

Just as the spy was about to object, his eyes met mine. He froze open-mouthed.

Damn!

The Time Master

I darted behind a passing Player, nearly getting tangled up in the flaps of his cloak. I took a few steps and went to stand next to a transparent store window.

"...You know very well that's impossible."

"And you think I don't? But it wasn't just one Seer who said it. We all know there's always one or two who get their prophesies wrong. But not all of them at once!"

"Anything else?" Hunter asked.

"Eriol is going to try to kill you today."

"I know."

"Then I won't worry about you. Good-bye."

"See you soon," Hunter replied, then added in the same level voice, "Come here. You think I didn't notice you?"

I turned my head. Hunter was looking directly at me.

Well, all right then. I'm coming. But you'll never find out that I rewound time to get that information.

"Are you done?" Hunter asked.

"Yes. I took an oath saying that now I'd be a sacred guardian of the rules of the Cesspit."

"That's not a joke. The Guards don't like to fuck around."

"But as I understand it, that doesn't stop everyone."

"Not really."

"Hunter?" I said. "What's a Chorul?"

Hunter gave me a long look. I'd never seen him so serious before. Then he said under his breath, so

that no one but me could hear him,
"It's the guy you killed."

Chapter 6

ANY EXPERIENCE that forces you to leave your comfort zone is frightening — getting a job, moving, meeting new people. We tend to think that novelty doesn't lead to anything good. The way we've always done things works fine, so why change? But then later, after you overcome a difficult stage in life, the one that came before seems less terrible. It's just another chapter in your life story that shapes you.

The first time I walked into the store for Players, my heart started to race. I was sure that everyone was going to point at me, whisper, and unmask me as a newbie. But the only person who lifted his head was the man behind the counter. And he looked at Hunter, not at me. Hunter nodded back, gave me some parting words, and went outside. I was left completely alone to wander the aisles which were overflowing with all sorts of gear.

Players were enthusiastically bustling about among the clothing. Some of them would go over to the guy at the counter, show him things, bicker, and retreat. In short, it was a typical thrift store. The only difference was that it smelled of dust here — not normal dust, but the kind that reminded me of cinnamon.

Well, what did I expect? After all, the clothing was enchanted. I picked up a tag that was attached to an ordinary-looking linen shirt.

Loose Garment.
+1 to Hand-to-Hand Fighting
+10% to regeneration of Stamina.
Price: 17 grams

That wasn't even the most expensive item. Naturally, the selection here was pretty good, but the prices left something to be desired. Maybe it was because we were far from posh places like Moscow. After all, everyone knows that Versace clothing is much more expensive in a provincial boutique than in Italy.

But Hunter had said that we needed to clothe me. There had to be some rationale to this. So I began to scour the aisles, searching out the cheapest items. I threw clothes over my arm as I went along; later I'd choose the ones that would do the least damage to my wallet.

And the kind of clothes they sold here… I really didn't know whether to laugh or cry. They looked like they all came directly out of some Peasant Spring 1789 fashion show. Most of the duds were made of an unadorned natural fiber: linen, cotton, wool, even jute. All I had to do was hold the small magic mirror next to them, and voilà: they immediately turned into relatively stylish synthetic jackets, skinny jeans, and Nike shoes. Charming!

"Hey, watch it!" a high resonant voice jolted me from my reverie.

Shit. I'd fallen so deep in thought I crashed into a Player — not particularly hard, but still not quite the best way to start a friendship...

...I stopped dead in my tracks just in time. A thin guy with pale skin and sparse dark hair did the same. Question marks and a text box reading *Magus* hovered in the air above his head. We simultaneously charged to the right and then to the left.

Unexpectedly for me, the Player smiled. "I'll go there, you go here," he said. When he was almost past, he added, "You a newbie?"

"Yes," I said, turning away and forcing my way among the aisles.

"Jan," said the Player, sticking his hand out.

"Sergei."

"I guess we're from the same neck in the woods. I'm also from Noggle. I lived there my whole life."

The whole puzzle suddenly came together in my head. So that's why he was so friendly. Noggle was the world of the Korls. I was a Korl, even though there wasn't a lot of Korl blood in me. But my appearance spoke for itself. So he decided...

"I'm not from Noggle. I'm from here."

"Hahaha," Jan laughed. "The Game really does a number on us. You get it? I'm just like you, only the other way round."

The Players who were standing nearby started to look at us. Some of them were just curious, but others were staring in open disapproval. Those were the type of people who thought that libraries should be silent.

I lowered my voice. "To be honest, I don't completely understand."

"Look, I'm a human who lived all his life in Noggle. And you're a Korl who's lived all his life in the Cesspit. Funny, eh?"

I started to grasp it — really grasp it. It turned out that Jan was feeling the same shock as I was, but in his case it must have been extreme. You go through your life thinking you're tall, blond, attractive. You can't go past a mirror without flexing your muscles. But then — bam, it turns out that you're a human whippet. So things weren't yet so bad for me, after all.

"I used to wonder all the time why I was so afraid of the cold," Jan went on. "Just like my mother. Everyone mocked me, saying that I was a sub-Korl. But that's what I am. Can you imagine how strong the human blood is in me that I don't even look like one of my kinsmen?"

I nodded even though to be honest, I couldn't really imagine it.

"Six months ago a few Players had a bit of a scuffle not far from my home. And ta-da! I woke up like this. At first I used to get really upset, especially when I found out that I could be killed just because I was also a Player now. Then I heard about the Cesspit. So I told my people, who were commoners, that I was going on a trip. Then I just came here. You have no idea how awesome this place is compared to Noggle!"

"Oh really?"

"Well, yeah." Jan started counting on his fingers.

"There's central heating, sewage, cars, TV, Internet...

For some reason I started liking my supposed homeland less and less. It looked like they had no creature comforts there at all. And on top of that it was really really cold. Not the kind of place I'd love to explore.

"But the coolest thing you have here," Jan's voice dropped nearly to a whisper, "is pornography."

I snorted. "Oh yes. It took humanity a long time to evolve to that stage."

"No, seriously. Where I'm from you rarely see a woman's bare arm. And God forbid if the Possessors find out that you thought something shameful."

"Possessors?

"The upholders of the law and morality. But that's for the commoners, not the Players. Anyway, you must be sick and tired of listening to me already."

You could say that. Jan was obviously a motormouth, but any information I could get was an advantage. I needed to get the lay of the land — or in this case, lands.

"Are you stocking up?" Jan nodded at the clothes I was holding.

It was a rhetorical question, so I didn't answer. But Jan examined the clothing like he was in charge, letting out a snort every so often.

"The most important thing to understand here is that you can get garbage or a treasure for the same amount of money. It's a thrift store. You've chosen garbage. Don't be offended. Come with me for a second. I saw something over there."

Jan dragged me toward a pile of clothing on the other side of the shop. He rummaged about and pulled out a knitted sweater with no neck.

"Hold this."

Damaged clothing of Speed.
+5 to Athletics.
+20% to sensitivity to the Air spell.
Price: 8 grams

"What's this sensitivity thing? Will air mages be able to smoke me more easily?"

Jan waved my question away. "Give me a break. These days you can count the number of good wizards on one hand. You can't do better for 8 grams with such an awesome addition to Athletics. Hold these pants."

He held out a simple piece of jute fabric, the kind that is usually used to hold potatoes. But these so-called pants also sported bizarre incandescent runes.

Rascal's Trousers
+3 to Bargaining.
+1 to Persuasion.
Price: 14 grams

"Keep your commoner shoes for now. In any case, you won't be able to afford anything good here. If I take a quick trip to Moscow, I might bring something back for you."

"Thanks for your help," I said sincerely.

"You're welcome. I used to be a newbie once, too. Also, I like helping because you see how much we have in common. It's like you and I ended up on opposite sides of the mirror. A Korl in the land of humans and a human in the land of Korls. You couldn't make that up. Well, Sergei, if you need anything, just let me know."

"How will I find you? How many houses down from the Gatekeeper are you?"

"Only newcomers live here. If you need me, call. You know how to use a phone, don't you?"

Jan smiled, making it clear he was teasing me. He was right: I shouldn't have stooped to Neanderthal level. I pulled out my cell phone. There was no signal, but it basically worked fine. I put his number in my contacts.

"See you," Jan shook my hand and headed to the door.

"Are you buying anything, man?" the shop assistant asked me. Or he could be the shop owner, I couldn't really tell.

He emphasized the word "man" ever so slightly, apparently hinting at my Korl features. I grabbed the clothes chosen by my personal stylist and went over to him.

"These. But there's something wrong with the price. There's a mistake."

"Is there? No, everything's right."

"Pants can't cost 14 grams. Eleven is more like it."

"Pardon me?"

"I'm saying that you could give me a discount."

I need to confess that I couldn't bargain to save my life. I was a lousy haggler. I hated going to markets because the skill of the seasoned merchants with their frostbitten fingers and smoky voices was way superior to mine. And in the supermarkets, the only thing you could contest was a price tag that didn't correspond to the receipt. So I was pretty nervous right now. Considering my zero level, I had good reason to feel that way.

"OK, 13 grams of dust for the trousers," the vendor looked at me disagreeably.

Your Bargaining skill has increased to level 1.

Good. It might have had something to do with my race's talent for Rhetoric, but what difference did it make? The rule of thumb is that if something ain't broken, don't fix it.

"There's just one problem. The pants are kind of long. Is there a tailor around here who can hem them?"

The clerk snorted and suppressed a smile. "Newbie?"

"Yes."

"Go behind the screen, change, and you'll see for yourself."

I marched into the fitting room, if you could call it that: an old mirror next to the wall and a curtain on a semicircle-shaped rod. I changed into my newly purchased clothes and examined myself. I looked rather humble, but overall not too bad. The sweater wasn't a sack, and I wouldn't have to shorten the pants: in fact, they looked like they'd been fitted by a skillful tailor for a festival of medieval reenactors.

I took out my little mirror. My reflection was wearing a pair of jeans and a trendy pullover. Funny.

Once I got outside, I bumped right into Hunter. And I noticed something interesting: if before the other Players had hardly paid any attention to me, now they were looking at us with badly concealed curiosity. Evidently my neighbor was a figure of some weight here.

He looked me over, nodded in satisfaction, and motioned toward the way out. "How much did you spend?"

"A little over 20."

"Not bad. Not bad at all. I thought you'd squander at least half of what you had. Why didn't you buy any shoes?"

"There wasn't a very good selection and they were expensive," I parroted Jan.

Hunter raised a quizzical eyebrow but didn't say anything. Had I managed to surprise him? Just you wait. I was just getting warmed up.

"Now let's talk business," he said. "If you need money, you can take a mission at the Syndicate. Come on, I'll show you."

We walked around the thrift store, plunging deeper into the maze of intertwined little lanes. Hunter stopped by a two-story building. There were at least as many Players here as on the square: Archali, humans, a few of those orange-skinned creatures, and a couple of the dark beings I'd seen at Tavern. But there were no Korls in sight.

Hunter went inside. I followed him. There was nothing at all there that showed the least hint of style. The wooden furniture that had seen better days; a bar, a weapon rack at the far end of the room, and a staircase in the middle leading up. The room was dominated by a black bulletin board with sheets of paper tacked to it.

"There aren't a lot of missions right now; you

need to come in the morning," Hunter explained, pointing at the sheets of paper.

"Can I take a look?"

"Of course."

I went over to the board and started reading.

Werewolf
Mission from the Order of Guards
Charged with: killing two commoners
Sentence: death
Proof of completion: head
Location: Smolensk Region, near the village of Merlino
Reward: 250 grams

Talsian the Blood Mage
Mission from the Order of Guards
Charged with: killing 3 Players and 26 commoners
Sentence: death
Proof of completion: head
Location: unknown
Reward: 2 kg

Four-leaf clover
Mission from the Order of Alchemists
Required: collect 10 plants that are celebrated as the luck of the leprechauns.
Location: Northern Ireland
Reward: 500 grams

Volot
Mission from the Order of Diplomats

Charged with: behaving aggressively toward Players, causing Players slight bodily harm.

Sentence: persuasion to obedience

Location: Siberia, where the Nizhnaya Tunguska and Chiskova Rivers meet

Reward: 600 grams

Chorul

Mission from the Order of Seers

Required: locate the site of the Chorul's murder

Location: Russia

Reward: 300 grams

Devils

Mission from the Order of Guards

Charged with: behaving aggressively, attacking commoners

Sentence: death

Location: in the vicinity of the local automobile factory. No commute required.

Proof of completion: devils' ears

Reward: 10 grams

Feral House Goblin

Mission from the Order of Guards

Charged with: aggressive behavior, impairment of commoners' psychological state

Sentence: catch and bring to the branch office of the Order of Guards

Location: The Grand Grocery Market

Reward: 15 grams

"So! The Seers have already gotten on it, I see,"

Hunter said behind me.

"Who are they?"

"The order of psychics, to speak in human terms. They're empaths and clairvoyants, if you will. They knew the Chorul was killed because they sensed it. But they don't yet know where it happened; they only have suspicions. For now..."

I imagined going to these Seers and telling them about the location of the murdered Chorul. Three hundred grams would just fall out of nowhere. But that brought up another question: what would happen to me after that? I just hoped they wouldn't lock me up in some secret underground lab to experiment on me.

"Why are some pieces of paper dark and others white? I could barely read about that mage, Talsian. The parchment is practically brown."

"See for yourself," Hunter said, motioning to the wall.

At that moment, a Player walked over to it, looked at the ads and pulled one off.

Then something strange happened. The piece of paper divided in two. Now it was simultaneously in his hand and on the wall. The one in his hand lit up and disappeared, while the one on the wall darkened.

Now it all made sense. That way you could tell which missions were more popular.

"How come no one's taking the feral house goblin or those devils? The pieces of paper are almost pure white."

"What, to run around town like a headless chicken for 10 grams?" Hunter made a face. "It's not worth the while."

"In that case, can't you just collect a bunch of

papers? Then when you happen to be in the right place, you just..."

"You're not the only smart one here. You can't take on more than ten missions at once. All that's left on the board is garbage, the unpopular missions. If you come in the morning, you can raise up to 40 or 50 grams without leaving the city if you work hard enough. Without putting yourself in danger, mind you."

"Hunter, you old Cabiri dog, I haven't seen you in ages!" an Archalus exclaimed, heading toward us.

While Hunter was thus distracted, I hurried over to the wall and tore off the two missions that applied to our city. The sheets of paper flashed and disappeared, leaving two notifications in the air to my right which too faded almost straight away. One said, *Devils,* the other, *Feral House Goblin.*

Hunter turned around, so I had to pretend I was studying the messages on the board. He quickly wrapped up his conversation with the Archalus and came over to me. He was clearly about to ask a question, so I started talking first. It's common knowledge that a good offense is the best defense.

"How come that some of them order you to kill the offenders while others just tell you to catch them or talk some sense into them?"

"That's because the decision is influenced by the differences in their intelligence levels. For example, devils, they are just... devils. Pointless trying to reason with them. But a house goblin or a mountain giant are perfectly capable of communicating with sentient beings. In which case everything depends on you. You shouldn't think that the Guards are harsh. They do their best to be fair."

"OK. And if you kill an evil creature, does it improve your karma?"

"If you're completing a mission, no. In that case the whole burden is on whoever issues the missions. Have you finished looking around?"

"I think so."

"Let's go. You've seen the most important things. You'll have plenty of time to study this place. You've been told about the laws of the Cesspit. Now I'll tell you the unspoken rules. For now try not to initiate conversations. You don't know what might offend an Archalus or an Abbas. Don't give them any attitude. And again, don't joke around. Not everyone will understand. And above all, try not to annoy anyone."

"If I quietly hang myself somewhere in a back lane, would that annoy anyone?"

"That's exactly what I'm talking about. Don't be such a smartass. It's easy to provoke conflict. Some Seekers intentionally go for that."

"What a boring place."

Hunter ignored my statement. "How's your job, all right?"

"Fine. It's my shift tomorrow."

"What do you do?"

For the first time since this whole Game stuff had started, I felt embarrassed. On the one hand, there's no such thing as a bad career. Uncle Nick himself wasn't exactly elite. On the other hand, I wanted to make a good impression on him.

But, as they say, that wasn't on the cards.

"I'm a warehouse loader."

"What are your hours?"

"Ten to seven."

"You should quit."

"What, just like that?"

"If you don't, you won't have the time to level up. As a Player, even if you're an errand boy, you can earn much more. Or are you an ideological loader?"

"Ideological? Is that a joke?"

Not a muscle moved on Hunter's face. "Of course. You're not the only one who knows how to be funny. Many Players in the Cesspit have jobs if they live in one place for a long time, meaning that they're on the books somewhere. Just so as not to attract the commoners' attention."

"OK, I'll give it a think. By the way, I have a question. At the Tavern they asked me if I wanted to pay in dust or cash. Can you change one for the other? I'm having some cash problems at the moment."

Hunter nodded. "Of course."

We returned to the square and headed to a small, round kiosk, like the ones where you buy tickets for city events. There was a slate board hanging above it with currency exchange rates written on it. Holy crap. 1 gram cost a whopping $11.50.

"We'd like to exchange some dust for cash, please," Hunter said.

A tiny mechanical scale appeared behind the grilled window. I couldn't see the money changer's face. But seeing as Uncle Nick was standing next to me, I might take the risk.

I took out the small bag and poured out 10 grams of dust. After a momentary delay, I was paid cash. They even gave me the petty copper change, every penny of it.

"I need to go," Hunter said, looking around

rather than directly at me. "If you finish your business before midnight, come by. If not, I'll see you the day after tomorrow. Good luck," he shook my hand and headed out of the community.

Two figures immediately set off after him. One of them must have been Eriol, judging by his orange skin.

It happened so fast I didn't even have time to react. Should I be a good citizen and warn Hunter? Unfortunately, three seconds wouldn't be enough in this case. I'd only attract attention. I wasn't quite ready yet to risk my own hide for my neighbor.

I pulled out my phone to call him but I still couldn't get a signal. Dammit! I ran out into the alley after the Players, but there was no one there. I reached the exit and nearly shouted with joy: my cell had signal now, two bars out of three. Better than nothing.

I dialed Hunter. Either his phone was off or he was out of range. Bummer!

I felt like shit. All I could do was hope that Uncle Nick was the seasoned Player he appeared to be.

I glanced at my watch. It was almost 3 p.m.. I needed to dash home, take a quick shower, and bolt to my parents' house. If I was late, the consequences would be so dire that they'd make death seem like a mere misunderstanding.

Chapter 7

THE HARDEST THING for parents is to accept that their children are growing up. They need to take their decisions seriously, learn to live with the mistakes they make because of their lack of experience, and stop talking down to them, treating them like adults instead. There are parents who undergo this rite of passage when their child is 16, and others who go through it when the child is over 20. My mother, though, still saw me as she always had, as her little boy.

"Sergei, have you lost weight? You look pale."

Of course I'm pale! I'm a Korl, aren't I? I nearly blurted out.

I looked around the entryway. Judging by all the shoes, my sisters had already assembled. It made sense for Darya: she was only 17 and still lived at home. But Lily, who was perpetually late, had also arrived. That made things awkward.

But what was with those filthy army boots? I looked at Mom questioningly.

"Uncle Denis just got back from an expedition,"

she explained.

That was amazing news. Uncle Denis stood out among my father's tiresome friends, his presence illuminating the memory of my childhood. He would burst into our mundane life, bearing a heap of gifts or just interesting things from his expeditions, and then disappear again. Uncle Denis was a geologist and he was one of those rare people who loved his job.

I went into the living room with a huge smile on my face and froze.

One of those rare people? You sure could say that.

Uncle Denis was a Korl.

Just like my father.

And here I was wondering how two such different people could have become friends. It was all so simple. You could call it a sort of genetic attraction.

"Are you gonna stand like that all night?" a blond Korl with familiar eyes asked in my father's voice.

"He's practicing for the part of the wife of Lot," Uncle Denis joined in. "Hey, Sergei!"

I managed to unstick myself and went to shake his hand, glancing around at everyone else. Strangely, the Korl features weren't very pronounced in my sisters. No, of course I could see that they'd changed: their hair and eyes had become lighter, but not much. Mom was just as she'd always been.

"Sit down, Sergei," she said.

I plopped down at the table.

"Nice sweater," Lily said.

"Did you get it in a thrift store?" promptly butted in my youngest sister — a.k.a. our family's trolling queen.

She had no idea how right she was. I decided to change the subject. "Uncle Denis, when did you get back?"

"Today. I'm fresh off the boat — or plane, rather. You can see how lucky I got. Finally I might get some human food."

"It's a good thing you showed up," Darya said. "Otherwise we'd be stuck listening to the latest news about the economy and about how Sergei has disappointed our parents," she put an imaginary gun to her head and pretended to shoot herself.

I found it odd that my father didn't react. It must be true what they say about younger siblings getting all the love. If I said something like that, I'd definitely be scolded. But in Darya's case, my father was pretending not to notice.

"So, Sergei, are you still disappointing your father?" Uncle Denis asked with a wink.

"I stay up at night thinking about what else I can do to let him down," I said.

"You've already done everything you need to," my father retorted.

"Stop," my mother intervened. "Why don't you take some salad? Denis, it has beans in it, just the way you like."

"Oh, I missed my chance with you, Nadia. I should have never let this chump chase after you," Uncle Denis chuckled. "I fell asleep at the switch. But then Sergei would be disappointing me now."

"What with all your traveling, he might still have been my son," my father said coolly.

The rest of our supper proceeded relatively calmly. Uncle Denis entertained everyone, Mom and my sisters laughed loudly, and even Dad had a good-natured smile on his face. It was perfect. No chance of me being thrust back into the limelight.

"Sergei, let's go have a smoke."

We threw on our jackets and went out to the balcony. Uncle Denis smoked greedily, taking deep tugs on his cigarette. Incidentally, that's also how he lived. He hated to do things halfway.

"Sergei, can be we serious for a minute? What're you up to at the moment?"

"Oh, I can't just sum it up like that."

"Please understand that your father isn't bothered just for the sake of it. He has his quirks, and there are lots of things I disagree with him about. But you're almost thirty."

"I'm quitting my job tomorrow."

"Are you really? What do you think you're going to do?"

"Freelance," I lied.

"What kind of abomination is that?"

"Uncle Denis, don't pretend to be clueless. I know that you're smart."

"Smart is as smart does, Sergei. OK, I'm aware of what freelance is. Could you be more specific?"

"A courier company. I'll give it a go, then I might hire a couple of people to help me. Just don't tell anybody."

Your Lying skill has increased to level 1.

"You know me. Silent as the grave."

I didn't regret my lie at all. So yeah, I'd lied. It wasn't even really a lie — more like a half truth. I really was quitting my job, and it was true that I would be doing little errands that were a bit like courier jobs. And I especially couldn't tell a clueless commoner the whole truth.

A new notification flashed open before my eyes. It hung in the air briefly, then began to fade.

The Wandering House Goblin mission has been updated.
If you catch the house goblin within the next 24 hours, your reward will increase by 15 grams.
Explanations have been added.

OK, what were these explanations? I mentally opened the mission and found the note at the bottom:

To enter the place where the house goblin lives, simply tell the commoners you work for pest control. If they demand certification, show them the paper that contains the mission.

"Cat got your tongue, Sergei?"

"I was just busy thinking about my life."

"Oh, you can't do that on a sober head. Thinking goes much better with some vodka. Let's go unload."

"Sorry, Uncle Denis, I need to run."

"Why, whassup?"

"Well, you see... there's this girl..."

Lying was like skiing downhill. Once you start, it's hard to stop.

"You've traded your friends for chicks?" Uncle Denis asked in mock anger. "That's what you kids do. In my time, half the girls' dormitory went through me.

Hm, I seem to be rambling a bit."

"D'you think you could cover my back?"

"You'll owe me one. I'm gonna pay you a surprise visit one day. And then you'll have to drink with me. Vodka — no, brandy."

"Please spare my liver."

"Something that's already dead can't die! I heard that on a TV show."

"Uncle Denis!"

About a half hour later, pleading urgent business, I escaped from the parental nest. My father was on the verge of getting angry, but Uncle Denis distracted him by launching into reminiscences of the good old days.

I couldn't help it. I was all restless and jittery.

The store where the feral goblin was supposed to be hiding was all of three blocks from my parents' house. I'd Googled it beforehand. Completing this task first was definitely worth it for me, since it would give me a bonus of 15 grams of dust, or around $170. Not bad.

I lit up a cigarette and punched "pest control" into the search engine. Aha. Apparently, there were a lot of complex methods to eradicate rats and other rodents. So the commoners mistook a house goblin for a rat? Was he really so tiny? Whatever. Let's go check out this Tom Thumb.

When I was halfway there, I realized that my breathing had gone south. I got a metallic taste in my mouth. The green Vigor bar was at zero. The message the system was sending me couldn't have been clearer: a healthy lifestyle would do me a lot of good. Very well. There was no way I'd quit smoking, but at least I might keep on drinking. Joke.

As if to spite the Game, I pulled out a cigarette, took a couple of drags and coughed until my eyes watered. Bastard!

"Are you OK?" a high-pitched voice asked me.

"I've been better," I admitted.

"Can I help you get to the bus stop? There's a bench there."

"Please don't. Freezing solid on the snowy sidewalk is my demise of choice."

I lifted my head and looked at my good Samaritan. I saw a simple Russian face: a bit wide, amiable, but at the same time attractive. A snub nose, enormous eyes, and flushed cheeks.

Faces like this are rare in the large cities where the fashion requires yellow-tinted complexion and dark circles under the eyes. The cheap Chinese down jacket, plain clothing... and on top of that, she was hardly wearing any makeup. Where had this oddity come from? The nuttiest thing of all was that the word "Altruistic" was floating above her head among all the question marks.

"You do realize that approaching strange men at night isn't safe, don't you?"

"But aren't you in a bad way?"

"Maybe I just randomly lure altruists like you, and then do vile, nefarious things to them?"

The unwitting Samaritan's cheeks grew even redder. No, I definitely liked her.

"But today I'll make an exception and save you instead," I said. "From myself. On one condition."

She frowned. This false anger of hers didn't suit her at all. "What's that?"

"We'll meet again at a more appropriate time of day and in a more appropriate place."

"In your dreams!"

"OK, then, let's make it so you know I play fair," I said. "If I guess your name, you go out with me. If I don't, you won't. I have a one in a thousand chance."

She wavered for a few seconds. But then some mischievous, reckless impulse seemed to stir in her. "You're on!"

"No cheating. If I don't guess, you tell me your real name."

"And I won't go out with you."

"Fair enough," I paused theatrically and massaged my temples, as though activating my special powers. "Lena."

"Ha," she said triumphantly. "You're wrong. It's Julia! So..."

I didn't listen to her finish.

Once again, I tried to look pensive and pretended to search deep within me. "Julia," I said tragically.

To say that she was surprised would be an understatement.

"Please don't say that your name isn't Julia. The astral ghost can't cheat."

"Are you really — what is it you call these people — a psychic?"

"Yes, in the fifth generation. No, scrap that. It's just that I have a talent for guessing people's names by looking at their faces."

Funny how I'd recently started to lie much more than before.

"So, did I win?"

"You did," Julia took out a cheap Chinese phone. "What's your number?"

I gave her my number, waited for my cell to ring, then added her to my contacts.

"Just one date," she said. "That's it."

"Am I really asking for more?"

"Well, then, see you."

That sure lifted my mood. Incidentally, while we were chatting, my Vigor had restored to its usual reading. I wasn't even upset about the charge points I'd wasted on rewinding time, even though they sure could help me in my upcoming confrontation with the house goblin.

I happily trotted the rest of the way to the Grand Grocery Market and stopped in front of it.

It was an old-fashioned self-service grocery store, a mothballed relic of the Soviet era complete with the crumbling refrigerator cases, sales clerks in light-blue aprons and aisle after aisle of half-empty shelves which had witnessed the collapse of the Soviet superpower. And here I thought those monsters had all died off, like the dinosaurs.

I activated the mission. When the paper materialized in my hand, I took out my little mirror and held it over the sheet. Heh! To an untrained eye, this indeed looked like an exterminator's license. Of course, the arrival of a rat killer at 7 p.m. could raise a few eyebrows — but then again, did my reluctant clients even know how these things were supposed to unfold? If the Game had given me a go-ahead, it probably knew better.

There was another odd thing. As I examined the paper in the mirror, I happened to catch a glimpse of the clothing I'd bought earlier. Instead of the stylish sweater, I was now wearing a bona fide brown and green uniform complete with a graphic of a rat inside a circle with a line drawn through it. Did that mean that our in-game clothing appeared different to commoners depending on the situation? Interesting.

I went inside and headed toward the most garishly made-up sales clerk, a woman with purple hair. She was surely at the top of the food chain in the hierarchy of these post-menopausal ladies. A bit like the shaman in a tribe of cannibals who always wears the shiniest beads.

"Good evening. I'm looking for your supervisor or manager."

"What do you want with her?"

I was right. As I'd guessed, this was the Cerberus guarding the passage. Now it was crucial that I play my role correctly. I couldn't mumble or overexplain because these alpha ladies always sensed one's weakness.

"I just need to see them. Otherwise, you can deal with the problem yourself. I have two other calls to make."

"Rose!" she shouted into the depths of the store. "Go get the manager!"

The manager turned out to be a heavyset woman of about forty. She appeared from near the storeroom, menacingly waggled her badly plucked eyebrows, and made her way toward me. Her entire bearing made it clear that I'd torn her away from something important. I needed to call on my talents and get ahead of her.

I pulled out the paper with the mission and was pleased to see the manager's expression change as she read it.

"Oh, we'd already lost all hope. Let's go."

"Why didn't you close the store when you discovered you had rats?" I thundered, starting to warm up to the role.

"Please don't shout like that," the manager whispered. "We haven't seen any rats. We only suspect that we have them."

"How can that be?"

"We have an old storeroom. Well, it's like a storeroom. It's just a room. We dump all the junk in it. Recently the workers have started hearing noises coming from inside it. It's a scratching sound. We went in and looked, but there was nothing there. So we decided it must be a rat."

I nodded. "We'll take care of it."

"How come you don't have a bag? How do you collect what you catch?"

"Let me take a look around first. Then if I find something I'll go out to my car."

We passed through a long, narrow corridor, descended to the basement and went toward the farthest door. It was encased in iron and snugly fitted to the jamb.

There was no way you could hear a sound behind something like that. How loud must this creature have been scratching?

The manager pulled out a bunch of keys and fiddled with them until she found the right one. Two turns of key later, we found ourselves in an impromptu storeroom, piled up with old cold-storage boxes and rotting wooden crates. A heap of filthy price tag holders was rotting in the corner. The place was quite big, around 20 square yards if not more.

"Let me take a look around," I said. "Shut the door. Whatever happens, we can't let it get out."

The absurd warning worked like a charm. The manager squealed. With an agility I didn't expect from her, she slammed the heavy door from the outside. That's what fear of God does to people.

I took out my phone, turned on the flashlight, and advanced slowly. I didn't touch my knife. The sentence said "catch," which meant this was an intelligent creature. So I'd need to come to an agreement with it.

"House goblin! House goblin! Come out now wherever you are, near or far."

I felt ridiculous. Here I was, a full-grown man walking around a basement trying to lure a house goblin out with a nursery rhyme. I guess I hadn't yet lost all my commoner reflexes. Even though I was now a Player, my psychological transformation was far from complete.

"House goblin..."

"Is that really how you summon a house goblin, blockhead?" a raspy voice asked. "You could at least put out a bowl of milk and be polite."

"Most honorable house goblin, please accept my apologies for not having studied your culinary tastes. Please excuse me. Try to understand and put yourself in my shoes. Please show yourself so that I don't have to keep talking to the air."

The Time Master

Your Persuasion skill has increased to level 1.

The house goblin appeared on top of one of the cooling systems that was lying on its side. He was no more than two feet tall, hairy, his eyes blazing with a yellow flame. If it weren't for the arms and legs, I would have mistaken him for a furry bun.

But the text box above his head didn't lie: *House Goblin* and *Unlucky Bastard.*

"Good evening. My name is Sergei. What's yours?"

"I don't have a name. House goblins have names, but I'm on my own now."

"I thought it was impossible?"

"Anything is possible. Pigs can get wings, if you know what I mean."

"The thing is, the Order of Guards has explicitly requested that I find you."

I can't pinpoint the moment when something shifted. There was a flash in front of my eyes, then I was flung at the wall. Holy shit!

"The thing is, the residents and salespeople are complaining about the noise."

"What am I supposed to do if I feel like crying? I was banished from my home and I had nowhere to go, so I holed up in here. I sit down and sometimes I howl or start to scratch."

"So why don't you find a new home?"

"As if a new home were mine for the asking, sir! D'you think you could invite me into your own house?"

I was about to refuse emphatically when a new mission message lit up to my right:

Feral House Goblin
Mission type: Variable

Option I:
Sentence: Capture and take to the branch office of the Order of Guards within 24 hours
Reward: 25 grams

Option II:
Sentence: Relieve the local inhabitants of the house goblin within 24 hours
Reward: 15 grams

Aha. So I wasn't obliged to turn him over to the Guards, after all?

Still, I had to get him out of here somehow. Brute force wasn't an option: this little guy wasn't just any dumb goblin. He seemed to be quite vulnerable. That meant I'd need to coax him out.

"And if I invite you, what will I get out of it?"

"A house without a house goblin is like a dinner table without a loaf of bread," the creature said, brightening up. I even had the impression that his voice was no longer as grating. "I can lend a hand with anything you need. I can cook and tidy up. And no burglars will ever darken your door while I'm in the house."

"Let's suppose I don't have a house. I live in an apartment block."

"Old build, new? Which period?"

"1970s, I think. Why?"

The house goblin sighed. "It'll have to do, I suppose. Now it's up to you."

I started to think. The many superstitions about these creatures couldn't have been all wrong. In the past, people thought that it was bad luck for a household not to have a house goblin. People would even poach them from their neighbors', then invite them along whenever they moved.

Naturally, until this point, I thought this was all legend. Now I could see that there was a lot of truth in old wives' tales.

"OK, you can come live with me. What's your name?"

+25 karma points.
Current level: -65.
You gravitate to the Dark Side.

The furry creature jumped off the cooling unit, came over to me, and held out a tiny hand. "I do have a name, but it's for my inner circle. My owners called me Bumpkin for the last few centuries."

"Nice to meet you, Bumpkin. I'm Sergei. Let's go. I'll carry you out so no one asks any questions."

I folded back the flap of my jacket, expecting objections, but the goblin sprang into my arms. I closed my jacket and started toward the door.

"Excuse me?" I called out to the manager.

"Yes! Already done? What did you find?"

"Just a mole who somehow got in. No idea how that happened. It got stuck in here, so it was wailing and scratching."

"Moles make noise?"

"It was in a tight spot, so it probably felt like crying," I repeated the goblin's earlier words.

"Is it... in there?" she pointed a chubby, sloppily polished fingernail at my bulging jacket.

"Yes."

"Did you..."

"No, it just died on its own. It crawled into the corner where it probably died from dehydration. It's strange that none of your people saw it. I'll just take it out now and no one will ever notice."

"Yes, yes please, thank you very much. You have no idea how much you've helped us."

She held out a bank note that she'd clearly gotten ready in advance. Had I had the cheek, I could have haggled a little. Just to level up the Bargaining skill, you know. Except that I'd done a pretty good job of raking in the rewards: I'd raised my karma, completed the mission and got myself a house goblin.

Speaking of which, he was beginning to stir unhappily. I grabbed the bill from the manager and rushed outside.

"Sit still, Bumpkin," I said into my jacket.

Since the shop manager was sponsoring my trip home, I caught a gypsy cab. I even managed to talk the price down to a quarter of what I'd just earned.

"What do you have there?" the driver asked.

"A puppy."

"Oh, I love dogs. I have two Dachshunds and a German Shepherd at home. Can I see him?"

There was such a menacing growl that the driver and I simultaneously stopped talking.

"He's nervous. He's not used to traveling."

"He'd better not soil my seats," the driver snarled.

We spent the rest of the trip in grievous silence. Only Bumpkin whined from time to time, apparently enjoying his role.

We made it home without any mishap. As I reached the entrance, I lifted my head and looked at Uncle Nick's windows. They were dark. I just hoped he was all right.

"D'you want us to freeze our asses here for much longer? House goblins don't like the cold," a voice came from under my jacket.

"It's all right. Keep your hair on."

I walked upstairs, unlocked the door and turned on the light, then reached under my jacket, helping him out. "This is where we live."

"We'll see," he said curtly and disappeared with a light clap.

I heard rustling under the bathtub, followed by knocking sounds coming from the balcony and bottles jangling in the refrigerator. Oh, right, I still had some beer left. I flung off my jacket, kicked off my boots, and went into the kitchen.

I opened a bottle while listening to the uneasy, almost ringing silence. What if I'd jumped the gun with this house goblin?

Chapter 8

MY MOM USED TO have a whole bookshelf of those esoteric books about "magick" and stuff. One of them claimed that while a person is sleeping, their spirit travels between worlds. And apparently if you're not careful when you wake them up, their spirit may not return in time.

You can laugh all you want, but had this been true, I'd have had major problems. Because my morning started with the crash of a frying pan falling to the floor.

Sitting bolt upright in my bed, I caught a whiff of an unusual smell. It was like singed hair mixed with something pleasant. I tugged on my trousers and headed toward the source of the noise.

I wish I were an artist, because the scene was a real beauty.

Tiny Bumpkin was standing on a stool by the stove, holding the frying pan in one hand and a piece of burned dough with trash from the floor stuck on it in the other. The table held a plate piled high with perfectly shaped pancakes, rosy and dripping with butter. All around this island of deliciousness, it looked as if Attila's entire army had just strolled through.

"I'll clean everything up, Master," the house goblin hurried to preempt me.

"I'm not your master," I replied mechanically as I scratched my head, examining the destruction.

"Yes, you are. I'm not some sort of heartless ingrate. You brought me into your home. I accepted the offer. So now you're my master. Should I put on some tea?"

"Yes, please."

I was about to walk out when something sparked in Bumpkin's hands. His furry body went up like a matchbox. Shit!

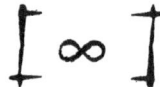

"Should I put on some tea?"

"I'll do it. Matches aren't a toy for house goblins. Give them to me."

I lit the burner and put the kettle on.

"Bumpkin, you really should make yourself look presentable. And fireproof. You need to cut your hair a bit. I have some scissors and a razor, if you need them."

"I'm no good like this?"

"No, you're not. Look," I said, pointing out a few scorch marks in his fur. Clearly the pancake preparation hadn't gone off without a hitch.

"OK, I'll think about it," he scratched the furry crown of his head.

As I stood in the bathroom brushing my teeth in front of the mirror, I got thinking.

I was a Korl with a unique development branch. A house goblin was living in my apartment. I lived next door to Hunter, whatever that was supposed to mean. And the world around me wasn't entirely how I'd imagined it to be. Yep, it had been quite a week.

Now it was time for the most important thing: dealing with my job.

Quitting is easy. But quitting without two weeks' notice is a task and a half, and all the more so when working with Bones, who was notorious for splitting hairs. Still, I already had an idea. The human mind is both simple and complicated. The key thing was to know the right spots to apply pressure to.

"Bumpkin, please try not to burn anything else," I called on my way out.

"I'll clean up a little," the goblin answered from inside.

"Oh no," I groaned.

Outside, the Professor and his friend the plumber were sitting on the bench chatting. Despite the early hour, they were already absorbed in philosophical talk, lubricating their brain gears with plastic shot glasses filled with some clear liquid.

"Love is the greatest thing that a human being can conceive," the Professor pontificated. "It's the apogee of his or her spiritual development, shall we say."

His friend nodded. "Love is a bit like a fur hat. Everyone has one, but more often than not, it's fake."

"You smartass! Let's drink to that."

I suppressed a smile, shook hands with them, and hurried to the bus stop. I trotted past the little café, nodding to Uncle Zaur on the way. He had stepped onto the porch and was smoking a cigarette.

Damn, that was it! Amid all the craziness of the morning I hadn't had time to smoke.

Without breaking my stride, I went to reach into my pocket when a notification appeared before my eyes:

Your Athletics skill has increased to level 1.

Logical. If I took up jogging in the morning, I'd be leveling up Athletics. That was a no-brainer. Except that I wasn't exactly an athlete.

Somehow or other, my hand holding the pack of cigarettes returned to my pocket. I was suddenly struck by doubt about the lifestyle I was accustomed to. More specifically, if I wanted to become a good — meaning, alive — Player, I'd need to make a bunch of changes.

As I was thinking about this, my bus arrived.

The old me would have spent the ride listening to music and scrolling through my phone, but now I just stared out the window the whole time. The city had been transformed almost to the point of being unrecognizable.

I tried to keep track of the changes. The first thing I noticed was that not all the stores for Players were located in the community. For example, the Tavern was far from the city center. And now I spotted different types of shops with curious signs. Some of them had nothing written on them — there was only an image of a magic staff or an open book.

The second thing I noticed was that there were more Players around than I thought. They were strolling along the streets, walking peculiar animals on leashes and talking between themselves.

Just as I thought about this, one of them got on my bus. He nodded to me like an old friend and got off three stops later. Admittedly, he seemed to be on his guard, judging by the fact that he didn't take his right hand out of his pocket.

The third thing I noticed were some behemoth creatures flying high in the sky. I couldn't tell if they were flying on their own or whether they were being controlled by people... I mean, Players. That was also food for thought.

So those myriad tales of dragons, unicorns, river sprites and other mythological creatures weren't mere tales after all. Just a part of the world that was observed by a few lucky commoners. Or not even by commoners, maybe. Who knows, maybe the Brothers Grimm were Players too? That would actually explain a lot.

The warehouse was silent when I arrived. It was my own fault for showing up a half hour earlier than usual. Even Marat wasn't sitting in his usual spot on the loading parapet. But Bones was definitely there. Our boss had this hangup of always having to arrive early. And today that actually turned out to come in handy.

"Sergei? Why so early?" Bones asked, busy dunking a tea bag into a cup in the storeroom.

"I need to talk to you, sir. It's serious."

"Have a seat. What's on your mind?"

"Well, it's about my head. I went to the hospital yesterday. They did an EMG and an MRI. The neurologist was good. He said they'd try to get a diagnosis quickly, but they think it could be ALS."

"What does that mean?"

"It's a nervous system disorder. It's incurable."

Your Lying skill has increased to level 2.

-15 karma points. Current level: -80. You gravitate to the Dark Side.

I'd spent all night inventing an illness. If Bones were even the slightest bit savvy about medicine, he'd see right through me. My lie ended up being too obvious and in-your-face. My entire calculation was based on that. For the record, there was barely any connection between my headache and change in muscle tone which was a true symptom of ALS. But no big deal, things were set in motion.

Did I feel like the lying bastard that I was? I sure did. A repugnant little worm had made its way into my soul. On the other hand, as cynical as it sounds, we all tend to use each other in lots of little ways. Including employers, who do use their workers. Had I been perfectly honest with him, that would only have delayed his decision... and hello, two weeks' notice.

"I don't know what to say," Bones muttered in bewilderment.

"What's there to say? My father's already made an arrangement with a hospital in Moscow. I'm going there next week. So, sir, I need to quit. It just that there's no way I can finish off the two weeks."

"What are you talking about?" Bones waved his arms. "I understand. Of course, it's a pity to lose a worker like you. But your health is more important. But there's no cure?"

"There's treatment, but it's not a cure."

We continued in the same vein for another couple of minutes, then I went outside. Bones promised he'd get my employment record book[10] filled in and ask the bookkeeper to issue payment.

I walked back to the bus stop red-faced, my ears burning. I knew I'd done everything properly and rationally. So why did I feel like shit? It was a good job I hadn't run into anyone on the way: my co-workers weren't exactly known for their punctuality.

I didn't start to relax until I was halfway home. No, I had done everything right, maybe not from a human perspective, but from the Game's point of view anyway. My world had changed; I could no longer live like I had before. Even if my lying were to be encouraged and transformed into a skill, I was on the right path. To be sure, it wasn't clear where that path might take me. As for karma, as I understood it, I could always work on it later.

Now for the most important thing: Hunter. I hoped he was OK. If he wasn't, I'd have to learn to manage on my own, without a Player — or Seeker, as they apparently called themselves — to help and guide me.

As if to mock me, the bus was taking its time — and just to add insult to injury, it broke down at the stop before mine.

I didn't have the patience to wait for the next one. In any case, I was no more than 300 yards away from home. So I set off at a run. It wasn't as epic as Forrest Gump's, and I slowed to a walk a couple of times, but I still managed.

When I reached my stop, one simple thing

became apparent to me: I may have been 25 years old but I was already a wreck. My side was splitting, my lungs were burning, and I was seeing all sorts of beautiful multicolored spots before my eyes. Yeah, I needed to change this.

As if in reward for pushing my body to its laughable limits, I was hit with a few new messages.

Your Athletics skill has increased to level 2.
You've reached level 2.
Available points: 3
Strength: 20 (x)
Intellect: 15 (x)
Fortitude: 20 (x)
Agility: 10 (x)
Stamina: 15 (x)
Rhetoric: 8 (x4)
Speed: 12 (x2)

Physical fatigue must have boosted my mental activity, because I immediately grasped the meaning of it all.

Every skill was directly tied to a specific characteristic. When you collected a certain number of skills, you advanced a level. From the looks of it, there were 3 points for each level. The more skills you leveled up from one characteristic, the bigger the bonus.

If my memory served correctly, I studied Illusion, Bargaining, Persuasion, Athletics, and Lying. And it turned out that all of them, except for Athletics, were related to Rhetoric. On the one hand, I needed to try to avoid imbalances. On the other, right now Rhetoric was the weakest characteristic.

I unhesitantly invested the available points in Rhetoric, Speed, and Agility.

After I'd caught my breath a little, I continued at a walk. My damned side wasn't getting better, clearly letting me know that taking up exercise at this rate was sure death to me.

Somehow I managed to reach my house. I looked at the abandoned bench, unlocked the front door, walked up an extra floor, anxiously pressed the bell, and...

Hunter cracked the door open. "Wait," he said, then shut it immediately.

Thank goodness. He seemed to be okay.

A moment later he reappeared on the landing, holding some keys in his hand. He went over to the nearest door, opened it, and went inside.

"What are you standing there for?" he asked softly. "Come on."

I followed him inside. "This your apartment too?"

"It is. Take your shoes off."

As far as I knew, this apartment had long been vacant. The owners had moved to Europe and were still trying to sell it. And still...

My amazement grew tenfold when I went into the main room, which most people would call a parlor. It had no furniture in it, just Roman shades on the windows. A thin gymnastics mat lay on the floor.

"This is where I keep myself in shape," Hunter explained.

"I see. You bought a whole apartment for that?"

"It's convenient — it's right next door. Of course, I had to fork out nearly 3.5 kilos of dust, but it was worth it."

He strolled over to the windowsill and began to pull out objects seemingly from thin air: wooden swords, daggers, a few ropes, and a pistol.

I recognized the Beretta. "That's Eriol's weapon!"

"Was," Hunter said calmly.

"So he's..."

"He's no longer around. The idiot thought he was stronger than me. He paid for that."

I started to think. Which abilities did you need in order to defeat an adversary with a gun?

"Take it if you want," he offered, pointing to the gun. In doing so, he gave me a funny look, not really a nice one.

"No, thanks. I've never shot a gun before."

"Lesson number one. Only fight with a weapon that you're capable of fighting with. Otherwise it could backfire on you. Hold this."

He tossed me a wooden sword. I managed to catch it. Feeling like an overgrown child, I took it in my hand and held it out in front of me.

Hunter lunged sharply, knocked my training bastard sword away, and threw me to the mat.

"What did you feel?"

"Pain."

"What did you feel when you picked up the sword?" he repeated, lifting me to my feet.

"Er... nothing really. What was I supposed to feel?"

"You should have felt your center of gravity, determined your areas of support and vibration, not to mention its weight. The sword is the greatest weapon ever invented."

"What about the gun?"

"The sword," Hunter coldly cut me off. "But you're not worthy of it yet. So we're going to train you in hand-to-hand and knife fighting. Soon."

"I'm all for that. When do we start?"

A quick uppercut knocked me off my feet. "We already have."

* * *

Is it a major task to walk down one flight of stairs? It is, if you've just been pummeled for two hours straight. To be precise, Hunter called this training. He must have been a frustrated sadist at heart.

Luckily for me, he had to leave before midday. He was on the books at a factory, but he could come and go practically as he pleased. The only thing was that he had to get there by 12 o'clock so he'd be seen during the morning check-up. That was the only thing that had saved me.

On the other hand, I had discovered the skills of Hand-to-Hand, Short Blades, and Blocking. We'd leveled Hand-to-Hand up to 5, Short Blades up to 3 and added a couple of points to Blocking as we did so. Now I knew a couple of the simplest ways of dodging the first blow and understood which side up you had to hold a knife. That's how Hunter had put it.

I stumbled home ready to drop — and immediately smelled something I was sure not to like. Well, it actually smelled great, like something meaty. But a little trickle coming out of the bathroom and the thunderous sound of overflowing water did not bode well.

"Shit!" I tore off my jacket, flung off my shoes and raced to turn off the faucets.

I was greeted by the sight of the overflowing bathtub with my clothes floating in it. I grabbed a bucket and a rag and started to mop the water off the floor. I'd come home just in time: another half hour and I'd have seen my downstairs neighbors in court. Luckily, the thick, tightly fitting old-fashioned tilework had saved my bacon this time.

It took me about 15 minutes to right things. The water seemed to drain suspiciously slowly even though the stopper was lying on top of the washing machine. Strange.

"Hey, Bumpkin!"

"What is it, Master?"

His voice was both frightened and strangely loud. I started and looked up.

The house goblin was sitting on the very top of the heated towel rail, looking as good as new. He'd shaved and cut his hair, so now he looked rather like a short, plump little man. It was just that his ears were a little hairier than normal.

"You tell me."

"I just wanted to give your laundry a quick wash. I didn't notice the water building up. It started pouring out. But I was confused."

"You were confused. And you leaped onto the radiator. You could have just turned it off. Never mind. It looks like the water trap is clogged. Let's take a look at it."

I waited for the water to drain completely, got

undressed, put the rag down, and started to unscrew the water trap.

At first I thought that a cat must have climbed into the sewer pipes and died there. Handful after handful of hair... where had it all come from? Unless...

"Bumpkin!"

"What is it?"

"Where did you put your hair after you cut it?"

"Nowhere. You have a little hole there. Everything disappears down it."

"Jesus. You *are* a Bumpkin, aren't you? Are you saying you've never seen a flushing system?"

"Nah. I've always lived in the country. My last master wouldn't let me go into the bathroom."

"Huh, I wonder why."

"What now, are you going to make me leave?"

He sobbed and wiped his nose. His huge, shining yellow eyes filled with tears.

"No, of course I won't. Just don't do this ever again, please. Look, here's the water trap. It's clogged. We can unscrew it, take out all the junk, and then put it back together."

"Oh, Master, show me, I'm a smart guy."

"Come here, take a look."

A half hour later, freshly showered, I was sitting in the kitchen eating scrumptious chicken gizzards fried with onion. I always thought my mother was the best cook in the world, but Bumpkin clearly planned to give her a run for her money.

"Where did you find them?"

"In the freezer. You ought to buy some things, Master. You don't have a bean foodwise. Me, I can survive a long time without food and I've seen worse.

But you, you might die. You're the skinniest Korl I've ever seen."

"Have you seen a lot of Korls?"

"Plenty," Bumpkin nodded from his perch on the stool.

"OK, I'll go stock up today. I have money — I changed some dust yesterday."

And now I'll head out and get some more for completing your mission, I thought. I strolled into the hall and picked up my jacket.

"Say, Bumpkin, why did you wash the clothes by hand?"

"How else was I supposed to do it?" he asked in surprise. "I looked around and your household isn't very well stocked. You don't have a bar of soap or a washboard."

"The washing machine didn't suit you?"

"Washing machine?" Bumpkin's eyes grew even larger. "Show me, please."

"I'll show you later. And please don't try to use it without me. And you know what, Bumpkin, please stay out of the bathroom for the time being, will ya?"

As I sat on the bus, it occurred to me that it might be a good idea to get a car if my earnings led me to a new level. Then I wouldn't have to endure the jostling on public transportation. Or maybe I should get a motorbike? I'd spent my whole childhood dreaming about having one.

The massive shape of another monster floated into view in the sky overhead. Could it be some sort of small dragon? Or what did they have there?

Lost in my reverie, I got off at the stop I needed and after some consideration, entered the familiar courtyard leading to the community.

My thoughts were racing, my stride was relaxed, and I was in a good mood. So the sharp pain in my back caught me off guard. And when a curved blade exited my chest, I nearly howled — more from surprise and amazement than actual pain. What the hell was going on?

[∞]

Chapter 9

THE CHINESE PHILOSOPHER Sun Tzu wrote that a war required a quick victory, not attrition. As it turned out, I wasn't the only one who had read his works: my assailant must have done so too. His swiftness made this perfectly clear.

Having managed to dodge the blow that should have killed me, I somersaulted and swiveled around to look at my adversary.

The Darkest One — as my Insight had identified him — was my height. Judging by the appearance of his hands, he was a human. I couldn't make out his face behind the hood he was wearing. Clearly he wasn't planning on striking up a conversation with me.

He stepped toward me and took a swing. I barely had time to stick out my hand. His knife's blade ripped through it. My own scream echoed in my ears.

I managed to dodge the blow. I think I even managed to graze the stranger's side with my moon steel knife. But he hardly noticed. He took a better grip of his own weapon and started toward me again. I only had one attempt left.

Another stranger appeared behind my adversary. Tall with chestnut hair, he was dressed like a Player in odd wool trousers and a leather jacket, but he had no name tag hovering above his head.

The Darkest One caught my gaze. He swung around and, sizing up the situation, dealt a mortal blow. His knife pierced the stranger's chest just below his throat. Immediately my assailant was sent flying in a cascade of sparks.

My savior was already gone. What the hell was going on?

"Either you're a dimwit or you're just greedy," a voice came from the end of the lane.

I turned toward it. The guy who'd just been killed by the Darkest One was standing there, alive and kicking and angry as hell. I could see that he wasn't talking to me. As he raised his hand, it exuded a crimson glow.

He was a wizard. I mean, anyone could be a wizard here, but this guy was the real deal.

The threat seemed to have worked. With feline agility, the Darkest One jumped to his feet and took to his heels. Neither of us were inclined to chase after him.

The guy came up to me. "Everything OK?"

"Sort of."

"What did he want from you?"

"I didn't get the chance to ask."

"What a lowlife," he shook his head. "Attacking newbs right by the community!"

I was caught up in my own thoughts and only half listening to him. Now there was a text box reading Mentalist above my savior's head.

I've never been a fool, so I promptly put two and two together. The guy must have specialized in creating projections of himself. That's what the Darkest One had just "killed." So this Mentalist guy leveled up as a wizard. Yes, he was a serious enemy.

"I'm Sergei," I said.

"Harph."

"Are you Greek?"

"No, Russian," he said with a laugh. "It's just that experienced Players give themselves new names, so that it's harder to trace them through their past lives."

Right, so that was why my neighbor was simply Hunter and not Nick. But Jan had introduced himself by his real name, hadn't he? Well, he was also a newbie. He wasn't a noob like me, but he'd become a Player relatively recently. OK, I'd make a mental note of that.

"Thanks, Harph."

"It's all right. Any self-respecting Player would have done the same. That guy is a scumbag. But I suggest you find out if this was just a random attack or it's someone with a grudge against you."

I nodded. I had already started to think along those lines. I wasn't that stupid, after all. He'd need a really good reason to attack me near the community. And he had a few. First of all, I'd killed a Chorul. Admittedly, no one had bothered to explain to me exactly what that was. Hunter would only say what he felt like saying. Secondly, I had a very cool development branch. No one other than Hunter knew about it. But if Hunter had wanted to kill me, even by proxy, he probably would have done it. That basically covered it. Or maybe all this ruckus was because of my Insight? No idea.

"Love your fighting style," I pointed to where the Darkest One had been standing not so long ago.

Harph nodded. "It was Thunder from the Sky. When you level up Destruction to 70, I'll teach you. Won't cost you much."

Yeah right. Can't wait. What wasn't much for a Player would take this warehouse loader decades to earn.

"Come on, let's go," he said. "Or are you going to stand here all night?"

We started across the maze of back lanes toward the local community. Although we encountered a few Players on the way, none of them tried to kill me. One of them even nodded at Harph.

Once we got to the square, we went our separate ways.

"I suggest you go see the Guards," he said by way of farewell. "If this was a random attack, it's better to report it. And if it was deliberate, all the more so. See you."

I watched him go. I had no intention of going to the Guards — at least, not now. That would just set the gossip mills in motion — what could that newbie have that was so valuable that another Player had attacked him? Revealing myself wasn't yet part of my plan. I had to consult Hunter and do whatever he thought best.

I strode confidently toward the Syndicate. It wasn't very crowded today. Maybe I had again chosen a bad time, but I only came across about a dozen

Players. Most of them were sitting at the tavern tables swigging beer, or something that looked like beer. A couple were hovering around the mission board.

I went over to see what new jobs were posted, and got a lump in my throat. The location of the Chorul mission now showed our city. And the piece of paper had darkened noticeably. That was a bad sign.

There were also some new missions available.

Sewer swamp spirits
Mission from the Order of Guard
Charged with: aggressive behavior, attacks on commoners
Sentence: death
Location: Sewers in the vicinity of the local automobile factory
Reward: 100 grams

Young treasure ghoul
Mission from the Syndicate
Charged with: embezzlement
Sentence: steal the treasure back from the ghoul
Location: Samara Region, village of Sosnovka
Reward: 1/3 of the stolen goods

Mad Barnyard Keeper
Mission from the Order of Guards
Charged with: aggressive behavior, mass animal slaughter
Sentence: Banishment or death
Location: Vladimir Region, town of Gorokhovets[11]

Reward: 50 grams

All the papers were already yellow and shriveled except for the Mad Barnyard Keeper mission. The one for swamp spirits had gone completely dark. Something else that surprised me was that the Syndicate could apparently issue a mission without any chargeable verdict. Had embezzlement become a crime in our country?

I gave it some thought and decided to take the Barnyard Keeper and swamp spirits. The latter's location was right here in the city, and the town of Gorokhovets a mere 60 miles away.

But just as I reached for the swamp spirits and touched the yellowed parchment, it crumbled in my fingers. What have I done now?

"Too bad," a dark-skinned Abbas behind me commented. "That girl over there is redeeming it."

I looked where the Player was pointing and found myself gazing right at an old friend: Artist_Chick, the girl I'd spotted at Tavern. She'd just walked out through a small door a little past the bar.

"That's where you redeem missions?"

"Yes," the Abbas replied.

I wanted to ask exactly how that worked, but he'd already lost interest in me and moved away. Well then, we'd just have to find out through trial and error.

I went over to the door, pulled it, and nearly collided with the girl. She sized me up in surprise, clearly not expecting to see me here, then floated past noncommittally. I was forced to make way for her.

Never mind. I needed to get used to the fact that I was still a nonentity to the other Players.

On the other side of the door I found a small office. It was filled with a large desk upon which stood a scale and a tall sharp spike with pieces of paper strung on it.

"What do you want?" an orange-skinned man asked me by way of greeting.

"To redeem a mission."

"So why are you just standing there? Give me the paper."

A snow-white sheet of paper appeared in his hand, containing all the information about the house goblin. I was expecting to be interrogated about what had happened to Bumpkin next, but the clerk didn't say a word. He read the paper, took out another scale, much smaller, pulled over a huge bag and measured out exactly 15 grams of dust.

"What are you standing there for? Take it!"

I pulled out my little purse and transferred the precious resource into it. Now I had 52 grams in total. Translated into human money, it was around $604. But I didn't plan on changing it yet.

I politely said good-bye to the Syndicate clerk who didn't respond, and went outside. I reflected for a few seconds, then went back to the board and pulled off the Mad Barnyard Keeper. All the other missions implied the need to fight, but I wasn't yet confident in my combat abilities. I already had the mission for the devils pending, its low reward clearly suggesting that it wasn't too challenging. Perfect to try my hand at.

I went outside and started to wander around. Hunter and I had only breezed through the community, but now I investigated it more closely. In addition to numerous shops, which I didn't look into because I didn't want to inadvertently part with my precious 50 grams, there was quite a bit of interesting stuff, such as the residences: The Order of Investigators, Order of Alchemists, Order of Guards, Order of Merchants, Order of Tamers. As far as I could tell, that was only a small portion of the Seekers' organizations. I was willing to bet that there were many more in big cities such as St. Petersburg or Moscow.

Further on, there were a few modest hotels and private homes on both sides of the road. At the end of the street stood a squat building with an indecipherable symbol over its double doors: a large circle with a narrow border of runes, its center crisscrossed with a complex pattern of straight lines. At first I thought they were placed randomly, but then I realized that each new one jutted out of the preceding one.

"*Haisa*, brother," a voice said behind me. "Have you decided to go on a little trip?"

I turned around and found myself face to face with Traug, the first Korl I'd ever met in this world.

"*Haisa*," I replied. "What do you mean?"

"You've come to the Gatehouse, so that means you've decided to go somewhere."

Right, of course. Traug had told me that he lived next to the Gatekeeper, hadn't he?

"Can we go in?" I asked.

Traug laughed. "Of course. These doors are always open to Players."

I pulled the steel ring and stepped inside. Traug followed me.

The place was relatively well lit by torches and bronze sconces filled with an oil-like substance. The place itself didn't have the same domed shape as it did from the outside.

I noticed a round annex by the back wall where the light was much brighter. Traug headed there; I followed.

"Here's the book," Traug said, motioning to a massive folio on a stand. "You can check it for all the places you can go to, as well as their descriptions and travel fees. Then all you do is pour the right amount of dust in the bowl," he pointed farther down, "stand in the center of the circle, touch the stone and say the name of the place out loud."

I was only half listening as I curiously studied the circle covered in runes. A small, flickering stone rose at its center. Behind it stood the Gatekeeper. He was one and a half times my height, wearing a full suit of armor tinged with blue, and leaning on a full-length shield. A closed helmet concealed his face.

"But what if you put down less dust than you need?" I asked, gazing at the Gatekeeper with acute fascination.

"Then nothing happens. You can't cheat him."

"Is he a human?"

"He's a Gatekeeper. They don't belong to any race. Accept him like you accept the sunrise or the stars in the sky."

"Can he hear us?"

"Of course."

"That's kind of creepy."

I opened the book and started to flip through the pages. Its contents were actually rather scanty. There weren't a lot of places where I could go, and on top of that, they all led to Purgator, without exception. I guess we really were off the beaten path. Finally, the cheapest trip cost 23 grams. And that was one way!

"Purgator," I said pensively, turning a page.

"It's a shitty place," Traug said, "stuck between Firoll and Elysium, so your choice is between a rock and a hard place. But it's the only way to get to the central worlds."

"You said that you don't go to Purgator anymore."

"Not to the large settlements, no. Too many Archali there. And in any case, I'm not planning to go there at all. You can live well in the Cesspit."

"Mm-hm," I said, lost in thought.

We left the Gatehouse 15 minutes later. In all that time, the monster hadn't so much as moved a muscle, looking suspiciously like a statue. Traug tried to invite me to some woman's called Elma, promising to get trashed, but I declined as politely as I could. I wandered around a little more, then went back to the central square.

I waited by the community exit until a large group of Players moved past, and then fell in behind them. It would be much better to encounter the Darkest One in a crowd than alone. Although my charges had been restored, I had precious little to offer against him.

Still, I didn't have to worry. We hadn't run into anyone apart from a scruffy mutt that limped past me on its own business. Once the crowd of Players entered the commoner part of the city, they began to part ways. I crossed the street and mingled with the commuters heading to the bus stop. I looked all around me but didn't spot anything dangerous.

I dialed Hunter, listened with grim satisfaction to the voice saying that the number I was trying to reach was currently unavailable, and slipped the phone into my pocket. Never mind. I'd have to wait until evening and just turn up on his doorstep, pretending I needed his help again.

On my way home, I remembered the promise I'd given to Bumpkin. I stopped at the supermarket and bought two bagfuls of food. You may laugh, but $70 was gone at the flip of a hat. I was cashless again.

I got home, stumbled into the hall, and nearly collapsed with the packages. I never understood why all those weightlifting competitions like the World's Strongest Man had participants drag massive stones. Where would they ever apply those skills? They should lug grocery bags instead. It would be much more interesting to watch, and it would better prepare them for life.

"What kind of meat is this?" the goblin grumbled in the kitchen, sorting through the groceries. "The beef is artificially colored and the cabbage is soggy."

"You should be happy I got that," I responded curtly. "I hope you haven't gotten into any trouble?"

"I didn't go into the bathroom if that's what you mean," Bumpkin said, looking at me seriously. "I just tidied up your room a little. And I fixed your pants. It's a shame to walk around in something so full of holes."

Face palm. How do you explain to a goblin that the holes in my jeans were there on purpose? That they're actually sold like that? He'd never understand. And his tidying standards? My room was now the epitome of army barracks: nothing out of place. The problem was, whenever I needed something now, it would take me a week to find it. I might consider giving Bumpkin a to-do list for the day, otherwise we wouldn't get too far.

I changed into workout clothes and tied my sneakers. "I'm going running. You can cook while I'm gone."

The goblin didn't reply. More precisely, he did, but with the same mumble. All right then.

Ever since my school days, sports and I had never got along. Or rather, we co-existed just fine on our own: sports were somewhere over there, and me over here. But things had changed, and now I needed to make up for that.

"Way to go, young communist!" the liquored-up Professor cried out to nearly the whole courtyard.

I wasn't surprised to see him. When you start getting involved in something you're not very good at, you can count on running into everyone you know. It's like when a woman runs out to the closest store without makeup on, she's sure to stumble right into her ex.

"I also used to run in the park, but now I only run to the liquor shop when it's about to close," the Professor said longingly.

I didn't listen any further to the tales of his athletic exploits. Stepping awkwardly, I ran out onto the street and took the busiest road, remembering the Darkest One. My plan was to reach the intersection and turn right, heading for the park which was two bus stops away. I could do a lap of the park and turn back, at an easy pace so my body could remember what exercise was.

Naturally, I overestimated my strength. I started dying even before I reached the intersection. And once I reached it, I just suffocated. And still I raised Athletics to level 3, after which it felt like I sort of got a second wind. "Sort of" being the operative word.

I didn't make it to the park. I honestly jogged one and a half bus stops and then croaked. Or rather, I first heard the coveted message:

Your Athletics skill has reached level 4.
You've reached level 3.

Predictably, it was followed by a small miracle as my stamina bar soared from zero all the way up. Still, the pain in my side didn't go anywhere. I tried to run some more and decided that I'd had enough for one day. Or as the case was, enough for the last five minutes.

What a nightmare. I was a wreck.

I returned home in fits and starts, running fifty to eighty yards and then walking and regaining my strength. Then I'd catch my breath and start all over again, sweaty as a metal worker next to a fiery furnace.

I walked a little more around my house just to save my face, seeing as not even twenty minutes had passed since I'd started my "run". As it turned out, there was no need for it: the Professor had already sloped off somewhere in search for more demon drink. Good.

The smells in my kitchen made me drool like Pavlov's dog.

"Another half hour," Bumpkin said, catching sight of my begging look.

OK. Struggling to lift my wooden limbs, I stumbled into the shower. Then I fell into bed. This so-called active lifestyle that people keep raving about is brutal.

On the other hand, I had to think of my level.

Available points: 3
Strength: 20 (x3)
Intellect: 15 (x)
Fortitude: 20 (x)
Agility: 11 (x3)
Stamina: 15 (x)
Rhetoric: 12 (x)
Speed: 14 (x2)

That meant Strength, Agility, and Speed. Only now had I noticed that I had 32 charge points compared to 30 at level 1. Which meant that each level added a point to it. Not much, but still.

In any case, I'd received 3 pt. to Strength. My Health was now at 45.

I was about to spend some more time with the settings when the doorbell rang. The serving spoon in the kitchen knocked against a pot and went silent. Bumpkin, too, had stopped showing any signs of life.

I got up, hauled myself to the door and looked through the peephole. Surprise! It was Hunter.

"Today I got attac — " I started to tell him as I opened the door.

"I know, I know," Hunter said as he walked in without waiting for an invitation.

It looked like he was coming right from work — I mean his human job. But it was still early. He removed his shoes, took in the kitchen aromas, and went straight there. I was left to straggle behind.

"Around thirty Players were killed in the city today. All of them were initiated not three days ago. Someone's looking for you."

I slumped onto a chair. "Holy crap."

"But that's only part of the trouble. Because of what happened, the majority of the Order of Seers will be coming here soon."

"Which of those things is worse?" I asked.

"All of them," Hunter answered curtly.

Chapter 10

PICKING UP a project where a professional has left off is a foolish and, generally, useless undertaking. For example, it takes an Indian rug maker years of hard work to finish a hand-knotted silk rug. And if, God forbid, something happens to him, all that amazing effort would go to waste because no one would dare finish what he started.

Even though I knew that, I still set about finishing the soup Bumpkin had begun cooking. What was I supposed to do? Hunter's unexpected visit had prompted my dear goblin into hiding: every now and again I felt his reproachful stare boring into me.

Meanwhile, Hunter was watching me with interest.

"So what about this guy, what's his name — the Darkest One?" I asked as I sliced some carrots.

"Where should we start," Hunter said thoughtfully. "First of all, thirty murdered Players in three days is a lot even for Moscow, let alone for our backwater. Everyone's been put on their toes. I think tomorrow there will be missions issued regarding the attacker. The Guards won't just sit and wait, either. Secondly, you said it was the Darkest One?"

"Yes. Do you know him?" I asked, my eyes tearful as I chopped an onion.

"The Darkest One isn't a name; it's a characteristic. That's what they call a Player whose karma has dropped to -5000 points."

"Wow. So he must be a really bad dude."

"Well, to stoop so low, all you need to do is kill 50 neutral Players. Either that, or... there're lots of options, in fact."

The words made me shudder. Fifty. I'd been lucky to cross his path and survive to tell the tale. Had it not been for Harph passing by...

"He's very strong," Hunter continued. "And I suspect that..."

"What?"

"That he could be a Wandering God."

I stopped chopping and gazed dully at the wall. A God wanted to kill me. How fantastical was that?

"Just try to keep your head down for the time being," Hunter continued. "In a way, having the Seers here will be very convenient. He won't dare attack anyone anymore if his actions can be foreseen."

"What do you mean?"

"The Seers are mostly empaths, but there are also a few clairvoyants among them. The closer they are to the source of an incident, the more accurate their predictions. Only a madman can violate the law under their nose."

"Why do I have the impression that there's a catch there somewhere?"

"Because they'll find *you* before you even know

it."

"Why on earth do they need me?"

"And who killed the Chorul? Who gained possession of the unique Avatar?"

"But I didn't mean it, man. If you told me what a Chorul is, you'd have made it much easier for me."

I was so desperate I didn't even notice I'd switched to an overly familiar tone with him. But nothing seemed to faze Hunter. He ignored the question and continued as if nothing had happened,

"Both the Darkest One and the Seers are looking for you. Except that the Darkest One has a simple motivation. He wants to get his hands on either the Avatar or your ability to rewind time. But I can't say the same about the Seers. Their objective is a mystery."

"They probably want to invite us to tea," I quipped, unable to calm down. "To cause us some grievous bodily harm, most likely."

"It's not so easy, I'm afraid. The Seers are very strong, but at the end of the day they're just an Order. With all due respect, as soon as an empath violates the law, there'll be lots of people who'll be more than eager to stab them in the back. The Guards won't just sit there doing nothing, ether."

"So why are they so feared?"

Hunter heaved a sigh and gave me a condescending look. "No one knows what the Seers want. That's where the problem is. And you should have respect for the power that you can't challenge."

"Yeah right. Like bow down to them."

"Or even better, just stay out of their way. I should abstain from visiting the community for the time being. Try to spend as much time indoors as you can. And if you do venture outside, try to stick to busy and crowded places. The Darkest One isn't an idiot; if he starts to mow down commoners, the entire Cesspit will be out to get him. Just like it happened to that blood wizard.... why do you have milk in that saucer?"

The non sequitur threw me off. Naturally, the milk was for Bumpkin. No matter how many times I'd told him to learn to use a glass, he had refused to do so. In the end, I had to do his bidding, pour some milk into a saucer and put it under the radiator in good old-fashioned house-goblin tradition.

"That's for my cat, isn't it?" I said.

"I didn't know you had a cat," Hunter said, looking me in the eye.

"He roams around outside. He only comes back once in a while to trash the place and disappear again."

"OK then," Hunter said in a tone that implied that he didn't really believe me. "Don't forget you have training tomorrow."

With that, he left. I shut the door behind him and went back into the kitchen, where I found Bumpkin swearing in front of the pot.

"What kind of hands were you born with that you cook such slop?" the goblin demanded, looking daggers at me. "Not even dogs would eat this."

"So why'd you bolt? You could have cooked it yourself."

"It isn't fitting for outsiders to see a house goblin. It's a bad omen."

"Aren't we superstitious," I answered, spitefully ladling some soup into my bowl. No matter how bad it might taste, now I'd eat it out of principle.

To my surprise, it turned out to be quite decent. Either because I'd taken up where he'd left off, or maybe I wasn't such a bad cook after all. In any case, it was edible. Bumpkin just snorted, pretending to busy himself with the dishes.

I sat there mulling everything over. Not being able to go to the community was a major disadvantage. I'd even say it was a really, really major disadvantage. Just when I'd made big plans for my own future prosperity, the Seers had to come out of the woodwork. I only had two missions now: the devils and the Mad Barnyard Keeper. I might deal with the latter tomorrow. But I could also take care of the devils before the Seers introduced their damned curfew.

The piece of paper in my interface hadn't changed color. I figured that no more than ten Players were interested in it, and they likely had a passing curiosity but weren't exactly bending over backward searching for the devils. The ten grams offered for the mission was a joke.

But I could really use that money. And I'd take on this mission in all seriousness.

To start, I opened my laptop and entered my city in the search bar, followed by the address of the automobile factory and the word "attack." That was what they'd been charged with, wasn't it? I searched for any incidents that took place within the last week. And that was no small feat, even if I say so myself.

Judging by the search results, the only thing that hadn't yet happened in our city was the Apocalypse. Or rather, there'd been none in the last week in this particular neighborhood. But everything else you could imagine had happened: someone had stolen the scales from the monument of Justice by the courthouse; a girl had exposed her breasts, causing a mass car accident, a boozer fell from the seventh floor but got away with only minor injuries due to his inebriated state, etc., etc.

It took me half an hour of searching to find anything useful for my purposes. An unpopular city portal reported an attack next to the St. Trinity Church where a pack of stray dogs had assaulted a young woman. According to eyewitnesses, the animals behaved oddly, not even trying to maul the girl, but rather attempting to drag her away. Luckily, a passerby had managed to fight them off, rescuing the damsel in distress.

There'd been two more similar events where packs of stray dogs had attacked an alcoholic and a local prostitute respectively. In both cases, the dogs didn't try to maul their victims, but instead attempted to drag them away.

"Yes, it's most likely the devils," a voice said behind my back. "They're attracted to fallen people."

"Fallen people?"

"An alcoholic and a streetwalker," Bumpkin explained. "I don't think their first victim was that virtuous, either. The devils are building a lair for their queen. They've just gotten started — that's why there are no real victims yet."

"Can you be more specific?"

"What can I be more specific about if I've already told you everything?"

"Tell me everything you know about these devils."

"What is there to know? They usually swarm

together in groups of five or six. They also have a queen, the only female in the pack. She rules the roost. The lair is always near water."

"What about the fiery cauldrons?"

"You've read too many stupid books. In Russia, devils have always lived by the water, in abandoned wells and under old dams."

"That makes sense. All the attacks happened by the Oka River."

"No, that can't be it. The Oka is huge. They're afraid of large bodies of water. It needs to be a small river or a branch."

"Here! The main water supply canal that belongs to the car factory," I said, pointing to the monitor.

Bumpkin nodded. "That's more likely. They must have holed up there somewhere."

"All we have to do is check out this theory in practice," I said, standing up.

"Bah!" Bumpkin grumbled, heading to the kitchen. "Don't you have anything better to do than wonder around looking for devils?"

Not bothering to reply, I hurriedly got dressed and dashed outside. I groped for my knife; it was still there. Which was pretty obvious, really: it couldn't have gone anywhere.

Bumpkin had said that the devils settled in groups of five or six. I had enough charges for three time rewinds. That meant I'd need to follow the ancient maxim of divide and conquer.

To be honest, the prospect kind of agitated me. I'd been in maybe four fights my entire life, but now I'd have to kill — or more accurately, exterminate. After all, devils aren't the same as human beings, are they? Still, this felt a bit like having to kill a cow or a lamb. No matter how much you love a nice piece of steak, when they give you a knife and bring you toward an innocent grazing animal, your hands will begin to shake.

I took the metro to Culture Park and got off before the St. Trinity. Instead of subsiding, my anxiety kept mounting — until an inspired thought struck me. If it were true that devils usually went for drunks, prostitutes, deviants and other society misfits, maybe I should kill two birds with one stone?

I looked around and spotted a small bar. It was one of those outdated places that looked like it had frozen at some point in the mid-1990s. The only thing that kept it going was the regulars.

When I walked inside, my suspicions were confirmed. Shabby wooden tables, threadbare curved-back chairs, an ancient TV mounted over the bar, and a bored bartender.

"What can I get you?" he asked.

There were no other waitstaff. Great. I leafed through the faded menu. Ordering brandy here would be more trouble than it was worth. It was most likely dodgy as hell: if it didn't blind you, it might turn you into some semblance of a city fountain disgorging bile and puke. Safer to get vodka.

"Twenty grams of Beluga and a pickle plate."

The bartender nodded, jotted the order down on a slip of paper, and took it to the kitchen. Less than five minutes later, I received a plate loaded with pickles, cherry tomatoes, wild onions, sauerkraut, and marinated garlic. The chilled vodka had been expertly decanted into a round-bellied carafe. Of course, at $15 it wasn't even close to being economical. That was the price range of a restaurant, not a low-class booze hole like this one.

Then it dawned on me that I hadn't smoked all day.

My hand acted like it belonged to a trained monkey, reaching for my pocket on its own. Talk about reflexes! A mere thought of a smoke was enough to undo all my good work.

No way. Had I had that twenty-minute jog for nothing?

I poured out a shot of vodka, gulped it, chased it down with a pickle, then began to munch on wild onions.

A deceptive warmth spread throughout my body. I looked at my watch. I still had time but I shouldn't drag it out. I wasn't here to have a good time, but to get pissed quickly.

I polished off three more shots in about three minutes and left the pickle plate unfinished. I must have set a record for speed in drinking alcohol. In any case, the bartender watched me leave with a surprised expression on his face. OK, all set, time to go hunting.

I made sure to leave my jacket unzipped so I'd be able to pull my knife out fast, especially because I didn't feel the cold anyway. It was either my Korl blood or the vodka coursing through my veins. I passed a few rows of gloomy five-story apartment blocks and headed to the industrial zone where the river was.

I walked at a leisurely pace, as though I were just out for a stroll. I even noticed a small sand beach in the distance. Still, I doubted that anyone would be out for a swim in the icy-cold waters of the Oka right now.

I reached the water supply canal where I faced a simple choice: a wooded area to the right or the industrial zone to the left. I scratched my head and opted for the wooded area. Somehow I didn't think these creatures would choose the industrial zone — they were far too lazy to even watch others work. No: they would probably choose Mother Nature.

The alcohol started to take effect. It wasn't that I was hammered. I mean, really, with six or seven ounces of vodka? Give me a break.

Still, my body felt weak. I moved more uncertainly — you could say I began to stagger a little.

That's when the devil and I spotted each other simultaneously. He was tiny — half my height — and black with floppy ears, long fur, and beady red eyes.

He obviously intended to beat it, and even took a few steps to the side, but then my acting talent took over. I pretended to stumble and dropped to the road, hiccuping loudly for good measure. The little devil stopped and began to wag his tail as though summoning someone.

Good boy. Come to daddy now.

And he really wanted to approach me, he did. Aw, the poor thing was trembling. He stamped his hooves, looked around, and squawked loudly a few times. And then he just waited.

Soon, three more devils joined him. Damn, I wasn't counting on such a crowd. But it was too late to scram. Watching them dart toward me, I realized that I wouldn't escape anyway. They'd just catch me and have their way with me.

I bent down, like an earth mage trying to gather

strength from the asphalt, while reaching for my knife. Now it was time for a little dance.

It's true what they say: the first impression is the strongest. And I liked that little devil, just like he liked me. That little fool was constantly trying to lunge forward, impatient for his friends to catch up with him. Now he was in the home stretch, just a few steps ahead of the others.

I had no fighting experience. I'd sparred with Hunter a few times, but that was probably all I could brag about — except for my old-days training with Uncle Denis. But I got lucky. I stood up abruptly and took a step forward, pointing my knife in front of me.

The blade entered the devil's flesh as though the creature had no bones. We looked at each other in surprise for a couple of seconds, then all hell broke loose.

The other devils started such a racket like they were a bunch of marketwives accused of cheating. Three nimble shadows darted along the asphalt, nearly disappearing from view.

What was that now? Propelled by reflex, I kicked the poor wretch in front of me and pulled out the knife. The devil fell over on his side, still alive but obviously in no state to interact.

I managed to take a step back, trying to get into something that resembled the stance Hunter had shown me. And I immediately got it in the face and kidneys.

Very well. Now we'd see who's the top guy here.

The Time Master

I grabbed the creature's hand — or rather, his paw — wrenched it, and stabbed him in the back. But I couldn't dodge the jab in my side. Judging by the blinding pain, my adversary had clearly dealt me a flesh wound.

Grunting, I rolled onto my side with all the grace of a sliced squid and wielded the blade in front of me. Dang, they were fast!

As if it were shot from a catapult, a furry lump flashed before my eyes and latched on to my throat. I felt hot blood flowing down my chest. My limbs started to convulse. How revolting!

The furry lump impaled itself on the knife which I was holding at the ready. The creature cried out, squealing and wriggling. But this time I managed to catch the devil by his tail, as the saying goes, and stabbed the creature blindly several times.

Your Short Blades skill has increased to level 4.

I swung round, readying myself for another attack. Still, the last devil bolted off like a bat out of hell, showing no intention of fighting.

Let him run. He'd take me to his kin, that's all.

I walked around the battlefield. The second brute had died but the first one was still in agony. I shuddered. If you extracted all the adrenaline that was rushing through me, you'd have enough to fill several one-gallon jugs.

I braced myself, went over to the devil, shut my

eyes and stabbed him in the chest.

Done. He was dead now. I wiped my forehead with my shaking, blood-soaked hands. My heart was beating on the double; my knees buckled.

I'd just killed three devils. I, who in his whole life had never hurt a fly (not counting mosquitoes and an occasional wasp), had just exterminated three living creatures.

I crumbled to the asphalt. I should have bought another bottle of vodka to go. I was literally falling apart.

Had it not been for my wounds, I might be still sitting there now. As it were, I caught sight of a flashing notification:

Health: 33/45

I sure was wounded. So I shouldn't be loafing around, really.

I stood up and took out my mirror. The reflection showed me the devils looking just like ordinary stray dogs: nameless mongrels with a touch of red in their coats.

I reopened the mission description. Could my memory be deceiving me? But no, it was there in black and white — or should I say, in binary digits?

Proof of completion: devils' ears

Just then I felt the unmistakable taste of vodka and pickles rising in my throat. I managed to get to the closest bush before I puked.

That was better. I clenched my teeth, strode

over to the devil, grabbed his ear and slashed it off, and then did the same to the other ear.

I slipped the rough, stubbly triangles into my jacket pocket. Don't think, just do it, I repeated to myself. I went over to the second devil, cut off the ears, and headed to the third one. A second wave of nausea came over me. Now I vomited the soup that had been the result of the joint efforts of a human and a house goblin. But at least I now had it out of my system for good.

A feeling of detachment set in. It was like everything that had just happened to me was just an illusion. Like I'd been sitting at home watching an entertaining horror film.

The idea made me feel less burdened. I conjured Light, turning my hand into a powerful flashlight, and checked out my surroundings. The runaway devil had taken off for the wooded area, which ran along the canal. So I slowly plodded in that direction.

I was careful. I knew I shouldn't rush. I only had two charge points left and I had to wait till they regenerated. So I wasn't in a hurry to chase after the only survivor.

Still, my Zen idea of "he who understands life does not hurry" fell apart when I noticed that my Health was slowly but surely approaching zero. It was now at 29. If only I had bandages to dress my still-bleeding wounds!

But at least my available charges were now at 20: enough for two more rewinds. I decided not to drag things out and take a risk. Ultimately, if it turned out too dangerous, I could always scram. Then I'd get myself back home and bandage my war wounds while Bumpkin would watch anxiously, oohing and aahing. There was no way I was gonna die next to that reeking waste pipe of a stream.

No sooner did I think this than I heard a shriek in front of me. I stopped and conjured Light.

The structure in front of me looked like a cross between a beaver dam and a wickiup made with tree branches, the sort children build to play in. Two devils stood in front of it, yelling blue murder.

I waited a bit longer, but no more devils came out to join this charming pair. Which meant they had no backup. Good. In any case, they seemed to be expecting me.

I advanced uncertainly, trying to ignore the pain. The problem was, Hunter had taught me to defend but not to attack. So when I attacked I was about as graceful as a hippo on a balance beam.

I went for them like a typhoon on steroids but failed to even ruffle my foes' feathers. They just dodged my attack, end of story.

But little did they know that I was different.

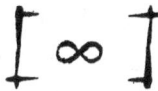

The devil leaped aside, surprised at my changing direction mid-flight, but I still managed to stab him. Sorry, old boy, that's exactly how these things happen.

I pushed aside the mortally wounded enemy and turned to the devils' lair. The last surviving devil raced at me like mad — but either his instinct for self-preservation wasn't working or he was simply stupid.

He stubbornly stood his ground, trying to strike back at me.

I performed the only trick movement I knew, which Hunter had just shown me without actually teaching me how to do it. Miraculously, my enemy fell for it. He stuck his neck out, finding himself within my reach. I took a wild swing, ripping his shoulder to pieces.

Screeching, the devil lunged forward, ramming me with his tiny horned head and knocking me down. Unfortunately, in doing so he impaled himself on my knife.

I pushed his body off me and sat up, waiting. There was no sign of any more devils. Unhurriedly I removed my foes' ears and stood by the entrance to the lair. The last thing I wanted to do was go in, but I had no choice.

I activated Light and saw a wide burrow under the wickiup.

Using my hand to light the way, I started to lower myself slowly. When I was in about three yards, the space widened. This was a real den, rather big and riddled with side tunnels. I stopped in the first chamber and looked around. The only thing I saw was a huge heap of rags on the ground. When I sniffed, the heap rustled.

"W-w-w-ho's th-th-there?" the rag heap asked in a good Russian.

"It's me," I answered for lack of a more intelligent response.

"P-p-p-please unt-t-t-ie me."

"And you are... ?"

"Exc-c-cuse my manners. I'm Litius."

A belated name tag appeared over the heap:

Litius
???
Mentate
???
???

I frowned. I'd heard about Mentalists, but a Mentate?

Just as I reached out to the rags in which my new friend was wrapped, I very nearly gave up the ghost in the best horror film tradition. Something rocketed out of a distant chamber and went for me. Actually, I knew who it was: the queen, the female devil the others had been protecting.

Caught by surprise, I thrust out both of my hands: one still casting Light and the other with the knife. Remarkably, it worked. The queen recoiled and went to cower somewhere in the darkness.

Without taking my eyes off the darkening chambers, I cautiously proceeded to untie Litius. Which explained why I didn't immediately look at my new friend's face.

As soon as I threw aside the rags, I was faced with a tied-up... well, I don't know how to say it. A human cheetah?

He had a long, thick tail, large hind legs, human hands that had four plump fingers, and a cat face. A lean, muscular beast.

I froze in surprise. "How did you end up here, man?"

"You s-s-see, I was looking for some b-b-b-blood moon st-st-stones. But those rascals had stolen some of them. So I had to find them. But they t-t-tricked me and attacked me on the sly, all of t-t-them, then dragged me here. If you free me, dear s-s-sir, I'll r-r-reward you handsomely."

Reward you handsomely? That's what I like to hear!

I cut his bonds loose. Litius crouched on his hind legs, rubbing his hands.

You've restored freedom to a Player who is neutral to you.

+50 karma points. Current level: -30. You gravitate to the Dark Side.

"Th-th-thank you."

"The queen is still in there," I said, pointing down the cave.

"H-h-hold on."

He dashed into the darkness. Soon I heard a scream that made my blood run cold. A moment later it went quiet. After another couple of minutes, Litius reemerged, stepping noiselessly along the earthen floor.

"Th-th-the stones," he announced, showing me some red pebbles. In his other hand, which he held out to me, were the devil's ears.

I accepted his gift and shoved it in my pocket. "Cool. Should we get out of here?"

"Y-y-yes."

When we got outside, I stretched, kneading my numb back, and turned to Litius. "By the way, what's a Mentate?"

That was obviously the wrong thing to say, because in an instant Litius' calm face turned into the anxious expression of a predator. He drew himself up to his full height and leaped at me.

Chapter 11

IN RUSSIA, lots of people seem to think that strong male friendships should start off with a fight. That was probably Litius' opinion too. Judging by his next actions, he definitely wanted to bond with me.

What do you feel when you see a 220-pound feline, all sinew and muscle, pounce on you? Fear? Despair? Panic? Probably all of those things at once. I mean, a human being has precious little to offer against an animal. In a fight between man and beast, it's the sharpest claws and the strongest teeth that decide the outcome.

Of course, that only applies to ordinary people, not Korls endowed with the Time Master development branch. I had my own trick up my sleeve. But only one, if the number of charges was any indication. So I needed to be alert.

Litius was nimble — amazingly, devilishly, phenomenally nimble. I envied his grace, the deadly beauty of a human cat. He would spring, landing on his hands, then touch his hind legs down and immediately kick off again, tearing toward me — or rather, directly into me.

The short, powerful blow blinded me. I nearly passed out, but still managed to...

There was no way I could dodge the blow, so I just dropped onto my back, watching his huge, muscular body fly over me. As adept as Litius was, he hadn't had a chance to react. He put his arms out and started to slow down, and that messed up his coordination — even though the momentum kept him moving forward.

His strong tail, as fat as a mooring cable, flashed in front of me. My hands reached out for it on their own. I grabbed at the tail, slippery with slick short hair, and was immediately propelled forward, trailing in Litius' wake. Still, I promptly rearranged my position and collapsed onto his back, pinning him down with my entire weight.

From that vantage point, I could now indulge in some small talk. "Are you sick or something? I've saved your butt!"

"You must have followed me... You were l-l-looking for me. You want to k-k-kill me or even s-s-sell me."

"Yes, that's why I dragged you out of that hole, so I could skin you at leisure."

"You know that I'm a Ment-t-t-tate."

"I think you're a wimpy alley cat. The sign said you were a Mentate. I don't even know what that means!"

After much struggling to escape my platonic but

firm embrace, Litius suddenly went quiet.

"I have Insight," I explained. "I can see information about everyone."

"Insight," I could hear a note of remorse in Litius' voice. "I'm s-s-s-sorry, I... I..."

"I'll let you go, but only on two conditions. First, promise you won't throw yourself at me like a soldier on leave at the sight of a half-naked girl."

"Exc-c-cuse me?"

"I mean, promise you won't try to kill me. And secondly, I want you to tell me everything."

"What ex-x-xactly?"

"Why you wanted to kill me. Do we have a deal?"

"D-d-deal."

I didn't release him immediately, just loosened my grip slightly. But Litius seemed to have changed his mind.

Still, I leaped aside and reached for my knife, just in case. It was unlikely that I'd have a chance to cause him any serious harm — my knife would all but graze his thick hide — but I wasn't about to give in just like that.

"Have you calmed down?"

"You really don't know what a M-m-mentate is?"

"Search me. And stop looking at me like Bill Clinton at Monica Lewinsky. I really don't know what a Mentate is. You tell me."

"Then you need to p-p-promise you won't t-t-tell anyone what I'm gonna say."

"Scout's honor," I said, raising my hand.

Litius slumped to the ground and covered his cat face with his hands in a weary, sad gesture. His shoulders started to tremble as though he were crying. It sort of frightened me. Watching women cry always flustered me, to say nothing of men. But Litius raised his head and calmly began to speak.

"I was b-b-born in Ullum, the world of the Beastmen. I m-m-mean, it wasn't our world at first. After we lost the Thirty-Year War, they started sending my kind to Ullum. Then it became known as the world of the Beastmen."

"Hold on. If you know about other worlds..."

"We know all about the Players, Gods, Avatars, and all the other worlds, both of Darkness and Light, as well as those which are called Hazy, the ones with black passageways between them. We know about everything. But humans still think we're inferior to them. They insult us and call us dirty alley cats, reptiles, and stinking fish," he gave a disappointed shrug.

"Litius, forgive me for pointing this out, but you've stopped stuttering."

"I only stutter when I'm nervous," he said with a sad smile. "So anyway, the only way to escape Ullum is by becoming a Seeker. Or a Player, as you call them here."

"And you became one."

"A group of Players got into a scuffle next to our settlement. Six of them were killed, so six new ones could take their place. I was one of them. But fate threw me for a loop."

"What do you mean? You wanted to escape from your world and you did."

"You don't understand. As if in jest, the Game assigned me the most valuable development branch of them all. It would have much better suited a mechanoid who have a natural aptitude for it — but instead, it was endowed upon a beastman. You know what I mean? I'm a Mentate."

"We're right back where we started. What does this mentalism or mentatiness or whatever, give you? What's the right word, anyway?"

"I can instantly memorize large volumes of information and operate with it. All kinds of knowledge come to me like the alphabet to a child who already knows how to read. Do you understand now?"

"So you're like a sophisticated computer on two legs — sorry, on four. What's wrong with that? You should be happy. This Mentate branch sounds like a dream come true."

"How many friends do you think I have? Or how many Players do you think have tried to kill or enslave me once they found out about my branch? You were surprised that I attacked you. But if a Seeker says 'Mentate' to me, in the next second he's either going to stab me or cast a spell on me. Which is why-"

I was all ears; I even crouched on the freezing ground: Korls couldn't catch a cold, anyway. Which was why I missed the moment when Litius darted toward me. His claws sank into my shoulders. I couldn't do anything even if I wanted to: my charges were still at seven, and my reaction times were lamentably inferior to those of my adversary.

I smelled Litius' hot, fish-scented breath. What in the world had those devils been feeding him?

"Swear to me..." he began.

"To do what — brush my teeth in the morning?" I asked, trying to turn away.

"I want you to swear that you won't tell anyone

that I'm a Mentate."

"And you'll believe me?"

"Repeat after me: I swear to Litius from Ullum that I won't tell anyone that he's a mentate."

"Oh, give me a break!"

"Swear."

"OK, OK. I swear to Litius from Ullum that I won't tell anyone that he's a Mentate-"

A bright light momentarily blinded me. I squinted. When I opened my eyes, Litius was watching me, looking pleased as the cat who got the cream.

"Now what?" I asked.

"Nothing. Now you really won't be able to tell anyone anything about me."

"What if I want to?"

"Then... let's not talk about the consequences. I'm so happy I have a friend now! You're the first Player I've met in a long time to whom I've been able to talk to openly."

Litius' eyes were beaming with happiness. If you asked me, friends like him rather belonged in a petting zoo, but I kept this notion to myself. Instead, I stuck out my hand, solidifying our crazy friendship with a handshake. I'd just need to go to the pet store to buy him a special bone to clean his teeth: that dismal smell was painful.

"I found something in the lair," Litius said, pulling a bundle out of thin air. "You might find it useful."

When I unfolded the bundle, it turned out to be a trench coat, old and tattered like the one Columbo used to wear in that old TV series. Still, its drab appearance was deceitful: this was a magic coat if ever I'd seen one.

Destroyer Mage's Trench Coat
Adaptable to owner's level
+100 to mana.
+7% to damage from all Destruction spells used by the owner.
+6% to absorption of all hostile Destruction spells.

And no disadvantages or postscripts in fine print. It was just a gift.

I put it on. I probably looked like a scarecrow in a cornfield in it. Whatever. I pulled out my mirror and took another look. Well, well, well. To an unsophisticated eye, the garment looked just like a regular sports jacket.

"The Lying Mirror," Litius said.

"I don't know, probably. Someone gave it to me. May I?"

Litius nodded. "Of course."

The funniest thing was that commoners saw Litius as a rather good-looking young man with wheat-colored hair, a small beard and a wide, amiable face. Despite its ordinariness, his appearance was quite memorable.

"How'd you pull this trench coat out of nothing?" I asked.

"All Seekers have storage units."

"Like those at the railway station?" I asked jokingly.

"Exactly. No one can take things from there without the owner's permission. Unless, of course, you're a top-level thief."

Hmmm. I looked inside myself, so to speak, and

poked around in the interface. In the left-hand corner I saw an icon that looked like a tiny bag. They couldn't have thought of a better place to put it, could they?

I opened it. It was empty.

"Where do you live anyway, in the community?" I asked, putting the little mirror into a pocket of my coat.

"No. As I said before, no one likes the Beastmen. Even if you're a Player. So I try to keep a low profile. I live among the commoners in a rented apartment. Here, take this."

He held out a business card: a plain white rectangle printed with a phone number, an assumed name, and a job title. Apparently, he was an IT security specialist. So!

"If you need anything, give me a call," he said. "I owe you. Or just text me."

"In that case, let's get out of here. I think I came from over there."

"That's right. If you trust the maps, there are only two places in the city where you run into this kind of configuration of the water supply canal. One is in the industrial zone and the other in the wooded area. In both cases you need to head northeast. Don't look at me like that — I'm a Mentate," Litius added, laughing.

I liked his laugh. It was soft, velvety and comforting, like the purring of a cat. After everything that had happened, it was just what I needed.

I activated Light and walked forward.

Your Illusion skill has increased to level 5.
You've reached level 4.
Available points: 3
Strength: 23 (x3)

The Time Master

Intellect: 15 (x)
Fortitude: 20 (x)
Agility: 14 (x3)
Stamina: 15 (x)
Rhetoric: 12 (x)
Speed: 16 (x)

Only two characteristics had coefficients attached to them this time: Strength and Agility. If my memory served me correctly, I used to level up Hand-to-Hand Fighting, Short Blades, Blocking, and Illusions. That last skill had only increased by a point, so no bonus was given to Rhetoric.

Unhesitantly I invested in Strength, Agility (seeing as there were bonuses), and Intellect. The latter gave an advantage to mana, and at some point I intended to become a wizard even though I was yet to unlock any skills related to that branch. So be it.

Litius and I parted ways at the bus stop. With a farewell swish of his tail, he bounded onto the bus as though he hadn't been imprisoned for weeks in the devils' lair. I sat down on a bench and anxiously felt my side. Although my clothes were filthy and stiff with caked frozen blood, the wounds were gone. Also, once I'd made a new level, the maximum amount of Health I could have had been brought to 60 and the Health itself, completely regenerated. Magic!

But I was wiped out — not so much physically as mentally. I'd met a Beastman, completed a mission, and got myself a magic trench coat. I was so drained I didn't feel anything apart from a desire to sleep off the hunt.

I opened the app on my phone and called a cab.

I wasn't in the mood to commute with the rest of 'em.

My apartment gave me a cold reception — literally. For one thing, the house goblin didn't run out into the hall to greet me. For another, the apartment truly was chilly, as though someone had opened a window in the...

"Bumpkin! Hello? What's going on?"

The room was quite a scene. A sheet of old fiberboard covered the now-paneless window frame. This little alteration of my room's design had significantly improved its air conditioning properties.

"Bumpkin!"

Something rustled in the kitchen. The culprit appeared before me, his head hunched between his shoulders, his eyes avoiding mine.

"What is this?"

"Fiberboard," the goblin answered grimly.

"Well look at you, you have quite the vocabulary! What's it doing there?'

"It's covering the window."

"Yes, I can see that. Why is it covering it?"

"I broke the glass," Bumpkin said, wiping his nose with his hand.

"And how did you manage to do that?"

"I was washing the windows."

"Ooooph," I collapsed weakly onto the couch. "Who washes windows in subzero temperatures?"

"I thought..."

"OK, OK. Where did you get the fiberboard?"

"From over there," the house goblin said, pointing to the wardrobe.

I frowned. My wardrobe wasn't known for any excessive storage space. It wasn't Narnia, after all.

I opened the wardrobe door and heaved another sigh. The crafty house goblin had ripped out the backing panel which now offered an excellent view of the wallpaper behind it.

"You're gonna kick me out now?" the goblin sniffed without lifting his head.

"Oh..."

To be honest, I'd love to. Really. But there were two things that stopped me: my pity for the wayward creature and Bumpkin's cooking skills. Even my mother didn't cook like that.

"You're safe... for now. Just please don't touch anything. Please."

Somehow I doubted my words had sunk in. Although Bumpkin had nodded, I could see that he definitely agreed to disagree. Forcing a house goblin not to do any housework is probably like forcing me not to drink beer. Talking about which...

I peeled off the trench coat and went into the kitchen. It wasn't exactly cold, but it was kind of brisk, enough to make someone want to knock back a pint or two. I clearly remembered buying a few bottles to help me get through a hard day — like this one.

Full of anticipation, I opened the refrigerator and...

"Bumpkin!"

"What's up *now*, Master?" the goblin asked, materializing on top of a kitchen stool.

"Where's the beer?"

"There wasn't any beer."

"The bottles were right here."

"Oh, that was piss, not beer. The brewer should be shot. I looked at it, sniffed it, and even tasted it. Your shop owner is a cheat. I poured it all down the drain."

"Oh, Bumpkin..."

I was dying to grab him by the neck and squeeze it gently until I heard it crack. Still, I managed to suppress the urge. Mentally commending my self-restrain, I filled the tea kettle and lit the burner.

"Don't you. Ever. Touch. My. Beer," I said coldly.

"Got it," the goblin replied. Now I could see that I'd finally gotten through to him.

We drank tea in a tense silence. Rather, I drank tea while the goblin sat next to me, trying to blend in with the decor. Yeah, karma's a bitch. I brushed my teeth, showered, and dove into my bed, which Bumpkin had unfolded. OK, I guess he was good for certain things.

I tossed and turned for a long time, staring at the ceiling and listening to the cars driving by outside. Thanks to the goblin, my apartment's sound insulation was now non-existent.

I finally dozed off an hour later. I had strange dreams, to put it mildly.

I was walking, but I couldn't see the road. I followed the soft sound of a melodious voice beckoning me. I knew it wasn't a trap. They were waiting for me there, up ahead. They'd been waiting a long, long time.

The darkness was almost tangible. It seemed to be touching me, trying to hold me back. Closing up all around me. And it wasn't happy that I was there.

I heard a soft knocking sound up ahead. The darkness hissed and shrank, retreating. I was now facing several beams of light slashing through the gloom. I could just make out the outlines of figures beyond them.

The Time Master

Knock-knock-knock. The light grew brighter. It caressed me, filling all the available space and chasing away the grim darkness.

That's when I saw them: three figures in long flowing robes. I couldn't see their faces. Their hands were hidden in the folds of their clothes.

The figure standing in front was holding a staff. He lifted it.

Knock-knock-knock. The last layer of darkness dissipated under the blows of the staff. I felt incredibly good, warm and happy.

As for the three figures, I now knew that I'd been looking for them all along. I'd been walking toward them for such a long time, without any hope of ever finding them, that I'd almost forgotten all about them. Now finally I was standing in front of them. They were so close, their outlines so dear and familiar. How could I have ever forgotten them? How could my memory have failed me?

The man with the staff took a step forward, shrugged off his hood and smiled. "We knew you'd come to see us!"

Knock-knock-knock.

I sat up on the unfolded couch. So it was only a dream. But it was so real. The three men looked just like that Chorul whom I'd — no, they weren't men, they *were* Choruls. Then again, I wasn't too sure. Was the figure with the staff a human or not?

I couldn't remember anymore.

Knock-knock-knock!

Shit. Someone was hammering on my door.

I grabbed the phone off the bedside table. Dammit! I was already 10 minutes late for my martial-arts class with Hunter. That's what a little fresh air does to the body. I'd been flat out for hours.

I stood up, pulling on my jeans as I walked to the door, and froze. Because at that moment, someone entered the room. And that someone was myself.

Chapter 12

THEY SAY THAT when you're losing your mind, you're the last person to notice it. Truth be told, this morning I had those thoughts. Not every day starts off with you sitting on your butt watching yourself walk into the room.

In every fantasy novel, when the hero sees his double, he kills him because he knows that he's the real person while the thing in front of him must be up to no good. So when I found myself in this situation, I acted almost on autopilot.

My knife was lying on the chair, covered by my sweater. I instantly vowed to leave it on top from now on so that I could whisk it out at a moment's notice. Because the milliseconds I'd wasted groping for my knife had decided everything. When I finally grabbed it, about to spring into action, I heard a voice say,

"Master, you all right?"

I hesitantly froze on all fours next to the chair.

"Bumpkin?"

"Who do you think it is? Oh, hold on."

A second later, the goblin was standing in front of me as if nothing had happened.

"What the hell?"

Bumpkin shrugged. "You were sleeping and I tried to wake you up, but I couldn't. And then this..."

A brief, insistent knock interrupted him.

"This," the goblin repeated. "So I shapeshifted into you just to open the door and chase him off. But then you woke up."

"You-" I cussed, scrambling up to my feet and heading for the door. I had a funny feeling I knew who it was.

My hunch was right. An angry Hunter was standing in the doorway.

"You're ten minutes late for your training," he snapped.

"Just a minute. I'll get dressed and come straight up."

He turned on his heel and started back upstairs. I slammed the door and barged back to get dressed like an injured moose ramming through the taiga.

"Tell me quickly, what's with all this shapeshifting shit?" I demanded.

"It's totally normal. All house goblins can turn into their master whenever the situation in the house requires it."

"What did you mean when you said you couldn't wake me up?"

"You were sleeping like a rock. That's how evil spirits sleep, or those who have no conscience. Dead to the world."

"We'll talk about it later," I said, bolting out of the apartment.

I don't like it when my morning starts abruptly like that. Ideally I'd take a bath, drink a cup of tea, and ponder the direction the country was going. Haste makes waste. But in all fairness, morning had ended long ago.

Also, Hunter turned out to be a rather ungrudging Player. I thought I could expect the harshest sparring session possible, but no. My mentor made me do a bridge stretch instead, forcing me to arch my back as far as I could. Whenever my body started tilting toward the floor, I'd shift my foot on the ground, adjusting my balance.

After twenty minutes or so, we finally sat down face to face and did the butterfly stretch. Hunter now showed himself to be even more strict, not sparing my stiffened tendons.

"Don't feel sorry for yourself. Stretch until it hurts."

"I'm str-et... ching," I grunted. "What's all this for, anyhow?"

"Just do what I say."

After another fifteen minutes or so, I received a rather surprising notification.

Your Athletics skill has increased to level 5.

"What's that for?" I asked. "We haven't done anything, have we?"

"Oh yes, we have. There's something important you need to remember. The more variety in training, the faster you'll see a result. Is that clear?"

"Not really."

"Look, you have the Athletics skill. How do you max it out?"

"Er... I could run, I suppose. Do some push-ups, whatever."

"Or chest presses, or barbell squats. That's the easiest way. But if you add on, say, yoga and acrobatics, things will go exponentially faster. That's the idea. That's how things work — not only in the game, but also in real life. Abundance in diversification. If you do the same exercises on the same muscle groups day in day out, the body will adjust to them instead of improving."

"Hold on. For example, I have the Light spell. It's part of the Illusions skill. Does that mean that I'll never reach level 100 in that particular skill if I limit myself to that spell alone?"

"Of course you will if you're persistent enough. Only by then, the trees might wither and the rivers run dry. But if you start to use Invisibility, Fear, or Harmony, the process will go much faster. You get it?

"I think I'm starting to understand. So if I want to level Athletics up faster, I shouldn't just jog, but do all kinds of exercises?"

"Exactly. Now get up. You've warmed up a little. I'm gonna show you how to tuck correctly. Do a few rolls and then try a somersault."

What I eventually did was anything but a somersault. Instead, I managed to perform a routine consisting of a one-and-a-half flop landing on my backside, a half-somersault landing with my face pressed to the mat, and a two-yard slip across the polished floor. Through these clumsy tricks, I managed to add 2 points to Acrobatics.

We finished the training session as we always did: combat with wooden knives.

"Have you decided on your direction yet?"

Hunter was breathing evenly, his movements smooth like those of a fish in water. I was swerving this way and that, blocking awkwardly and gasping as I was already completely out of breath. I was dripping in sweat; my muscles were begging me for mercy. I struggled to remain standing through sheer will — the quality which was probably what turned a boy into a man.

"Mage," I answered curtly, thrusting my knife which sliced through the empty space where Hunter had just stood. "Combat... mage."

"Good choice," he knocked one of the knives out of my hands. "But you won't have an easy road ahead of you."

With a fake swing, I thrust from below. Unfortunately, Hunter was prepared. So he wanted to play that game, eh?

I missed him by an inch. His reaction time was out of this world. And he seemed completely relaxed. He was calm and even-keeled, as if he were just sitting there enjoying a meal rather than fighting.

Your Short Blades skill has increased to level 5.

That was the last thing I heard. Hunter did a foot sweep, sending my body to the ground like a sack of bricks.

"First you need to learn to fight on your own, without your abilities. Then your abilities will make you invincible. That's all for today. I'll be expecting you tomorrow. And one more thing: keep your phone with you."

That last warning seemed odd, but I didn't say anything. My cell phone was always on me. Hunter was the one who was usually unreachable.

"I have a question," I said. "I heard something about, what are they called now... Hazy worlds, yes. With black passageways."

"Who'd you hear that from?" Hunter asked guardedly.

"A Player told me," I said truthfully.

"The Hazy worlds are a place where there's no light nor rules. They're populated with monsters. Players rarely risk poking their noses there."

"Do the Choruls live in a world like that?"

Hunter frowned. I'd already figured out that he didn't much like talking about the Choruls. I was prepared for him to dismiss our conversation, but after thinking for a few moments, he responded.

"The Choruls live beyond two of the Hazy worlds. That's why Players have rarely found their way there. And the few fortunate ones who have, got sent packing. The Choruls don't like outsiders."

"What about the black passageways?"

"That's enough for today." Hunter turned away, making it clear that he wasn't going to say much else.

I went downstairs to my apartment and finally had a proper wash and a shower. The tea kettle was already boiling in the kitchen which smelled heavenly:

the goblin had cooked an omelet. Not an ordinary boring omelet, mind you, but one that seemed to be made of milk clouds. Never mind the omelet: Bumpkin could even take cheap store-bought teabags and put an original spin on them. But I didn't want to praise him. Instead, I feigned dissatisfaction and began grilling him.

"So, we have a goblin shapeshifter in the house, eh?"

"Master, you insult me day in and day out. First you called me a human and now a shapeshifter!"

"We're a little touchy, eh? Can you only turn into me or into any human?"

"It's not shapeshifting. It's transformation. It's like smoke and mirrors," he explained. "I'm telling you, all house goblins can do it if the situation requires. But we can only take on the guise of our master."

"Hm. That's actually quite convenient."

Bumpkin tensed. "How so?"

"You broke the window. Now you're going to replace it."

"I'm not leaving the house," Bumpkin asserted.

"You don't need to. You'll turn into me, or transform, whatever you call it. You'll let in the glass-cutters and check their work afterwards. I'm going to pop out now and order the glass. Oh, and by the way. What do you make of this?"

I took out the paper with the mission to catch the Mad Barnyard Keeper. Bumpkin scanned it and then looked at me.

"Barn hands do lose their mind when they're abandoned."

"Barn hands?"

"Barnyard keepers, as you call them. House goblins call them barn hands. In the past, every rich home had its own barnyard keeper. The house goblin took care of the house and the barn hand took care of the yard — he made sure the cattle didn't fall ill, the well didn't get flooded, and the locusts didn't get into the crops. So he's one of those."

"What do you mean, abandoned?"

"The house goblin must have run away but didn't take the barn hand with him. That also happens. Either the master died or he kicked the house goblin out. He probably died, I think."

"Why do you say that?"

"Because if he kicked him out, the house goblin would have taken his barn hand with him. The barn hand is like a little brother. But in this case, most likely, the master had died, and the house goblin mourned until he got confused in the head and left the household. So it was like the barn hand was abandoned."

"So why didn't he leave himself?"

"That's the thing," Bumpkin said, raising a meaningful finger. "The house goblin is attached to the master and can't be without him, while the barn hand is attached to the house goblin. That's why the poor thing is suffering."

"OK. So how do we find this barn hand?"

"It couldn't be simpler. Just go straight to the household where the master died recently. You'll find him there."

Easier said than done! I Googled the town of Gorokhovets. It only had a population of 13,000 — a trifle by Russian standards. Hm... it might actually work. Somehow I didn't think people were dropping like flies there.

I searched for their registry offices. The town only had one, how awesome was that? I just needed to come up with a believable story. No big deal. I could think it over on the way.

While I was at it, I researched glass cutting services. Damn. According to the map, they were nearly halfway across town.

I put on my freshly washed Player clothes and headed outside. How would I have time to do all the things I had to do?

By the entrance I predictably ran into our inebriated literati under the Professor's enlightened leadership.

"Greetings to you, my dear young man."

Mr. Petrov was at the apex of intoxication. No wonder: it was already past midday. All self-respecting gentlemen of his ilk had already had their share of booze.

"Hi, Mr. Petrov. Do you happen to know of a glazier nearby?"

"I do," the Professor's playfulness immediately fizzled out. He grew serious, climbed to his feet, and walked over to me. "Cross the avenue and go another block, until you hit Gorky Street. Then turn left and it's the second building. The entrance is from the courtyard."

A ten-minute walk, in other words. I hurried out to the street in the direction indicated.

Uncle Zaur was standing by the entrance to the café at the intersection. With a helpless wave of my hands, I raced past him. It wasn't my fault I now had a master chef in my own home. I wouldn't be surprised if I put on a few pounds in the foreseeable future.

The glass-cutting shop was exactly where the Professor had said it would be, even though it hadn't shown up on Google Maps. So much for modern technologies. They were no match for native knowledge.

In all fairness, maybe the reason it wasn't listed was because no one would even think there'd be a workshop here. I found it in a house basement, long and drab; the shop must have been set up there at least thirty or even forty years ago. Dusty panes of glass, wide tables; a few mirrors displayed by the wall. No living soul in sight. What a nuisance.

I wasn't about to leave, though. I kept walking. Finally, farther on, I found a gray-haired grandpa with a sparse beard sitting on a rickety stool. The old boy was holding a glasscutter, about to set to work on a mirror lying in front of him.

???
Skilled Craftsman
???
???

"Hi," I said. "Are you the owner?"

The old man lifted his head, peered at me, and nodded.

"I need some glass."

"What sort of glass?"

"Er, like this..." I attempted to pantomime with my hands.

"Don't you have the dimensions?"

I cursed myself silently but just shook my head.

"I got it anyway," the old boy said. "You need 22 by 45. That one over there is 24. You can take that. Cut it at home. That'll be $6."

"Can't someone come install it?"

The old man scrutinized me again. "They might. My slackers will be back soon. But they'll overcharge you. I know them. How far is it?"

"It's only a ten-minute walk," I said, giving him my address.

"It might cost you another $9," the craftsman said confidently.

"Excellent. How about I pay now?"

"All right."

The old man stood up, went over to one of the small tables and pulled out a stack of receipts. He ripped off a sheet, picked up a pen, and started to fill it out.

"You can settle up with them directly for the work," he said, holding out the slip of paper. "Hold on, take down the foreman's number. His name is Mark. Here you go," he marked down my name and address, went over to the glass, and taped the slip of paper on its edge.

Phew. One problem less now.

I went out into the street and tried to figure out how I'd get to Gorokhovets. I still had around $30 left in my pocket, and I'd need to use $9 of that for the glass repair. According to my phone, an Uber to Gorokhovets would cost $22. Then I'd have some expenses once I got there.

I needed to find a way to cash some dust. Through Litius? That wasn't an option. He didn't seem to frequent the community. There was also Traug, but he didn't have a cell phone — it was like he was still living in the Stone Age.

Who else was there? Jan? Of course! I had his number and he seemed like a decent guy. I didn't think he'd rip me off, especially because we were like brothers in misfortune. He was an inadequate human and I was an inadequate Korl.

As soon as I pulled out my phone, it started to ring. Bones. Huh. That was interesting.

"Hello?" my voice promptly transformed from lively to weak.

"Hello, Sergei," I heard Bones' voice. "Am I calling you at a bad time?"

"No, except that I just got back from the hospital. They did some tests."

Your Lying skill has increased to level 3.

"Hm... well, I'll come right to the point. We've filled out your employment record and issued payment. As soon as you have some time, you can stop by. Or I'll swing by your place if you can't come."

"No, no, don't be silly," I said, probably too hastily. "I'll take a taxi and drop by."

"Great. See you soon."

I put the phone back in my pocket. Well, I guess the money issue had just resolved itself. My backpay wouldn't make me rich, but for today's operation that should be enough with some to spare.

That meant I needed to go to work now. But I had to pop back home first.

Judging by the source of all the racket, the

drunken symposium of our house's intellectual elite had moved over to the neighboring courtyard. I ran into my house, calling a taxi on the way. I put some money on the bedside table and instructed Bumpkin about the upcoming visit.

"So who's coming?" he asked, visibly nervous.

"Just some people, to replace the glass. Here's the receipt and here's some money. Just transform into me and supervise their work."

"Oh no, no, no. Not good. It's a bad sign for strangers to see a house goblin."

"They won't see you, will they? They'll see me. It's no good you argue."

My phone dinged, letting me know that the taxi was already waiting for me. Well, that was quick. Also, the driver was a real nice guy.

We drove through the city in silence. No gut-wrenching Russian rap on the radio blaring about wrongly accused convicts whose weeping mothers were waiting for them at home. The driver didn't chatter about how customers were idiots, the operator was a jerk, and anyway this was only a temporary job. The cab didn't even stink of some sickly-sweet deodorizer that cabbies usually hang over the dashboard.

I had no problem talking him into taking me all the way to Gorokhovets. Talk about good luck. I'd chanced upon a perfect cabbie.

It took us ten minutes to reach what was now my former job. After another fifteen minutes of pretense, my employment book and $215 were already sitting in my pocket. Bones then caught me by the bookkeeper's and tried to slip me the money he and the loaders had collected. I almost had to fight him off.

It's one thing to lie, but quite another to profit from someone's best intentions.

When I got back in the car, I was crimson, my cheeks burning. I didn't begin to calm down until we were nearly outside the city. I took out my phone and looked up the Gorokhovets City Hall website. I clicked on the person I was looking for and started reading about him. He was the chairman of the city's Assembly of Deputies and a member of the ruling party — in fact, his whole appearance made it clear that he'd been around the political block a few times. Perfect for what I had in mind.

The highway was almost empty. We got there in an hour and a half, and I even squeezed in a little nap. Finally, the driver pulled up in front of the building where I had to do my errand. I paid him, reluctant to dismiss him. I'd still need to drive around the city and then get home somehow. But a paranoid person inside me was whispering that I shouldn't be using the same car.

I climbed out. The old Renault revved up, tearing out of this godforsaken hole. Have a nice trip, man.

I turned to the white two-story building that must have been erected a good couple of centuries ago. The sign on it read,

Bureau of Vital Statistics and Archives Department of Gorokhovets District

I took a breath and started for the entrance. Let the day's main event begin.

Chapter 13

S AY WHAT YOU like, but the apple never falls far from the tree. Problem families haven't given us a lot of Nobel laureates. Of course, there are rare exceptions which only prove the actual rule. People are strongly affected by their environment. I remember a lady friend of mine who once got a job working with an all-male group and just a month later she was cursing like a trooper, she knew the Champions League schedule by heart, and she genuinely didn't understand where the second sock of the pair kept going.

And when people get jobs in government agencies, they change in surprising ways. All the humane and genuine parts seem to be washed out of them, replaced with statutes and bureaucracy. Comprehensible words like "you should" are transformed into "the filer of the application must as soon as possible..." Meanwhile, their eyes take on the steely, cold gleam of a confident predator.

This was precisely the specimen I faced when I went up to the counter. Or rather, she desperately wanted to appear like that. She was very young, probably no older than 25; a bit chubby, with cute pink cheeks, trying very hard to emulate her older colleagues' professionally resentful glares.

I shot back a look of disparaging calm. "Good day," I said confidently, looking her straight in the eye.

"Hello."

"What's your name?"

"Svetlana."

"So, Svetlana, you should have received a call about me."

"I didn't get any call. Who are you?"

"I'm Sergei. But that's not important. What's important is who sent me. I'm from Colonel..." I paused and added in a quiet voice as though I were sharing a secret, "Nozdrev. Have you heard of him?"

Svetlana nodded. Most likely, she really had heard of him. This was a small town. Colonel Nozdrev had been at the helm for decades. In the early 1990s, he'd managed to jump on the bandwagon just in time, quitting the Communist party and joining the current ruling one. And despite his advanced age, he clearly had no plans to call it a day.

"The elections are coming up," I continued in the same hushed, confidential tone, "and we've started to hold some PR events. You know what I mean?"

An affirmative nod. I looked around. We seemed to be alone.

I must have looked and sounded too suggestive for comfort, but that was only an advantage for me. "I'm in charge of one of those events. We want to feature a struggling family with a recently deceased breadwinner. We'll film the Colonel arriving, chatting with them, and helping them out. To make it clear that he cares about his constituents."

The girl was listening to me so attentively she didn't even blink.

"So we need a list of people who died in the last month. We'll look at the list and choose a suitable candidate."

"I can't do that," the girl said, shaking her head.

"Svetlana," I heaved a deep sigh. "We can do it all officially. The result will be the same. It's just that neither I nor the Colonel need that. Perish the thought that anyone gets wind of it. And this way," a few well-worn bills materialized in my hands, "everyone will be in the black."

I laid the money on the table in front of her.

Your Lying skill has increased to level 4.

The startled girl looked at the money. No, she hadn't been working here long; she wasn't yet corrupted by bribery.

"It's a win-win situation." I continued. "The Colonel remembers a good turn and knows how to be grateful."

Your Persuasion skill has increased to level 2.

A tiny hand shot up onto the table, fell on the bills and quickly slid back. Svetlana looked around nervously, fixed her hair, and nodded.

"Wait a moment, please."

I expected her to hand over some battered manila files or ancient archival books. But my outdated ideas of the way they did things in the provinces couldn't have been farther from the truth. Svetlana stared at her computer for a while, then printed a sheet of paper containing ten names with the date of death and registered address of each of them.

She crossed out a few of them. "Here, these are from the last month," she said, handing me the list. "The ones that are crossed out were old people who lived alone. They're not what you're looking for. All the other ones have families."

"Thanks, Svetlana, you're a peach. I hope I'll see you again soon."

Of course, that last statement was a big fat lie, so clumsy it didn't even added to my Lying skill. I wasn't likely to run into this girl anywhere anymore.

I hurried outside and opened the paper. I'd also lied when I said I wanted names of people who'd died in the last month; I was only interested in going back a week. The mission had been issued only recently, so that meant the head of the household couldn't have died that long ago.

And in fact, one of the crossed-out names turned out to be the one I needed: Olga Nikiforov, year of birth 1938, year of death...

I skimmed down to her address and punched it into Google Maps. It turned out to be close enough to walk to, especially because the weather was good. Well, a small snowfall seemed to be in the air, but to me that was like a pleasant warm drizzle.

Gorokhovets was impossibly small and charming. It was cozy and old, just like a holiday postcard. Awash in monuments, it had long become a historical monument itself. All the cars, lampposts and electric cables looked so out of place there.

I was so enchanted by this provincial town with its onion-domed churches, fancy baroque mansions and slightly ramshackle 19th-century houses that I nearly missed the street I was looking for and had to turn back.

Things were already simpler here. The street was lined with tired broken-back log cottages that had once been well built. The paint on their shutters was peeling, the carved ornaments on their roofs cracked and withered. The barking of guard dogs broke the oppressive silence. Good dogs: they sensed the presence of a stranger.

I went up to Mrs. Nikiforov's house and stopped. It was just as Bumpkin had described it: a big house and a courtyard with outbuildings. There were no lights on. Svetlana had been right: the old lady must have had no apparent heirs. Still, I soon made out a chain of tiny barefoot footprints in the fresh snow, leading to a nearby shed.

I didn't bother with the gate: I had no idea how to open the wretched thing, anyway. I just leaped over it and immediately ducked down for fear of the neighbors spotting me.

I ran over to the house, stood up straight and pulled out my little mirror to check the footprints. Just what I thought: they appeared to belong to a cat. Clutching my knife, I slowly walked toward the shed. There was no lock, just a rusty iron hook on a loop. I took it off, activated Light, and barged in.

It was dreadful. It looked like a wild animal had been confined here. The walls were covered in deep scratches and streaks of blood as though someone had been dragged inside by force. The few garden tools kept in the shed were strewn all over the place, a bench lining one of the walls was completely smashed. Hadn't the mission said something about a mass slaughter of animals? Evidently, everything must have happened here.

I looked around closely. A tiny old man the size of a small dog cowered in a dark corner. He was scruffy and disheveled, with red eyes and long fingers. He was wiggling back and forth, mumbling something under his breath.

As I approached, I managed to make out the words.

"One-Eye, how can I live without you? One-Eye, my dear friend... One-Eye... oh, One-Eye..."

"Hello there."

The old man raised his head, gazed at me expressionlessly, then emitted a heart-wrenching scream that made the birds perched outside shoot up into the sky.

"One-Eye! One-Eye!"

"What are you shouting for? Really. Stop now!"

"One-Eye... he abandoned me," the creature started muttering again, dropping his head. "He ran away. No house goblin, no barn hand. One-Eye, oh, One-Eye!"

A notification flickered in front of my eyes, updating the mission. Not this again!

The Mad Barnyard Keeper mission has been updated.

Dispose of the barn hand as soon as possible. In case of delay, the amount of the reward will

decrease by 5 grams per hour.
Explanations have been added.

I opened the explanations.

There are two ways of getting rid of the barn hand. Either find him a new home or kill him.

Oh, great. Thanks a bunch for the tip. Find him a new home? Was that a joke or something? I definitely wasn't taking this psycho back home; one lucky house goblin was well enough for me.

I reached for my knife. If I remembered rightly, Bumpkin was one hell of a fighter. He didn't remember his attacking me, of course, because I'd managed to rewind time just at the last moment. Now let's see if a goblin helper is anything like his bosses.

I pulled out my knife, readying it. The creature was oblivious, mumbling something about One-Eye and his treacherous betrayal.

In one swift swing, I buried the knife in his hunched back.

Blood gushed everywhere.

Mission accomplished.

You've killed an intelligent being that was neutral to you
-50 karma points. Current level: -80. You gravitate to the Dark Side.

You've gained the ability: Obedience
You've gained the spell: Summoning of a Sheep Dog.

Not bad.

All would have been fine and dandy, except the creature's head dropped back. Our eyes met.

His dying gaze was filled with pain.

Shit. Shit, shit!

I managed to deflect the blow at the last moment. Then I sheathed the knife and walked out of the shed. I was dying for a smoke or even better, a drink.

All right, but where was I supposed to find him a home now? I desperately needed Bumpkin's advice. That meant going home and then coming all the way back here. That would be at least four hours of travel, which meant 20 grams of dust: an inexcusable luxury.

Having said that...

I took out my phone and scrolled down to Mark, the glass fitters' foreman. I couldn't imagine what he'd think about me. But then, what did I care? I didn't even know the guy.

The phone was ringing, great.

"Hello? Are you glazing the window at Dementiev's place right now?"

I could sense confusion on the other end. He was obviously looking for the receipt.

"Yes, I'm at Dementiev's. We're about ready to leave."

"This is a matter of life and death. Please put him on the phone."

"What do I do?" I could hear Bumpkin's annoyed voice. "Talk to who? Where?"

"Bumpkin! Hi."

"Yes. I mean, hello."

"Just listen and don't say anything. Well, listen first and then you can talk. We need to decide what to do about this barn hand. His mistress has died, just like you said. And it looks like the house goblin has bailed, too. What should I do?"

I couldn't imagine what the glaziers were thinking about me — or rather, the house goblin — if they were listening to the conversation. He gave me complete instructions. He told me to get some milk and find a big country house with a well-groomed homestead, then added a few tips on how to strike up a conversation with the owners and their house goblin.

Yeah right. Provided they didn't have me committed.

A couple of minutes later, I finally hung up. I went back to the road, climbed back over the gate and looked around. There were no well-appointed houses around here; they all listed to one side and had clearly seen better days. Only the one I'd just been to didn't look so bad — apparently, thanks to the care of their rogue house goblin.

I walked all the way back to the intersection where I finally found what I was looking for. A decorative pebble path led from the electronic gate to a spacious three-story mansion built with stone slabs. Several neat outbuildings were lined up behind it; a couple of luxury cars were parked in a wide driveway. Nothing too posh or in-your-face — just a modest little shack probably belonging to one of the local administration. Bribery might be a crime but it sure did pay.

According to Bumpkin, over time even the most beautiful house would fall into decay if it had no house goblin. This edifice must have been here for quite a while but it still looked like new. That meant it must have had a goblin.

OK. Let's go get the refreshments.

The local "supermarket" was just a dilapidated hole in the wall, its dirty windows displaying a messy array of cookies and candy. A thin, fortyish woman was keeping military watch by its single narrow aisle. She looked guardedly at my purchase even though there was nothing of note. Just a bottle of milk, some plastic plates, and a pound of chocolates. If I bought any less, it would look too suspicious.

I went back to the mansion. Thank God Gorokhovets was only a small town. In my city, there'd be all sorts of cameras installed all around the fence's perimeter, but here you could do whatever you pleased, particularly since there was no one around. On my whole trip to the store I'd only run into one local denizen.

The steel fence was nice and strong — another sign of the house goblin's vigilant care, — but its bars were around six inches apart, enough for me to stick my hand through. I set a plastic plate on the ground behind the bars and poured some milk onto it, then lay a chocolate next to it. Looking like a complete imbecile, I started whispering the summoning spell Bumpkin had taught me,

"House goblin, house goblin, I've got something nice if you help me out with your wisest advice."

I wouldn't have been surprised if nothing happened. But a door slammed softly in the house. A fur ball rolled out and headed directly for me. At first I thought it was a cat, but then I made out small hands and feet.

The local house goblin was stockier than mine. Clearly, he'd had a much better life.

He beelined for the milk and began lapping it up just like a natural cat before turning his attention to the chocolate. He didn't look at me until after he'd taken a big bite of it.

"What do you want, Seeker?"

"I have business to discuss. What should I call you?"

"Hush."

"Sergei," I said, offering him my hand.

The goblin wavered for a split second but shook hands with me anyway.

"So as I was saying, I have some business to discuss. I heard that a woman died here recently. Mrs. Nikiforov."

"I know," Hush said, nodding.

"She had a house goblin and a barn hand."

"That's right. One-Eye and Goody."

"Well, things are not at all good right now with this Goody, I'm afraid. One-Eye abandoned him and ran off. Now the barn hand is all alone."

"Is he really?" Hush said, surprised. "I wondered what was going on. I thought One-Eye was too harsh with him, that's why he was crying. House goblins take their masters' deaths hard."

"If you heard things like that, why didn't you check in on him?"

"One-Eye and I were at loggerheads. When it comes to housework, he's the best, but he has a crappy personality. You can't go visit someone else's house goblin without his permission. It's not good form."

I chose not to dwell on house goblins' code of good manners. That's not what I'd come here for. "Well, One-Eye isn't around anymore. Apparently, he abandoned the place. And the house is no longer his."

"That's what happens," Hush agreed.

"And his helper will lose his mind without him."

"He will," the goblin agreed again. "And then he'll become feral and will do all sorts of mischief."

"Not if you take him in..."

Hush nodded so quickly it was like those were the words he'd been waiting for. "My household is only small. No livestock worth mentioning apart from the dog and turkeys, but it's better than nothing, I suppose. We need to get back to him fast before the others find out — er, I mean before poor Goody goes completely nuts."

Gotcha! That meant that not every house goblin had his own barn hand, and they were prepared to fight tooth and claw for the right to have one. Still, who was I to object? I was getting my cut out of it anyway.

"Let's go, then!"

Hush leapt onto the high fence, shook all over like a cat about to plunge into frigid water, then jumped down to the ground.

He took a couple of steps and clung fearfully to me. "What are you standing there for? Let's go. I can't stay here long."

"Why not?" I asked as I set off toward the defunct old lady's house.

"We don't like to leave the house. A house

goblin loses his strength when he's away from his nest. They say that if a house goblin spends a week without his home roof, he'll forget his name and lose his strength."

Hush chattered nonstop. Maybe he was babbling in order to rid himself of his fear of being outside his home, or maybe he was just a motormouth. Most likely he was trying to assuage his fears because the closer we got to our destination and the farther we got from his house, the faster he yapped.

Finally, we stood in front of the fence.

"Stay here and don't go inside if you value your life," Hush told me. "No matter what happens. You'll only make it worse."

The next moment he was already sitting astride the fence, turning his head this way and that. Then he hopped down, reached the shed in two feline leaps and slipped inside.

I listened tensely. A woman passed by, clearly a local, so I hurried away from the house. After about five minutes, I came back, but Hush still hadn't returned. I just hoped he was out of harm's way.

And of course, like always, I jinxed it.

"One-Eye!" a voice screamed.

The shed shuddered as though a grenade had exploded inside. My knees shook with the impact.

My first thought was to get the hell out of there as fast as I could. But nothing happened. I was afraid the neighbors might panic, but they hadn't.

A couple of minutes later Hush and Goody emerged.

The house goblin was leading the barn hand like an invalid dosed up with tranquilizers, holding him gently but firmly by the shoulders. It looked like the creature had accepted his fate, peering under his feet and not even muttering.

When they got to the fence, Hush hesitated, lifted the helper onto his shoulders like a sack of potatoes, and leapt over, barely making it under the weight.

I pulled out my mirror. The scene was hilarious. It showed a big fat cat carrying a small, sick kitten by the scruff of its neck. But when you looked at the semiconscious barn hand, the last thing you wanted to do was laugh.

In this state we reached Hush's house. The house goblin slid through the bars, pulled Goody after him, and turned to me.

"Wait here, good man. I'll be right back."

You've helped a barnyard keeper find a new home.

+50 karma points. Current level: +20. You gravitate to the Light Side.

Whew. Finally, I was in the black. So one barnyard keeper was worth five old ladies crossing the street. Even though there was more profit in this, I'd take the old ladies any day. House goblins' helpers were rather neurotic.

Hush returned alone, happily bouncing from foot to foot.

"Thank you, my good man. Now Goody will get better in no time. I'll take care of that. Why does any creature get depressed? Because he or she has nothing to do. But if you keep a person or house goblin busy with the smallest task, they might forget their old malaises."

No, no matter how you sliced it, Hush was still a chatterbox. I nodded my agreement, all the while wondering what the house goblin was trying to get at with his speech.

"I don't really have any money. But here..."

Hush reached out his hand which held a small amount of dust. Eyeballing it, I estimated that it was around 10 grams. But before I had a chance to reach out my sticky fingers, something started to happen to the dust. It shriveled up, as though it were alive, and started to quickly solidify, releasing a whitish smoke. Six seconds or so went by, and instead of the little handful of the Game currency, a tiny, bright crystal lay on the house goblin's palm.

"This is for you."

I took the cold polygon and nearly yelped in fear as it crumbled in my hands. What kind of a joke was this?

You've mastered the Smoke and Mirrors spell.

"Take care, my good man," Hush shook my hand and trotted back to the house.

Smoke and Mirrors, you say? I continued to stand there, still gathering my wits. Well, at least now I understood how spells were passed along. I remembered Harph saying that as soon as I leveled Destroyer up to 70, he'd teach me Thunder from the Sky. What did that mean? Apparently, selling spells wasn't the vendors' prerogative: Players could do it too. Of course, it wasn't an excuse to be overusing and abusing them because these crystals were apparently fashioned out of dust, which made them rather pricey. And something deep inside told me that the coolest spells must cost a lot of dust.

I opened the interface.

Smoke and Mirrors (Mysticism) significantly reduces the chances of being spotted.
Works only on living things.
Range: 3 yards.
Cost: 20 mana points.
Duration: 30 seconds.
Warning! This spell doesn't affect the living things whose Mysticism skill is higher than the user's.

Well, this wasn't bad. Like, really not bad. But now it was time to think about more pressing matters. It was already 2:50 pm, and I was sixty miles from home. Not good.

I turned off Hush's street and headed toward the center of Gorokhovets, even though the expression "headed toward" was strange in this context: it only took me seven minutes to get there and another couple to Google the local taxi service. Predictably, based on the meter I had to pay four bucks more than what I'd paid to get here.

I smiled as I pressed "Accept". One ruble in, two rubles out. Ah, the perks of provincial life.

My second driver was a mirror image of the first: a swarthy frizzy-haired southerner in a dirty sedan. The radio was blasting while he kept trying to shout over it. Unfortunately for him, I didn't want to engage, responding with monosyllabic words until I busied myself with my phone. I actually wrote a letter to Julia — the girl whom I'd met near my parents' house. I needed to follow up on her promise to get together.

She replied almost immediately along the lines of *I always keep my word*.

"*When?*" was the only thing she asked.

To that I replied cryptically, "*Soon.*"

Feeling perfectly content, I put my phone away, laid my head on the headrest and slept the whole way. I didn't open my eyes until the sedan jerked for the last time and the driver slapped me on the shoulder.

I'd been delivered safe and sound — but not to my own building: I'd deliberately told him to stop at the neighboring one. First of all, it looked like I was developing a taxi habit — something my nosy neighbors might not appreciate. And secondly, what if the driver could be traced back to me? No, it was best not to take any chances.

As I watched the car drive away, I mechanically pulled my cigarettes out of my pocket, extracted one and raised it to my lips, then tossed it away. Damn that!

I strode to my house. It was already dark. The streetlights had already been turned on, their gas discharge bulbs gradually warming up. The cars' turn signals were blinking. People were hurrying home after having begged off an hour early. Life was good. Now I'd get up to my place, and Bumpkin would undoubtedly have cooked something delicious....

My serenity vanished in an instant. I was walking past my house along the sidewalk lined with bare, wintry trees, when a Player appeared in front of me. There was nothing wrong with that, had it not been for the text box hovering above his head. It contained a single word that made my blood run cold:

Seer

Chapter 14

I T'S COMMON KNOWLEDGE that misfortune breeds misfortune. If a pipe bursts in the bathroom, the valve to turn off the water is also sure to break. Or you'll run out of money for your phone. Or the repair man's van will get a flat tire right after it pulls away. Yep, Murphy's law in action.

And that's just what happened to me at this moment. No sooner did I spot the Seer than I immediately did the only thing I could do.

I stepped to the right and hid behind a bare tree which in theory was wide enough, especially seeing as it was dusk now. With only one reservation: the Seer was heading my way.

And he wasn't the only one.

Shuffling along laboriously, the Professor was crossing the street from the other side. He was as drunk as a person could be. But that wasn't the worst part. The worst part was, he'd already caught sight of me and clearly intended to engage me in one of his highbrow discussions.

Oh yeah. Just my luck.

Staggering, the Professor raised his arms in greeting and opened his mouth to say hello. I thrust out my hand, and, driven by some sort of inner confidence in my powers, cast the Smoke and Mirrors spell.

Your Mysticism skill has increased to level 1.

The Professor stumbled and lost his footing. He looked around dimly, and spotting a new target, set off toward the Seer.

"Excuse me, young man. As fate would have it, I must ask for your help."

"Pardon me?" the Seer asked in surprise.

"I mean," — hiccup — "the three Moirae, the Greek goddesses of fate who're forever spinning the thread of human lives..."

Uh oh. The Professor was on a roll.

I peeped out from behind the tree. The Seer was standing at an angle to me, an amused smile frozen on his lips. In front of him, the Professor pontificated animatedly, enlightening him on the subtleties of Greek mythology. I knew that he was also well-versed in Roman, Egyptian, Anglo-Norman, and Scandinavian religions — but I didn't stick around long enough to hear where his speech was headed.

I surveyed my surroundings again. I was exactly halfway home. I couldn't take the path in front of me. That meant I'd need to go back — and ideally, make it quick. It was obvious that the Seer didn't enjoy his patrolling mission because he now directed all his attention at the Professor, patronizingly chuckling at his particularly amusing pearls of wisdom.

Now.

I dashed across the lawn — if you could apply that word to the patch of muddy soil next to the sidewalk — threading my way past the trees like a half-crazed rabbit. Only a couple of seconds later, I heard the Seer's hesitant voice behind me,

"Hey! Stop!"

Yeah right. Nothing short of a handgun could stop me. Which was actually quite a possibility. The Seer could have had all sorts of things on him. He could launch a fireball or just fire a real gun at me. You just didn't know with these guys.

Luckily, he didn't. As I took cover behind the corner of a building, I glimpsed the Seer running after me down the sidewalk.

I froze. What could I do now? I had nowhere to hide. The store was straight ahead; to my left was the foundation pit that I knew so well. Cars were flashing by but no one would stop for me: fights were a common occurrence in these parts. Who really wanted to risk getting involved?

Should I make a dash toward the foundation pit? I might just as well get down on my knees right now and yell, "Sir, please don't kill me!"

I felt some kind of righteous anger well inside me. This was probably what our ancestors used to call valor. The Seer was now expecting his prey to run away, thinking he'd catch up with it. I could do something to alter that plan.

I pressed myself to the wall and listened intently until I heard the approaching clatter of footsteps. My pursuer's rosy, pudgy face loomed out of the darkness right in front of my eyes.

Take that!

The punch came out pretty well, knocking my adversary off balance. Still, it wasn't quite as I'd expected. No big deal — I could try again.

This time I invested all my strength into a right hook. I even thought I heard a crunch.

Your Hand-to-Hand Fighting skill has increased to level 6.

The Seer slumped to the ground and didn't appear in a hurry to stand up. I checked his pulse, just in case. He was alive. I didn't get any more notifications, so I figured he'd live.

I got my ass in gear and dashed back home, via the courtyard this time. I dove into the lobby, slammed the front door behind me, heard the magnet lock click, and nearly slid down the wall.

My knees were shaking and my arms were covered in goosebumps. They'd tracked me down. They'd found me... or had they?

What was the probability that the Seers would be strolling right next to my house? Not very high. On the other hand, why was I so sure it had anything to do with me? Maybe they'd just found the foundation pit where the Chorul had met his demise? That scenario was also entirely possible.

I could hear footsteps upstairs: someone was

coming down. Trying to look as nonchalant as possible, I went to meet them.

It was Victor, Lydia's husband. While I was somewhat formal with her, he and I had a more cordial relationship even though there was a bigger age difference between us.

"Oh, hi, Sergei. I thought you were at home."

I tensed up. "Why?"

"There's music playing in your place."

"Ah, I just ran to the store," I glanced at my empty hands and added, "To get some cigarettes."

"I've also been sent to the store," Victor said cheerfully, as if running errands was the entire purpose of his life, then stumbled down to the lobby.

I took out my knife and continued upstairs. Music playing? They might be waiting for me at home. I really needed to get the hell out of here. That would be a much more sensible thing to do, except that there was a Seer outside, and he'd probably recovered by now.

At the same time, hey, this was my house. I didn't have another one. If someone had broken in, all I had to do was politely ask them to vacate the place. I might even give them a kick in the butt to speed up the process.

I stopped by the door and furtively pulled at the handle. The door was locked. Victor had been telling the truth, though — there was music playing. I couldn't quite make out what it was.

How odd. I took my keys out as quietly as I could, unlocked the door, and pushed it in.

"*Kalinka, kalinka, kalinka maya! Eh, kalinka, kalinka, kalinka maya!*" was coming out of the living room.

Don't get me wrong: I have lots of respect for Russian folk songs. It was just that today I wasn't really counting on hearing any in my apartment.

Without removing my street shoes, I slowly approached and peeked into the room.

I nearly burst into laughter. The scene was a beauty.

Bumpkin was sitting on the folded couch with his legs crossed. He was waving his right hand like a conductor while pressing his left hand to his forehead — all the while, singing along. Or rather, he was opening his mouth, repeating the words after the choir.

I decided to stop lurking. As I entered the room, one of the floorboards creaked under my foot. The house goblin jumped so high he very nearly hit the chandelier overhead.

"Are you okay, Master?" he asked, staring at my knife.

"You're playing the music too loud. The neighbors are complaining. They asked me to talk to you," I joked, putting away the knife.

I went over to my laptop. It was switched on, the search engine sporting the words "feel-good music" in an open tab. "You know how to use a computer?"

"My last master taught me. But that was before I..." he faltered.

"Before you what? Come on, spit it out."

"Before I spilled some water on his *campucher*. I didn't mean it."

"Of course you didn't. Would it be any other way with you?"

I walked around the apartment, checking to

make sure that a hurricane named Bumpkin hadn't destroyed anything else. To my surprise, everything was in order. The window had been fixed. I saw three bucks on the bedside table: apparently, the goblin had bargained the foreman down even more.

The aroma of beef Stroganoff coming from the stove drove me wild. I didn't even wash my hands. I dished out a plateful of exquisite, finely chopped pieces of meat, and as Bumpkin shrieked in protest that the sauce was supposed to be warm, I started to eat.

The house goblin watched me fearfully, like you'd look at starving African children who have been sent humanitarian aid. I didn't bat an eyelid. So there was nothing for Bumpkin to do but turn away and boil some water for tea.

Huh, and what if I decided to level up my new ability? I reached out toward the house goblin, who was standing with his back to me, and cast Smoke and Mirrors.

"Are you experimenting, Master?" Bumpkin asked without turning around.

Well then. I guess that settled it: the goblin's Mysticism skill must have been much higher than mine.

I spent the rest of the day just fooling about. I played Heroes of Might and Magic III for a while, did a few sets of push-ups in the futile hope of upping Athletics, and added a few stretches for good measure. I also wanted to practice casting Light in order to level up Illusion but reconsidered just in time, realizing that it might be noticeable from outside. So I went into the bathroom and practiced it there instead.

I must have looked a sight: half naked, in boxers and a trench coat, illuminating the confines of my bathroom with my hand. As my mother would say, all dressed up with no place to go. And in the end, it was all for nothing. A half-hour later, having spent all my mana, I hadn't received a single point. Wonder if it might have something to do with the usefulness of the spell that was used?

I went to bed in a bad mood, expecting a serious conversation with Hunter.

The morning sun greeted me in the kitchen as I devoured a plateful of fluffy homemade waffles. Today not only had I not overslept, but my dreams were normal and not memorable in any way. I spent some time reading the local news just in case, but I didn't see anything of note, so at the scheduled time I went upstairs to Hunter's.

"Sit down and get into butterfly," he greeted me.

So much for talking to him. Uncle Nick looked angry, and he didn't bother to hide it. He paced around, acting like he was occupied with something important — but to all intents and purposes he was only moving stuff around.

"Tell me about it," he said finally, sitting down in front of me.

In theory, there was no reason for me to hide anything. So I told him all about my misfortunes the night before, skipping the trip to Gorokhovets.

Hunter listened impassively and silently, shaking his head from time to time.

"The Grand Master of the order sent Magister Oliverio here," he finally said. "He usually oversees Western Europe, but Magister Velemir left for Mechilos for some discussions, so Oliverio had to come instead. He brought around thirty Seers with him. As far as I understand, most of them are empaths, but rather strong. It took them all of an hour to find the place where the Chorul had been killed."

"So I can expect them at any time?"

"It's more complicated than that. You didn't have a chance to leave traces, not counting the Seer's broken nose. Why are you surprised? Yes, you broke his nose."

"What do you mean?"

"It's easy for them to track the Chorul's information matrix because there're none of that kind in the Cesspit. All you need to do is tune in to the right channel. By the way, right now there's no mission issued that would mention the place of the Chorul's murder. Know what I mean? With you, it's a little harder. You're a human — your Korl blood is diluted to say the least, — and most of the Players in this world are also humans."

"Cool. Does that mean I might sit it out?"

"Yes, and that's exactly what we're going to do. You'll sit tight at home for about a week and then we'll take you to Purgator to see a friend of mine. We can't do it now; it's not a good time."

"The community is the only place I can't go."

"It's not the only place where there are Gates and a Gatekeeper. OK, get up now."

He didn't say another word. He proceeded as he always did, starting with hand-to-hand fighting, and then with knives. I made a new level in Hand-to-Hand and two in Short Blades.

I squandered the rest of the day. In the past I wouldn't have given that any thought, but now the inaction stressed me out. When you're cozy and warm at home, you can't level up skills, which means you can't level up overall. And to be honest, in just the first day of my forced idleness I did everything I could possibly do. I played a game for a while, watched some series for a while, and in the evening even turned on the TV[12] and felt my brain rot even as I watched the national programs.

The only thing I understood for certain was that I was slowly turning to mush, like a fish that lay in the hot sun for a whole day.

Sitting around at home for an entire week was out of the question.

On top of that, I had that idiotic dream again. The same darkness and the three figures in front of me. But this time I was standing still and they were walking toward me. I was roused by Bumpkin who was poking me anxiously: according to him, I'd been sleeping like the dead again.

I had my training, after which my mood was as low as could be. I didn't level up a single skill. It might have been my mood or maybe my body had indeed "adapted" — but Hunter was much crueler than usual, and at the end of the training he told me I looked fried.

Bumpkin was the only happy one. Why shouldn't he be? His master was at home and in need of his care. Except that I risked turning into a walking muffin top if it went on for much longer. I had enough food for a week and a half. In any case, I couldn't go on like this.

Julia put the final nail in the coffin of my craving for freedom, texting me a laconic message:

Did you change your mind?

The Time Master

I furtively slipped on my trench coat so the house goblin wouldn't protest, and crept out into the lobby. I paused on the landing for a few moments, looking at the courtyard through the filthy window. Kids were playing by the slide; at a distance, teenagers were smoking on a run-down bench, practicing their cussing. A few men were repairing a Niva SUV next to some not-exactly-legal garages. The place was crawling with commoners: not a single Player in sight. Touch wood.

I went outside- but instead of heading to the street, I walked through the courtyards, skirting the school grounds. I was so nervous I desperately wanted to smoke. I went so far as to take out a cigarette, knead it in my fingers, and sniff it. I imagined how good the first drag always felt.

Then I broke it and threw it away. No way. I was stronger than that.

I approached the bus stop from the other side. I stood there for a while and looked around. No signs of Seers anywhere. Impossible. Somehow I didn't think they'd decided that lightning doesn't strike twice in the same place: they were bound to leave someone here. There was also the possibility that all of them might still be hanging around the foundation pit. But in that case, I would have noticed someone next to the building. Weird.

With a spring in my step I headed over to Uncle Zaur's café. I shook his hand and much to his surprise, only ordered a coffee: a nasty, foul instant drink whose only natural ingredient was water, and simply because you can't sit in a café without ordering anything.

I took out my phone and dialed Julia. She picked

up almost instantly. We agreed to meet half an hour later at the Woodlands.

The Woodlands? Did she really want to go to the park in the winter? Was she also a Korl or something?

It wasn't a very long ride, anyway. I'd have enough time to finish my coffee.

"Hey, minnow, wanna do a three-way split?" [13]

Minnow? Oh, right, to commoners I was still this scrawny guy who didn't look his age. A definite drawback of Uncle Zaur's little café was that there was no dress code. As a result, it attracted a motley crowd.

"No, thanks."

"Why not? Who do you think you are, fucking Prince of Wales?"

It was too bad there was no way to just make him disappear. But... maybe I could do just the opposite?

I reached out my arm and cast Smoke and Mirrors.

Your Mysticism ability has increased to level 2.

My potential drinking buddy gave me a dull look, then turned away and sat down at a nearby table.

Fantastic. Had I had just a little less of a conscience or a less scrupulous upbringing, I would have gone in for thieving. With a spell like this I didn't need anything else, provided I didn't end up on CCTV cameras.

I finished my coffee and went outside. Once again I took every possible precaution — but it was like the Seers had decided to troll me a little. I waited for the bus and rode to the park.

When I got off, I ran into a little corner store and bought a box of Raffaello. I arrived at the Gorky monument 10 minutes early.

Julia appeared with the punctuality of the English queen. No, I hadn't been imagining things when I met her in the dark. She was a knockout.

"Hi."

"Hi. Flowers weren't quite right for the weather, so here," I said, holding the chocolates out to her.

"How do you know they're my favorite?" she asked with a smile. "Nothing like them to grow some fat on my butt."

"You could eat twenty of those boxes without ruining your shape."

She blushed and so did I, embarrassed at my clumsy compliment. I wanted to rewind time but then reconsidered. I could handle this.

"Some place you've chosen," I said.

"Why? I often come here for a walk."

"Aren't you scared?"

"What's there to be scared of? I have a green belt in tae kwon do."

I learned plenty more interesting things about her. For example, she went to an industrial technology school on scholarship and was finishing up. She lived with her parents. Not married. Clean criminal record. Little Miss Perfect, in other words.

"You're shivering," I said.

"No, I'm OK."

"You may think I'm a nerd, but let's go find a warm place instead of walking in the cold."

Julia shook her head. "I'm not going anywhere

with you."

"Oh please. Do I look like a rapist? How about a movie?"

We left the park happily. I called a taxi on the way. A couple of minutes later we were sitting in a toasty car, and ten minutes after that, standing in line at the theater. All the movies playing looked crappy, but I couldn't have cared less what we saw. I bought tickets, led her to the bar, and practically had to force her to get something.

My jaw practically dropped when she asked for some salted popcorn. Holy shit! Things like that can't be mere coincidences. We ordered two buckets of salted popcorn and Cokes, and went inside.

I couldn't stop thinking about the Seers, the Chorul, and the entire situation I'd fallen into. But at the same time, I felt happy and at peace with myself just sitting beside Julia. It was as though I'd known her for a hundred years.

The movie exceeded my expectations — that is to say, it was exceptional garbage: a brainless action blockbuster with three obscene jokes and eighteen toilet ones. But not even that could ruin our good mood.

"I'll get us a taxi," I said outside.

"Let's take the bus," Julia suggested, averting her gaze. "It takes longer."

Did I need to say anything more? Well, probably.

I walked her to her front door.

"Thank you," she said.

"What for now?"

"For guessing my name."

She kissed me on the cheek and fluttered into

The Time Master

the lobby. I unfastened my trench coat to cool down and stomped toward the bus stop.

Sorry, Misters Seers. You won't get me. Especially because I'd come up with a plan.

I took out my phone and found the contact I was looking for.

"Litius? Hi dude. I need your help."

Chapter 15

A S THE RUSSIAN proverb goes, you're better off having a hundred friends than a hundred rubles. Meaning that you can always turn to a friend in need. I wouldn't say I had a lot of money. And people weren't exactly lining up to be my buddies. But as it turned out, I didn't need a hundred friends: two proved more than enough.

"Hey," Jan said, shaking my hand.

"Hi."

"Here," he handed me a slip of paper.

I stared at the map of the community depicted in the best traditions of primitivist art. That is to say, it looked as if a three-year-old child had scribbled it.

Jan shrugged. "Sorry, I don't have the Calligraphy ability."

Calligraphy? I made a mental note. I really needed to expand my list of skills. All I had at the moment was Insight. Not exactly the worst of abilities, but still.

"So it's this building?" I pointed to a cross on the map.

"Yes. The Magister himself doesn't go out. And the Seers don't return until nighttime. They spend the whole day poking around the city. People are spreading different rumors."

"Like what?"

"That someone killed a *Kvorull*. And he was some sort of a top gun or something like that."

"Chorul," I corrected him. "So I guess you don't know what that is."

"No, no one ever talked about anything like that in Noggle. Nor here, at least not until now... so where's your expert?"

I wasn't going to tell Jan that Litius wasn't an expert but just a brilliant creature with an amazing memory. For one thing, it was none of Jan's business, and for another, I simply couldn't break the non-disclosure oath. I had no idea what might happen to me if I did.

"He's on his way," I said.

We were sitting in a cheap tavern — one of those places where you couldn't tell whether it stank of piss or beer. For some reason Litius wouldn't let us visit him at home. Rather, he would have let me visit, but when he heard about Jan, he began stuttering and ultimately refused to have us come over. In short, he started to act like an ignorant Beastman.

"There he is," I said, sitting higher in my chair.

Jan stood up and offered Litius his hand. Apparently, Jan knew nothing of the scorn that Players had for these catpeople. Or rather, he hadn't yet had a chance to imbibe it. Since Noggle was near Ullum, Jan used to see a lot of Beastman Seekers after he'd been initiated, so to him that was quite normal.

"Did you g-g-get it?" Litius asked.

"Here," I said, holding out Jan's artwork.

Litius didn't laugh at the sight of the clumsy drawing. Rather, he nodded approvingly, running a finger along the paper.

"Can I get you something?" a server had materialized next to Litius.

"A beer, please," he said. When the girl had walked away, he gave us a long look. "Please don't s-s-say you were expecting me to order some m-m-milk."

"Well, to be honest..." I began.

"No, Sergei," Jan shook his head. "They may be animals but they drink like fish. Sorry about that."

"It's all right," Litius shrugged. "It's true. I would have said we drink like pigs. Anyway, look at this."

I leaned over the table and noticed that Litius had stopped stuttering.

"The Seers have taken over the third building to the left of the Syndicate. You can't reach it from the main entrance."

"Shit. So much for all the trouble."

"But," Litius said, raising a finger, "you can access it along the roofs of the neighboring houses, starting from the commoner district.

"Sorry! My name's not Spiderman," I said.

"But you have a mage friend," the Beastman pointed out.

"I'm not Spiderman either," Jan said, shaking his head.

"What's your Witchcraft level? Do you know the Ivy spell?"

"It's thirty-eight. I do know Ivy, and I also know Wild Ivy and Poison Ivy. But why-" Jan stopped mid-word, his eyes wide open. He looked first at me and then at Litius.

"Damn man, you're a freakin' genius. I never would have thought of that."

"Can someone explain?" I demanded. "What's with this Ivy thing?"

"It's a spell. It conjures up — surprise! — ivy," Jan explained. "It's a combat spell usually used to either immobilize or strangle your opponent."

Litis nodded. "In this case you'll cast ivy from one roof to the next. Then just walk across it," he picked up his beer, lapped it up quickly with his tongue, and then guzzled the rest in two huge gulps. "And you'll keep doing that until you get to the Seers' residence."

"Cool," I nodded. "That's what we'll do, then."

"Sergei," Jan said, elbowing me. "Are you sure this is worth it? If it doesn't work, it'll be our heads on the line."

"That's why you two aren't coming. I have no intention of blowing your covers. The Seers are looking for me and they won't rest until they find me. The only option I have is to pay them a visit myself. But it needs to be impromptu and without warning, just a quick chat with their boss. Preferably involving strong arguments," I lovingly stroked my knife, looking pensively at the two.

"I hope there are no Prophets among them," Jan said.

"A Prophet isn't omnipotent," Litius pointed out. "He or she can't consider all the options. But the Oracle is something else entirely."

"Then I hope there are no Oracles among the Seers."

For some reason, my response made them

laugh. Not chuckle or smirk as well-behaved gentlemen are supposed to: no, the two guffawed like a pair of donkeys.

"You can be sure that there's only one Oracle in the Cesspit," Jan said. "And he doesn't belong to any Order."

"In that case, this mission can succeed," I said, getting up and shaking their hands. "See you tomorrow."

Jan nodded. "Two p.m."

I took all the necessary precautions on the way home: I rode one stop too far and walked back across the maze of backyards until I came to the semi-legal garages behind my house. I went into the lobby, walked up the stairs, and unlocked my door.

I was greeted by silence permeated with the breathtaking aroma of deep-fried dough. I shut the door, took off my jacket, and practically ran to the kitchen.

A plateful of sweet wafer rolls sat on the table, still soft and clearly mouth-watering. Never mind the condensed-milk filling was missing. I knew very well why: it's been a while since I'd shopped for one of those delicious white cans[14].

"Bumpkin, you'd better own up," I said with my mouth full. "What have you done this time?"

"Nothing really," I heard from somewhere in the air either above or behind me. "I just dropped something."

Then it hit me: there was no music playing. I didn't hear any of those Russian folk songs that the house goblin loved so much.

I darted into the living room and turned on my

computer, my fingers still greasy from the rolls. I spent a couple of agonizing minutes waiting, but fortunately there was no reason to be anxious. Everything was fine.

"Bumpkin, come here."

The house goblin materialized next to me.

"What did you break?"

"I dropped it," my freeloader answered curtly and pointed at the television.

My so-called television was supposed to symbolize the long and winding road of progress. It was one of the first LED ones bought secondhand together with its heavy stand. I wouldn't say that I used it often, as it was hardly a necessity.

I turned it on and immediately saw some defective pixels on the left side of the screen, right where the channel's logo belonged. It was actually more fun this way, trying to guess what channel you were watching.

"*Vera, you misunderstood me,*" an actor babbled on screen.

"J*esus! Can one get anything to eat in this house?*"

Aha, that was *The Voronins*, a brain-dead excuse for a sitcom. Therefore, this was STS.[15]

Click.

"*...both the civilization and all knowledge of it sank into oblivion. Its traces weren't uncovered until the early 20th century, strangely coinciding with the time when Rockefeller became one of the wealthiest men on Earth,*" a voiceover pontificated.

I couldn't name the exact program, but the channel just had to be REN-TV.[16]

Click.

"*And that's why it happened the way it happened,*" intoned an obese ex-celebrity.

TNT.[17] Click.

"*They themselves sponsor terrorism and all sorts of lowlifes and then they say we're the bad ones. That's twisted logic.*"

This was either Channel One or Rossiya.[18] Whichever option you prefer.

I pressed the red button. The screen went black, but I also pulled the plug out of the socket for good measure.

"You know what, Bumpkin? You didn't do anything bad."

For the rest of the day I did a little studying, texted with Julia for a while, ate the rest of the wafers, and nearly died from a burst stomach.

In the morning I even woke up with a smile on my face. Bumpkin was puttering around in the kitchen, my phone showed a few new messages from my new crush, and instead of feeling fear in the face of a bold plan, I was actually quite confident of my powers.

"Why are you glowing?" Hunter looked at me warily.

"I just got enough sleep."

My Lying skill didn't level up this time, which meant Hunter hadn't believed me. He motioned me to the mats, and our usual training began.

In fact, today I was in top form. Naturally, when it came to hand-to-hand, I was still no match for Hunter. But when we switched to knives, I managed to parry a few complicated blows that in the past I would have missed.

The Time Master

Your Short Blades skill has increased to level 8.

"Not bad. You have a knack for weapon fighting."

I couldn't believe my ears. Was he praising me now, for the first time since we'd been working together?

"If you keep up with that, we'll move on to swords pretty soon."

That was quite a change! The only question was how I was supposed to carry a sword in public. It would be pretty conspicuous, wouldn't it? A knife was much more unobtrusive.

I laughed. I was an idiot, wasn't I? What was my bag there for? That's why I'd never seen a single Player in the community wearing full armor or clutching a battleaxe. You could stash everything away in your inventory.

With that, we bid our good-byes and went home. A little later I looked through the peephole on my door and saw Hunter go downstairs, heading to work. If the truth were known, I should also come up with some sort of cover story. On the other hand, he was obliged to live a double life. How could you explain to people why a grown-up man still far from retirement age wasn't working? You couldn't. On the other hand, there were plenty of young people like myself loafing around doing nothing.

I waited until I had to leave and crept out into the lobby. Bumpkin tut-tutted disapprovingly by way of goodbye. I walked past the school to the next bus stop over and rode to the community — or more precisely, a little past it. I went around it from the side of the old commoner buildings, where I met up with Litius and Jan.

"Here," Litius said, handing a piece of paper to Jan.

It showed a sketched diagram of the buildings. It wasn't like Jan's childish drawing, but a proper scheme with starting and ending points.

"If everything turns out OK, call me in three hours. If not, then..." he made a helpless gesture.

"Got it. We'll get to the house and then Jan will leave."

Jan nodded in agreement. We may have been friends, but he wasn't signing up to be a suicide case.

"If the shit hits the fan, we don't know each other. Okay? Should we get moving?"

We stepped into a small courtyard with a dilapidated sandbox at the center, two parked cars — a rusty Moskvich and a small Toyota — and a few dead branches of a young poplar poking through the cracked tarmac. Judging by the state of the battered two-story buildings, the residents were obviously waiting to be rehoused.

"I hope no one sees us," Jan said worriedly.

"I have Smoke and Mirrors if anything happens," I said just to calm him down.

I chose not to tell him that its range was short and it only worked on one person. It would be useless against a crowd of gawkers.

Jan went close to the wall and reached out his hand.

A thick, sprightly green shoot appeared on the ground in front of him, breaking through the pavement. Submitting to his will, it looped several times, taking the form of something like a staircase, then stretched upward.

"Let's go," Jan said quietly. We clambered up the plant onto the sloping roof of the house.

"Litius, stay here. Take this," I held out a slip of paper with a phone number on it. "If anything happens to me, call this person. His name is Hunter. Tell him everything."

Litius didn't have to be told twice. He wasn't exactly jumping at the chance to cosplay running along roofs and chasing pigeons.

Jan looked down and waved his other hand, destroying the Ivy. The plant wilted like a bush shredded with garden clippers. Jan reached out and waved his right hand again, casting Ivy on the neighboring building.

We set off together, crouching down, as if that would help. It was rather frightening to say the least. Even though the stalk was covered in small, tiny bristles, you couldn't quite call it hard. It caved in under our feet and sort of floated away down below.

On top of that, when I'd almost reached the neighboring roof, a notification flashed before my eyes.

Your Stealth skill has increased to level 1.
You've reached level 5.
Available points: 3

Strength: 26 (x2)
Intellect: 16 (x2)
Fortitude: 20 (x)
Agility: 17 (x4)
Stamina: 15 (x)

Rhetoric: 12 x3)
Speed: 16 (x3)

You've improved your current branch. You may decrease the number of charges used by one point for each use or increase the duration of the rewind by one second.

This abundance of information made me lose my balance and almost come crashing down. Jan grabbed me, dragged me onto the roof and gave Litius a thumbs-up, signaling that everything was OK.

"What's up with you?" he demanded angrily.

"Just a sec."

First I invested in Intellect — seeing as it had been sort of stuck; Agility, since I got such a big bonus; and Rhetoric. What did it say about the charges? Now I had 34 of them. Even if I decreased the number of charges by one point, I still had enough for three rewinds, not more. That meant I should increase the duration of the rewind.

All set, now I could travel back four seconds. You'd better watch out, whoever you are!

"Everything's fine. Let's go."

Jan nodded. I tried to walk around the roof to see if I could do it. These damned old houses! It was so easy to fall to our deaths — all it took was for you to let your mind wander for a split second.

I crouched — not because I was trying to level up Stealth (there was no one here to hide from, was there?), but in order to be able to latch on to the roof with my fingers if I slipped. Finally, we reached the edge. Jan looked at the map, then at Litius, nodded, and cast Ivy again.

Before stepping onto it, I looked around. The place was just too remote for my liking. Far ahead, I could make out the entrance to the community. In front of us lay the last commoner building, one story taller than the previous one.

With the agility of a tightrope walker, Jan climbed the stalk and waved his arm. I just hoped I wouldn't receive any notifications.

And I jinxed it, didn't I? Talk about the devil.

Your Acrobatics skill has increased to level 3.

I was already glad I didn't get bombarded with more messages. Jan checked the map and waved again.

This roof was nothing like the other ones. For one thing, its surface was flat and even: you could lie down on it and sunbathe if you wanted. Next, it offered an excellent view of the community. If any hapless commoners ended up here, they'd just see a bunch of dilapidated buildings — while we saw Players moving in and out in every possible direction. Archali, humans, Abbasses, even an occasional Beastman and a weird-looking creature I'd never seen before, all covered either in bark or in some green growth. Shame I wasn't able to take a good long look at him. There were also a few Guards.

Jan yanked me by the arm, pointing first at the map, then at Litius. The Beastman was looking at us intently, like before — I would even say too intently. Never mind. What did we have here?

This building proved much longer. When we got

to the end, I realized that we were on the edge of the central square.

"That's the house we're looking for, over there," Jan said, pointing at one a couple of buildings down.

"How are we supposed to get over there?"

"The spell is called Levitation. I've improved it, but..."

"But what?"

"I haven't yet leveled it up completely. Normally, you can only use it on yourself. I, however, wanted to make it a combat spell, so I modified it to be able to cast it on an opponent in battle. For now it only works for three seconds."

"Tell me what we need to do."

"Just take a running jump, and then I'll catch you with the spell."

"What do you mean by 'catch'?"

"I mean catch."

"To be honest, I don't think it's a good plan. Do you?"

Jan shrugged. "I don't know. Litius seems to think so. The most important thing is for you to make it to the opposite roof."

"And then what?"

"There's not a lot of space between the other two buildings. Also, the Seers' residence is one story lower."

"Oh great. And here I am hoping that Litius thought with his head and not his posterior."

"He did think. He made a scheme on a piece of paper and did all the calculations. He said you should make it."

"Well, if he says so!"

But it was too late to back out. Well, I suppose I could, but who knew when I'd ever get another chance like this?

"OK, so what do I need to do? Just jump?"

"Wait. You need to wait a moment."

He was right. Even though we were still some distance away from the square, Players would occasionally pass by below.

The right moment came twenty minutes later. Jan slapped me on the shoulder, "Go."

And, well, I went.

I accelerated and jumped. At least I didn't scream. I must have looked like someone having a heart attack on a roller coaster.

But Jan didn't let me down. When I was still about five feet away from the roof, I became weightless, as if stuck between this reality and some other world. It was an odd feeling, like I was a naughty kitten lifted by the scruff of the neck.

But I didn't get the chance to get used to the feeling. Bam! I fell onto the roof, smacking my chest. It looked like I'd indeed made it.

I turned to Jan who gave me a thumbs-up. The joker. Grunting, I stood up and staggered to the opposite edge of the roof.

Your Stealth skill has increased to level 2.

I sure needed that now. It did in fact seem to be possible to jump all the way. It was no more than four yards away. I'd just needed to be quick. I'd be spotted — that much was certain.

I took a few steps back and ran.

Crack!

The bone-snapping sound was so loud that I'm sure even Bumpkin had heard it back in my house.

Only then did I scream.

The agony! Blinded by pain, I didn't even realize at first that I could rewind time.

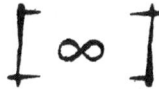

Only after I'd stepped and lifted off the roof, did the agonizing pain release me. My memory came back — and with it, I realized what I'd done wrong the first time.

A video I'd watched three years ago flashed through my mind — an interview with a freerunner. He was talking about the importance of shifting your balance when you fell so that you wouldn't fight gravity.

Bingo! I landed on my toes, reached out, and somersaulted to a stop.

Your Acrobatics skill has increased to level 4.

That's how I should land in the future: nice and easy. I sprang to my feet and ran to a small garret that led inside. I climbed in, fearing that the door might be locked. But I was in for a crazy streak of luck.

I drew my knife and dashed into a long corridor on the top floor. I had two more rewinds in reserve. I quickly took in my surroundings. The residence wasn't meant for the likes of me, I could see that. It was all oak doors, decorative MDF wall panels and brass lamps hanging from the ceiling.

If only I could figure out where the Magister was.

The Time Master

There was no way there'd be a sign hanging on the do...

I tried to rub my eyes — that was exactly what was hanging there, a black sign with white lettering that read *Magister*.

Feeling as if this place was the center of something inconceivable, I inched toward the door. I pulled it and it gave.

It was dark inside. Little light penetrated the windows hung with thick curtains. All I could see was the outline of a massive figure in an armchair.

"It's about time," said a raspy, old-sounding voice. "I was starting to think you wouldn't come."

Chapter 16

A GOOD PLAN is when the things actually follow your well-conceived scenario. A bad one is when new glitches just keep cropping up, forcing you to improvise. And a truly useless plan is when you realize that it makes up part of someone else's clever little scheme.

Judging by the stranger's confident voice, my arrival hadn't surprised him. What a bastard! He didn't even twitch.

"Who are you?"

"It says it right on the door: I'm the Magister."

With a click of a switch, a lamp went on on a tiny table next to the chair, illuminating the owner of the raspy voice. He was an old, chubby man with darkly tanned skin and green eyes.

The Magister looked intently at me for a few more moments, clearly waiting for something, and then burst out laughing.

"Sorry, I love pulling people's legs. I thought it would be fun to put up that sign. Well then, let's begin!" he lifted a finger, apparently as a summons.

The Time Master

Cold hands clamped down on my shoulders from either side of me.

Well, well, well. So you thought you got me, didn't you?

"I thought it would be fun to-""

Without waiting for him to finish, I swayed to the left and immediately jerked my elbow up. I heard a crackle, followed by a scream.

Your Hand-to-Hand Fighting skill has increased to level 7.

Bingo. I rolled aside, whipping out my knife in the process, and turned to my attackers. So, who's the first?

It turned out that I had three adversaries: two humans and an Abbas. Actually no, scrap that. There were two of them. The Abbas was already doubled up on the ground, clutching his face. Courtesy of my Insight skill, I knew the two remaining fighters' identities: one was *the Master,* and the other *Wittechar,* whatever that was supposed to mean.

The one known as the Master reached his arm out in front of him, mouthing something. A fiery sword appeared in his hand.

Dammit! I was down to my last time rewind.

"Stop! Stop!" the Magister jumped to his feet. "Stop now! Artan, take Nicholas out. Yulo, just stay where you are."

The luminous sword disappeared instantly. The

Master grabbed his wounded colleague under his armpits and dragged him toward the door. I recognized the second guy as the poor bastard I'd clobbered earlier next to my house. Judging by the barely visible symmetrical bruises next to his eyes, his nose must have been broken at least a few days prior. He'd probably used magic to heal himself. It might be a funny coincidence, but it looked like I'd just made yet another enemy.

But that wasn't what I should be worrying about right now.

The Abbas stayed in the room along with the Magister who sat back down and started to nervously drum his fingers on the armrest.

"Put your knife away. By the way, where did you get a weapon made of Lmoon steel? Anyway, let's take things one step at a time. Sit down. If we wanted to hurt you, Artan would have shredded you in an instant."

That was far from a sure thing. He may have an instant but I had four seconds of potential advantage.

"Sit down already! We need to have a chat."

He indicated a chair behind me. I looked at the open door through which the two Seers had just left. Following my glance, the Abbas reached out and slammed it shut.

Very well, then. Let's have a chat. I sat down but didn't put my knife away. I'd love to know where the room's windows opened up onto.

"What do you need?" I asked.

"The same as you — information. Let's do it this way: you tell us everything you know, including about the Chorul."

"And what's in it for me?"

The Magister laughed. "Yulo, you hear that? He wants to bargain. All right. Then I'll answer your questions."

"All of them?"

"All of them. Just don't forget the race characteristic of the Abbas. What, you don't know? They can detect any lie."

"And what's gonna happen afterward?"

"I don't know. You'll go to a bar and drink some vodka. You do drink vodka in Russia, don't you?"

"Yes, and we sleep with bears. So you're gonna let me go, then?"

"What we need is information, not your savaged body. So what do you say? Is it a deal?"

"Deal. But you need to swear..."

My phrase seemed to have baffled Oliverio. He slapped his knee and burst out laughing.

Your Persuasion skill has increased to level 3.
Your Persuasion skill has increased to level 4.

"You're a quick learner! OK, I swear to the Chorul's killer who was born in the Cesspit that I won't deliberately harm him unless under a threat to my life or the Order's existence, or unless he presents mortal danger to this or any other world."

He wasn't born yesterday, was he? It was clear this wasn't his first rodeo and he knew the importance of the fine print.

I squinted from the bright light that enveloped the Magister, sealing his oath. Very well. Now we could talk.

"What do you want me to tell you?" I asked.

"Everything. Starting at the beginning. Who are you and how did you become a Player?"

"My name is Mikhail..." I began brazenly.

Hearing that, the Abbas clicked his tongue. The black growths on his head twitched.

Okay, okay, just checking. "My name is Sergei..."

It turned out that talking was indeed my thing. Maybe if I'd been born two or three thousand years earlier, I would have become the second Homer. I recounted everything in detail. A few times, I wanted to embellish the events just to make myself look like less of an idiot, but the Abbas kept clicking his tongue, forcing me back onto the path of truth.

After about ten minutes, the Magister knew all about some of my escapades. However, I'd told him nothing about what had happened in the foundation pit. Ditto for Hunter, Bumpkin, and everything that had followed, except for a few insignificant details and probing questions on my part.

"So that's how you do it," the Master said, scratching an eyebrow. "I admit that when I saw it, I was confused."

"When you saw what?"

"How you rewind time."

"No one can see it. For you, the future I rewound no longer exists."

"You need to understand that I'm a Prophet. Not the most powerful one, of course. We can focus on a particular person in order to see the possible alternatives of their future. That requires maximum concentration and years of practice developing your abilities. Anyway, I won't bore you. As soon as you came in, I saw everything you could do. And then..."

He trailed off, looking at me closely as if in hesitation, then continued, "A white spot appeared in the future, exactly during those four seconds, and you dropped out of my visions. That's never happened to me before, ever."

"So what now? You gonna send me to a lab as a guinea pig?"

"No, of course not. Still, I think that you're in possession of a much more powerful weapon than you realize. And I don't want it to be used to harm the Cesspit or any other world."

"I had no intention — "

"Sergei, I'm afraid no one's gonna ask your opinion here. You killed a Chorul — that's something no one has ever been able to do. That's not within the powers of a Player, let alone a commoner. It seems to me that the whole setup has been carefully and very subtly orchestrated."

"Could you at least tell me what Choruls are?"

"Ah, that's complicated," Oliverio said, scratching the bridge of his nose, "but I'll try. This may sound like a fairy tale, but beyond the black passageway that stretches past two consecutive Hazy worlds, lies Archaeth, the world of the Choruls. It's mysterious and little studied because..."

"Because the Choruls don't like outsiders."

"Exactly. But that's an understatement. They can't bear them. Their level of tolerance for migrants is zero," the Magister smiled. "Many Players, including Wandering Gods, have tried different methods to infiltrate Archaeth. But they've always failed."

"Because the Choruls can rewind time?"

"Not quite. What happened with you is more of a mutation. I don't know the reason for it — whether it's your race, or more specifically, the mix of races, or just pure chance. As I was saying, no one has ever killed any Choruls because they know everything that's going to happen to them in the future."

"How can that be?"

"Imagine you're a young child. You approach a river to cross it by a flimsy bridge. But you know where and when that bridge in front of you is going to break."

"Like déjà vu?"

"You could put it that way. Choruls live their lives simultaneously in the past, present, and future. They exist in all dimensions. You can't kill a Chorul because he'll know you're going to try to. He's forewarned..."

"And therefore, forearmed."

"Exactly. So what happened with you is unusual, to put it mildly. And it attracted a lot of unwanted attention."

"What are you talking about?"

"The attacks on you and other Players. What did you say the name of your attacker was?"

"I didn't say anything."

"So tell me, then."

I shrugged. It wasn't much of a secret, especially because I still didn't quite understand a lot about their power games.

So I gave him the name.

"The Darkest One?" the Magister repeated eagerly. "That could be helpful. That means we really are looking for a Wandering God."

"What do you mean, you're looking?"

"Well, of course. We really don't want such an

ability to land in the hands of a powerful but unscrupulous Player. There was a strong probability that you'd come here to see me. All we had to do was make it possible for you to reach us. Which was why we began looking for that lunatic under the Guards' guidance."

"And? Any results?"

"None at all. He seems to have disappeared from the face of the earth. He's definitely been here: I can still detect his vibrations in the places where he's been, but there are no traces of where he might have gone. It just doesn't make sense."

"Now what?"

"I'll send all the information to the Grand Master," Oliverio took out his phone.

I spotted the blinking WhatsApp icon. Was this for real? They communicated things like this through WhatsApp?

"He'll decide what to do next," Oliverio continued. "But knowing him, we'll stay here for the time being to monitor the situation, so to speak."

"What about me?"

"I don't know. You can go get a drink at the Syndicate. They've just had a delivery of Nogglean ale, I hear. Or you can go home. It's up to you."

"Can I go? Really?"

"Do you think I'm not going to keep my word, especially since I took an oath? Yulo, please see our guest out," he ordered without waiting for me to answer. "And if you find out something important or if you need protection, the doors of the Seers' home are always open to you."

The Abbas stood up and headed unhurriedly

toward the door. He had an unusual gait: his limbs were slightly twisted forward, so he sort of bobbed as he walked.

He glanced expectantly at me. I had to get up.

"Good-bye," I said, remembering my mother's lessons in good manners.

"I hope to see you soon, Sergei," the Magister said, nodding at me.

We went into the corridor and descended the staircase. There was some activity by the front door. A few Guards were having a heated conversation with Artan, the Master with the luminous blade. Rather, they were trying to get in but he wasn't admitting them. The guy with the twice-broken nose was sitting next to the Master on a stool by the front door. He wasn't convulsing from the pain anymore — evidently he'd already been healed — but the way he looked at me made it clear that we weren't going to be friends.

"Yulo?" Artan asked.

The Abbas made a few complex gestures, pointing first at me and then outside.

Dammit! The guy was mute!

"Everything's fine," the Master explained to the Guards. "Just a little misunderstanding. This is our guest and friend. He's just a little quirky. He likes to attract attention, so he came in through the roof."

Well not quite. Attention was the last thing I wanted. That's why I wasn't about to dispute him. It would be better to slink out and get myself away from here. I nodded to the Seers, elbowed my way past the Guards and exited onto the central square, barely keeping myself from breaking into a run.

I looked up. Jan was nowhere in sight. OK, I'd

wait for them here. On second thoughts, I'd wait in the Syndicate and combine business and pleasure.

There was hardly anyone inside: mostly humans, with just one Archalus sitting by the door. There was also that Artist_Chick girl sitting back on a chair in the corner and scribbling something in a large, tabloid-sized sketchbook.

I went into the tiny office next door, fished out two slips of paper with the missions and held them out to the orange-skinned creature. But before he meted out the 60 grams of dust I was entitled to, I read the notification that popped up.

*You've completed three missions. You've earned the designation **Syndicate Messenger**. You now have access to missions in neighboring worlds.*

A new marking showing the location of the Syndicate building in the closest city has been added. In order to view it, you need the Cartography ability.

"Hello! You gonna take your dust or what?" the clerk demanded.

I scooped up my 60 grams without even rejoicing at the sudden windfall. I had now amassed more than 100 grams, which meant I could probably afford something interesting, including spells and abilities. But right now I had to focus on any missions to the neighboring worlds. I was more interested in them than in anything else.

I shuffled back into the main room and went over to the bulletin board. New messages had appeared alongside the old ones: they were the same size but written on orange paper.

Beholder
Mission from the ruler of the city of Brem
Charged with: killing 20 commoners and Players
Sentence: death
Proof of completion: an eye
Location: northwest of Brem, Singing Cave
Reward: 900 grams

Five-Headed Hydra
Mission from Commander Sabnak of the fifth legion of Firoll
Proof of completion: one of the heads
Location: two leagues south of Ubetrain
Reward: 4 kilos

Holy War
Mission from Commander Archail of the second legion of Elysium
Task: place yourself under the orders of Archail to raid Ubetrain
Location: camp near Ubetrain
Time remaining: 9 hours
Reward: 500 grams (issued in the event of a successful raid)

If I understood the first mission correctly, you'd have to go out and kill a beholder. But the second listed no charge at all. What exactly had that hydra done wrong? There was also something nebulous about the last one — you were supposed to place yourself under the orders of some Archail guy to raid a city or stronghold.

I don't think so! I was no one's cannon fodder. Based on the stories I'd heard, Firoll was what we on Earth called hell, and Elysium was heaven. Very well, let them wage war with each other. I wasn't about to get in the middle.

A posting down below caught my eye.

Letter to Fibbian
Mission from the researcher Savial
Required: Deliver a letter to Fibbian
Location: 800 paces along the northern Valley of Silence trail from the Gates
Time remaining: 1 hour 8 minutes
Reward: 60 grams. Return travel to Purgator covered
Level restrictions: under level 10

Perfect. A delivery job from A to B, easy peasy. Ideal for visiting a world for the first time. I'd take that one.

To complete the Letter to Fibbian mission, you need further instructions. Please address yourself to Savial.

Where the hell was I supposed to find this Savial? I looked around and spotted the Archalus still sitting by the door. He was now beckoning to me.

"Hi," he said, sticking out his hand when I got close to him.

"Savial?"

"Yes, that's what they call me. I saw you tear that paper off. Look, I need to deliver a letter to my friend Fibbian. I can't do it myself. I'm waiting for a guy I need to close a deal with. And the letter needs to be delivered as fast as possible. Think you can do it?"

There was something a bit off about him. He was tall and massive with beautiful folded wings. But he was too fidgety. He didn't stop waving his arms as he babbled on in double time.

In the end, he produced a little bag of dust, so heavy that I started to drool involuntarily. He was obviously a merchant.

"I'm going now," I said. "I just wanted to wait for my friends."

"If we don't deliver the letter to Fibbian now, we'll lose a lot of money. He's busy at the excavations. So, what do you say?"

He thrust a hand into the bag and took out a handful of dust.

"Thirty-four grams for the trip. Fibbian will pay the return fare. Do we have a deal? You won't have to do anything. Just take the mountain trail, and it'll take you to my friend. OK, I'll pay you eighty instead of sixty. But it has to be done ASAP."

I won't say I didn't have my doubts. I had no idea what Purgator was like. On the other hand, if there were excavations going on, that must mean there was lots of life there, including Guards who could protect me if needs be.

Also, the money issue was no small thing. Eighty grams was a lot. On top of my hundred and ninety — that was a lot more than two thousand bucks. Damn...

The Time Master

"I'll do it," I said. "Will I get it done under an hour?"

"Of course. If I see your friends, I'll tell them to wait for you. What do they look like?"

I only described Jan. It was unlikely that Litius would come into the community, anyway. I took my 34 grams' fare money and listened to his orders again.

"Have you ever traveled between worlds? No?" Savial's eyes lit up. "Then you need to remember this. The place is called the Valley of Silence. Put the dust in the bowl in front of the Gatekeeper and say the name of the place where you want to go. You need to say it loudly and clearly. Then you'll travel there. Go directly to Fibbian. Give him the letter, wait for his reply, take the dust for the return trip and go back to the Gates. Do the same thing as you did before, but this time say *Sorrow*."

"Sorrow?"

"That's what this place is called," the Archalus said with a helpless gesture. "Then come back to me. You'll give me the letter and get your reward. Can you remember all that?"

There was in fact a lot of information, but I nodded.

"Here, take this."

Savial held out a wax-sealed envelope. "That's it," he said, waving his hands at me. "Go, go."

I guess I was stuck now. I made my way outside and rushed directly to the Gatehouse. I ran in, slightly out of breath, beelined to the statue, and poured the dust into the bowl.

"Before you set out, I'd like to warn you."

I started. I'd never seen a talking statue before.

256

"There may be dangers lying in wait for you in the world where you're going. Do you still want to take the path of the Seeker?"

I thought it sounded like an odd question, but I nodded anyway.

"On the way to the other world, all objects created by commoners evaporate. You can leave them here and pick them up later."

Got it. I took out my phone, money, and keys and placed them beside the Gatekeeper. Now I was ready.

"Where do you want to go?"

"To the Valley of Silence."

"Come closer and touch the Gates."

If I wasn't mistaken, the Gates were the rune stone at the center of the platform. I went closer and touched it lightly.

The giant statue set aside the sword in its left hand and reached out its right hand, making a fist. Some of the dust flew out of the bowl as though it were lifted by an enchanted wind. It sparked, overflowing with colors, and even seemed to be radiating warmth. The dust gradually gathered next to the Gatekeeper's right hand and he then reached out to touch the stone.

It felt like being punched in my chest. Everything happened fast, almost lightning fast. One second I was inside a rather shabby but illuminated room, and the next second I was outdoors, in almost complete darkness.

A cool wind made my trench coat flutter; my bare feet almost instantly started to freeze on cold rock.

Bare feet? Oh shit! My shoes were regular Ralph Ringers — in other words, ordinary commoner shoes. So just as the Gatekeeper had told me, they'd evaporated. Running was going to be fun.

Where was I going to be running to, actually? I turned around to ask the local Gatekeeper, since they were so talkative, and tensed up.

There was nobody there. The circular symbol was there, and so was the stone inside it. But the main character was missing. And the bowl wasn't just tipped over; it was shattered.

I had a bad feeling about it. I took a few steps in search of the northern path and stumbled on a few cobblestones. That cheered me up a bit. I walked about a dozen yards and found that the trail disappeared just as abruptly as it came into view.

On top of that, somewhere far ahead of me, I heard an irritating scraping noise coming from with the impenetrable darkness. It sounded like some giant was sharpening enormous knives with a diamond wheel. Holy shit, what kind of world was this?

Chapter 17

THE HUMAN BODY has certain physical reserves that can kick in under stress. We've all heard of cases where a feeble woman lifts a car to pull out her child from underneath. Or when a man with an injured spine ignores the pain and gets himself to the hospital.

Or when a stupid Player who ends up God knows where musters up his willpower and tries to survive.

Of course, that last one was me.

Despite the pitch darkness, I didn't risk casting Light for fear of attracting attention. My feet were standing on cold, dark ground. A massive crimson moon hung in the sky.

But that wasn't all. I didn't know what was going on with this world, but it had two satellites: a blue one and a red one. The blue one was so small I only noticed it by pure chance.

Damn, I shouldn't be thinking about that. How was I going to get out of here?

Valley of Silence? That was an overstatement,

really, as I could hear loud screeching sounds coming from somewhere nearby. Still, I was indeed standing in a rocky valley squeezed between two mountains. A narrow trail led downward, apparently to the place where I needed to go look for Fibbian — that is, if Fibbian really existed. I was starting to have major doubts about that.

Meanwhile, the sound kept getting louder. I looked around and spotted a small boulder that barely reached my waist. I dove behind it just in time.

A creature that looked like a giant praying mantis rolled onto the portal site. It had a thin, extended body, more legs than you could count, a fidgety head, and dagger-sharp front feet, which it was scraping together, making the screeching noise.

Famulus
???

Judging by the few question marks, this beast wasn't top class. But that didn't mean that I could sneak up on that thing with my toothpick of a weapon, and even the time rewind wouldn't be much help here. I checked it just in case: it had 19 points of charge already. Excellent. Still, that didn't make things any easier.

The famulus turned its head in my direction, no mistake about it. Its angry faceted eyes focused on me. The creature started to scrape its feet harder. Shit, did it sense me or something?

My hands started shaking on their own accord. My legs grew weak. I wanted to bolt, but it felt like my legs belonged to someone else.

Just then the Gates flashed open, interrupting the praying mantis' preparations for his evening meal. The portal stone burst into flames, disgorging a girl onto the platform. I knew her — it was Artist_Chick.

She held out the sketchbook that she always carried, thrust a hand into it and pulled out a gleaming black pistol. The page shriveled up and crumbled to ashes as though it had been set on fire. Yet the pistol remained in the girl's hand.

Bang bang bang bang!

My ears clogged. All the shots merged into a single drawn-out, droning sound that bored into my brain. The famulus began to squeal, wiggling its mandibles, and sprinted into the darkness.

Everything happened in a matter of seconds, so fast that I didn't have a chance to register everything. Meanwhile, Artist Chick had already spread out a long, taped-together sheet of paper that had an elaborate drawing on it.

I went closer and saw that it was a picture of a spear, depicted in such intricate detail that would have made the finest draftsmen of the past weep with envy.

The girl's fingers touched the paper, sinking deep inside the sheet and turning into a two-dimensional pencil sketch of a hand. Immediately the girl pulled her hand back out. But now she was holding the spear — yes, the spear that had only just been a mere drawing.

The paper shriveled, darkening, and crumbled to ashes.

"Hold this," she said angrily, "in case more famuli show up."

Reluctantly I took the spear. "What am I

supposed to do with it?"

"Hold it in front of you and try not to get yourself killed," she said, leafing quickly through the sketchbook until she found the page she was looking for.

But this time she didn't pull anything else out. She merely stretched her arms in front of her. The sketchbook disappeared; the girl was now holding a sword in her right hand and a short staff in her left.

"If you follow me you'll have a chance of surviving the Red Moon. You can't stay here."

"What's the Red Moon?"

The girl pointed upward as we walked. "What do you see?"

"A moon... a red one."

"Any other questions?"

"Why do we need to survive it?"

"Just because! Even the youngest child in Purgator knows not to roam the Wild Lands when the Red Moon is out. That's when all the monsters become stronger. Our time is the Blue Moon. Don't forget that. It might come in handy if you do survive."

"So do you watch over the newbies or something? You make sure nothing happens to them?"

She must have found my questions amusing because she stopped walking and turned around, smiling. "Yeah right. And then I catch you and watch over you again. Hunter paid me to take you to the closest city and bring you back. He paid me well. Are you his son or something?"

Hunter? How had he found out about this? And so quickly? "Was he alone?"

"No, he was with some guy. A short, scrawny type."

Jan! So that's where he'd disappeared to. He must have thought I was in trouble and went back to Litius. And Litius must have called Hunter just like I'd asked him to. In any case, that was quick! When I call Hunter he usually doesn't answer the phone. I was sincerely grateful to him, anyway, because if this girl hadn't shown up, right now I'd be getting to know the famulus from the inside.

"Artist_Chick..."

The girl swiveled around and fixed me with a stare. It flustered me.

"No one calls me that. Call me Arts."

"As in Arts and Crafts?" I joked, but immediately shut up because there wasn't a trace of irony in her eyes. If you're bad at humor, don't try. "OK, Arts. So where are we going?"

"There," she said, pointing in front of us.

"All right. If you say so."

I examined the weird stabbing weapon I'd so suddenly acquired.

Copy of the Ilitian Merchants' spear
Summoned weapon
Time to disintegration: 1 hour 59 minutes 12 seconds.

I turned it over and tried to toss it in the air. The spearhead was sharp. You could use something like that to clip the fingernails of certain antagonistic Players. A very good copy. Counterfeiters, eat your heart out.

"Can you draw an assault rifle?" I asked.

Arts gave me a condescending look as though I

was trying her patience, then smiled at her own thoughts. "You don't understand. I can draw anything, even an atomizer from one of the central worlds. Only it won't work."

"Why not?"

"To summon an object, really summon it, you need to know its design in every detail. I spent almost a month on the pistol. The breechblock, mainspring, operating spring, hammer, firing pin... you need to draw all the details. Then I pass over on top of it with another color. You get it?

It was all very complicated. I looked at my spear with new appreciation. The small notches in the wood, the scuffs on the tip — they looked like it had really been sharpened. If you didn't know, you'd think it was real, not summoned.

"If you draw something and only stick to the outward appearance, you'll just end up with a mock-up," she added.

"Is this your main development branch? Artist?"

"It's bad form to ask a Player about their specialization, remember. You'll get smacked on the face or worse. If they want to, they'll tell you themselves. But I shouldn't hold your breath."

"Why not?"

Arts rolled her eyes. "Are you so simple or just pretending? Curious idiots don't last long here. The Game is the worst place for friendship. You either survive alone or join an Order. But even if you join an Order, no one guarantees your safety. Once you start to create problems or just get in the way..."

To finish her point, she drew her thumb across her throat. "Naive individuals like you die immediately."

"How am I naive?"

"Well, you grabbed a mission without even asking yourself who it was from, even though it said in black in white that it was for dummies," she snorted. "It was limited to players under level 10. Whoever wrote that, didn't want a strong Player to take the mission."

"Why not?"

"The Wild Lands are only dangerous for an inexperienced Seeker. Of course, you meet all kinds of monsters here. Like Alphas, for example. But if you know what to do, you'll reach the nearest city with no problem. Alive," she gave me a meaningful look. "But Players like you end up in Rachnaids' jaws."

"Was that the creature we saw? It said it was a famulus."

"That's right. All those creatures are called rachnaids. Their nests consist of famuli, which are the servants, an Alpha, and the Mother. The Alpha is the Mother's personal bodyguard. He's chosen from the largest rachnaid, and then the Mother feeds him with her milk or whatever those insects have. Over time, the Alpha grows a thick shell of armor."

"I hope we don't run into that one."

"That's unlikely. They usually don't leave the Mother's side. They only start roaming about when the colony is in danger. Wait a second...." Arts stopped and peered into the darkness.

We'd already descended a long way from the Gates platform. If the brisk wind was any indication, the mountains here weren't very imposing after all. I wondered what lay farther on. Plains?

"Do you need light?" I offered. "I have a spell."

Arts looked at me skeptically, then nodded. "All

right. Over there."

The sharp light made my eyes water, so I had to shield them with my sleeve. It took me a few seconds to adapt and get a good look at our surroundings.

You wouldn't really call it a road: more like a trail, hard and rocky (which I already knew courtesy of my bare feet). It was lined with boulders and pieces of massive stone blocks which at one point must have crumbled down from the mountains above. Arts was pointing to one of them.

At first I didn't see anything of any interest about it. But then I noticed the edge of a webbed wing protruding out from the safety of the boulder. Someone was lurking behind it.

The ball-shaped tip of the girl's staff grew red-hot, as if someone had held it in a forge for an hour or so.

Arts advanced a couple of steps. "Come out, Kabirid! I can see you."

The webbed wing shrank behind the boulder.

A few seconds later the Kabirid reluctantly emerged and approached us. He was a powerful creature, more than six feet tall; his red skin appeared singed. He had small horns on his forehead and enormous wings on his back. But while Archali wings look just like birds' wings, the Kabirids seemed to have bred with bats. This stranger's body was human down to his knees, ending with goat's trotters. I couldn't take my eyes off the sight.

"Who are you?"

"Fib... Fibst. My name is Fibst."

Fibst, ???

???
???
Liar
???
???

The question marks next to the name indicated that Fibst wasn't his real name. But that was how he introduced himself. On top of that, the Liar characteristic put me on alert.

"I think he's bluffing," I said to Arts.

"I know he's bluffing," she said loudly. "Right, Fibbian?"

The Kabirid's eyes bulged as though he'd been accused of cannibalism. On the other hand, who knew? Maybe that was totally normal among his kind?

Our new acquaintance made a sharp gesture with his hand. I felt like someone had slit my eyes with a knife.

"Aaaahh!"

I heard the sound of a rockfall nearby, followed by an inhuman growl and the cracking of bones. Then all was silent.

A small hand lay comfortingly on my shoulder.

"Was I just blinded?" I asked.

"Just wait a bit."

Indeed, my eyesight gradually returned. The hazy outlines of my surroundings emerged from the darkness, coming into focus. Finally, the world regained its original color.

"What was that?"

"Blindness. Don't you understand? It's pretty rare. Such a shame I couldn't kill him."

"Where'd he go?"

"Gone with the wind, as the movie says. Those Kabirids have no manners."

"Why didn't you go blind?"

"I did. I just got my sight back fast. My Stamina is high and has all the abilities that come with it."

Of course she didn't say what those abilities were. By her own admission, Players didn't share things like that. Never mind. I didn't care, anyway.

I scrambled back to my feet. I hadn't even realized that I'd dropped to my backside — so naturally, now I had to get back up.

"An Archalus chummying up to a Kabirid!" she sniffed in contempt. "Unbelievable."

"I don't quite follow you. I mean, I don't follow you at all."

"The Archalus who sent you here with the letter is obviously an accomplice of that fib-telling Fibbian, if not his friend. Where's your letter? Open it."

I took out the sealed parchment and turned it reluctantly in my hands. It was still someone's correspondence, you know.

Arts ripped it out of my hands, tore open the seal, and held up a pristine sheet of paper. "Here you go," she tossed it aside. "The letter is just a ruse. The Archalus recruits newbie Players with the promise of some decent money — decent for a newbie, of course. He sends them here where they most likely fall right into the hands of the rachnaids. Then they get robbed and eaten."

"So what do those two — the Archalus and the Kabirid, as you called him — get out of it?"

"It's all very simple. The creatures kill the

Players, and after some time the Kabirid collects everything they dropped — dust mainly. You wouldn't get rich doing it, but a couple of kilos in a few days is still a couple of kilos. Plus the loot. The two bastards would then lie low for a while and move on. Rinse and repeat. We really should report it in the nearest city. They're probably already wondering why they've been having a lot of new Players showing up recently."

I listened to her open-mouthed. Holy crap, what a scheme. How do you trust angels — I mean, Archali — after this?

The truth was quite sobering. Here I was, a naïve little nerd who expected his new dream world to be paved with rainbows. I seriously believed that its denizens saw their purpose in helping the weak and righting the errant. Reality was much simpler and more cynical.

If there was a way to profit from a fellow Player's death, someone would certainly take advantage of it. If there was a way to rob said fellow Player of a spell or ability, someone would do it.

My incredulity must have been written all over my face because Arts said,

"Not everything is so clear-cut in the Game. It's only in books where angels are good and monsters are bad. Here, you're gonna meet Archali with such dark karma they'll make a Kabirid blush. There are Abbasses who have betrayed their own people. Genies who bargain with Ifrits. Things aren't black and white here, not in the way you're used to, anyway. Oh, look. The sun's coming up. Finally!"

I didn't see any sun or whatever they had here. But she was right: the sky over of one of the mountains had gotten lighter. The gloom was gradually receding, taking my remaining anxieties with it. The Red Moon became fainter, no longer hanging somberly above us.

A scorched valley covered in sparse vegetation opened up below. Arts was heading toward it.

"We'll get to Virhort by midday," she said. "It's a piddling little town — not a town even, more like a fortress spilling out of its limits. It's a ghastly hole, but they still have Gates and a Gatekeeper. They also have a Kabirid governor who's sympathetic to lost souls like you and I. The important thing is to avoid crossing paths with the ruler of the community."

"You mean their sachem?"

"You could say that. This isn't the Cesspit, so things are different here. Purgator is unfortunate enough to be stuck between Elysium and Firoll, the two worlds that are constantly at war with each other."

"Between a rock and a hard place."

"Exactly. There's no official direct route between them. You need to go through Purgator. So the two armies seize Purgator cities one by one, whichever army is the closest. They capture the ones that are geographically strategic, of course. There are still a few big cities in the north, far enough from the theater of war to be able to develop, after a fashion. But nobody ever ventures there — neither the Archali nor the Kabirids, let alone Players. The city inhabitants are an aggressive bunch — they'll kick your butt to hell and back. You'll be lucky if you get out of there in one piece."

"And this Virhort, who does it belong to now?"

"Good question. Last time I checked, it belonged to the Archali. But I haven't been here ever since the Red Moon rose — and a lot might have changed in these couple of weeks. But don't be afraid. Virhort has nothing to do with Players' communities. What's going on in the city doesn't concern us. Almost."

"Arts," I said hesitatingly, "could you maybe draw me some shoes?"

She burst out laughing. "I can only draw clogs in a hurry, wooden ones like they wear in Holland. Fancy some?"

Wooden shoes? I looked down at my dust-covered feet. No, thanks. Apparently, I'd have to grin and bear.

Arts froze. "Shut up."

I wanted to say that I wasn't talking but obeyed anyway.

She looked around anxiously. With each passing second her face became more worried. She turned back to the valley we had left, and I thought her eyes were going to pop out of her head.

"What's there?"

"A real mess. I'd say more: a freakin' shit of a mess," Arts said, adding a few stronger words.

I didn't know what to say to that. I just didn't expect this kind of language to come out of her mouth. Up until now she'd sounded all so educated and well-mannered. What could possibly be happening back there?

I peered at a gleaming spot of light rapidly approaching. The sound came later: the familiar screeching noise that made me shudder. I wanted to hunker down somewhere and not come out until it was all over. The scraping of the sharp front feet against each other sparked panic in the depths of my being.

The only thing keeping me from dropping everything and taking to my heels was Arts' presence.

Those damned rachnaids.

"You distract the famuli," the girl commanded. "It looks like there are only two of them. Just hold the spear out in front of you and don't let them come close. Got it?"

I nodded quickly without taking my eyes off the approaching creatures.

"If you can, just hit it over here," she grabbed my head, turned it toward herself, and pointed to a spot on her throat. "That's one of the few places where they're vulnerable. Or on the legs."

I listened; I think I even managed to remember some of what she said. Hit them on the feet or under the head. It couldn't be simpler. It was all so simple... all of it...

My thoughts dissolved faster than I could think them, because in this trio of rachnaids there was clearly a leader. It was one and a half times larger than its cousins, with thick chitinous sides, huge feet with dagger-like filaments on them, and a powerful dark head.

The huge boulders tumbled like weightless garbage under his limbs. This robust creature wasn't so much running as floating through the valley in front of his counterparts. His long mandibles were wildly seizing the air, as if they were looking forward to capturing their impending prey. His faceted eyes reflected the rising sun.

"What the hell is that?" I asked quietly.

"The Alpha," Arts said, raising her staff.

Chapter 18

THERE'S A CLICHÉ that before a person dies, their whole life flashes before their eyes like a movie. Either my life would only make for a boring B-flick, or I didn't deserve a full feature, but instead of a full-length film I only saw a screenshot of Bumpkin's wafer rolls on my kitchen table. Would I ever eat them again?

Lost in these thoughts, I missed the moment when Arts transformed. One second she was standing there in her ordinary clothes — a sweater, pants and worn-out leather boots — and then she was wearing some weird-looking armor. The pauldrons, knee guards, and breastplate were made of an unusual dark metal; the rest was just light leather armor.

Did that mean that you could carry around a full set of armor in your bag? That made sense. Armor is only limited by the weight you can carry, but it doesn't affect reality in any way. So you travel light until you face the first danger and then poof, you're a knight in shining armor, bar the horse.

Arts staff was so incandescent hot now that it

hurt to look at it. When the Alpha approached, the staff flashed one last time and spouted a brief spurt of flame. Strangely enough, the fire seemed to have noticeably cooled the rachnaid's ardor. The leader crashed to the ground, tucking his feet under himself.

Arts ducked to the side, toward the stones, leaving me alone. The remaining two famuli who until now had kept a safe distance tore toward this reluctant new target. OK, time to really get a grip. Just like Arts had said — I had to hold the spear in front of me. Check. Now what?

Defying my expectations, the rachnaid soldiers didn't fly at me in a cavalry charge. They were clearly familiar with spears and even displayed something like a strategy. While one of them distracted me with fake attacks, the other one began to circle me. No, my sweeties, that's not the way it works.

I didn't even notice that my hands had stopped trembling. I stood confidently with my bare feet on the rock, bending my knees slightly, just like Hunter had taught me. Admittedly, he hadn't told me how to handle any mutant insects. So I'd need to adlib.

Not waiting for the other rachnaid to get all the way around me, I attacked. Not sure if you could really call it that. I merely took a small step forward and poked the spear into the snout in front of me. I did it gently so as not to break my guard.

The rachnaid shrank back without even trying to defend himself. I soon understood why: while we were thus waltzing around, the other rachnaid was inching his way toward my back.

Little did he know.

The vulnerable spot that Arts had mentioned

was a slightly protruding, drooping pouch on his neck. And it wasn't protected by the hard chitin. I glanced at how many charges I had: they were fully restored now. That meant it was now or never. If I slowed down, they'd tear me to pieces between the two of them.

I did a fake thrust, then jabbed with my spear as hard as I could. The rachnaid didn't croak; he only twitched his head, avoiding the blow. Immediately the other one attacked me from behind.

Step forward, fake thrust, jab. This time I didn't aim at his head — I pointed the spear at the thin air just next to it.

I heard a shuddering noise like the sound of a wineskin being ripped in two. A revolting green goo flowed down the spear.

Your Pole Weapon skill has increased to level 1.

Your Unarmored Combat skill has increased to level 1.

I let out a yell, realizing what had happened. Swinging round, I held the spear out in front of the rachnaid's bloody claw. Shit! He still managed to graze me. I tried to thrust the spear at him but the creature effortlessly dodged it.

My wound ached. Under any other circumstances I would have already collapsed to the ground grabbing at my bleeding hand, and called for help. But that would be useless here. No ambulance would come to spirit me away.

I had to earn my right to live.

The rachnaid must have decided not to drag it out. Perhaps that was how his companion's death had affected him, or perhaps it was the taste of my blood, but it was as though the creature had gone amuck. He barged at me, apparently unconcerned for his own safety. He would have trampled me had I not remembered what Arts had just told me. After two unsuccessful attempts to hit him, I stabbed him in the closest foot. That worked pretty well.

Your Pole Weapon skill has increased to level 2.

The rachnaid didn't wound me anymore. However, because of all this waltzing, my Vigor had dropped below 20%. My strength was about to run out; I was a ready meal for them now. And the rachnaid looked as if he was just warming up. I needed to do something, and fast.

I thrust my left arm forward, casting Light. Of course, I wasn't counting on the blinding effect that the Kabirid had demonstrated a little while ago. According to Arts, a spell like that was quite rare. My plan was simple. It was dark all around — the sun had just begun to rise, barely peeking from behind the mountain. The light might disorient the rachnaid: who likes to be pulled out of a dark room into a brightly lit space? That might help me gain two or three seconds.

It turned out that my head was good for something other than blabbing. It sometimes worked like that in critical situations.

The insect stretched out his front legs and froze. I stabbed him. It was hard: my right arm nearly went numb while I raised the weapon. I'd thought that thanks to my agility work I'd be in good shape. As if!

The vile goo went everywhere. The rachnaid collapsed, very nearly smothering me. But I survived.

Your Pole Weapon skill has increased to level 3.

I looked around for Arts. A shiver ran down my spine: things weren't going very well for her. The Alpha truly lived up to his name. He barged like a tank, only delayed by occasional flashes of her staff. At this point, the staff was no longer spewing a flame, just spitting out an occasional feeble light.

As for Arts, she seemed to dance gracefully around — you'd be hard pressed to call it fighting. Just watching her made me jealous. Step, turn, dodge, jab, lunge forward, another jab.

However, it was obvious that things weren't adding up in her favor. Her sword wasn't powerful enough to harm the creature's feet, let alone his body. After every thrust, the Alpha gave out a yelp that made my blood run cold. Still, Arts' blows seemed to only give him mental discomfort.

Also, he must have hit her a couple of times: I could see blood on Arts' armor. Every time the girl swung round, claret would splatter everywhere. She wouldn't last long at that pace, unless she had thirty pints of blood in her body instead of the usual ten.

Despite everything, I wasn't in a hurry to step in. For one thing, my Vigor was almost down to zero. If I ran over there now half dead, five minutes later I'd be gasping for breath. Also, I needed to observe the Alpha and figure out his weaknesses. Finally, I was scared shitless. I never would have thought that I'd go to kindergarten, make it through school, graduate from university, find a job, all this only to discover that everything I'd learned was useless because I'd just end up having to fight this monster. How was advanced math going to help me now?

Meanwhile, the Alpha was applying pressure. He kept doing the same thing over and over again. Whenever Arts attacked him, he simply clung to the ground and snapped his sharp front feet, trying to seize his adversary. There was only one solution: try to accomplish what I'd failed to do with the other two, namely surround him between the two of us and have a go at him from both sides until we achieved the desired result.

But everything turned out to be much more mundane. The creature simply didn't notice me. I stabbed him a few times in his chitinous rear end, under his gut and then in the feet — but only that latter maneuver finally made the Alpha pay attention to me.

He half-turned toward me, gave me a studying look, then kicked me — gave me the boot, literally.

Your Unarmored Combat skill has increased to level 2.

By the time I read this notification, I was already sprawled on my back six yards away from the Alpha. The bastard didn't even turn around to finish me off. Somehow that felt insulting.

Grunting, I scrambled back to my feet, picked up my spear and staggered toward the creature. Never mind. Just you wait-

Once again I stabbed him in the foot and received another kick in the chest. This time, I managed to tuck midflight and rolled away.

This time, stepping aside wasn't enough — I literally had to leap away. That threw me off balance for a moment. Shit. What a waste of charge points.

But then the monster's kicking foot straightened completely. I had plenty of time. I took a swing, investing all my rage into the blow, and jabbed the Alpha in the leg.

Your Pole Weapon skill has increased to level 4.

Except that the creature had no respect for my success. He jerked, finished his turn, and struck with another foot.

This time I hit my head on the rocks and spent some time lying sprawled on the ground. I also noticed that my half-cocked attempt at levitation had dropped my Health by one-third. Or it could also be caused by my wound, you never know. My whole sleeve was now wet and heavy with blood.

I was also saved by the fact that the Alpha's sharp limbs were directed at Arts. Otherwise, I would have already been dead as a doornail. I needed to keep going.

With a somewhat misplaced tenacity, I stood up and raised my spear. There was nothing I could do; if that creature finished off Arts, he'd make quick work of me.

Meanwhile, Arts seemed to be sort of jittery. She kept casting meaningful glances at me, mouthing something.

"What?" I shouted.

"Your knife! The moon steel!"

Was she serious? I couldn't get to him to the length of my spear, and she wanted me to use the knife? The creature would just gobble me up like a mid-morning snack. On the other hand, the situation was a bit desperate. If we didn't break the back of this fight, it would break our own.

I tossed the spear aside and started to inch toward the creature.

Your Stealth skill has increased to level 3.

The Alpha didn't really see me as a threat. I crept up as close to him as I could, staring at his horrifying legs. Each one was as thick as two of my own. They were twitching, distributing the body weight as the monster moved.

What could I do? My knife was far shorter than his leg. But judging by Arts' pleading look, I had to do something pronto.

Never mind. I was already getting used to having my ass kicked.

I took a swing. The knife penetrated the Alpha's back foot like it was made of melted butter. What was that now?

Your Short Blades skill has increased to level 9.

A bloodcurdling scream echoed over the slumbery valley. The disgusting goo gushed under my feet, mixing with my own vomit.

Then something struck me from above.

"Run!"

Arts' scream sank in my dimming consciousness.

This time I didn't miss it. I hacked out with my knife and, ignoring the flashing notifications, promptly recoiled.

The Alpha's agonizing screech made my blood run cold. My neck went stiff; my legs felt like they belonged to someone else. But stopping now would amount to death. We had to run.

My wound started to ache, filling me with a leaden weight which dragged me to the ground. Run. My tongue, rough and dry, stuck to the roof of my mouth. Ru...

My bare foot hit a sharp rock. I screamed. Blood went everywhere; the precious little number of hit points I still had now began to drop even further. The ground suddenly became very close as I collapsed. Wasting valuable seconds, I crawled after my knife, grabbed it and turned around, ready to face my death.

But my death was in no rush to meet me. On the contrary — it took to its heels, absurdly dragging a seriously wounded leg as it headed to the mountains. The Alpha was retreating.

Shaking all over, I stood up and sheathed my knife. I gingerly took one step, then another, and hobbled over to Arts. She'd already removed her armor and now was wearing her pants and a short linen top without a sweater — apparently, for fear of soiling it with blood while examining her own wound. It looked nasty: deep, ragged, stretching all the way from her side to her abdomen. I was truly afraid this was the end of her.

But Arts was clearly in no hurry to die. An almost imperceptible plume of blue smoke shot out of her hand and landed on her abdomen. Was it some kind of a healing spell? She cast it a few more times. I wouldn't say the wound had repaired entirely, but it shrank considerably and was no longer bleeding as before.

"My Regeneration level is low and the spell is weak," she explained through parched lips when I reached her.

Arts crouched and reached up for her sketchbook which appeared out of thin air. She found the page she was looking for and pulled out a vial filled with a dull, brown liquid. She pulled the stopper out with her teeth and greedily clung to it.

"That regenerates your health?" I guessed.

"Yes. I tried to draw a regeneration potion, but it had some funny particles floating in it. I couldn't get the color right, either, so it didn't work. Come here."

She lightly touched my torn trench coat. The same pale blue spell emitted from her fingers. My health score flickered and stopped dropping.

I pulled off my clothes: just as I thought, my wound had closed up. Only a light pink scar served as a reminder of the damage. It probably hadn't been as serious as I thought.

"Now what do we do?"

"Now," said Arts, going back to the sketchbook and pulling out an ordinary gauze bandage, "you'll have to dress my wound. We need to survive until we get to Virhort. They'll patch us up there."

When I'd taken Basic Medical Skills at university, they taught us to give injections, perform CPR, and apply bandages. Wish I could remember any of it now.

"Do you have another bandage or some cotton?"

Rice reached into the sketchbook and produced another strip of gauze. I folded the first bandage several times and placed it on the wound. Arts groaned; still, she kept her eyes open, watching all my movements. Not that I did anything special, though. I gently wrapped the bandage around the wound, ripped the loose end lengthways with my teeth, and tied it in a bow.

You've taken the first step toward acquiring the Healing ability.

You've helped a Player who is neutral to you.

+20 karma points. Current level: +40. You gravitate to the Light Side.

"OK," Arts said. "Now we should make it to Virhort."

The next thing I knew, she was already dressed in her usual attire. Her clothing seemed to have appeared out of nowhere. Not that I was a pervert, but

I found myself unintentionally admiring her body.

"How about you help me up," Arts said, jolting me from my thoughts.

I offered her my arm. She leaned on it and stood up with a groan.

"I'll just go get the spear," I suddenly remembered and staggered away to the spot where I'd wounded the Alpha. When I got back to her, I asked, "Do the rachnaids drop any loot?"

She didn't understand right away, but then she shook her head. "We could take their mandibles, I suppose. But it takes a long time to cut them off. And I'm bleeding."

I nodded. Whatever. I offered her my arm again, but she moved away from me, took out her sketchbook and pulled out a walking stick.

Proud, are we? OK then, she could walk by herself if that's what turned her on.

"Phew, it's a good thing we got away with that," I said, deciding to make conversation.

"That's the third one," Arts said through clenched teeth.

"Third what?"

"It's my third wound in all the years I've been traveling between worlds. Even on the man-made central planets," she broke off midsentence and looked at me angrily. "And then I almost died in Purgator because someone got the idea to go for a stroll under the Red Moon."

"No one asked you to come in after me. You could have said no."

"Greed will be my undoing," she grumbled.

I smiled. "You could say that."

In one sense it was true — no one had asked her to rescue me. She'd signed a contract without reading the fine print, so to say. But on the other hand, I was indirectly responsible for her wound. Had it not been for Arts, one Sergei Dementiev would probably already be feeding worms. Or more likely, the rachnaids wouldn't have left anything for them.

But to my delight, Arts didn't intend to hold a grudge.

"Where'd you get the moon steel?" she asked.

"A friend gave it to me."

"Don't forget that Hunter has no friends. I don't know why he gave you something so rare, but he obviously did it for a reason."

"It's really rare?"

"Did you see me fight? I couldn't get the sword into that creature once. During the Red Moon, the chitin is the best protection from spells. Apparently, it starts to produce some kind of substance that only moon steel can penetrate — or an orichalcum sword. But you won't find orichalcum anywhere, and moon blades are extremely rare these days, too. I've only ever seen one in my whole life, and it belonged to some real vile character. If only we had a couple of those...."

"Then what?"

"The Alpha wouldn't have gotten away, and we could also find the Queen."

"Why would we need it?"

Arts rolled her eyes. "Use your head."

She paused, thinking, then continued, "There are four days left until the full Red Moon. That means that the Queen will soon be hatching. That explains why the Alpha was chasing us. He's overcautious, and

I'd wounded one of his scouts."

"This Queen, what kind of loot does she drop?"

"Eggs. You can sell one for fifty grams. And there are at least two or three hundred," she fell silent.

I could hear the sound of a clanging cash register in my head. Two hundred... two hundred eggs equaled ten kilos of dust. And that was... let me see...

"So how come no one hunts for them?" I asked.

"Because their lives are more important to them. Venturing into the Queen's lair during the Red Moon while the Alpha's on the prowl? I don't think so!"

"Yeah, but he's wounded now, isn't he?"

"It doesn't matter. He's still very dangerous. For a mission like that you'd need a mage healer, a mage destroyer, a scout with the tracking ability, and a couple of good fighters with the right weapons. In other words, it's a hassle."

"But can't a mage be a healer?"

"Theoretically, yes. Why?"

I didn't say anything, pondering the most lucrative business in Purgator.

Arts must have read my mind because she snorted. "If you value your life, don't even think about it. You can't defeat an Alpha. And you won't be able to put together a team. You just don't have the right connections. Here, everyone's for themselves. You get it?"

I nodded with an inner smile. That remained to be seen. I did have a team — they just didn't know they were a team yet. All I had to do was introduce everyone to each other.

We walked the rest of the way in silence. I'd already wholeheartedly regretted rejecting her offer of clogs. At this point I would have been happy with any kind of footwear. My feet were bleeding, and my right sole had been cut against a sharp rock. So it goes without saying that I was ecstatic to spot the little city or fortress or whatever it was on top of the mountain.

I was ecstatic indeed – until I glimpsed a tiny dot in the sky. It stayed suspended there for some time, then rushed toward us. I could already make out the powerful white wings, the closed helmet ablaze in the sun, and the shining breastplate. The creature's arms and legs were unprotected.

The female Archalus landed about twenty paces away from us. She conjured up a huge two-handed sword and held it in front of her.

"Stop right there, you dark bitch."

She clearly wasn't talking to me. At least, what was it the message had said? Didn't I "gravitate to the Light Side?"

This particular Archalus seemed to know Arts. And apparently that wasn't an advantage.

Chapter 19

THE ABILITY TO BEHAVE properly in a tricky situation is the most valuable thing a person can learn. We're not born with this: this skill comes with time, and most important, with experience. As far as I could tell, Arts clearly had it.

"I'm no darker than you, Ilia," she said confidently. "Did you guys lose the city again?"

"Those damned Kabirids came down on us like ashes from the Black Mountain. Urful's legion attacked at dawn. They brought a pack of Cerberi with them. You know what those creatures are like under the Red Moon. But never mind that. Wefeil has already gone to get the griffins. Speaking of the moon, what are you," she looked at me hesitantly but added anyway, "what are you two doing prowling around the valley?"

Arts began to speak in a strange language, twittering like a bird. I couldn't understand a single word of what she said. But the Archalus was listening intently. As Arts continued her story, the winged woman's face changed expression. First it betrayed scorn and contempt which was soon replaced by surprise and finally, complete disbelief.

Your fame has increased to 1.
Your reputation has changed to Nutcase.

What the hell was that? While the girls twittered sweetly — this was the only way to describe their conversation — I opened my interface. I poked around until I found some messages under my characteristics.

Fame influences the character's recognition across all worlds. It is required for controlling settlements and armies.
Reputation subconsciously influences the other Players' opinion of you, triggering either goodwill or, alternatively, rejection. Seekers with similar reputations may come to an agreement more quickly.

This was all fine and dandy, but why on earth was I a Nutcase?

The female warrior smirked. "So you're the newb who decided to take the mission in the Wild Lands during the Red Moon?"

Ilia
???
???
Paladin
Gravitates to the Dark Side
???
???

"It's just that I didn't have time to study your

astronomy."

"And you're the one who wounded the Alpha?"

Actually, I'd also killed two other rachnaids. But I thought it best not to overemphasize that."Yes, he just happened to be in the wrong place at the wrong time."

The Archalus stepped forward, almost looming over me. "How did you do it?"

Arts' words came back to me: *Players don't talk about things like that.*

The Archalus swung her two-handed sword as though it were but a feather. The blade stopped less than half an inch from my neck. "Fancy a bit of tough love?"

Was she threatening me? Well, we'd see who'd win that battle.

I parried the sword with my spear which then carried on through with the momentum. I took a step forward, but Ilia proved faster. She let go of her sword and elbowed me nice and hard. The bitch!

I parried the sword and promptly let go of my spear. Crouching to dodge another blow, I drew my knife, straightened up and pressed the blade against the Archalus' throat.

Your fame has increased to 2.

The Archalus' eyes widened in surprise. "How

did you do that?"

"I thought we agreed to each have our own secrets."

"All right, human. Enough playing around!"

Her tone was so firm there was no room for objection. I put my knife away. The Archalus picked up her sword.

"You only have a few hours, Arts. After that, I won't bother to differentiate between who's in the city. Either get out or take shelter in the local community."

"We'll only need an hour," Arts answered.

The sword Ilia was holding disappeared. She crouched down, then soared into the air. Only now did I notice a few silhouettes hovering high above — probably her escorts.

"Are they going to attack the city again?" I asked.

"Of course. You heard her. They're waiting for the griffins now, then they're going to seize the city. A little later the Kabirids will retake it again."

"Why are they at war?"

My question seemed to have puzzled her. She thought for a bit and then shrugged. "They've always been at war. Their feud is probably older than that of cats and dogs."

"Another question. You said that she was darker than you. I saw that myself, too. But how is it possible?"

"Why not? Didn't you learn anything from the Archalus who gave you the mission?"

"Him I can understand. But she's in the Elysium army, isn't she?"

Arts nodded. "She's captain of the second company of the fifth legion."

"So how is it possible that a Dark Player can join the angel army?"

"I told you before that things aren't so clear-cut here. It's hard to be a commander. Sometimes you have to issue very cruel orders. You can't do that and remain all so lily white. Her Karma doesn't get in her way, at least not in Purgator. On the contrary: the dark Archali often create diversions in Firoll using Disguise. Just like the Light Kabirids do in Elysium. If she's urgently summoned back home, Ilia can raise her karma pretty quickly. It's not hard although it's quite burdensome."

Yeah yeah. Cute and cuddly creatures riding marshmallow unicorns. On the other hand, what did I want? This was a war between angels and demons. It would have been strange if things were simple here.

"Come on, let's go. We don't have much time."

So the two feeble Players set off for the mountain.

As we walked, something odd had happened. The spear I'd been leaning on as I walked suddenly disappeared – or rather, crumbled to the finest ashes. Apparently, its summon time had run out.

We stepped out onto a well-trodden dirt road that led to the city. Now we could get a good look at its tall spires. In some places they were intact, in others destroyed. A few poor shacks outside the city wall were smoldering.

A pair of demons were standing by the gates: tall, monstrous, fascinating winged creatures.

They were a spitting image of that Fibst (or Fibbian) guy we'd met earlier. If all demons looked alike to me, did that make me a racist? In any case, these boys were striking. They wore huge, bony, spiked pauldrons, knee guards with skulls on them, wrought steel boots and imposing breastplates decorated with the image of some strange beast which must have been the symbol of the legion the Kabirids belonged to.

"Halt! Where are you from?" one of them asked.

???
Summoner
???
???

"We're from the Cesspit. We got here two hours ago. We'll be leaving in an hour."

"You look a lot like Archalus snoops."

"We look like someone who will tell Urful that his worthless lackeys aren't letting Players into the community."

"You may pass," the Kabirid grumbled.

"Urful is not a bad demon — compared to the others, obviously," Arts explained. "He never hassles Players. He understands that it can backfire. But their squabbles with the Archali are theirs alone."

Hm. I wouldn't be surprised if it turned out that this Urful gravitated to Light. Everything was so mixed up here.

As I pondered life's ironies, I tried to examine the city. Either it was the most sparsely populated place ever or everyone had gone into battle. We came across lots of Kabirid patrols but few orange-skinned city residents who looked at us with open animosity.

"There aren't a lot of people here," I commented.

"Most Purgs went to hide in the surrounding villages. The ones who are still here had nowhere to go. Or they're working for the demons. It's a strange war here. They'll spend a month or so fighting for this little city, then they'll abandon it and switch their attention to another one. Then the Purgs will come back."

"The Purgs – you mean, the locals?"

"Yes, but no one ever calls them 'Purgatorians'. Just Purgs."

"They're exactly like humans. It's just that they're orange."

"That's the sun that's here," Arts said, pointing to the sky. "It looks just like ours. But that's what it does to your skin."

Aha. So Donald Trump must have been a Purgatorian too. "Hold on, I'm just starting to get this. Do they realize we're Players?"

"Of course. There are no protective pillars here."

I stopped dead in my tracks. "What are protective pillars?"

"They sort of accumulate magic energy. In some of the worlds the pillars do mass distractions of commoners. But the pillars in Purgator were destroyed a long time ago. It was a price to pay for the permanent war."

Curiouser and curiouser. I peered at the city that seemed to be still stuck in the Dark Ages. A lot of us idly fantasize about how we would have lived in the era of chivalry: we would have indulged in jousting tournaments, praised the king's virtues and entertained the fair ladies of his court. And there I was, walking barefoot on the filthy cobblestones which stank of urine, and the only thing I wanted more than everything now was to go home.

"That way," Arts said, pulling me after her.

"That way" turned out to be the mountain. Literally. The road stopped at a small gate cut into a cliff and then forked, leading toward a castle to our right.

But Arts forged right ahead, under the mountain. That's where the local community was apparently set up. I could see Players of different races, a few houses and a couple of Korls at the entrance who nodded to me cheerfully as though I were an old friend.

Light penetrated through an opening in the top of the mountain, so neatly cut it appeared to have been sawn off with an angle grinder. I couldn't believe my eyes.

"Whenever shit hits the fan, the community just shuts the gates and that's it. They're enchanted, so no one can break through them. No one even tries. The Kabirids and Archali are one thing and the Players are quite another. Come on. Over there," she motioned to one of the little houses.

The wrought iron sign with a picture of a test tube indicated that this was where the alchemist lived. The door was hard to open, as though it didn't want us there. It was dark inside.

"Hello? Anybody alive here?"

"That's how you enter a crypt, not a shop," a voice said inside.

Darkness parted, revealing a short man shuffling toward to us. He was either a dwarf or a gnome — I couldn't tell which. The man was illuminating his way with a lamp — but instead of oil, the lamp held a tiny winged creature. Whenever it started to flutter against the glass, the light would beam brighter.

"Arts," he said, cheering up. "What brings you to our hole?"

"Ask him," Arts said, sitting carefully on a chair next to the counter. "Tartr, I need the Healing essence."

"Where am I supposed to get that?" Tartr asked, raising his arms. "Let me take a look at you."

Arts shed her clothing until she was just down to her top. Since I'd put the bandages on her, they'd become soaked in blood and now were a dirty crimson. She didn't look good.

"Ouch," Tartr said, gingerly unraveling the bandages. "Who did this to you?"

"An Alpha. In the Valley of Silence."

"I'm not surprised. Why would you go there when this moon is out? Oh boy. Did you cast a spell on yourself? Good. It's not really that bad. I have an ointment that just might.... Bretta!" he screamed, his voice suddenly hideous and shrill.

I flinched. A voice answered him in the same manner from the depths of the shop, making me jump,

"What do you want?"

"Bring me the Elufrian ointment!"

"There's none left."

"What about in the stockroom?

A brief pause. "No!"

"What about in the lab?"

There was a barely audible shuffling of feet. "No!"

"What about in the basement with all the chemicals?"

There was a sound of a heavy lid dropping, followed by the creaking of stairs. "No!"

"Go look in the cabinet."

I suppressed a smile. They reminded me of an elderly married couple who stockpiled several years' worth of supplies. It could be anything: toilet paper, soap, canned food, salt.

I must have guessed right about the old married couple thing. It turned out that Bretta was of the same race as Tartr: she an Herbalist and he an Alchemist Experimenter. A family shop.

"Hi, Arts," she said flatly.

She didn't give me so much as a glance. She put down a vial containing a dense, acrid substance and turned to leave.

"What's with your friend?" Tartr asked Arts, pointing at me.

"He cut his foot. There was also a small wound on his hand, but it's not serious."

"Bretta, you need to clean his wounds too."

"He's a Player. He can do very well without."

Only then did it dawn on me that there was no glowing aura around her. She was a commoner!

"Bretta, just fetch me some water, will you?"

Bretta muttered something but left and soon returned with a jug of water and a basin. She indicated where I should sit down and began to wash my feet.

I felt uncomfortable to say the least. I'd spent my whole life taking care of myself. But the time in which to protest had already been lost. And you couldn't solve this kind of problem in four seconds.

In the meantime, Tartr had smeared the ointment on Arts' wound, waited a few minutes, then wiped it off with a cloth.

Holy cow! The wound had already closed. Without any spectacular show of sparks, flashes of light, or other special effects. The most powerful magic turned out to be perfectly mundane.

"Come here," Tartr turned down toward me. "Pfff, that's nothing. Take off your trench coat."

The ointment felt cold when he rubbed it on me. Even worse, it stank. That's the lack of justice in the universe for you. If you want to be cured, you need to drink something bitter and repulsive. If you want to lose weight, you need to eat tasteless things by the clock. It sucks.

"That's it. What are you doing roaming around barefoot, young man?"

"It just happened."

"Bretta! Bring me the Boots of Solophon."

"Why are you yelling? I can hear you. I'm standing right here," Bretta echoed, shuffling away.

At this point, I realized that although I didn't have any particular feelings for Bretta, I sincerely sympathized with the old man. And I noticed that this impression had formed almost instantly, as soon as I entered the shop, and not after he helped me.

Was it because he was an alchemist — a nutcase scientist and a fellow soul in his own way? I could only speculate.

Bretta came back, hurling a massive pair of leather boots on the floor in front of me, at least three sizes bigger than my 11.

The Boots of Solophon
+4 to Medium Armor

+10% to an attempt to successfully create or modify a spell.
-1 from Athletics

The latter deduction must have been due to the item's weight. Bretta could barely lift them. But on the whole, they were even kind of cute. They almost looked like they came from the latest Paris Fashion Week.

"A mere fifty grams."

Arts snorted but didn't say anything. I gathered that she wasn't going to interfere just like when we'd run into the Archalus, watching her two friends fleece me. Still, no matter how crazy the old man must have thought I was, I decided to bargain.

"Fifty grams?" I snickered. "For that price you'll be trying to sell these oversized clogs for the rest of your life in these backwoods."

"Name your price then."

"Ten grams. And that's only because you helped us."

"The smudge of the ointment that healed your foot and hand cost ten. Forty-five."

"Forty-five is the most you'd get for everything in this room. Fifteen!"

I didn't even notice the moment when I'd begun to enjoy the process. I didn't generally get satisfaction from bargaining. But in this case I really went for it. And it wasn't because I was a penny-pincher or something. I just suddenly went with the flow. And the more I managed to knock the price down, the more of a buzz I felt.

In the end we agreed on 28 grams. A pretty good price for a pair of boots.

The Time Master

Your Bargaining skill has increased to level 2.

The moment I put them on, they predictably shrank to fit my own feet. I stood up and stamped my heels. The boots felt perfect — almost like they'd already been broken in. I was willing to bet they wouldn't give me blisters.

"Put it on my tab, Tartr," Arts said, standing up and heading outside. I only had a chance to nod at the old man. He answered in kind, clearly satisfied with the deal.

"Where to now?"

"We're going back. We need to get out of here as fast as possible."

"Where's the Gatekeeper?" I asked brusquely, acting like I was an old hand at interworld travel.

"Over there," Arts said, pointing.

I would have been able to figure that out myself if only I'd looked a little closer. It was a broad, squat building with that same unusual symbol in the shape of an intertwined circle, exactly like the one in the Cesspit – or rather, on Earth.

No sooner did I point my healed and shod soles that way when two Players appeared before us. According to the text boxes hovering over their heads, their names were Bodyguard and Rock. What could this possibly mean?

"Arts, the ruler wants to see you."

"Hey, we've only been here for 10 minutes," Arts said, making a barely perceptible hand movement. I realized she was reaching for her sketchbook. "I'm taking care of his business. I'll pop by to see him soon. Why?"

"He asked us to bring you to him."

"OK, OK. Will you wait here?" she asked, turning to me.

The guards switched their attention to me. Which must have been exactly what Arts had been waiting for. She quickly pulled out her sketchbook with the hand already stuck in it, and tossed it to me.

I heard a quick click and then another. The guardians were now standing handcuffed. Clever!

I caught the sketchbook in mid-air and was about to run off with it when someone tripped me. Smart bastards…

I leaped up, dodging the blow, and rushed after Arts who made a dash toward the Gates. The guards quickly recovered from their astonishment. Although the handcuffs slowed them down a bit, they were still close at our heels.

We barged into the Gatehouse and sprinted to the stone.

"Quick, get the dust out!"

"How much?" I shouted, in no state to converse calmly.

"Thirty-two grams."

Without looking, I poured the right amount into my palm. Arts had already thrown hers into the bowl.

Right then, our pursuers sprinted in. We hadn't made it!

But help arrived from an unexpected quarter. The Gatekeeper, who until now had been duly standing as still as a statue, took a step forward. He very nearly crushed me, so I had to bend down.

The giant stepped over me and walked out of the circle. "Attacks on Players in this residence are prohibited and punishable by death!"

Oddly, his voice was different here. Were the Gatekeepers actually living beings rather than automatons? In fact, this one looked a little shorter than the one earlier. Or else the Gatekeepers had already become familiar to me? Makes you wonder.

But our two handcuffed pursuers wasn't in the mood for idle pondering. They flew out of the room like a cork from a bottle of champagne.

The Gatekeeper calmly went back to his spot. Even his silence breathed with a stern, mighty power.

"Give me your hand," Arts said, looking toward the door.

If you say so. "What did they want?"

"I forgot to tell you that I'm in a little dispute with the ruler of the community in Vir... well, here. That's it. Stop talking now. *Sorrow,*" Arts said.

I was cannonballed out onto another portal site.

I looked around. Everything around me was just the same. Nothing had changed. The familiar place, the same dim light, the Gatekeeper. Except for the fact that the door leading outside was closed.

Did it not work?

"Where are we?"

"Home," replied an angry male voice.

Hunter stepped out into the light.

Chapter 20

ACCORDING TO MY Mom, children will never understand their parents until they have children of their own. Neither will teenagers listen to adults until they become adults themselves.

Before, I'd never given much heed to her words. Only now had the sheer truth of it finally dawned on me.

I could easily see the situation through Hunter's eyes — and I really felt like giving myself a good hiding. What else were you supposed to do? You spent days training this kid, telling him everything he should know in order to live a happy and hopefully long life, and he ends up pulling a stunt like this on you, dashing off like a headless chicken to Purgator — and during the Red Moon, of all times!

A good hiding? A kid like that deserved a good old-fashioned thrashing with a Red Army belt!

Still, Hunter said nothing. What's more: he now seemed to have lost all interest in me. He took Arts aside and spent some time questioning her about the whole incident, then handed her some dust. Rather a lot of dust.

In the meantime, I walked over to the Gatekeeper. If the truth were known, I didn't expect him to talk to me — but I had no one else to ask.

"Last time I used this, er, Gate, I left some stuff here. Like, a bunch of keys, you know, and also some money and a cell phone... oh sorry, a phone is this thing that looks like a sort of rectangular piece of plastic-"

I promptly cut my mumbled explanations short as the statue threw its hand in the air. Not to slap the annoying human across the head, no. It was in fact pointing to one of the walls.

I turned my head and saw a bowl sitting in a small niche dimly illuminated by one of the torches. I walked over to it and looked inside.

Oh wow. Everything was present and correct: the keys, a couple of crumpled bank notes and the phone. I scooped them up and stepped aside.

Excuse me? Where was the niche now? It had been here only a moment ago! I reached out and felt the smooth, flat surface of the wall.

"Sergei? Let's go," Hunter called.

I turned round. Arts was already gone. I hadn't even had the chance to say thank-you.

We stepped outside, into the freshness of the morning. I took in a loud, wheezy lungful of air. Judging by Hunter's shuddering as he wrapped his coat tighter around himself, it was way below zero. The street was deserted, if you didn't count the Guard who'd just walked past us. The Seers' residency, however, seemed to be burning the midnight oil as all the windows of all the stories were ablaze.

"The Grand Master's flying in today," Hunter said. "That's why they're all jumping out of their skins to receive him properly."

"How do you know?"

"I have my sources."

"So they must be getting ready to go to the airport, then."

"From what I heard, the Grand Master doesn't trust mechanical devices. Also, there're things much faster than planes, even if the Gates are closed for some reason."

We'd already reached the exit from the Community when I slapped myself on the forehead, remembering. I had virtually no dust left — and only had a couple of grand in local money[19].

"I need to change some dust."

"Get on with it, quick," Hunter replied.

I trotted toward the round kiosk. Despite the early hour, the scales materialized almost straight away behind the little wicket. The exchange rate had also grown a notch. Not much, only about $0.70 per gram, but that was still something.

Shame I had so little dust left. Only 38 grams, how was I supposed to conquer other worlds on such a pittance? Having said that, I already had the first inklings of a plan.

"Hurry up!" I heard. "The Grand Master will arrive any minute!"

The exchange kiosk was quite close to the Seers' Residency. It looked like someone in there had left the front door open a crack. In any case, I could hear the Magister's voice.

Something must have clicked in my head —

don't even ask! — because I found myself heading for the building.

I was already approaching it when I slipped on the icy pavement and very nearly kissed the sidewalk. Or rather, I did kiss it and even dislocated my ankle — at least that's what it felt like.

Why "very nearly"? Simple.

I gingerly walked around the slippery bit of the sidewalk, keeping an eye on the number of the remaining charges. Only 18. They'd only just started to grow after my lucky escape from Purgator.

Never mind. I had to be careful, that's all. I only had one available cooldown left.

"Artan and Ulo will come with me," I heard Magister's voice from behind the door. "I've checked our route, there're no nasty surprises there. I'll leave Bular in charge here, right? We should be back in a couple of hours. Nicholas, would you please go and get us three mounts? They should be in the community stable."

So they even had a stable here, eh? I didn't think I'd heard any horses neighing. Apparently, I'd missed a lot when exploring the area.

Okay, I'd heard enough. I'd better make myself scarce.

Unfortunately, I didn't get the chance to follow up on the idea. The door swung open, letting out my good friend — the one I'd been so unfriendly with during our first encounter next to my house — and whose face I'd roughed up again not so long ago.

I shouldn't have hesitated. That was my main mistake. Never mind. Better late than never.

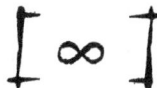

"Nicholas, would you please go and-"

This time I had to think quickly. I couldn't escape by running: they'd hear me. They'd see me, anyway. Unfortunately for me, this Nicholas was quick on the draw: he was already opening the front door. All I had time to do in this situation was grab the door handle and slam the door closed, then run for my life.

"My nose!" a scream from behind the door sliced through the matinal silence.

He must have collapsed where he'd stood, blocking the exit. That was a blessing in disguise, meaning no one chased after me.

"What's going on there?" Hunter asked.

"Just some brawl next to the Syndicate."

"Idiots. Just wait till some guards come and beat some sense into them. Come on now. We need to talk."

I nodded, trying to slow down my racing heart. As we headed toward the commoners' part of town, I must have turned round and checked the street at least five times. No Seers in sight. Even though I had no idea yet how I was going to explain myself to the Magister, I gradually calmed down. I'd think of something.

A deserted city is a beautiful place. The very first early risers, still groggy from sleep, were just making their morning coffees. A feral dog walked calmly down the street, wiggling his ears and feeling perfectly safe from humans — of which there were none, if you disregarded the occasional car whose driver was much worse for wear.

The city was asleep, bar two wide-awake resolute babushkas — one of them grim, with the X-ray stare of a customs officer, the other busy rolling her trolley bag. The two must have been heading wherever old ladies normally head to at this ungodly hour: to the hospital, or to the market, or to the other side of town to get that special-discount-70%-off-catering-size-bags of Basmati rice.

"Wanna take a cab?" I offered, watching the two purposeful old dames.

"It's a long conversation. And it's not meant for prying ears. I really don't want any cabbies to eavesdrop."

Either he had some special ability or he was plain lucky, but the bus arrived in less than two minutes. One of the two old ladies perked up and began collecting her stuff but the other one told her it was the wrong line. So we were perfectly alone in our seats at the back. The sleepy female conductor floated toward us like a frigate past a flock of fishing boats, handed us our tickets and departed back to her very special seat which other passengers aren't supposed to occupy — at least that's what the notice on its back said.

"Come on, spit it out," I said, looking out the window. "I know. It was stupid of me. But I'm gonna find this sonovabitch Archalus if it's the last thing I do."

"You won't. He's a fly by night. When this beastman of yours called me, I went straight to the Community. It's a good job Arts was there!"

"Uncle Nick- er, Hunter? Why are you helping me? Just don't give me that bullshit about not wanting to attract attention to yourself. I could buy it then, but now everything you do disagrees with what you say. It's as if you have some personal interest in... in me."

"I do and I don't."

He fell silent. The pause was so pregnant with meaning that I turned toward him.

"He came to see me," he finally said. "Before all this happened."

I tensed up. "Who did?"

"The Chorul. He gave me the knife and the mirror. And... he told me how it was going to be. He told me everything."

"You don't want to say he wanted me to kill him? Why would he do that?"

"He didn't tell me. I think he was following orders."

"But you can't order someone to die, surely?"

Hunter shrugged. "Choruls. You never know with them. If they did, they must have had their reasons."

"Well, that makes me part of someone's plan, doesn't it? If only I knew who it was. They don't seem in a hurry to show up and tell me what to do next," I paused. "You. You did offer to help me. Why? What else did he give you?"

Hunter smiled. "He told me how I'd die."

"He what?"

"Okay, okay, I'm gonna tell you something. Have you ever heard about the Oracle?"

"I think so. My friends spoke about him. They said he was the only one of his kind in the Cesspit. They also said he wasn't affiliated to any existing Orders."

"He's actually a Player — but then again, not quite. He's a god — but he's neither Wandering nor a Resident one. He's actually the weirdest old god I've ever seen."

"Why so?"

"Things like wealth or power don't seem to interest him. With his abilities, he could live anywhere, in any of the known worlds. Still, it's been years since he moved here and seems quite happy living in the sticks. Any Player can come and talk to him, but they can only do it once. And they never know what the Oracle's gonna tell them. So basically... I too went to see him. It was a long time ago. This world was different then. You wouldn't have recognized any of today's countries or governments."

I tensed up and pricked up my ears. Hunter wasn't the talkative type. So when he decided to divulge something you'd never hear from other Players, you had to pay attention.

"I was young and arrogant. I considered myself the best Seeker ever born. I thought I deserved taking the Divine route. The only thing I feared was death."

"So you asked him when you were going to die."

He shook his head. "No," he said with a smile. "I asked him *how* I was going to die."

"And what did he say?"

"He said it was up to me. Then he added that I'd die in my student's arms. That's exactly what he said."

He paused, then added as if in a trance,

"*You'll die in your student's arms.* It was a long time ago. A very long time. I am who I am now. And I haven't had a student in centuries."

I almost stopped breathing, afraid of disrupting

his flow. My next-door neighbor — or was he my mentor? Didn't he teach me the ropes and train me as best he could?

"It wasn't until I spoke to the Chorul," he said. "He explained it to me. He told me everything. In the end, I thought it would be stupid trying to escape one's fate."

"What did he tell you?"

"That old story of Perseus and his grandfather King Acrisius, remember[20]? Meaning you can't escape fate. Everything's predetermined. The Choruls, they have a very special relationship with time. He told me about your mission. And I saw his point. I knew he was right."

I leaned forward. "So what's my mission, then?"

"That I can't tell you. If I do, I'll disrupt the natural flow of time. I can only do what I have to do: namely, try not to let you croak before your time comes. Despite your best attempts to the contrary. Come on now. We're getting off on the next stop."

The next stop? That was quick. Surely the traffic-free morning hour must have had something to do with it. As well as the subject of our conversation, which was entertaining to say the least.

Hunter didn't say another word for the rest of our trip. I had a funny feeling he would now keep radio-silent for at least a month. Only when we'd reached our house did he motion me to stop.

"Wait two minutes, then go in. I don't want any commoners to see us. I cast Oblivion on my wife — it's a nasty old spell but I had no choice. And you still have a training practice tonight, don't forget."

I glanced at the interface clock and groaned. I'd

missed the night's sleep. Trying to catch a few brief Zs now would be an offense to my exhausted body. Doubtful I'd be able to get out of bed afterward, let alone be fully functional.

I lingered, waiting, then staggered toward our house. Hunter and his paranoia! There was no one in the yard. I could hear a single car motor warming up, and even that had been started with a remote control, bless this wonderful invention.

I climbed the stairs to my floor, unlocked the door and turned the lights on.

"Alive, thank God," Bumpkin gasped, inspecting me. "What happened to your coat?"

"I've been hiding in the bushes peeping at some naked ladies. When they saw me, I had to fight them... off."

"Very funny," the house goblin shook a disapproving head. "One-liner of the century. Come on, boss, take it off. Those ladies must have been very angry with you. They've ruined everything — your coat... and look at your jumper... I mean, the sweater! It's ripped right through! Come on, take everything off now."

Too tired to protest, I peeled off the damaged clothes and stumbled into the bathroom. I spent some quality time in the shower, washing away the dust of Purgator, then cleaned the bathtub and turned the taps on. While the water was running, I walked over to Bumpkin busy mending my trench coat and retrieved my cell from the pocket.

Holy moley! Thirteen missed calls? Two of them were indeed from my mom. The remaining eleven, from Julia.

I wrote my mom a lengthy text message, telling her that I was perfectly fine and reassuring her that it was my defective phone playing up. I already knew from experience that a brief "I'm fine, thanks" wouldn't cut it with her. Been there, done it, suffered the consequences.

Now Julia was a different matter entirely. I hated starting a new relationship with lies. And still that was a better option than making her think I was a total nutcase. "Sorry babe, I just popped out to this parallel world and got a bit tied up there fighting demons..."

Oh, no. I texted her saying that I'd had to go on a business trip and that I'd left my phone at home. I apologized for not letting her know. Now if only I could come up with a sufficiently believable job.

Before I could think of anything, I saw that my message had already been read.

Your Liar skill has improved!
Current level: 5

Talk about luck! Because this was an incredible, formidable piece of luck. Julia didn't nag or preach to me, she just said she'd been worried, that's all. Said she'd been afraid I might have changed my mind. I tried to turn it into a joke, saying that it's against a gentleman's code of honor to dump a girl before he'd seduced her. In the end, we set up another date for tonight.

Just think that only a few hours ago, I'd been on the run from the minions of the Community's Governor, surprised an Archalus, wounded an Alpha and smoked two rachnaids. And now here I was, asking a girl out as if it were the most natural thing in the world.

The funny thing was, I wasn't really surprised. For some reason, it just felt normal. My life seemed to have gained a bit of color, that's all.

"Here you go," Bumpkin carried the trench coat pompously into the room as if offering me the crown jewels.

I studied his handywork. It was indeed very neat: if you didn't know it was there you wouldn't notice anything. I spent another couple of minutes fingering the sweater's sleeve but couldn't even find the place where it had been ripped.

"Nice boots," Bumpkin's voice rang with envy. His eyes glinted wetly.

Yeah right. Dream on. I'd won them in an honest haggle.

I climbed out of the tub, toweled myself dry and pulled my clothes back on. After a moment's hesitation, I put on the boots too, which by now were polished and shining. I just didn't like how Bumpkin followed them with his watchful gaze.

"Okay, show me what you've cooked. I need some reinforcements to face another training session."

Bumpkin made himself scarce. The rattling of pots and pans echoed through the kitchen. Seven minutes later, I was eating the best meat patties in my life, neat and so tender that I managed to bit the fork a couple of times. I'd love to know how he does it, the bastard.

"Bumpkin, you're too good for words. Thanks. Mind slicing some more bread for me?"

The house-goblin turned crimson. "Oh, that's nothing, boss."

Either embarrassed by my praise or for whatever other reason, he made a strangely clumsy movement. The bread knife slid out of his hand and dropped to the floor. Not dropped even — its tip actually hit my boot's toe.

Your Mid-Range Armor skill has improved!
Current level: 1

It was a good job the knife hadn't pierced the leather!

A new system message saved Bumpkin from my righteous anger:

You've reached level 6!
Points available: 3
Strength: 26
Intellect: 18
Endurance: 20
Agility: 21 (x3)
Stamina: 15 (x3)
Eloquence: 12 (x3)
Speed: 16

That was a no-brainer. They've made the choice for me already. I invested the points into Agility, Stamina and Eloquence. My Vigor had reached 40. I also received one extra charge.

Every new level gave me this awkward feeling that my progression wasn't going right. Where were my destructive spells? Where were my level-100 Intellect and my tons of mana? I had to buy it all for money — and the state of my wallet, although still in the black, was dangerously close to what meager capital I'd started with.

On the other hand, I'd done a bit of traveling. I'd seen other parts of the world. I'd also earned some quite priceless experience. I really should check the task board. But as some book character used to say, the only thing you got through hard work was a pain in the butt. In other words, completing tasks was a long and tedious endeavor. I had to come up with something else.

So that's exactly what I did for the next few hours that were left till my practice, straining my poor brain until all the straw started coming out, bristling with needles. The best thing I could think of was come to my friends and humbly beg them for help.

On the other hand, hadn't Litius said he'd been happy to find a friend? I hadn't forced him to say that! He'd just have to put his money where his mouth was, wouldn't he?

That was it, then. Once I'd left Hunter's place, I'd give Litius a ring and try to extort... how much? Good question. I needed enough for all the skills and spells as well as the fare for the entire group.

Apparently, fools seldom differ, because the moment I reached for the front door, my cell vibrated. The name, Litius, lit up under the generic caller's icon (I hadn't had the chance to take a picture of him yet, for obvious reasons)

My need for him was pretty obvious. But what would he want from me?

"S-s-sergei? Sergei..."

"That's not how you use this thing. First, you need to say "Hello, may I speak to-"

"Sergei, p-p-please tell me it w-w-wasn't you..."

"Yesterday? I'm afraid it was. It's still me now."

"Please t-t-tell me it wasn't you who d-d-did it!"

I tensed up. Whatever had just happened, Litius seemed to blame it on the humble me. "What did I do?"

"Killed... the Seers..."

"Are you kidding me? You know very well I just spoke to them. Everything was fine when I left. Didn't Hunter tell you?"

"Not then. *Now*. We've just heard that almost the entire Seers' Order has been massacred. S-s-sergei, please tell me you're not be-be-behind it? Because that would make me your ac-c-complice. Sergei..."

I switched off the phone and slid down the hallway wall. What was it I'd said? My life seemed to have gained a bit of color?

That was the understatement of the century.

Chapter 21

ACCENTUATE THE POSITIVE, as shrinks say. Like, if you lost your legs in a traffic accident, you could learn to walk on your hands in no time. Awesome, eh?

I'm exaggerating, of course. Still, the idea had a point. Not in the leg-losing-traffic-accident kind of way — but positivity definitely had its fortes.

Take the Order of Seers, for instance. According to Litius, it had been massacred, which meant that there was no one left to keep the Darkest One at bay. There was nothing positive about this, only negatives. But by the same token, Hunter had canceled my practice. He thought we'd better report to the Community and sort it all out ourselves. Just in case they did accuse me of stuff.

Still, my mood was anything but rosy. In fact, I was so jittery I even started frisking my pockets for some cigarettes. Old habits die hard. Luckily for my wellbeing, the contents of my pockets had disappeared during my portal jump to Purgator.

Hunter flagged a gypsy cab. The very first car

stopped for us without even asking how much we were prepared to pay. He must have had some ace up his sleeve — a magic trick, maybe? And it didn't stop there: as we rode, the cars in front of us hurried to change lanes, clearing our path. Talking about magic.

I pulled out my earbuds and clicked on a random song in my playlist. It turned out to be Glen Campbell's *Southern Nights*. Perfect. The reggae guitar had a soothing effect on my nerves. I even dozed off — for what felt like a brief moment.

Hunter shoved me awake. I glanced at my watch: we'd made it here in no time. I even double-checked our driver but no, he didn't look anything like Samy Naceri[21].

The driver appeared sincerely surprised by our request to pull up by the house's gateway without driving up to the front door. Still, he drove off without commenting on it.

I pulled out the knife.

"Put it back," Hunter said.

Okay, okay. Keep your hair on.

I was about to enter when he motioned me to stop, pointing at a road sign attached over the gateway. Or rather, something that resembled a road sign. It was round, made of galvanized steel, but it had no pictogram on it. Instead, a warning ran across it:

The players with The Darkest One karma reading are temporarily banned from the premises.

I pulled out the pocket mirror and checked the message again. It was a regular No Entry sign. So it wasn't my imagination.

"Overcautious idiots," Hunter grumbled. "You need Observation Skills to notice it, anyway. In any case, who do they want to fool with this message?" he shrugged, then walked in.

And that was just the beginning of it. Two men stood in the archway marking the entry to the Community. One of them was easy enough to recognize: you don't see black-masked dudes in long flowing robes very often, unless they're Community guards

And next to him stood... well, well, well. If that wasn't Artan, the fake Jedi with his fiery sword.

My heart raced; my skin began to prickle as if pierced by thousands of needles. I had a very bad feeling about this.

And right I was. Artan's pupils dilated; he stepped toward us. Despite Hunter's warning, my hand reached for the knife; I'd all but rewound time.

But instead, Artan did something I least expected him to: he bowed to Hunter. And his sword was still sheathed. Very well. It meant we could hope to have a talk.

He turned to me. "The Grand Master and the Magister want to speak with you."

"I've got nothing to do with it."

"Nobody says you have," he replied, apparently surprised.

"Can we go, then?"

"Absolutely."

As we walked, I turned back a couple of times, expecting him to change his mind. Still, Hunter's composure seemed to have had a soothing effect on me.

We entered the main square which was — how can I put it politely — a very unusual sight. The entire Community was swarming with Players. Archali, Abbasses, humans, Korls, even two Kabirids, dammit, and a very weird creature — either a cyborg or a human hung with tubes and steely parts. And Guards — Guards everywhere.

"Come now," Hunter grabbed me by the hand and dragged me through the crowd.

For a brief moment, I thought I'd glimpsed Litius' face — or his muzzle, rather. Was he here as well?

We hurried down a street past the money exchange kiosk until we reached the Seers' residency. Hunter knocked the front door which opened almost straight away, revealing Yulo behind it. The mute Abbas stepped aside, gesturing us to enter.

What I saw made my blood run cold. The entryway was lined with neat stacks of clothing: some boots, a shirt, a few pairs of pants, a sweater, a pair of shoes... they took up the entire length of the corridor all the way to the stairs.

I felt a lump in my throat. No points for telling whose clothes these were — they all had belonged to the dead Seers. I recognized a few items I'd seen on Nicholas, the unfortunate bastard whose nose I'd broken three times.

A shiver ran up my spine.

"He didn't take anything," the Magister's voice came from the stairs. "He didn't even bother to collect all of the dust. Come up here, please."

I hurried past the, how can I call them — remains? Not really. Once a Player died, he or she dematerialized completely, leaving nothing behind.

These were more like tragic reminders of what one day could happen to any of us, especially those who travel between worlds.

The familiar room wasn't locked. I paused, waiting for Hunter, then the two of us walked in.

The Magister was in the room. A Seer stood with his back to us, staring out the window. Mysterious, are we?

???
Eternity Weaver
???
???
???

The stranger turned round and looked at me, then at Hunter. He smiled.

Against my best judgment, I was surprised. By simple elimination, if Yulo was here and Artan by the Community gates, this had to be the Grand Master, even though I'd imagined him as a frail ancient man — admittedly wise but suitably gaunt with age. But this man...

Let's begin by saying that he appeared to be at least ten years younger than the Magister. He was fit, his complexion white with just a hint of crow's feet around his eyes. His bespoke business suit added him an air of commandeering elegance.

Dammit! I'd bet my last grain of dust that this was his in-game gear. I'd love to know the name of the tailor who could make something that awesome.

"Nice to see you, Hunter."

"Likewise."

"How long has it been? Ninety years?"

Hunter nodded. "Something like that."

"And your friend here is Sergei?"

"He's my student."

"Is he really?" the man's voice rang with surprise. He turned to me. "Very well. I'm the Order's Grand Master. You've probably heard about me."

"I might. I think they said something like that in chess news."

I immediately felt a strong aversion to him. He was too groomed, too polished; in other words, fake. Strangely enough, although the Magister hadn't made any effort whatsoever to be likeable, my first impression of him had been very positive. And here, the opposite was true.

"Very well," the Grand Master gave me a meaningful look, "please take a seat. We need to talk."

I posed my posterior on the already-familiar chair and fidgeted on its jacquard seat, feeling admittedly out of my depth. Hunter's impassive presence felt somewhat soothing: he looked just like an English lord contemplating his next cricket match.

"We've been attacked," the Grand Master said. "It happened when Oliverio left to meet me. All of the Seers were slaughtered. What's more: it was one of the Seers who killed all the others."

Hunter frowned. "A traitor?" his face turned grim. "Or..."

"Exactly. A Player in possession of the Destroyer God's Avatar. One capable of controlling any living creature."

"I thought the Destroyer's Avatar was lost?"

"So did I. It has been a while. Did you hear what

happened the last time a Player had the Destroyer's Avatar? Did you hear what he did?"

"I sure did. From what I heard, it was a miracle they'd managed to stop Shiva at the last possible moment."

"According to the Oracle, that's exactly how it happened."

"But why would the Destroyer attack your order?"

"I think it's part of his plan. Everybody knows he's after one particular Player. This one here," the Grand Master theatrically raised his hand in the air and pointed his finger at me.

"Is it about his development branch?" Hunter asked.

"The funny thing is, it isn't. That's exactly what I thought at first. Given some practice, his ability to rewind time can become a killer weapon. But when I tried to read the past, I caught a glimpse of some of the Darkest One's thoughts. He's after the Avatar."

I very nearly jumped in my seat. "You can read the past! That's right! That's what Eternity Weaver means!"

The Magister suppressed a smile.

The Grand Master cringed. "How insightful."

"But that makes no sense," Hunter said, ignoring my words. "Why would the Darkest One want the Savior's Avatar if he's already the Destructor, anyway? You can't wear an opposite-karma Avatar, it's a simple as that."

"Think, man, think. Who can use both Avatars simultaneously?"

Hunter fell silent, his face strained in thought. He

seemed to be trying to solve a math problem which was easy and tricky at the same time, as if the obvious answer evaded him.

"I thought he'd left this world?" he finally said.

"Well, he's back now. I'm pretty sure it's about the Avatar. Savior and Destructor are linked together. When this player had found the Avatar, the Other One sensed it straight away."

"Gods are not almighty," Hunter said. "You can fight them."

"You can. And you should. I just wanted to make sure you knew who your student was dealing with. Just think what might happen if He collects both Avatars."

"Well, in that case I feel sorry for the world where it happens. Or any other world, for that matter. What are you planning on doing?"

"Well," the Grand Master grinned, "if Artan killed Sergei, that would be an ideal solution. He's an expert with long-bladed weapons, his magic resistance is decent, and he already has a Warrior's Avatar affiliated with Light."

Hunter nodded. "In other words, he's capable of using Savior's Avatar."

I wanted to jump off my seat and scream. WTF was going on? Had they forgotten I was still here? The way they were deciding my fate you'd think they were discussing who to slaughter for the festivities: me, or the fatted calf.

"Artan is a good match for Him," the Grand Master said.

"He might even win," Hunter added, "in which case he'll acquire a third Avatar, making him the most powerful Player in the Cesspit."

"After the Oracle, of course."

Hunter nodded. "Sure. After the Oracle."

"But even if we broke our oaths and went against Cesspit laws, defiling the Seers' reputation in the name of peace-"

"I wouldn't let you do it. Sergei has his own path."

"Do you know it?"

"Yes."

"Very well. In that case, we'll wash our hands of the whole matter. The Seers are not in danger anymore, anyway. Oliverio has already read his future."

Hunter turned to the Magister. "What about the Darkest One?"

"He disappeared," Oliverio replied. "It feels as if he's left this world but we do know he's around here somewhere. He's amongst us. You know very well how it happens."

"In that case, we have little time."

"If you ask me, the Darkest One already knows which one of the Players harbors the Avatar. I'm surprised the boy is still alive, to tell you the truth."

The *boy*? Did he think he was the big guy?

"As long as *I* know this, I'll take care of it. Leave it all to me," Hunter rose to his feet. "I'm not saying goodbye."

"Likewise. Have a nice day."

Seeing Hunter head for the exit, I also jumped to my feet and hurried after him. We didn't say a word as we walked past Yulo. On an impulse, I nodded to him — and much to my surprise, he nodded back.

"Hunter, wait! Can you tell me what's going on?"

"That was only a game he was playing. The Darkest One knew you had Savior in your possession. He knew who you were. So he had all those initiated Players slaughtered just to have an excuse to summon the Seers. Then he destroyed their Order just before their Grand Master arrived. Who in turn did his bit of eternity-weaving and saw he'd done it."

"I don't really understand. Why would he do that?"

"He wants Savior. That little is obvious. But not only that. Ever since he found out that you and I stick together, he changed his plans. He knows you're my student now. So he showed us his true power. He wanted us to know there's only one thing that can defeat him."

"Which is?"

"Gramr."

"*Grammar*? Sounds easy enough!"

"Well, it's not. Gramr is the name of the sword that used to belong to a great Player who went on to become a God and met a tragic death. I found it by chance and immediately realized the power it possessed. The Darkest One knows about the sword, and it's the only reason he hasn't killed you yet."

"You mean that he's waiting for you to leave in order to fetch the sword so he could kill you first, and then kill me next?"

"Not necessarily in that order. But that's what it boils down to, yes. That's his plan. He's the most cunning Seeker I've ever heard of."

"In that case, wouldn't it be a good idea not to do what he expects us to do?"

"Maybe not, but once he realizes we've foiled

his plan, he'll just kill you and drop off the radar. Which is why I absolutely need to fetch Gramr."

"Do you have it here?"

"What an idea! That's not the kind of thing you keep around you. It's in a safe place. Too safe, actually."

"So what do I do in the meantime?"

"Just keep it cool. Stick to your usual schedule. We don't want Him to smell a rat. I'll be back in a couple of days," he slapped my shoulder and trotted toward the Community gates.

Oh, great. Just what I didn't want to happen.

My head was heavy. I needed to sit down and give it all a good ponder. But the moment I thought about it, someone gave me another slap on the shoulder.

"There you are, brave warrior," Jan's grim face loomed into view. "So you decided to play it safe too, I can see?"

"What do you mean?"

"Apparently, there's a serial killer on the loose. The one who massacred all the Seers. From what I heard, the Community is the safest place in the city now. Hopefully."

"Hopefully being the operative word. I don't really know much about it, but according to the Grand Master, the Darkest One can be anywhere. And there's nothing you can do to identify him."

"Can't say I like all this hoopla," Jan said. "I think I'm gonna make myself scarce. I might leave in a couple of days, go sit it out in some other city. Or in Purgator even."

Dammit. That essentially put a lid on my get-rich-quick plans.

"Where's Litius?" I asked.

"He's with his buddies over there," Jan pointed.

He was right. So stupid of me not to have noticed him earlier. Litius was standing in a group of his brethren next to the lane leading toward the sachem's house. That's if the word "brethren" could be applied to a lamb-man and a lizard-man. Interestingly, the lamb-man was holding a small spiky creature on a leash.

Like, an animal walking an animal? What kind of racist thoughts were these?

To add to it, Litius was doing just that: standing. The beastmen didn't seem to be engaged in any form of conversation or whatever. It must have been danger that had forced them to stick together as a group. Which apparently didn't imply they were to become friends.

"Follow me," I told Jan. "We need to talk."

I walked over to our feline companion and his group. "May I steal your friend?" I gave him a confident tug on his sleeve as if it was the most natural thing in the world.

The other beastmen didn't seem to care. The little spiky thing did growl though, pulling on its leash until it hung in mid-air.

"Need to talk," I repeated to Litius.

"Where?" Jan asked.

Indeed, we were standing right in the way of a busy human traffic. Not the best place for the kind of conversation I had in mind.

"What if we go to the Syndicate?" I offered.

Jan chuckled. "Where do you think they're all

329

going?"

"Or to a shop."

"That's what everybody's doing now, buying up weapons and potions."

He was right, dammit. Having said that... I did know of one other place.

"Let's go," I said.

We were already halfway there when Jan perked up and caught up with me. "Pointless going to the Gate," he said. "It's absolutely packed there."

"I'm not going to the Gate. Or rather, I am, but not quite," I said, confusing him further.

True, the Gatehouse was quite popular today as the most faint-hearted of the Players hurried to leave the Cesspit which suddenly wasn't so safe anymore. Well, whatever turns them on. Personally, I didn't consider Purgator a very cozy place, either. Not during the Red Moon, anyway. But they were already overtaken by a mass hysteria, lining up to get out.

We stopped just short of the panicking queue. I walked over to the second house on the right and knocked.

"Go screw yourself, shit for brains!" a voice came from behind the door.

He wasn't in a hurry to open up, was he? I knocked again.

"I'm gonna kick your head right in so that your ass will stare at Elhvell!"

Judging by his tone, Elhvell wasn't a particularly nice place, either. I heard the clinking of bottles, followed by heavy footsteps. The door swung open.

The sight of the half-naked Traug was sufficiently scary for me to shrink back, as did the nearest part of the waiting line which hurried to arch away. My friends, too, took a few steps back.

"Ah, it's you," Traug's voice softened. "*Haisa*, man."

"Haisa to you too. You said I could speak to you if ever I needed help."

"Well..."

"Didn't you say that Korls should stick together?"

"So they should," he heaved a sigh, enveloping me in stale alcohol fumes. "Come on in, then."

"Er... I'm not alone," I stepped aside, allowing him to take in the figures of Jan and Litius.

Traug's studying gaze slid over the beastman, then lingered on the magus. Finally, he nodded. "Get in, all of you."

He stepped aside to let us pass. "If any fucker knocks on this door again, I'll smear his brains on my toast!" he barked to the waiting line.

The last thing I saw was the sufficiently motivated queue hurrying to move to the opposite side of the street.

"Take a seat," Traug snapped at us.

I looked around. Where did he want us to squat, actually? Whatever free space there was, was taken up by all sorts of junk: old glass, crushed boxes, scraps of parchment and bits of broken pottery. Interestingly, Traug wasn't that squeamish, judging by the empty bottles of local booze sitting next to the finer wares served up by the Syndicate.

"What's all this?" I asked. "Was it your birthday yesterday?"

"As if," Traug wheezed. "There's nothing to do

here, is there? It helps me to kill time. Finding proper work here is real hard. I have to keep myself busy somehow. There's nothing worse for a man than doing nothing."

His scarred but powerful chest heaved as he sighed. There was so much strength pent up in this compatriot of mine! And most importantly, this strength was waiting to out.

"Now," I began. "I think I've come up with a way to raise a lot of dust quickly. It's not the safest of ways, I have to admit, but it can be done. We already have a team: a mage healer, a beastman scout and a Korl warrior. All we need now is a wizard."

Chapter 22

hAVING A GOOD balanced team is half the battle. Robert Oppenheimer used to have his Engineer District which was later called the Manhattan Project. Thomas Edison had Menlo Park; Katy Perry has her Christian music label. Although I wasn't as lucky as this undoubtedly most talented singer of our time, I wasn't doing so badly, either.

I was sitting at Traug's, drinking Buds and contemplating the meaning of life while Jan and Litius were outside keeping an eye on the Community gate. Traug and I were supposed to replace them after half an hour.

I glanced at my phone. If the Player we needed hadn't turned up within the next hour, I'd have to split. I still had the date with Julia to make.

Still, it looked like Traug wasn't meant to venture outside today. With a short knock, Litius stormed into the house. "He's there!"

"Where is he?"

"At the enchanter's."

"And Jan?"

"He's following him."

"I see. Now, get on over to the Syndicate and try to grab a table, by hook or by crook. I'm gonna get him. Hopefully."

I ran outside, wrapping my trench coat around me. Okay, let's think. The enchanter lived in the fourth house from the other end of the street. I'd never been inside but I'd been past it a few times, so I knew more or less where it was.

The sight of Jan hanging about the front door was confirmation enough.

"Is he inside?" I asked.

Jan nodded. "He is."

I psyched myself up and walked in.

The enchanter's house was just an old Russian-style log hut like many more in our town — but unlike them, it was still in one piece. In fact, it appeared to have been recently built.

I lingered in the dark hallway for a while, then went through to the living room. It was hung with swords and staffs, lined with scrolls and absolutely packed with Players crowding around the enchanter: a rather short man of undetermined age.

I located Harph straight away. He stood humbly with all the others, not trying to talk over them, and patiently waited his turn. A few Seekers were just hanging aimlessly about the house, just like I was. Interestingly, no one even tried to touch any of the items, let alone steal them. Either their respect for the enchanter was so great, or they were simply scared of his retribution. Whatever the reason, the crime rate in this particular part of the Community was 0.0%.

The Seekers' needs were all different. One

asked for his staff to be recharged, another wanted some protection to be cast on his armor. Yet another one wanted his sword to spew fire. You could say that the Darkest One had our peaceful backwater quaking, that's for sure.

The Enchanter used some crystals to help him. As I understood it, they were some sort of mana batteries. He would take one and fumble with it, then activate it, and bang! — the weapon or the piece of armor in need of charging would flash momentarily while the crystal opposite it would go out.

Finally, it was Harph's turn. He and the enchanter spent quite some time examining some silver amulet with a blue stone in it. At first, Harph appeared to be asking his advice; then he started pointing at the item, arguing under his breath. In the end, they seemed to have come to an agreement — either about the price or about the method of charging the item.

Finally, the enchanter activated the amulet. Harph measured out some dust, shook the enchanter's hand and headed for the exit.

As he walked through the hallway, I approached him. "Hi."

"Eh, hi," he zoned out for a couple of seconds, apparently trying to remember me, then his eyes came back into focus. "Ah, it's you."

"It's me," I said, unwilling to deny the obvious. "I have a business proposition for you."

"That's a bit rich coming from a nutcase," he said with a dismissive little smile.

That was strange. When we'd first met, he'd appeared rather normal. And now he seemed quite aloof. Why on earth would he call me a nutcase?

A cold shiver ran down my spine as I realized. My damned reputation! Hadn't the message said in clear digital language that it was supposed to have a subconscious effect on other people? So naturally, this mentalist would treat me as a Nutcase. Bad timing, really bad.

"We need a wizard to escort a group to Purgator."

"Have you ever heard of..."

"Yes, yes, I know. It's Red Moon," I hurried to interrupt him. "But it's a sure deal. The group is ready. All we need is you."

"Okay, let's presume — mind you I said *presume* — that I accept," he gave us a wary look. "What's in it for me?"

This was the most delicate part. As my fellow compatriot, Traug had shared with me a few secrets pertinent to such raids. There were two ways you could pay: by either offering a percentage or a fixed rate. The first option implied that the raid leader decided on each team member's cut of the loot. Naturally, his own share would be slightly higher. The second option guaranteed a Player either a particular item or a set amount of dust. In which case, he lost any claim to whatever else the raid might procure.

"We all get the same. My own cut won't be any higher than other group members'. Alternatively, it's a one-off fee of..."

I paused, thinking. This was a tricky one. I could neither offer too much nor too little.

"Half a kilo of dust," I finally said.

"Well... What's the length of the contract?"

"A day, two days at the most."

I'd already thought about that. This way we could come back just in time for Hunter's return. Especially seeing as the Darkest One was now in Cesspit — while we would safely escape into Purgator.

"Who's on the team?"

"Traug the Korl as a warrior, Jan as a mage and Litius as a scout."

"That crazy boozer Traug is the only one I know out of the whole bunch. You know what I think? You've got yourself a shitty team, dude."

He shook his head and turned, apparently about to wander off. Which was why I blurted the first thing that came to my head,

"And Artist_Chick!"

He stopped and turned back to me. A look of surprise spread over his face. "Arts? Is she with you?"

'We've already been to Purgator together not so long ago. That's when we discovered our... our *objective*."

It looked like mentioning her had turned our conversation around.

"Well, if she's with you..." he paused. "I need more information."

"All the others are already waiting for us in the Syndicate. We could talk right there."

"All right. Let's go."

While we trotted over to the mission building, I was racking my brain thinking how to approach Arts. I hadn't spoken to her about this. I actually hadn't even planned to ask her along. But I couldn't retract my words very easily now. I could only hope that she'd be inside and that I'd somehow manage to talk her into it.

As soon as I entered the building, I heaved a sigh of relief. Arts was sitting at her usual place all alone, ignoring the surrounding bustle. What's more, she was lolling over one chair, leaning against the wall, with her feet up on another.

She was busy drawing as usual. Despite the shortage of chairs, no one dared to come over and claim one of hers.

"Wait here," I said to Harph, pointing at the table occupied by my team.

Traug, bless him, had managed to procure a table — the fact that it was located by the entrance didn't matter seeing as a lot of other people couldn't get a seat at all. He'd even managed to cling on to a spare chair.

With a nod to Traug, Harph took a seat at the table while I headed toward Arts, trying to keep my cool.

"Hi," I said.

I pulled the chair from under her feet and sat down. She stared at me, slightly taken aback by my brazenness. But what could I do? I had to make it look as if we were old friends, at least from a distance.

"I have a proposal for you. A real serious one."

"Yeah right."

"I've put a group together, just like you said I should. A scout, a healer, and two warriors. Over there," I pointed at the table by the entrance.

"Congrats," she replied dryly and returned to her sketchbook.

"You coming with us?"

"No, I'm not," she snapped without taking her eyes from the sheet.

"Didn't you say there was a whole lot of money to be had there?"

"First you need to kill the Alpha."

"I have an idea."

I hurried to tell her about it, casting occasional glances at Harph who was sitting sour-faced staring in our direction.

"Okay, let's presume it works out," she lifted her head from her sketchbook. "What's it got to do with me?"

"You're an experienced player. You've been to Purgator. You know what to expect from it."

Also, Harph wouldn't go without you. And he's the one I probably need the most.

"What's it worth?"

"Everybody gets the same cut. Me included."

"Throw in five percent of your own cut, and I'm in."

What a cheek! It would be great to cut her down to size. The problem was, Harph would then do an about-turn too. Which meant that my so-called raid might be over before it even started.

So I clenched my teeth and nodded. "Fine."

Arts cheered up. The sketchbook disappeared from her hands.

"What's going on over there?" she nodded at my group sitting at the table. "Are you guys already working it out?"

"Exactly. Let's go and join them."

We picked up our chairs and headed over to the other table. It was a bit cramped but in the end, we all had enough elbow room.

Harph switched an uncertain gaze between me

and the girl. Finally, he couldn't keep it up any longer. "You really coming with us?"

Arts nodded. "Sure."

"Oh well. In that case, it might just work out. Let's get on with the contract, then. I'll take my fee in dust. 200 grams now and another 300 on completion."

"Agreed," I replied calmly as if I wasn't the one with only 38 grams of dust in my bag.

Your Persuasion skill has increased to level 5.
You've taken the first step toward acquiring the Leadership ability.

"Now tell us. What's the raid's objective?"

I invested all of my gift of gab into my spiel, paying special attention to the fact that we'd already managed to wound the Alpha. Then I explained how exactly I intended to get him killed.

At first, Harph listened warily, but closer to the end of the conversation, he gave a few reserved nods. "All right. I'm in."

"In that case, you'll get your fee tomorrow at the Gatekeeper's. We'll port out tomorrow at dawn."

"Local time or Purgator's?"

Shit. I hadn't even thought about that.

"Purgator's," Arts replied.

"W-w-which is n-n-nine thirty-s-six l-l-local time," Litius made a prompt calculation.

"In that case, see you at nine-thirty by the Gatekeeper's," I said, trying to play the boss.

Surprisingly, nobody raised any objections. Neither Harph nor Arts played too hard to get, apparently unwilling to show their superiority. Traug was the only one who actually spoke up,

"You could stay at my place if you wish," he said to the girl. "I live close by."

"In your dreams," she replied. Only then did she turn to me. "See you tomorrow."

Harph didn't hang around, either. With a nod, he headed toward the exit.

The only thing that worried me now was that the two of them — Arts and the mentalist — might rip me off. But I didn't get the chance to dwell on it as some semblance of a chart appeared in my interface.

Hire Agreement

Jan: 20% of the proceeds
Traug: 20% of the proceeds
Litius: 20% of the proceeds
Arts: 25% of the proceeds
Harph: 500 grams (200 grams advance pending)

This looked almost as cool as a public tender offer. The bold print meant that it was almost as good as done. As soon as I paid Harph his advance, his line would turn bold too. But that would require some more brainwork.

"Wait up, you guys. I've got a question for you."

Jan grinned. "A million-dollar one?"

"Yeah, sort of. Have any of you got any spare cash? I'll pay you back as soon as we're home. I'll swear an oath on the Game, if you wish."

The thing was, according to Litius, seeing as I was the group leader (albeit stripped of all the bonuses), who do you think was supposed to pay for all the porting? That's right: the poor little bastard Sergei. Now let's do a bit of math. Six people traveling to the Valley of Silence, that's 204 grams. The return trip from Virhort, another 192. That's not counting Harph's 200 grams.

Jesus.

"Not a problem," Traug reached into his inventory, produced a fistful of dust and poured it onto the table. "No, wait. I still need a bit for tonight."

With these words, he withdrew a small pinch of dust — 63 grams, by my estimation. He brushed it off the table into his hand, then threw it back into his bag.

"Everything's fine for a good man," Jan said, lobbing his purse onto the table. "Take it all."

Oh wow. Another 207 grams. Now we were cooking!

It was Litius' turn. He cast a wary glance around, then began producing tiny bags from under his clothes, one after another, hiding them under the table.

"Here," he handed me five fat purses under the table. "I h-h-hope th-that s-s-s-suffices."

The moment I took them from him, I knew it was half a kilo. I dumped them into the bag with the rest of them. How interesting. It definitely didn't look as if he'd given me his last dregs. I'd love to know what this undercover feline millionaire was up to.

"Thanks a bunch, guys."

"Think nothing of it," Traug waved me away as his gaze scanned the Syndicate hall, alighting on a woman by the bar. He got to his feet, smacking his lips. "All right, see you tomorrow, then. I have some unfinished business here."

"I need to dash too," I said, shaking hands with Jan and Litius. "See you tomorrow."

I rushed outside. Business is all well and good, but it was getting close to six o'clock and I too had some unfinished things to see to. Not things even, but rather something very pleasant to look forward to.

I stopped under the arch and checked if there was anyone following me. Someone could have seen me accepting all that dosh, you know. About a dozen Players brushed past, some entering the Community, others leaving it, but I didn't see anyone tailing me.

Having said that... why would I even think of that? Only a complete idiot would contemplate attacking a fellow Seeker at this point. The place was absolutely teeming with guards. They'd just grab you and beat the shit out of you.

I reached the bus stop and glanced at my phone. I finally had signal and with it, several messages from Julia, all of them saying that she might be a bit late. I replied, reassuring her it wasn't a problem.

It was actually even better this way. I could just hang about on the bridge for a while. It was a bit of a shame we hadn't agreed to meet closer to my place.

Oh well. No good crying over spilt milk. I'd thought it might be easier for me to get back home afterwards. Never mind.

I got onto the arriving bus — or rather, I jostled my way in, because it was absolutely packed. And off we rattled.

With every new stop, the bus was getting fuller until finally we were packed in like sardines in a can. I stood by the handrail, trying to shrink myself into a plastic separator by the exit. It was a good job I had the dust safely stashed away in my inventory: you could easily be relieved of all your possessions in a crowd like this.

Just as I was thinking about this, a dowdy middle-aged woman screamed next to me,

"My purse! My purse is gone!"

I didn't get the chance to get a good look at her. What I did see was a young guy who made a dash for the opening doors. Either he had some quirky metrosexual tastes or the bright-red leather purse studded with rhinestones that he was clutching wasn't his own.

No, dude, I'm not going to chase after you. I have better tricks up my sleeve.

My hand closed around the back of his hood before the woman had even had the chance to start screaming. The guy tried to jerk himself free — but only ended up attracting more attention to himself.

"My purse!"

What happened next was even more interesting. The crowd which only a moment ago had been clambering over each other had now parted. The dowdy woman with the sergeant major's voice elbowed her way toward the hapless thief. She was wearing a pair of glasses, a coat and a red beret. Furious, she snatched her purse from the guy's hand and started beating him over the head with her handbag. As I was still holding him by the hood, it took me a while to realize I was now a witness to an assault.

"We need to call the police," someone in the crowd suggested.

This prudent suggestion had a sobering effect on the lady who stopped using her handbag as a hammer. I let go of his hood, and the thief took off through the doors. After a few seconds, the doors shut and we drove on.

"Thanks," the woman nodded, then turned away to face the handrail.

You've helped a Commoner who is neutral to you.

+20 karma points. Current level: +60. You gravitate to the Light Side.

Gradually, the crowd knitted back together, once again filling all the available space. Some were muttering something about "these youngsters" while others started fumbling with their smartphones as if nothing had happened. The woman in the beret alighted at the next stop; a couple of stops later, everybody seemed to have forgotten the whole issue.

I spent the rest of my journey without any further incident. I glanced at my watch: I'd actually arrived a little bit early. Considering what she'd said about being late, I still had time to go and buy the tickets. I joined the line to the box office.

"Hi, how's your day?" the girl behind the till said, her face a clear indication that hers wasn't going so well.

"Great, thanks. Which film is coming up where you have a completely unsold back row?"

She gaze momentarily went blank. "What, the

whole row? How many tickets do you need?"

"All of them," I said.

Before, I never would have done anything like this. This was the most ridiculous of all splurges. But either the heap of dust was burning a hole in my pocket, or the thought of the loot I would have gotten off the Queen. Especially because I had plenty of time-rewind charges now.

"It's *Fifty Shades Freed*," the girl said in a softly obsequious voice, as if conspiring with me to commit a minor offence.

"Great, give me the whole back row."

"It's a romance," she tried one last time to talk some sense into me.

"The back row, please," I repeated.

"Wait a moment... It'll be forty-eight bucks."

"There you go."

"Very well. *Fifty Shades Freed*, Screen Four, seats one, two, three, four..."

"Up to seat fourteen," I finished for her as I peered at her computer screen, picking up the roll of tickets.

I ripped off seats seven and eight, and put the rest in my pocket. Just as I did so, Julia finally appeared.

"Hi," I gave her a peck on the lips.

"Hi. What's showing?"

"Apparently, some cool new movie."

Your Lying skill has increased to level 6.

Okay, okay. At least now I knew the film wasn't up to much. That might save us a bunch of time.

We spent another twenty minutes hanging around the multiplex, chatting about nothing in particular, then returned to Theater 4. It wasn't very busy: it was a workday, after all, and the movie — if you could call it that — had been running for a while. Girls of every possible age made up the bulk of the audience. Not that that bothered me.

We honestly watched a few trailers, after which the back-row magic did its trick. I tried to kiss her, and she definitely wasn't against it. Only when my hands started wondering, did she lay the law down. I didn't insist.

All things said and done, I did like the film. The setup, the development, the climax — everything was good, if not a little arousing. Some like it hot, you know.

We left the theater slightly disheveled and more than a little turned on. Julia pressed her body against mine while I tried not to think about inappropriate things. We had some pizza on a terrace and hung about the theater for a while, silently this time, after which my girl said she needed to go home.

The cab driver seemed to cast disapproving looks at us, apparently on the verge of telling us to get a room. Still, the traffic-free roads made it a short journey. We spent another twenty minutes standing by her front door, complaining that the film had been too short. Finally, Julia went upstairs to her apartment.

I came back home feeling hot, all bright-eyed and bushy-tailed. Bumpkin solemnly announced that the master of the house was "a little worse for wear". And when I declined his offer of a dinner, he turned dark as a cloud. He trudged around the apartment grumbling that his travails weren't "appreciated". The good old goblin seemed to have really taken offence.

It took me a long time to fall asleep. At first I spent some time corresponding with Julia. After she'd gone to bed, I began fantasizing about all kinds of liberal stuff. In the end, I missed the moment when I'd dropped off to sleep.

My phone alarm seemed to have gone off the moment I'd closed my eyes. Shit! My eyelids felt as if they were packed with broken glass.

I rubbed my eyes and sat up on the bed, trying to get a grip. Why had I had to set the alarm to 7 a.m.? I had a funny feeling it must have been done by a stranger, not myself. I had to go back to bed and sleep it off properly. I had lots of things to do and no one but myself to do them.

It almost worked. My head very nearly hit the pillow; then I opened my eyes, fully awake.

That's right. I had to arrive at the Community way before our departure. I still had a few things to sort out before setting off on our Purgator raid.

Chapter 23

THE BEST INVESTMENTS in the world are those you make in yourself. You're the least likely person to betray or disappoint yourself. The time you spend on furthering yourself is bound to pay off a hundredfold.

Which was why this was exactly what I was going to do today.

Compared to yesterday, the Community was deserted. The few Players who scuttled between the houses ignored each other completely, all businesslike. Then again, why did that surprise me? It was still early. Also, the fact that there were six guards posted around the square must have had something to do with it, as well as the occasional silhouette of a Seeker.

I walked past the Syndicate and stopped at the last street. From where I stood, I could actually see the exit. Did that mean that the Community was open-ended? Oh well, you live and learn.

Here, the small houses were considerably shabbier. You could tell that nobody bothered what they looked like. Following Traug's instructions, I carried on until I reached the house I was looking for.

I stopped. This was an old brick building with a sagging front porch. It might have belonged to a 19th-century Russian merchant, had common citizens ever installed themselves in the Community.

The sign over the front door said,

Rumis' Magic Emporium

The man who was sitting under it smoking a regular cigarette had orange skin. That made him a Purg: a native of Purgator.

"Hi," I said. "Are you Rumis?"

"The very same. Who are you?"

"I'm Sergei. I'm here on Traug's recommendation."

"I see. Come in, then," he stubbed his cigarette out and flicked it into a giant cast-iron trash can.

In the meantime, I gave him a closer look.

Rumis
???
Spell Modifier
Gravitates to the Dark Side
???
???

The fact that I'd begun seeing two stats instead of one had nothing to do with me. It was simply because Traug had told me a lot about this vendor. Apparently, he was a constant turncoat, serving the Kabirids first, then defecting to the Archali, then back to the Kabirids. In the end, he'd ripped someone off big time and split into the Cesspit where he bought himself a shop and kept a suitably low profile. But despite his background, he was a head and shoulders above the rest in what he did best: making and selling modified spells. At least according to Traug.

We walked through a small hallway past a staircase into a big room. I noticed a few chairs, a tea urn on the table, and a tall pulpit like those used by university professors. There was another small room behind a curtain, just big enough to accommodate a bed.

Rumis hurried to pull the curtain close and mounted the pulpit. "Come on now, give me your hands."

I walked over to him and gingerly offered him my hands. Rumis squeezed them.

The world around me went out.

I found myself in pitch-black outer space. I could barely make out the familiar constellations. Planet Earth hovered below.

A list of skills was scrolling in front of me: Map Making, Observation Skills, Linguistics, Perception, Lability, Charisma, Logic. Interestingly, my Insight wasn't on the list. I'd already gathered that it was a very rare skill.

Each of them was clickable. I started pressing the ones closest to me.

Map Making (Intellect). The ability to memorize the locations the Player has been to in order to preserve them in his or her mind in the shape of maps. For a certain fee, maps can be put onto pieces of

parchment or transferred to Seekers.
      Cost: 100 grams

      Linguistics (Intellect). The ability to learn the languages of other worlds. For a certain fee, messages in other languages can be put onto various items.
      Cost: 100 grams

      Lability (Agility). The ability to improve the body's natural maneuverability as well as the speed of stimulation cycles in nervous and muscular tissues.
      Cost: 300 grams

      Charisma (Elocution). The ability to endear oneself to both Players and commoners (excluding the cases when one's reputation clashes with both sides).
      Cost: 500 grams

      According to my earlier mental calculations, I had about 155 grams of dust to spare. The rest I'd have to spend on our travel fees and Harph's advance. So I wasn't in a position to splurge. I wanted to buy some spells, too. Which meant I'd have to choose between Map Making and Linguistics. Probably, the latter.
      The moment I thought that, I was dumped back into our reality. There I was again, standing in front of Rumis in his pulpit.
      "So you've chosen Linguistics, then?"
      "Apparently so."
      "Don't just stand on parade. Give me the dust."
      Of course. I reached into my bag and produced a big handful of the precious substance. Exactly a hundred grams; I'd measured it bang on.

I wasn't even surprised when the dust in Rumis' hands began to transform into a large crystal. The shop owner kneaded it in his hands, adding new grains of dust, until it turned bright yellow and began to glitter.

I also noticed that some of the dust escaped the process as Rumis deftly dispensed with it, secreting it in his invisible inventory.

"Take it."

Gingerly I accepted the crystal. Holding my breath, I watched it falling apart in my hands until there was nothing left of it.

A new skill appeared in my interface:

Linguistics (Intellect). Your current Intellect level allows you to select up to ten of the most common languages within the semiotic system of one particular race.

The list of racial semiotic systems you have come into contact with:

Humans
Archali
Korls
Beastmen
Kabirids
Purgatorians

Please select the semiotic system you would like to study.

As I didn't even know which race I should be friends with, I hesitated between the Korls and the Archali. Then I reconsidered. Whatever my choice, I was temporarily bound to the Cesspit anyway. Apart from an occasional raid, humanity was my family at the moment.

> *The semiotic system selected: Humans*
> *Languages available:*
> *Chinese*
> *Spanish*
> *English*
> *Arabic*
> *Hindi*
> *Bengali*
> *Portuguese*
> *German*
> *Japanese*
> *Lahnda*

The sheer value of this gift made my head spin. For a measly 1150 bucks, I could instantly learn ten of the most popular languages on Earth. No registration needed, no jumping through hoops. Online language schools, eat your hearts out. Naturally, being Traug's friend had played a big part in it: I wouldn't be so sure that Rumis was quite so accommodating to his less frequent customers.

"Anything else?" he asked.

"I need some spells."

"Upstairs," he pointed over to the staircase.

Fine. I didn't mind. I didn't expect Rumis to follow me, though. I thought I'd be served by somebody else. And once I'd climbed to the second floor, I was even more surprised.

The room was huge and devoid of any furniture, if you didn't count the few scruffy mannequins and a row of battered paper targets on the walls. An identical pulpit rose at the room's center. No, not identical: this one was much shabbier.

"I'm warning you straight away: once you've bought it, you can't use it more than three times. If you break a window or pull down a wall, you'll have to pay for it separately."

"All right, then," I nodded, not really understanding what he was on about.

"Give me your hands."

This time, rather than in the icy void of outer space, we found ourselves standing on a picturesque river bank: green grass, cows grazing in the distance, a soft breeze playing with my hair. Shit. It was all so real.

Still, I had no time to take it all in. I needed to select some spells. Here, they were grouped by skill:

Illusions: Search, Courage, Sharp Eye, Valor
Transformation: Flesh of Stone, Balance
Sorcery: Battle Knife, Raising the Dead

It took me some time to realize that the actual list of spells was huge, and these few were only the active ones available to me. It probably had something to do with a respective skill's level. Once I'd sufficiently leveled up Sorcery, there'd be more spells available.

I checked a couple of those.

Healing of Minor Wounds (Regeneration).
For the Player's personal use only.
Cost of use: 20 pt. mana.
Cost of learning the spell: 30 grams.

Courage (Illusions). Adds 30 pt. to both Health and Vigor.

> *For the Player's personal use only.*
> *Cost of use: 50 pt mana.*
> *Duration: 60 sec.*
> *Cost of learning the spell: 60 grams.*

Okay. What about attack spells?

Destruction: Feeble Flame, Ice Arrow, Electric Arc, Depletion, Combustion.

The stats of the first three were absolutely identical, the only difference being that the first one burned your target, the second one froze it solid and the third one, gave it an electric shock. The fourth one depleted your target of its Vigor on contact — it sounded awesome but was too expensive both to use and to buy.

Now the last spell was quite interesting.

Combustion (Destruction). Sets your target on fire, dealing it 4 pt. damage per second.

> *Cost of Use: 40 pt. mana.*
> *Duration: 60 sec.*
> *Cost of learning the spell: 150 grams.*

Compared to it, regular Fire was much more modest.

Fire (Destruction). Creates a fireball which deals 40 pt. of one-time damage.

> *Cost of use: 45 pt. mana.*

Cost of learning the spell: 30 grams.

That didn't make sense. Judging by this, Combustion was a much better option. Not the quickest way of cracking your opponent but much more effective. The problem was, I could only afford one of the simplest Destruction spells. I had to choose between the first three.

I gave it some thought. Fire was a bit trite. I wouldn't be surprised if everyone here had protection against it. Ice... not too special, either. But as for electricity... what is it they say — waste not, want not?

I selected Electric Arc.

I found myself back in the house. Once again Rumis proffered me an expectant hand.

There, take it, you greedy bastard.

A few moments later, I took a new crystal from him which immediately disintegrated in my hands. To my delight, I was now the proud owner of three new spells.

"Try to aim at the mannequin," Rumis said ruefully. "No more than three attempts, remember."

I didn't have any more mana, anyway. And even that was thanks to my trench coat.

Never mind. Let's do it. Time to check what this amazing spell could do.

I extended my hand with the palm facing the mannequin. My hand instantly heated up, an irregular white arc leaping from it over to the mannequin. The air quivered. A black dot appeared on the wooden surface of the statue at the point of impact.

Immediately I got myself commended. Not by Rumis, no. By the Game.

The Time Master

Your Destruction skill has increased to level 1.

Not bothering to read the whole message, I cast the spell again. Another black dot appeared on the mannequin which this time made it sway.

I cast a doleful look at my remaining mana. Just over a third left. I absolutely needed to level up Intellect, by hook or by crook.

I cast the spell one last time.

Your Destruction skill has increased to level 2.

"It's a good job you didn't take Fire," Rumis said happily, putting away the fire extinguisher he'd produced from under the pulpit. "I'm sick and tired of those pyromaniacs! Never mind. Come back when you level up the skill to 10. I'll either modify this spell for you or sell you a new one."

He put on a poker face, making it apparent that if I was done, I could clear off. I'd already noticed that the Purgs were not the friendliest of races. On the other hand, there was no telling what would have become of me had I been hunted by both the Acrchali and the Kabirids.

Outside, nothing had changed. I glanced at my phone. They must have had some powerful magic jammer in the Community because here my phone could only serve as a gentrified pocket watch. I still had some time before our RV. I could, theoretically, go and check the other exit to the town. But honestly, I just didn't feel like it. So instead, I ambled back to the Syndicate.

Surprisingly, a third of all the tables were

already taken. Don't these people ever sleep? I stared curiously at the cyborg, studying the tangle of tubes and all the linkage and printed circuits fused with human flesh. As far as I'd gathered, this was a creature from one of the more advanced central worlds. How on earth had he turned up here?

I ordered a jug of beer which only cost me one gram, curious to try proper beer out of a wooden barrel. I sat at an empty table, poured myself a mug and sipped it. It's not for nothing they say that the first mug is always the best. It quenches your thirst while satisfying your taste buds. Everything after that is just getting pissed.

The beer was all right. It was different: slightly bitter and stronger than usual, but it agreed with me.

Naturally, I wasn't going to get drunk. I just needed to while away the time. Unlike the Players' inn in town, this place had no TV, so here the only option was this most ancient of entertainments.

I sat so that I could see the bulletin board. It was quite full. Lots of the missions had gone dark because there'd been plenty of Players here just recently, but they were still active. For instance, the blood mage one had turned almost claret.

But that wasn't what interested me.

Harpies
Mission from the Oracle
Charged with: aggressive behavior and attacks on commoners.
Sentence: death
Location: Crete, Greece
Proof of completion: the harpies' claws

The Time Master

Reward: 200 grams.

Crete? That was a bit of a trot. The fee was nothing to write home about, either. But that wasn't what had drawn my attention to it. It had been issued by the Oracle. It wasn't every day that he issued tasks to Players.

I walked over and pocketed it.

I spent some more time in there, then got up and left the building. It was a shame to leave more than half a jug of good beer behind. The guys from my 'hood would never have understood that.

Litius, Arts and Jan were already waiting for me at the Gatehouse. We exchanged a few meaningless phrases which betrayed our nervousness, then quickly fell silent.

Three minutes before we were supposed to leave, Harph finally turned up. He just nodded and stood next to us.

"Before I forget," I dug both my hands into my bag and drew out 200 grams of dust.

He took it without a scruple in the world. His name on my group list was now printed in bold. Now we were all set.

"So where's this Korl of yours?" Arts asked, leafing impatiently through her sketchbook.

I glanced at my watch. She had a point. I wouldn't say that Traug was the central character in our group but according to him, he was a decent warrior nevertheless. "One moment."

I walked over to his front door and tapped it lightly. No reaction. I thumped it with my fist.

Something clinked inside. The bed creaked. "Go

to hell!"

"Traug! We're all waiting for you!"

There was a moment's silence, followed by a crashing noise. It sounded as if our new friend had barged for the door with all the force of an atomic icebreaker, ignoring all the obstacles in his path.

"Traug!"

"I'm coming, okay? One moment!"

Traug's bare torso appeared in the doorway. If I wasn't mistaken, the girl sleeping on the bed was the one I'd seen last night at the Syndicate.

Traug lived up to his word: he got dressed in no time, rushing around the house like a wounded bear. His bedmate ignored all the racket.

Finally, my fellow countryman tumbled outside.

"Don't you want to leave her a note?"

Traug shrugged it off. The rest of the group wasn't too excited to see us — or rather, him. Even the always cheerful Jan wasn't smiling. As for Arts and Harph, they were almost looking daggers. It was a good job Traug had a thick skin which allowed him to ignore all the unfriendly stares.

"Let's go," Harph said. "The sooner we get started, the quicker we'll finish."

Never a truer word said in jest. We entered the building and approached the Gates. We even had to wait in line behind two orange guys and a human all of which seemed to be going to different destinations, or so I gathered by the names of the locations.

Finally, it was our turn.

"We need to put the dust in the bowl, stand around the rock and hold hands," Arts instructed me, noticing my bewilderment.

The Time Master

I almost burst into tears when I had to part with the dust. 204 grams! You could buy a skill with this money or even several spells. But it couldn't be helped: I'd already set the process in motion.

I walked over to my group. They stood in a circle. The only things missing were the long tie-dye robes and some idiot humming to psychedelic music.

Harph's hand lay on my right shoulder; Jan's on my left.

"Now touch the stone. You know what to do next."

I sure did. I lay both my hands on the rock and uttered,

"The Valley of Silence."

This time everything happened much faster. The dust rose over the bowl with a flash, blinding me. It only lasted a few seconds; then I sensed a fresh touch of wind on my face.

When my eyesight came back, I was facing the rocky platform and the trail which led downward in the crimson light of the Red Moon.

In the morning sunlight, the place didn't seem so terrifying. If anything, it appeared deserted, even abandoned, rather than foreboding. The powerful wind whistling through the mountain peaks like some relic monster was the only hint of its true nature.

"Arts? Can I have a spear, please?"

The girl laid her sketchbook on the ground and produced a chain of sheets. She reached inside them and pulled out a spear.

Oh. Last time it had been bigger, hadn't it?

A copy of an Ekhitte aboriginal spear

Summoned weapon
Time to disintegration: 1hr 59 min 58 sec

"And a length of rope, please."

When I got hold of it all, I pulled out the knife and began to fumble with it. It had seemed much easier in theory.

"Give it to me," Traug grabbed the knife.

He took a sword out of his own bag, laid the spear on a rock and hacked at it with all his might. The spearhead and part of the shaft flew aside but no one rushed to pick it up. Traug used the rope to securely tie the knife to the shaft and gave it back to me.

I studied my modified summoned weapon, with my knife replacing the spearhead. The spear itself had become much shorter, about six foot or so. I pulled at the rope. The knife didn't wobble. This was the weapon I intended to kill the Alpha with.

"That's it," I said cheerfully. "Now it's all up to our scout. We're gonna find their lair, kill them all and retrieve their eggs. Litius? What do you think?"

"Over t-t-there," Litius pointed to one side, then headed off confidently in that direction.

Chapter 24

IT'S LONG BEEN KNOWN that one man's meat is another man's poison. Not because some people are sturdier than others, of course. All it means is that what is habitual for some can be uncomfortable for others.

That's exactly what happened now. The path which had been perfectly serviceable for the rachnaid killed by Arts earlier that morning, wasn't exactly passable for us. Or should I say, it was completely impassable? The wretched creature with his stick-like legs had no problem walking where we'd already been struggling after the first measly fifty yards.

The descent was steep, too. The slightest lapse of concentration could send you flying into the abyss. Which very nearly happened to me.

"Please don't do that again," Jan said, grabbing me by the collar. "Suicide is the worst thing you can think of right now."

"Why?" I asked, crouching in fear.

He laughed. "If you die, who's gonna get us back? I don't have one grain of dust on me."

"You're not in a hurry, are you?" Litius shouted angrily.

Our beastman was the only one who didn't seem to have any problem with the rocky terrain. He leapt deftly from one boulder to the next in huge bounds, sniffing the air as he peered around. Then he would turn back to us, waiting for his clumsy and less speedy partners.

We descended into yet another ravine, framed by a mountain on one side and jagged cliffs on the other. I noticed the semblance of a road that led up through them. To my question why we couldn't take it, Litius replied with a curt "Too long."

Yeah right. And if I fell to my death now, that would be quicker, would it?

"Over there," Litius pointed below. He already felt quite at home here and had even stopped stuttering.

"What is it?"

"An old mine. Can't you taste something nasty in the air?"

Actually, he was right. I even had the impression this wasn't Purgator but some polluted industrial zone near Chelyabinsk[22]. You couldn't take a full lungful. At least now I knew what caused it.

"Ellurium deposits," Litius said. "As far as I know, this entire region was rich in it. Further on, there should be some abandoned smithies. That's why they kept the Gate nearby. They used it to transport the finished weapons to other worlds."

I turned round, "Arts? Have you heard anything about these mines?"

She shook her head. "It must have been a very

long time ago."

"So," Litius continued, "the rachnaids chose these mineshafts for their dwellings. They have plenty of tunnels leading in all sorts of directions which improves their mobility."

"Does that mean we'll have to climb down?" Traug asked anxiously. "I'm not good in enclosed spaces."

"Aha, so our brave giant from the North is a big claustrophobe?" Arts asked innocently.

"No, I'm not," Traug said, taking offence. "If you absolutely have to know, I prefer women."

The only person who hadn't uttered a word throughout the whole trip was Harph. I actually had the impression that he'd begun to regret his decision. Still, two hundred grams he'd received from me were a power to be reckoned with. There was no turning back now: he had to complete the contract in full.

"There're some scratches on the rocks by the entrance to the mine," Litius shouted from below. "The rachnaids have passed this way. I can smell their droppings."

Arts screwed up her nose and donned her armor. Traug too hurried to equip. One moment he was a normal person — or should I say Korl — and the next moment he was a giant in full armor and Vendel helmet, holding a round shield in his left hand and a longsword in is right. Had I worn dentures, they would have dropped to the ground in surprise.

Litius and Harph were the only raid members who hadn't transformed. Actually, not quite. Harph did don some sort of cloak and hung an amulet around his neck. I recognized it as the one I'd seen at the spell modifier's place. Everybody was getting ready to fight.

"I can hear some noise inside," Litius said softly when we'd climbed down.

I peered at the thick wooden beams and the shaft's black mouth. I really didn't feel like going there blindly, even considering the spell that I had.

Harph stepped forward. "I'll go take a look."

Before we could say a word, he'd split into two identical figures. One remained immobile where he'd just stood while the second one took off and trotted down the shaft.

After about a minute, Harph's immobile figure sprang to life and turned to us. "There're lots of tunnels down there. Some of them make up part of the original mine while others must have been dug by the rachnaids."

"We have plenty of time till sunset. We need to explore it all properly. Do you have enough charges to do this again?"

"Well enough," he said, then forked off again.

We didn't have to wait too long: fifteen minutes at the most. By then, Harph had been down the tunnels eleven times with an occasional break to tell us about whatever he'd seen there. The most important part of his intel was the fact that he'd found three famuli which definitely appeared as if they were guarding something. The fastest way to get to them was via the new passages dug by the rachnaids. But there was also another way, slightly longer but somewhat safer: through the shaft's original tunnels. This would give us some room to maneuver.

"Well, let's go," I said, my voice faltering.

It was scary. Very scary. I remembered my

earlier encounter with the rachnaids. Even the thin scar on my shoulder which had healed rather quickly thanks to the magic and Elufrian ointment had now begun to throb. Either it was my overwrought imagination or maybe I could really sense the monsters.

Still, I had to advance. Sergei the Nutcase who'd had the cheek to call up the raid had no right to betray his fear. He couldn't seek support from his friends. He couldn't quiver. Instead, he was obliged to coordinate the attack and lead his men... or rather, his creatures.

"Traug, you take point. I'll follow. Arts and Harph after me. Jan and Litius, you bring up the rear."

That was actually quite simple. Traug clad in armor head to toe was your typical tank. So he was going to take the blows. I... well, I was probably still more of a warrior. That's why my place was next to him. Arts was a battle mage and Harph, a classical wizard. Jan had already shown himself as a healer. A quite unusual one, but still. But Litius... as I'd already gathered, he was a rather average warrior. He carried a short sword in his hand although he hadn't changed his clothes. Let's leave him in Jan's care.

I extended my free hand and cast Light, then nodded to Traug, pressing the spear to my chest.

Traug raised his shield and walked unhurriedly forward with a kind of savage grace. I followed.

Here deep down the mine, I struggled to breathe. Ellurium dust crunched between my teeth, leaving an unpleasant aftertaste. I had a stitch in my chest; my heart was throbbing. Then again, it could be the adrenaline rush.

We walked to the end of the main tunnel, past the twisted wreckage of mine carts, half-buried tools and heaps of miners' lamps with broken glass lenses.

On Harph's suggestion, we turned left. Here, the darkness was so impenetrable that even my Light couldn't dispel it. So Harph cast one of his own spells — admittedly an unusual one but it did work. In his case, it was his whole body, and not just his hand, that began to glow. The spell appeared similar to mine: he must have modified it to suit his own needs.

"They're quite close," Harph said.

"I hear them sh-sh-shuffling their feet," Litius said softly. "They're c-c-coming for us."

"Very well," I said, trying to will myself to stop shivering. "We'll face them here."

Tactically, the advantage was on our side. The tunnel wasn't wide enough: definitely not enough to allow more than two rachnaids to pass at a time. Traug and I were going to meet the enemy head on, making sure they didn't fight their way past us to the rest of the group. And our fire power would give us a considerable edge in this confrontation.

That's exactly how it happened. There were actually three famuli. Two of them immediately advanced while the third one hovered restlessly behind their backs, making nasty noises and impatient to join the fray.

This time their tactics differed considerably from the last time when the famuli hadn't appeared to be in a hurry. Now they descended upon us like angry wives on a payday.

Traug didn't budge. Razor-sharp claws slid off his pauldrons, unable to find a place to penetrate them, and started hammering against the shield. Traug didn't shift an inch.

My own opponent, apparently doubtful of the power of human weapons, allowed his momentum to drag him onto my makeshift spear, ripping his belly open in his attempt to get even closer to me. I ducked aside to avoid the blow which only grazed my shoulder.

By saying "only" I mean "clawing me all the way to the bone". I screamed with pain, afraid of passing out, then rewound time.

I crouched and dug the spear shaft into the ground at a sixty-degree angle. The spearhead turned green with slime. I didn't even have to aim it in the pouch under his head: apparently, the Alpha wasn't the only rachnaid who suffered from allergy to moon steel which sliced through their flesh like hot knife through butter.

Your Pole Weapon skill has increased to level 5.

Your Short Blades skill has increased to level 10.

You've achieved Mastery in the following skill: Short Blades

Mastery level: 1

Every fifth blow in a series of attacks will result in a crit.

I glimpsed the creature's sharp claws and mandibles fleeting over my head as he hadn't yet realized that his prey had escaped him. The rachnaid slid forward along the ground, ripping his belly ever deeper. I watched his life ebb away as his body bled nauseous toxic slime.

I heard a short clap which sent the rachnaid's dying body flying into the depths of the tunnel. I turned my head. Harph was standing behind me, his hands outstretched. In the meantime, Arts was firing away at Traug's opponent.

"Magic almost doesn't work on him," she said. "Wretched Moon! We can only deal physical damage."

Traug must have heard her because he moved resolutely forward, swinging his sword time and time again in a series of decisive blows. I heard the crunching of bones, followed by the creature's scream as one of its fighting legs gave way. Traug attacked it again; this time the famulus began to limp.

The surviving rachnaid went for me but was stopped by a white shroud which dropped onto the monster from above. It was clearly another one of Harph's spells. Although it hadn't dealt much damage, it had considerably tamed the monster's ardor.

Immediately a tiny green shoot appeared between the rocks, rapidly growing in size. In just a few seconds, it entwined the famulus completely, immobilizing him, then began to constrict him until his bones crunched. The creature squealed.

"Now!" Jan shouted.

"I'm on it!" I ran over to the monster and thrust my spear into its head. It made a foul sound like sinking a knife into a potato.

And just to remind you, it took me exactly five blows to kill it. A coincidence? I don't think so. It must have been my new crit bonus at work.

The Time Master

Your Pole Weapon skill has increased to level 6.

I looked around. A few paces away, Traug had already overcome his own victim's defenses and was finishing it off, sending slime sloshing all over the place. The creature's legs jerked in an attempt to cover itself from the blows; half of them were already broken, the other half chopped off. For a brief moment, I felt sorry for the bastard — but only until the agonizing monster used its mauled legs to make one final thrust, aiming to sink its mandibles into Traug's neck. With envious reactions, Traug threw his shield up, then continued to hack at his enemy.

"Enough, you!" Arts shouted. "Can't you see you've already caved its head in? That's exactly why I can't stand Korls! You love to run amok!"

'Run amok?" I repeated.

"It's one of their racial traits," the girl explained. "You humans have Intellect and Eloquence. And they have Amok which lowers their intellect but improves their strength and reaction times."

Oh, great. Did that mean I'd borrowed all the worst from both races? As a human, all I had was Eloquence but no boosts to Intellect. And as a Korl, I'd missed out on Amok in favor of cold resistance. Just my luck, I suppose.

'Okay, what now?"

"I'll go and see," Harph said, splitting again.

This time he only made two sorties, after which he rejoined us. "They dug a narrow passage from this tunnel, ending in a huge cavern guarded by six famuli. The Alpha is guarding the other exit."

"I'd venture a guess that he's guarding the Queen," Litius said. "And if so, he won't move unless there's a direct threat to either him or her. And as for regular guards, we could lure them out."

'Exactly," Harph agreed. "The big one didn't give a damn about me. He kept watching me but he stayed put. But the other famuli kept following me and even tried to attack me."

"One more thing to consider," the beastman raised a hairy finger, "is that rachnaids are constantly communicating. They already know that we've invaded their territory and killed their own. Another thing I'd like to point out is that these creatures learn remarkably fast."

"Hopefully, not too fast," I said. "Harph? Which one of your spells has the longest range?"

"Falcon's Arrow. It's an aimed shot with a range of a hundred and fifty yards. I have a few which have a longer range but I can't guarantee their accuracy."

"Good enough. How far is it from the passage to the cavern?"

"About twenty-five yards. You actually can see the cavern from the tunnel."

"Excellent. We'll all stay here while you aggro one of the guards. The passage is narrow; there's no way they can get through it all together. We'll stand our ground and make mincemeat out of them."

Nobody seemed to object. Guided by Harph, we cautiously made our way to the passage. Traug probed inside and immediately returned, confirming the information about the six rachnaids posted about fifty paces from the exit.

Now it was Harph's turn.

"Make it quick. Cast your spell and come straight back," I said.

He smirked, his whole countenance making it clear that his battle experience far outshone my own, and moved forward. We stayed behind in pitch darkness.

I stretched out my hand and sent a mental command, casting Light.

Arts reached inside her sketchbook and produced a hand grenade, of all things. It looked like an old pineapple grenade but with smooth round sides.

She must have read something in my stare. "What now? Yes, it's a Russian RGD5."

"You don't happen to have anything else like this in your book?"

"I might," she replied softly.

I would have continued asking questions, and I sure would have found out a few more interesting things, had it not been for a sudden burst of light as Harph returned.

"I've aggroed him," he said, bug-eyed.

Litius waggled his ears, listening in. "They're coming."

"I'm gonna lob it," Arts said as she tugged out the pin, then did exactly what she'd said she would do.

It was one hell of an explosion. My ears were still ringing when the first rachnaid showed up. Granted, he was limping — but apparently you couldn't stop these with a piffling RGD5 grenade.

It was a good job that Traug had been standing directly in front of me. Admittedly, he too was concussed but at least he was wearing armor and not a tatty trench coat mended by a goblin. The rachnaid's claws made a screeching noise against Traug's armor as the creature attacked him not once or twice but four times — and only after that did Traug finally wake up and move his butt to assault the enemy.

Just then our wizards joined in, too. Arts doused the famuli with a good dose of fire while Harph was showering them with some killer air spells. The first rachnaid was repeatedly thrown in the air; his body was singed but he kept getting back to his feet, assaulting our tin can a.k.a Traug time and time again.

At this point, I finally came back to my senses, took a better grip of my spear and began advancing.

I stood directly behind Traug and started dishing out blows at the creature's flitting legs. Not all my blows earned me points but those that did land were real beauties.

Your Pole Weapon skill has increased to level 7.

Just as I received the message, the creature's razor-sharp front leg came flying through the air. The rachnaid screeched, trying to rear up, but Traug's sword sliced through his most vulnerable point directly under his head. He must really have known a thing or two about these things' anatomy.

The rachnaid's body was still warm and convulsing when another famulus headed toward us. Traug stepped aside, giving him a chance to get out of the passage, and only then did he attack the wretched insect. At that point I noticed that my knees had stopped shaking as the battle had turned into a regular tactics practice. You aggroed a mob, killed it, then aggroed the next one.

I killed the second one single-handedly with an accurate blow to the head. Honestly speaking, I'd been plain lucky. It was only the second time in my life that I'd used a spear so I was far from being an expert. But at least I could handle it with confidence.

We'd almost finished off the third monster when I heard the angry roar of what sounded like a tiger.

"We're surrounded!" Jan shouted.

The old me wouldn't have known what to do. He would have probably frozen in place or started mumbling something incoherent. But the new me didn't hesitate a second.

I took two steps back and swung round. "Traug, don't let him through! Harph! Arts!"

I hadn't needed to say anything. Harph had already cast his signature Thunder from the Sky, the one he'd used to defeat the Darkest One. Now it was just as spectacular, sending one of the new arrivals tumbling head over heels back into the far end of the tunnel.

I hurried toward another one which was giving Litius a hard time. Our beastman was growling and throwing feints, but his fur was covered in blood. I noticed at least four deep cuts in his hide.

The rachnaid swayed, trying to avoid a blow from a new opponent, but I had the most serious intentions regarding him — short of offering him a wedding ring.

One accurate blow did it; the next moment, my

spear was pointing upwards with the rachnaid's head already impaled upon its razor-sharp tip. Because as he'd ducked, he'd literally offered himself to my knife.

Your Pole Weapon skill has increased to level 8.

Your Short Blades skill has increased to level 11.

The other famulus who'd already recovered from his short but impressive flight suddenly tripped up a mere ten paces away from me and dropped, entangled in Jan's ivy creepers. He struggled furiously for a while, realizing that his number was up, then quietened down as he watched me approach him slowly. He might have hoped for mercy — or he might have realized that any resistance was pointless. In any case, mercy was the last thing on my mind. I whacked him in the head with a spear, then finished him off with two more blows.

"Jan, heal Litius!"

Our beastman was in a bad way. He hadn't even tried to get back to his feet, lying limply where I'd left him. The ground under him was dark and sticky with blood. His eyes didn't focus on me but stared into space over my head.

"Jan!"

"Wait up, for crissakes!" Jan shouted back. "I'm out of mana!"

"Take this," Harph said, hurling him his amulet, the one he'd received from the enchanter.

Jan clenched it in his hand. Immediately a green shoot began boring its way through the tunnel's rocky floor, so thin it was almost invisible. It had broad leaves and a pink bud that kept swelling. Finally, it bloomed, releasing a cloud of off-white pollen tinted with crimson, which instantly filled the air.

I watched in amazement as Litius' wound began to close, leaving hard scabs behind.

"Here," Arts hurried to his side. She reached into her bag and brought a vial of bright red liquid to his lips. From what I gathered, she hadn't drawn it but must have spared it from her own emergency stocks.

"There, there. It's gonna be fine," she said softly, pouring the liquid into Litius' mouth. She then felt his pulse and looked up at me. "He's alive. He'll pull through."

Only now did I begin to shake. Really, it felt like I was outside in minus forty wearing nothing but my underpants. I'd very nearly lost a team member... a fellow human being... or rather... ah, dammit, Litius *was* human, whatever you say. I hadn't taken all the eventualities into account. I'd made a mistake in planning our advance.

Strangely enough, that's when I received another message:

You're on your way to receiving a new skill: Leadership.

But it wasn't the right moment to wallow in self-pity because Traug was still fending off the last Rachnaid. I hurried to his side and chopped off one of the creature's legs. As the famulus began to list, he failed to see the sword blade that struck his head. The blow wasn't fatal but it was enough to disorient him, resulting in another blow from my spear.

Your Pole Weapon skill has increased to level 9.

We did away with the last of the Alpha's guards without resorting to any special tricks. Traug aggroed him while I finished him off with my moon-steel blade.

Only then did I turn back to check on Litius. He stood upright without seeking any support. Granted, he staggered a little but at least you could see he was okay. Jan was busy next to him, doing his shaman's thing.

'We can't get through here anymore," Traug wheezed, breathing heavily. "Their bodies are blocking the passage."

I turned to Harph. "Where are those other passages they made?"

"Logically, they should all lead to the cavern. But to get to them, we'll have to go back."

"We don't have much choice. I don't see us moving all these bodies. They're all intertwined."

We waited for Litius to recover somewhat, then headed back the way we'd come. Harph wandered off on another recon, then returned. According to him, the coast was clear.

We then squeezed through a passage so narrow as to allow only one person at a time. Traug took point. I brought up the rear, having learned my lesson the hard way.

It was indeed a much longer hike. We walked along the winding tunnel for another half-hour until it finally led us to the cavern which Harph had told us about.

"I don't think it was the rachnaids who built it," Litius began to pontificate as soon as he'd recovered. "This cavern appears to be a natural formation. All the famuli have done is tweak it a little by digging a few tunnels and..."

"Shush," I said, casting wary looks around. "Harph? Where did you say the Alpha was?"

"Over there," Harph replied, pointing at the broad tunnel at the back.

"He's not there anymore," I shared my understated observation with him.

"Guys, I think I know where he is," Jan said under his breath. "Look up, but do it slowly."

The last thing I saw when I raised my head was the long legs of the rachnaids' leader coming for me.

Chapter 25

VEN THE SHARPEST knife in the drawer doesn't cut very well sometimes. The best-laid plans of man can go awry. Unless you're the Oracle, of course.

How was I supposed to know that our death might assault us from above? The rachnaids had neither wings nor cobwebs. There was no possible way they could have descended upon us from the ceiling.

Having said that, the Alpha hadn't exactly descended: he'd quite simply dropped, burying one of his combat legs into Harph and piercing his body right through.

Harph's gaze glazed over. I and all the others were swept off our feet by the monster's chitinous shell.

I needed to act quick!

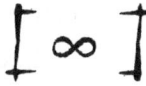

"...I think I know where he is," Jan said.

"Up above! Spread out, quick!" I shouted as I darted and rammed Harph out of the way.

The Time Master

We collapsed onto the ground as the Alpha came crashing to the floor behind us. I swung round, picked up my makeshift glaive and held it out in front of me, casting a quick glance to check on my team.

Traug was on his knees, picking up his shield. Arts was reaching into her sketchbook. Litius growled and stepped aside. Jan was casting another spell.

The good news was, everyone was still in one piece. And the bad news...

The bad news was towering right in front of me: huge, angry and lethal. The only thing that still kept me alive was the moon steel which the Alpha must have sensed. At first he tried to get to me but immediately screeched something in his insect language.

And I was still trying to figure out just how to fight him. According to our plan, we were supposed to engage him after which I would stab him like a freakin' pin cushion, excuse my French.

The problem was, our plan involved cornering him which now seemed a bit problematic.

Still, despite all the hassles, I saw a tiny green shoot forcing its way through the rocks under him. If only we could distract him for long enough!

I thrust the spear forward so that its tip hit the monster's chitinous chest. The blade clanged as it glanced off. Not good. It looked like my moon steel couldn't do jack against the Alpha. I had to aim for his leg or the vulnerable spot on his neck.

Seeing the spear deflected, the rachnaid went

for me. His sharp front leg flitted before my eyes. I was just about to rewind time again — I had enough for one more activation, counting the charges already restored — but the Alpha seemed to slow down.

He struggled again, but the growing ivy held him tight within its grasp. The amulet in Jan's hands was vibrating, shining brighter than the local sun, while Jan himself continued to work his magic.

Still, our luck didn't last. The Alpha swung round, ripping the ivy apart. All I had time to do was poke him a few times in his backside without much effect, after which I swung my makeshift weapon in the air, chopping off one of his legs.

I heard one hell of a crunch. The rachnaid momentarily lost his balance. Still, it lasted but a second. Soon he turned back to me, disregarding my moon steel which he now viewed only as a nuisance.

Traug tried to attack him from the other side. Without turning, the monster kicked him so hard that Traug flew against the wall and crashed to the ground.

"Harph, cast *Windstorm!*" Art shouted as she reached into her sketchbook for something I couldn't yet see.

Harph promptly did as he was told, forcing the Alpha to crouch lower against the force of the hurricane. In the meantime, Arts had already found what she'd been looking for and was now laying the sheets of paper on the ground. The item she was about to produce must have been huge, by the looks of it.

The result didn't disappoint. Arts stood up, holding what was arguably the second most famous Russian weapon after the AK-47: the Soviet-era handheld anti-tank grenade launcher with a khaki-colored wooden stabilizer and black muzzle. I couldn't take my eyes off such a powerful weapon in the girl's delicate hands.

Arts deftly lifted it to her shoulder, took aim and squeezed the trigger.

The fiery flashback extended from behind her right shoulder, making everyone squeeze their eyes shut. A loud explosion resounded about twenty feet away from me, just next to the Alpha's backside.

When I came round, I was lying on the ground feeling around me for my spear and staring at the thrashing monster. It looked like he was dying. Although the weapon had failed to completely destroy his chitinous armor, it had ripped it apart. Clots of green slime were escaping through the cracks.

The problem was, the Alpha apparently intended to take as many of us with him as possible.

I could see that his every movement was an agony for him. Still, he headed confidently for Arts.

Harph was trying to bring him back down with his air spells; Arts was spraying him with generous amounts of fire — but the Alpha was intent on avenging himself.

At this point, I must have completely forgotten my sense of self-preservation. I stumbled back to my feet and, ignoring the pain in my body and the ringing in my head, dashed forward, trying to approach Arts in a roundabout way. Unfortunately, by then there were barely ten feet left between the two. Ignoring all the others, the monster raised his sharpened claws when I rose in front of him.

In one brief blow, I buried the spear tip under the Alpha's head.

You've helped a Player who is neutral to you.
+20 karma points. Current level: +180. You gravitate to the Light Side.

The monster wailed and jerked his head, trying to lift me off the ground with my spear. It didn't work: the spear shaft just disintegrated, vanishing into thin air.

The wretched summoned weapon! My knife was still sticking out of the Alpha's neck — and he was still alive and kicking... literally.

Shit. This looked like suicide but I'm afraid I had no other option.

I sprang from where I stood onto his outstretched leg. The monster froze in disbelief at my insolence. Leaning against his shell, I clambered to my feet and hurried to retrieve my knife — then received an almighty clump around the back of my head for my troubles.

Not waiting for myself to faint from the agonizing pain, I rewound time.

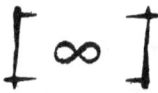

I sprang onto the Alpha's outstretched leg, waited and feigned a blow, then crouched. His front leg wafted past my hair, leaving only a whiff of fetid air in its wake. I jumped again and grabbed at my knife's hilt with both hands.

Your Acrobatics skill has increased to level 5.

Due to my weight on the knife, its blade ripped

through the monster's body even further, dousing me with cascades of stinky green slime. Finally, my knife stopped halfway through his neck, halted by something hard inside.

My fingers slipped off the hilt; I fell to the ground. I immediately rolled to the side, afraid of the Alpha collapsing on top of me. It was good timing, too, because the dead creature's head landed a mere foot away from me.

I breathed heavily, staring at the fallen monster. It felt like the whole excruciating fight had lasted less than a minute. I still couldn't believe we'd smoked him. Although initially I'd indeed expected us to overcome him, but when our plan had gone pear-shaped, my confidence had taken a dive.

Arts crouched next to me. Her face betrayed the same surprise as mine must have done.

"Killing the Alpha — and during the Red Moon, of all times..." she shook her head.

"Why didn't you tell me you had an RPG[23]?"

"I did. You asked me if I had something else in my bag."

"You could have taken me out, too."

"I didn't, did I? Don't worry. It wasn't my first time."

"Too late to shit yourself now," I climbed back to my feet. "How can we move this bastard? I need to get my knife back."

"Not a problem," Traug walked over to us. "Gosh, man, you stink."

He was dead right there. I wasn't smelling of roses. I was all covered in the green slime and could still feel the bitter quinine-like taste on my lips. Also, I'd ripped my trench coat again. Bumpkin would moan at me, that's for sure.

In the meantime, Traug easily lifted the monster's head. I hurried over and retrieved my knife.

"Stand over there by the wall," Harph said as he came over to us. "We're gonna give you a scrub."

Had I known what was going to happen next, I definitely wouldn't have obeyed him. Still, the sensation of the slime running down my body was too disgusting.

As soon as I'd stood in the place they'd showed me, I was hit by a powerful jet of water. My breathing seized up. I stood with my arms outstretched in front of me, spluttering and trying to breathe at the same time. It took me almost half a minute to adapt to it; then I even tried to help them, washing off the gunk with my own hands.

"It's cold," I said, my teeth chattering, as soon as the waterboarding procedure was over.

"In a moment," Harph said in a meaningful and not exactly unthreatening tone.

This must have been the Windstorm they'd used on the Alpha. Admittedly, I didn't like it much, either. My body was pinned to the wall until my vertebrae crunched. True, the water cascaded off me so that in less than a minute, the front of me was already dry.

"Turn round so I can dry your back."

"No way," I protested, imagining the rocky wall sink into my chest. "It'll dry just fine on its own. The worst that can happen is I catch a cold."

"No such chance," Arts replied, busy over the Alpha. "Players don't get sick."

The others, too, had already begin taking the

monster apart. Traug was holding the creature's head in his hands, studying its mandibles. Jan was trying to saw one of the Alpha's legs off with the sword he'd borrowed from Traug. Harph, too, once he'd realized I had no more need of his laundry services, beelined for the monster's corpse.

"Interesting," Traug said. "Only a minute ago he was absolutely immune to any weapon, and now he crumbles apart like dry wood."

"The Red Moon only empowers living things," Arts said, filling a vial with some of the monster's body fluid.

"Where's Litius?" I asked.

I had a point. Litius was the only one of us who hadn't taken part in the slaying of the Alpha. And now I couldn't see him anywhere at all. Having said that, this place didn't abound with hiding places.

"Litius!"

"I'm over here," his voice came from above.

I looked up. I couldn't see a thing in the dark. I stuck my arm out and cast Light.

Your Illusion skill has increased to level 6.

Litius' hairy head was peeking from behind a large ledge in the ceiling about twenty feet up. By the looks of it, there was still plenty of space left between the ledge and the ceiling.

"There's a passage here that leads up," Litius said. "It starts in the back tunnel and circles the room. That's how the Alpha got to us."

"Come down, will ya?"

Litius nodded. In one graceful feline leap, he

landed next to me. I looked up again. The mind boggles. I might have to ask him about his racial properties. He definitely had some very interesting Agility skills.

"Are you done taking the deceased apart?" I grinned, feeling the initial shock of defeating the monster dissipate. "Harph, we need to find the Queen."

"Got it," Harph replied, then split again. His doppelganger hurried toward the back tunnel.

"So, Arts, what else have you got in your magic sketchbook? You don't happen to have a tank there, by any chance?"

"No, I don't," she replied calmly, studying the vialful of green slime against the light. "In actual fact, I should be given a higher cut. It took me six months and a lot of blood to draw this wretched RPG."

"I'm afraid we've already discussed everything and signed the paperwork, period. Thanks for the RPG, anyway."

She rolled her eyes and smirked, letting me know where I could stick my appreciation.

I took one last look at the fallen Alpha. He was a sad sight. Gutted, with his head chopped off and half his limbs missing, he no more resembled the awesome insect which only a few minutes ago had instilled the fear of God into everyone.

"I've found her," the real Harph came back to life. He turned to me and repeated, "I've found the Queen."

"Just how dangerous is she?" I asked Arts.

"Without her minions, we could take her with our bare hands."

"Nobody else around?"

Harph shook his head. "Absolutely no one. The problem is, there's a really weird spot there."

"Which is?"

"I'm gonna show you when we get there. I can't pick up everything my copy perceives. All I can sense is that it's not good news."

"What are we waiting for, then?"

I only had 4 pt. charge left, but that should be enough considering we weren't in danger anymore. No good hanging around: the sooner we started, the quicker we'd finish.

We set off toward the back tunnel. Harph reactivated his modified Light spell. Gradually, as it began to wear off, darkness took over.

This place didn't differ much from where we'd just come from. The tunnel made by the insects wended its way down. I second-guessed its descent when my ears got blocked, making everything sound dull and muffled. How strange. We couldn't have been that far down. I pinched my nose, closed my mouth and breathed out sharply. My ears popped as my eardrums returned to their regular position.

"Here," Harph stopped. "Can you feel it?"

Arts shuddered. "Sure."

"Someone forgot to shut the fridge door?" Jan said with an almost imperceptible smile.

Even Litius' fur stood on end — apparently, in an attempt to conserve body heat. Traug and I were the only ones who eyed our fellow raiders in surprise. It was slightly colder here, sure. This mountain must have seen much worse drafts than this.

"Wretched Korls," Arts shuddered again, noticing our bewildered gazes. "I'm not going any further."

"That's exactly what I was talking about," Harph said. "It's weird, don't you think? There's something in this tunnel that causes temperature to go up and down. And what's even more interesting, this effect doesn't go right until the end of the tunnel. Wait a sec."

Once again his copy trotted forward. After a while, the real Harph came back to life and went on,

"That's right. There's a small room over there, about thirty feet in diameter. That's where the source of the cold is. It must be some artifact. And the room itself... it wasn't built by the rachnaids."

Arts tensed up. "What do you mean?"

Harph shrugged. "You need to see it. I can't explain it to you. I couldn't see it under the layer of ice but it looks like there's a rock there which had been dressed perfectly square. There're also some shattered columns at the room's center. Everything's covered in ice so I couldn't really see very much in the dark."

"An underground city?" Litius asked, scratching a pointy ear.

Arts almost jumped with excitement. "It must be really old!"

"The mines were built about four hundred years ago," Litius began, losing his cool. "And ev-v-ven then th-th-they didn't f-f-find it..."

Harph nodded. "It must be at least a thousand years old."

"Sorry to interrupt your archeological discussion," I began, "but in order to get to the Queen, we need to get past this historical monument."

"Easy," Traug shrugged. "We can go, you and I.

The Time Master

The Korls don't give a damn about cold."

Well, thanks a bunch, Mr. Compatriot. I really didn't feel much like diving down a tunnel affected by some weird artifact. The fact that Traug was going with me made me feel a bit better, of course. Two dead bodies are always better than one. Still, I'd rather I share the experience with all my group members, including Arts with her magic sketchbook.

"I wonder if it could be disabled?" I said, staring down the pitch-black tunnel.

"Artifacts lose their properties once destroyed," Litius pointed out.

"I see. Arts, can I use your RPG?"

"What's wrong with hitting it with a rock, like our ancestors did?" she replied.

"Very nice of you. Come on, Traug, let's go. You go in front. I'll follow. Oh shit, you can't see anything, can you? Okay, I'll go first. Just please try to keep up.

I cast Light and stepped into the gloom, leaving behind a group muttering in low voices.

After another sixty feet and a couple of twists and turns, my and Traug's footsteps were the only sounds in the tunnel. The uneven sandy walls felt harder than rock, ice peeking out of an occasional crack. It looked like this place had long suffered in winter's grip.

The further we went, the frostier it got. At a certain point, Traug asked me to stop and removed his armor, putting it into his bag. He simply couldn't proceed any further in it. Our breathing misted, sending clouds of vapor up to the ceiling. Our eyelashes, moist with tears, kept sticking together. It was so cold that my teeth began to chatter.

I cast Light again and wrapped myself tighter in my trench coat.

Your Illusion skill has increased to level 7.

The room in front of us looked like a tiny round closet in an apartment block abandoned by its management. The walls here were covered with a thick transparent layer of ice. Pack snow crunched underfoot.

Indeed, a broken fragment of a column imprisoned in the ice rose at the room's center.

"It seems that there's a lake overhead," Traug nodded at the ceiling. "That's where the water is coming from."

"You'd better tell me where to look for the artifact," I said, using my glowing hand to peek into the gloom.

"Wait up. I'm looking."

Then a strange thing happened. It was as if I was being summoned by something — or someone. They weren't calling out to me using any known language, no: I heard the call within me. Not a sentient call even but rather like a pulsation that I sensed.

Obeying the command, I turned round and pointed my glowing hand, illuminating part of the frozen wall.

And there I saw it, trapped under a seven-inch layer of ice. It looked like a rock of a rare azure hue.

"Traug! Over there!" I pointed at the object. "You think you could get it out?"

He shrugged. "Easy."

Traug put his sword away and took a small

hatchet out of his bag. He took a swing and started hacking off pieces of ice with a fervor worthy of a champion mountaineer. He did a great job of it, removing whole chunks of ice with every blow. By the time I had to recast Light, my fellow Korl had already got down to the rock.

His greedy little mitt reached out to retrieve it. Then he screamed in agony.

"What's up?"

"I burned myself!"

I looked at his splayed fingers and shook my head. If anything, it was a frostbite. His hands had turned purple, with two of his fingertips covered in blisters.

That made no sense. How could you get frostbitten so quickly?

"Just you wait, you bastard," with yet another swing, Traug whacked the obstinate rock with the blade of his hatchet.

I'd expected anything other than what happened next. The back of the hatchet fell to pieces. Traug stood there staring dumbly at the shaft he was still clutching.

I must have completely zoned out. Logically, we had two solutions. We could either go back and tell all the others about the weird artifact, or we could carry on toward the Queen, kill her and retrieve the eggs.

Still, I chose a third way. Ignoring common sense, I reached for the azure-colored rock and pulled it out of the wall.

How strange. It actually felt lukewarm in my hands as if I'd picked it up from the bottom of a tropical sea.

"What the-?" Traug said, bug-eyed, still nursing

his frostbitten hand.

I didn't reply, transfixed as I was by the artifact. Which seemed to be looking back at me.

Arthall (Divine Stone)
It looks like you've already met.

"Let's go back," I said, putting the rock into my bag.

The artifact obediently sank into the inventory as if it had finally found its proper place. The summoning light it exuded became slightly stronger, as if begging me to hold it again. There was something dangerous about it, and at the same time enchanting. And the ease with which I'd procured it was admittedly frightening.

Chapter 26

A S EVERYBODY KNOWS, seagulls are the greediest creatures on Earth. So many children's tears have been shed on the planet's beaches over the ice-creams stolen by those flying gluttons. So many hotdogs have been snatched from their buns by those harbingers of the Apocalypse. So many boats have been plastered with the droppings of those screaming monsters which can eat anything from soap to French fries.

But now those cute birdies could take a leaf out of Art's book. Because the moment the girl had heard of my discovery, she turned into Gollum's twin sister.

"Come on, show me!" she demanded, forgetting all courtesy.

I turned to look at Traug. He shouldn't have mentioned the rock. Finders keepers. And now I'd have to tell them the whole story.

Never mind. We were a team, after all.

"Here," I reached into the inventory and laid Arthall in my hand.

"It's so pretty... ouch!" Arts jerked her hand

away. Her fingers turned purple, erupting in blisters.

That'll teach her the difference between taking a look at something and actually touching it.

With her good hand, Arts reached into the bag and pulled out a small tin pot. Instead of a fancy rejuvenating cream as you would have thought, it contained some Elufrian ointment, no less.

"When did you manage to get that?" I asked in surprise.

"Does it really matter?"

"Traug, would you come here, please? Arts will give you a heal too. You will, won't you, Arts?"

Our most important group member nodded without taking her eyes off her wounded hand.

"And still, why can't the rock do you any harm?" Harph asked, as if thinking out loud. "What did you say was in that message?"

"I didn't say anything," I cast an unkind look at Traug who pretended he hadn't noticed it. They were right in saying that a Korl is like a town crier. I didn't mean Traug in particular, but you get the idea.

"According to the message, I've already come across this rock somewhere before," I said.

Arts shrugged. "Bullshit. It must have been lying around here for centuries. And you've only just become a Player. Also, judging by the damage it deals, it's indeed a Divine stone. And you just picked it up as if you handle such artifacts every day. You're not a god, by any chance?"

"I wasn't this morning," I said seriously, shaking my head.

Harph shrugged. "Then I don't understand."

"It might be that the guy whose Avatar Sergei

received had indeed come across this artifact before. You never know, he might even have owned it."

"What kind of Avatar was it?" Traug suddenly asked.

'Oh guys, give it a break," I said. "An Avatar! Where would I get that?"

Litius watched me intently, his feline eyes focused on me. Judging by the fact that I hadn't received a new level in Lying, no one had believed me.

"You don't have to tell us if you don't want to," Arts said, confirming my suspicions. She'd just finished treating Traug's hand. "We can discuss this wretched rock some other time. The Queen's waiting."

"Finally some words of wisdom," I said. "Let's go."

That got me thinking. Apparently, a Divine Avatar had a memory of its own. That's what gave me this feeling about the rock. And that's why I'd received the message that I had: "looks like you've already met". That seemed like the only logical explanation of my possible connection with Arthall. This was a Divine Stone, and I was pretty sure I wasn't any kind of deity. Now Savior, or whoever had owned the rock beforehand, was a different story.

I'd love to know how it had ended up here. Had it been discarded or hidden? And what could it do?

Just as we walked past the room where we'd found the rock, a drop of water fell from the ceiling onto my nose, disrupting my train of thought.

"The ice is melting," I commented out loud. "Don't you think it's a bit quick?"

We stopped. Arts looked up.

Harph touched the wall. "It's really melting.

That's because the artifact's no longer there."

"We need to dash," Arts said, turning to us. "All that frozen water has to come from somewhere."

"You're right," I said. "Litius, you stay here. You're the fastest out of all of us. If something happens here, run and tell us. Come on, quick!"

You're on your way to receiving a new skill: Leadership.

We hurried on. According to Harph, we didn't have far to go: only another hundred and twenty feet or so. The tunnel continued to meander downhill like the thoughts of a corrupt official caught in corpus delicti.

"Now why didn't the rachnaids get frozen when they walked through that room?"

"They're not really susceptible to fluctuations in temperature," Arts replied who in the absence of Litius took up his role as a walking Wikipedia.

"They why haven't rachnaids spread over all of Purgator?"

"First of all, Purgator isn't the only world inhabited by rachnaids. Just so that you know. Secondly, some Players do manage to kill them, only not during the Red Moon. And thirdly, they have their own way of propagating."

"What do you mean?"

"Listen here. Did I tell you how many eggs can a queen lay?"

"A few hundred?"

"So you see. Those few hundred eggs produce about fifty new rachnaids. One of them always becomes a female although I don't know how exactly it works. Another one becomes the Alpha, and all the others, their minions."

"Did you say fifty? There were a lot fewer than that here."

"E-e-exactly," Arts drawled. "The whole process of growing a new generation of rachnaids is based on cannibalism. First, the newborn devour the remaining eggs. Then, as they get bigger, they turn on their weaker siblings. By the time they form a fully grown group, all that's left is the Queen, the Alpha and about a dozen famuli."

"Nice," I said.

"If everything goes well, the two groups split. The old one retains its territory while the newly born one wanders off looking for new feeding grounds."

"And if it doesn't go well?"

"Then the stronger group devours the weaker one."

"Our zoologists back on Earth would freak out," I concluded.

"It's here," Harph cut us short.

The tunnel widened, forming a large cave. Now I really could believe that this was the rachnaids' clumsy work. There wasn't one stalactite left in sight: everything had been smashed and leveled.

The Queen was sitting at the center of the room, surrounded by a clutch of oblong eggs. Then again, she didn't really deserve a capital "Q". The rachnaids' leader resembled a giant slug with a pair of long antennae and a broad fat body lined with hundreds of tiny feet. The body itself was protected by a chitinous shell.

On seeing us, she emitted an ear-shattering

screech and began to back off toward the far wall.

Bastard! She was trampling our eggs!

"Gosh it stinks," Arts said, holding her nose.

She was right. The air in the cave was unbearably fetid. I thought at first that it was the slug that had emitted these foul effluvia but then I saw a pile of rags and bones heaped up at the room's center.

"It looks like the rachnaids brought her whatever creatures they'd managed to kill," Traug commented, unfazed. "So there might be some useful items in that heap of junk."

Harph cringed. "You seriously wanna go and dig through that? Rachnaids mainly kill newbies. I don't think you're gonna find anything interesting there."

"If you don't look, you won't find out," Traug replied, drawing his sword. "But first we need to sort out the Queen."

Nobody stopped him. The slug was so nauseating that none of us had any desire to approach it. So if Traug had taken it upon himself to go and finish her off, so much the better.

Unhurriedly he approached his squealing victim, took aim, then gave her slimy head an almighty whack. The blade glanced off, striking up sparks from the rocky floor.

He took another swing but with the same result. The wretched chitinous armor and that Red Moon! It looked like I might have to get my hands dirty too.

"Let me do it," I reached for my knife, trying to suppress the nausea in my throat.

Traug stepped aside without going too far, so that he could protect me if needed. He even pulled his shield out. Still, in the end he didn't need it. Since I was a little boy, I'd had the habit of doing unpleasant chores as fast as possible. Three... two... one... zero!

I sprang over to the Queen and buried my knife up to the hilt into her armored shell. The blade went through it like butter, splattering me with strange yellow slime. Was it her brain?

The slug squealed louder, then fell quiet.

You've liberated Virhort and its surroundings from the pillaging Rachnaids.
+300 karma points. Current level: +480. You gravitate to the Light Side.
Your fame has increased to 3.

I shared the information with my team
Arts laughed. "You're a victor with a capital V!"
"Meaning?"
"It looks like Virhort's Mayor had issued a mission to kill the rachnaids," Harph explained. "And you've just completed it, by the looks of it, even though you didn't take it on."
"Which means you're gonna get zilch for it," Arts concluded.
"What makes you say that?" Harph said. "You can always negotiate. It depends on the levels of your Trade and Eloquence skills, of course. Alternatively, you could seek out the Player who accepted the task, and share the reward with them."
"Exactly my point," Arts said. "Somehow I don't think his Trade and Eloquence are any higher than 20. And I know this so-called Mayor. He's a smooth operator. He won't give Sergei a single grain of dust. Also, in order to negotiate, you need to know how much

the mission was worth to begin with. So I shouldn't hold your breath."

If the truth were known, I wasn't upset in the slightest. True, I could have earned a few hundred grams of dust — or more, even. But I wasn't going to lose any sleep over it. Not when I had all those precious eggs lying underfoot which could guarantee me the life of Riley for the next few months.

I picked one up. It was soft and springy. Bigger than an ostrich egg, if you asked me. They could stuff their mission. I might have a chat with their Mayor anyway, just to learn the lay of the land.

"Let's just collect the eggs and get the hell out of here," I said.

We spread out and started filling our inventories with the loot. Excluding Traug who bent over the heap of rags, rummaging unsqueamishly through it. That was another thing I wanted to know. If you got killed by another Seeker or sentient being, you simply dematerialized, like that Chorul had done. But if you got killed by a monster, your body stayed put. Why?

"Traug, sorry to spoil your fun, man, but let's collect the eggs first. Then you can scavenge to your heart's content."

He nodded and headed for the nearest clump. I was about to follow when I noticed a hilt sticking out of the heap of junk. You couldn't mistake it for anything other than a weapon.

Overcoming my disgust, I reached in and pulled out a short sword, about 25 inches long. Its double-sided blade was eaten through with rust. But the funny thing that had drawn me to it was the fact that its guard was shaped as two wide curved petals on each side. If you looked at it closely, it resembled the infinity sign.

What was that if not sign from above?

Black Imperial Katzbalger
Origin: Roin Province
Material: Roin steel
Charmed to increase the damage dealt to positive-karma Players.
Warning! The sword is damaged. -43% to damage. A good blacksmith might bring it back to its original glory.

It looked like the person who used to own this Katzbalger hadn't been a very nice individual. He'd probably been supporting the dark side. Still, the sword hadn't helped him much against the rachnaids, had it? What he'd really needed was something with increased damage to insects.

Almost unbeknown to me, my hand slid the sword into my bag. One moment it was there and then it disappeared. I walked over to Traug and started helping him load the eggs.

We'd almost finished when I head Litius shouting in the tunnel. Soon he emerged, his tail twitching nervously.

"It st-t-t-tarted! Th-th-the ice!"

"The ice what?"

"It's m-m-melting!"

"Let's get out of here a bit quick!" I commanded.

Traug eyed the eggs greedily. "There're only a few dozen left!"

"Even your life ain't worth that," Arts said, heading for the tunnel.

"Come on, quick," I nudged the recalcitrant Harph. Jan had already got his act together and was waiting next to Litius.

Our way back was a struggle. Firstly, we now had to walk uphill. Initially, we tried to run but our Vigor plummeted, forcing us to slow down. Gradually I caught up with the more experienced team members who too had begun to slacken their pace. The worst thing was, the weight of my invisible bag was hindering me just like a real one would. I soon realized why when I saw a notice in my interface:

Load: 365/570 lbs.

That could land me a job as a courier, I suppose, seeing as I could now carry almost 600 pounds. But considering how uncomfortable I already was, even 400 lbs. might completely exhaust me.

When we reached the artifact room, I finally realized what Litius had been talking about. The ice wasn't just cracking: it was crumbling even as I watched, coming off the walls in large sheets. The water was now literally running off the ceiling.

How strange. The ice just couldn't have melted so fast.

Still, the fact remained that we had to get out of here pronto. We all must have developed telepathy skills because we unanimously rushed out. A couple of minutes later, we'd already reached the slain Alpha.

The mountain rumbled thunderously as if awakening from its century-long slumber. Water gurgled, filling the tunnel.

"Come on, no point hanging about here," I

awoke the others from their stupor. "Let's get out before the mountain comes crushing down around our ears. You can never tell how many tunnels there are and how they're all joined up."

Still, I didn't have to be so apprehensive. Less than an hour later, we finally emerged from the shaft into the light of day which was admittedly rather orange.

I was happy as a pig in shit. Happy to re-enter the fresh air which I'd missed so much underground. Happy to see this stupid moon which remained crimson even at daytime. I was even happy to see the large billygoat which was staring at me, his tiger's head crowned with two sharp twisted horns.

Wait a sec. What the hell was this animal supposed to be?

Antalope
????
Unruly

"What's this, for crying out loud? What do *they* think they're doing?" Traug said, apparently as surprised as I was.

"These bastards aren't afraid of anything," Harph said. "The Red Moon is their time. Okay, let's just sneak past him."

"Can't we just shoo him off?" I suggested. "There're six of us and we're all armed. We'd just ripped a whole bunch of rachnaids apart. And this guy is all alone."

"That's what you th-th-think," Litius spoke. "Antalopes are never solitary. They always group together in herds. So if you attack one of them..."

"Then very soon we'll have to deal with the whole bunch," Harph concluded.

"In any case, we need to get to town before the sun goes down," Arts said. "We don't want to be wandering around under the Red Moon. Today is the last day of its cycle. Which means that all the nasties will be out and about."

"I agree," Harph said. "We have to be in Virhort before sunset."

"In that case, we'll have to be moving," I said, "even if we have to make a detour."

"You're dead right," Jan said.

"So what are we standing here for?"

"Because if it's like that, we'll have to clamber back up."

Still, the dilemma offered its own solution. With a resounding roar, the creature took off.

"One second," Harph said, splitting again.

After about thirty seconds he was already back. "He did leave to warn the herd," he said. "There're thousands of them there. Hurry up! We need to break through before they arrive."

We walked around the mountain heading for the valley. I could see a dozen antalope about two hundred yards away, all looking warily in our direction. And to our left, far ahead, the mass of the herd was already bearing down on us.

Jan frowned. "Do you think they might attack?"

"Hardly," Litius replied. "They may be predators but they never attack sentient beings. Also, don't forget there're quite a few of us."

"There's our problem," Harph said, pointing at

the moon. "The Red Moon makes even the most pacific of creatures run amok."

"By the way, the sign over that antalope's head read 'Unruly'," I added.

"Exactly. It looks like they're heading toward the river. All we need to do is try and get to that far hill before their whole troop blocks the entire valley."

"Let's get a move on," Arts said, reaching for her sketchbook.

"I wish I could oblige," I said, "but my Vigor drops too quickly. It takes it less than a minute to deplete."

"That's all because of your weight," Traug said. "Give the eggs to me. My inventory's not even a third full."

I didn't play hard to get. Relieved, I loaded the whole of my 150 lbs. onto Traug's sturdy shoulders. Or to be more accurate, I transferred them into his inventory. It didn't look as if my compatriot had even noticed the difference. His Strength must have been mind-boggling.

Now things started to go better. We set off at a fair pace, occasionally breaking into a trot, as we gave the antalope's avant-garde a wide birth. We'd managed to cross their path before the arrival of the main herd.

"How many of them are there?" I asked.

"A couple of hundred," Traug said confidently. "Too many if you ask me. I've never seen so many of them here."

"It's the last day of the Moon cycle," Arts added. "They're all out for a slap-up feast."

We were sitting on top of a high hill. About three hundred yards below us, the antalope herd flooded past, completely ignoring the cowering humans. From time to time, some of them would stop to confront each other; others simply roared, ignoring the challenge. The bulk of them, however, kept moving peacefully forward.

"There's something over there," the ever-observant Litius said, peering ahead.

Traug laughed. "I bet there is. Tons and tons of half-baked venison drunk on the madness of the Red Moon."

"That's not what I mean. Over there," Litius pointed with his hairy paw.

Now I too could see a man's outline which approached the herd at a considerable speed. The antalopes must have noticed him too because they lowered their heads, pointing their horns at him. He was only several paces away from them. A few more, and he'd be-

Dumbstruck with amazement, I mumbled something unintelligible. The man had suddenly disappeared, gone in a split second. His shadow continued alone, flitting over the ground. It *was* his shadow, wasn't it?

"There's only one Seeker who can turn into his own shadow," Arts' calm voice rang with jealousy. "It's Hunter."

Chapter 27

CONFRONTED with a miracle, people always react differently. Some fall into a stupor while others become hysterical while yet others turn pale and try to find a logical explanation to what they've just witnessed. Which isn't a bad thing, either. No matter how hard I'd tried to convince myself of the existence of all the multitudes of development branches within the game, each one weirder than the next, I too froze open-mouthed.

The shadow kept coming nearer and nearer, stealing along the scorched earth covered with dry grass. The antalopes appeared just as surprised as we were. They roared anxiously, shaking their horny heads from side to side as they sniffed the air, not even realizing that the man who'd made them so restless was already in their midst.

Arts even stepped out in front in order to be the first to greet him. Litius frowned; in contrast, Jan's face dissolved in a smile. Traug and Harph were the only ones who just blankly stared at the fleeting shadow.

"It looks like I might get a dressing-down," I said in a low voice. "Unbelievable that he found me here."

"Well, what did you want?" Arts replied. "You can't hide from him so easily."

"It's all right," Harph said in a calm voice, looking somewhat detached. "I'm gonna take him out now."

Before we could say anything, he threw his hands in the air and cast some crazily powerful spell. A cloud appeared in the sky, directly above Hunter. It dropped to the ground, enveloping him as well as the nearby antalope.

Hunter's shadow shuddered. Once again the figure of my neighbor materialized, lying face down on the ground.

"You shit for brains!" Arts spat as she darted toward the fallen Seeker.

"Harph, what's the matter with you? It's our Hunter!"

Harph just stood there with a nonchalant look, staring at what he'd just done.

Pointless to reason with him now. I dashed after Arts, shouting to the others as I ran,

"Follow me! We can't let the herd near him!"

By the time we'd approached my mentor, the antalope had already recovered from their initial shock and were on the hoof. Staggering and snorting, they were shaking their heads, trying to come back to their senses. Judging by their blood-shot eyes, they much have blamed everything that had just happened on the man lying in their midst.

Arts had already managed to reach into her bag and equip her armor as she ran. She now launched a pre-emptive strike with her staff right in front of the nearest tiger heads. She stepped next to the prostrated Hunter and drew her sword.

Litius promptly stepped on the other side, crouching and growling his fury. Even Traug's full armor and raised shield hadn't hindered him from getting in front of me. As soon as we got back, I'd have to do something about my physical shape.

Your Athletics skill has increased to level 6.

I stepped in front of Hunter and bent down, panting. He hadn't dematerialized yet which meant he was still alive. I could see him stir and open his eyes as he climbed back to his feet. That was already a good thing. The only thing left to do was to sort out the infuriated antalope.

To say that our situation was difficult would be an understatement. The herd heaved as all those incredible animals started to move all at once, surrounding us in a dense semicircle. We only had one option: to retreat back toward the hill. Still, I had a funny feeling that the moment we began to back off, the antalope would go for us.

"Don't kill any of them, for crissakes," Hunter grunted as he climbed to his feet. He was still staggering but on the whole, he was in one piece. "They'll take us apart if you do."

"It's easy for you to say," Arts said, her back pressed against mine, as she swung her sword at the advancing tiger goats.

A thunderous bang came from the opposite side of our little defensive circle as one of the more impatient antalopes smashed his horns against

Traug's shield. Still, Traug wasn't born yesterday. As soon as Hunter had issued his warning, he'd put his weapon away, freeing up his right hand. Now he used it to grab the headstrong animal's twisted horn, then stepped to one side and took a swing, sending the antalope flying.

Traug grinned, stepping back toward us. "It's a good job cows can't fly."

I didn't find it funny at all. Five Players against a couple of hundred animals beefed up by the power of the Red Moon. I had a funny feeling that the setup wasn't in our favor. Actually, why were there only five of us?

I turned around and looked back at the hill. Two figures were standing upon it, coolly watching our approaching demise. I even got the impression that they had no intention of interfering.

What was that now, a mutiny? Or some personal grudge against Hunter? I thought that Jan had been happy to see him arrive. I knew he'd seen Hunter the first time I'd got to Purgator, which meant that the two had already met. Harph, however, might not have done so because it had been a while since Hunter had turned up at the Community. But in that case, what had possessed him to cast that stupid spell?

"Don't attack them," Hunter said under his breath.

"B-b-but they're g-g-gonna attack us n-n-now."

"No, they won't. They'll be waiting for him."

"For whom?" Arts asked.

Hunter didn't need to reply. I saw the herd's alpha male from afar. He towered a good head and shoulders above all the others, his chest broad and powerful, his horns massive and blunt from years of infighting. All the antalope in his way lowered their heads in submission with every step he took. Even I could sense the powerful aura of confidence and control exuded by this proud animal.

> *Antalope leader*
> *???????*
> *???????*
> *Invincible*
> *???????*

"But this one, he *will* attack you," Hunter said, stepping forward.

A sword materialized in his hand. Hunter raised it to eye level. Did he really want to stop the herd's leader with this piece of steel? Don't get me wrong: the sword wasn't bad as far as swords go. Maybe. Then again, maybe not. It was a rather plain weapon, crude even, as if the blacksmith had hastily fashioned it on the eve of battle.

Hunter took another few steps forward to break away from our group, then stopped dead in his tracks. He was waiting for the leader: the alpha male confident of his invincibility, the great warrior strongest amongst all antalope. Unconquerable.

The leader stopped a mere fifty feet away from his intended victim. There was no anger nor hatred in his gaze: he eyed Hunter the way a butcher who's about to set to work eyes a carcass hanging in front of him.

Then he moved forward in a confident gait,

slightly faster than he'd been moving before, and gaining speed with every new step. The sight of the horned monster galloping toward you made you quake in your boots. I had a lump in my throat.

All Hunter did was disappear.

Or rather, stealthed up — or became his own shadow, maybe. I might be mistaken in my terminology but what I did see was the dark silhouette of a man with a sword dashing toward the bull.

The animal seemed completely nonplussed. He was used to fighting opponents who were visible and could put up an honest fight. Head to head, horn to horn.

The antalope leader stopped and sniffed the air. He even turned in the direction of Hunter's lurking shadow. Still, my mentor was quicker.

He materialized with his sword already raised to strike. In one clean swoop, the herd leader's long twisted horns thumped to the ground. Now the bewildered animal looked like a regular tiger goat, his head topped with two short stumps. His gaze now betrayed terror and dismay.

Hunter disappeared as promptly as he'd materialized. His shadow flitted toward us. Before I knew it, he stood before me, his sword lowered.

I didn't get the chance to pose him any of the questions I meant to ask him. How had he ended up in Purgator, when only recently he'd sworn never to set foot here again? What kind of shadow ability was this? And finally, what had just happened? The fight, the bull's severed horns...

To tell you the truth, I didn't even get the chance to breathe, let alone say anything, when everything around me quickly became hell again.

The bull's horns lay on the ground, quivering slowly from side to side. Finally, they stopped moving.

That's when all the other antalope attacked their leader. Several pairs of horns hit his powerful flanks at once, forcing him to his knees; countless hooves trampled over him. The more brazen ones were already ripping large chunks of flesh from their former leader. The entire herd was now trying to get to the dying animal in order to tear off a lump of flesh for themselves.

They seemed to have forgotten all about us.

"Let's get the hell outta here," Hunter said under his breath.

We were witnessing a veritable mayhem as ordinary herd members stampeded in their attempts to get to their stricken leader, trampling each other, breaking bones and ripping through flesh. We promptly retreated to the base of the hill. Only now did we finally feel relatively safe.

"Hunter, I thought you said you weren't going to travel between worlds anymore?" I asked, putting my knife away.

"And I thought you said you weren't going to stick your neck out. The fact that I said that you weren't in any immediate danger didn't mean that you had to join the Darkest One on his Purgator raid."

"What do you mean?" I asked, uncomprehending.

"Look up."

What did he want me to see there? It was only Jan and Harph standing on top of the hill. The latter had retrieved his amulet and was now busy casting something powerful. The guy was completely off his head.

A translucent cloud enveloped the top of the hill, then spread about a hundred feet in all directions.

Arts gasped. "Anti-magic!"

"What?" I asked quietly.

"Nobody else's spells will work here now, whether cast by a wizard or by a charmed weapon," she put her staff back into her bag.

"Expect for weapons made by a god," Hunter said, playing with his sword.

"Can someone explain to me what Harph is up to?"

"It's not him," Hunter said. "Your friend is only obeying somebody else's orders."

I peered at Jan which admittedly wasn't easy from this distance.

My hair nearly turned gray.

Admittedly, my former friend also looked a lot worse for wear. In the short time it had taken us to rescue Hunter, his face had become deeply furrowed. Black circles framed his eyes, his cheeks gaunt and sunken. You could barely recognize the cheerful magus I used to know.

But that wasn't the main thing. My Insight had now allowed me to see this Player's only characteristic.

There was no mistaking. I was looking at the Darkest One standing atop the hill.

"It took you a while, Hunter!" the fake Jan shouted from above. "I was already about to kill all those idiots. Apart from your precious student, of course. How else am I supposed to lure you in?"

"No need to lure me in, Two-Face. As you can

see, I've come of my own free will."

"Ha!" the Darkest One's voice rang out over the valley, remarkably strong and clear in contrast to his appearance. "So it must have been that idiot Grand Master who told you, wasn't it? Good. It means that everything went according to plan. Never mind. Now I can finally get rid of him, as well as all the other Seers. I don't need them anymore."

"I'd already known before he told me. All the Grand Master did was confirm my suspicions. Which Player could have gone on a killing spree and still evade the Seers as if he didn't exist? It took me some time to think who that Player might have been, but in the end, I did remember."

"Not a Player! A God!" the Darkest One snapped. "I'm over two thousand years old! Don't you dare dis me!"

"Oops, sorry. I didn't realize you were so sensitive."

"Who is Two-Face?" I asked Arts quietly.

She waved my question away. However, the subject of my curiosity had heard me.

"I'm your death," he chuckled. "I am one of this world's oldest procreations! Oh sorry, I didn't tell you my full name. It's not Jan but Janus. Janus the Two-Faced, as your mentor has kindly introduced me."

"So what the hell do you want?" I demanded, struggling not to betray how shit scared I was.

"Peanuts, really. When you had the outrageous luck to have killed that Chorul, you inherited his Divine Avatar. Which is so rare that I sensed it right across four worlds at the time. I have a long history with Savior, actually. A long time ago, I already tried to take his Avatar off him. But he hoodwinked me with his fake death and escaped. So I wasn't gonna miss a second chance."

"For a god, he yaps too much," Traug sniggered.

The Darkest One ignored the remark entirely. "In my millennial travels, I met a Player who told me a thing or two. Humans can become very talkative when they think that the information they offer might help them survive. So he told me lots of interesting things. Like the fabled blacksmith god who lived in Cesspit. And Gramr, his famous sword which could penetrate any defense. He also told me about its four keepers, only two of which were still alive. Oh sorry, did I say two? One, of course. I forgot to tell you that the talkative guy's name was Jisra."

Hunter gnashed his teeth. How strange. He seemed to struggle to suppress his fury. He must have known that Jisra guy very well.

"So when I finally came to reclaim the Avatar and saw the sword's last keeper standing next to its carrier, I decided to kill both birds with one stone."

I wasn't happy to hear him refer to me as a thing. Still, this wasn't the right moment to voice my objections. I cast a furtive glance at my number of charges left. Only 18. Barely enough to rewind time just once. And my enemy was clearly not easy.

"So all I had to do was arrange for Hunter to go and fetch Gramr himself once he'd realized who he was dealing with."

Jan finally deigned to look at me. His gaze made me shudder.

"Because you see," Jan went on, "your mentor has the naivety to believe that this sword might give him a chance to slay me."

"Enough of your blabbering," Hunter said, heading for the hill.

"If you say so. Harph, kill him."

The skies rumbled. A bolt of forked lighting reached out, striking the exact place where my mentor had stood only a split second ago. His shadow was already running uphill, zigzagging like a hare chased by hounds.

I'd long realized that Harph was a good and experienced wizard. Now I was witnessing another proof of his art. As soon as he'd noticed that his opponent had activated invisibility, he cast the same spell he'd used earlier, sending a cloud that billowed down to the ground.

Although I could see that Hunter wasn't seriously hurt, the cloud had unstealthed him. He somersaulted, then continued up the hill.

"We should help him," Arts said.

What a girl! Even though she knew that her staff wouldn't work on the hilltop, she still couldn't help herself. I couldn't have agreed more. We needed to help him. But how were we supposed to do that? With my ridiculous excuse for a penknife and just one charge left between all of us?

If I'd thought that my team members would embark on an extended discussion of our tactics, I was wrong. Unlike Janus, they weren't in the mood to shoot the breeze. They just darted up the hill, all of them.

"Spread out and outflank them!" Traug shouted as he broke into a run.

"The probability of my meeting a lethal outcome is especially high today," Litius said sadly.

Before I could reassure him, he leapt forward, overtaking Traug, and headed to the back of the hill in order to attack the enemy from the rear.

Arts wasn't in the mood for talking, either. Ignoring me, she took a swing with her sword and beelined for Harph who was launching everything but the kitchen sink at Hunter.

I braced myself. Come what may!

I drew my rusty sword and took my knife in my left hand in the best Spanish fencing style, then ran after all the others. I stumbled and slipped several times but I did make it to the top.

It looked like I was late. When I finally ground to a halt with my Vigor down to 30%, the battle was already all but over.

Litius was growling as he rolled around on the ground, his shoulder ripped to shreds. I was pretty sure he'd been the first to attack and had paid for it. Arts was lying on her back some distance away from the action, her chest heaving slightly. She was unconscious but still alive.

Traug was still trying to fight the Darkest One but even my untrained eye could see who was gonna win.

Despite all my hatred for Janus, I could appreciate his swordplay. The grace with which he blocked Traug's lunges, dodged and counterattacked was exemplary. Had it not been for Traug's armor, he'd already been lying on the ground with his throat slit. As it was, Janus had shown remarkable clemency by punching him in his exposed Adam's apple unprotected by the armor.

But maybe I spoke too soon about clemency.

Traug was lying on the ground, bug-eyed, holding his throat. The Darkest One was just about to give a coup de grace when I turned up.

I came running at him and poked him with my Roin-steel blade, ready to rewind time at a moment's notice.

My amazement was so great I even forgot to breathe. The Darkest One didn't even try to defend himself. Although his in-game clothes were quite good, he was still an easy target for a sword.

I was even more surprised when my sword met with an invisible barrier.

"You're so stupid, my boy," the Darkest One laughed. Forgetting all about Traug, he turned and stepped toward me. Mechanically I shrank back. "Why do you think your mentor ran off like a headless chicken to fetch his sword as soon as he knew about the arrival of the Destroyer god in Cesspit? The Destroyer Avatar has an interesting characteristic: its carrier can't be killed with a regular weapon. Know what I mean?"

He didn't have to waste his breath. I'd already worked that out. The only thing that worried me now was what to do — or more precisely, where to run to. I'd already missed my opportunity to rewind time so now I had to wait for him to attack me. The problem was, what would happen next?

"And seeing as the sword is now here, and so is your mentor," Janus faked thoughtfulness, pretending the idea had only just crossed his mind, "then it looks like I don't need you anymore. Now I can finally reclaim the Avatar which belongs to me by right, becoming the greatest god that ever lived. The Dark god with a

Destroyer Avatar and the Light one with that of Savior. The two-faced god in possession of the opposites in both power and strength. The one who can turn into anyone he wants."

"You do love to yap, don't you?"

I swung round. Hunter was standing over the slain Harph, holding the bloody Gramr in his hand. His face scared me. Devoid of either fear of cruelty, it exuded steely determination. He didn't look human now. More like a preprogrammed killing machine.

"Sergei, step aside. It's not your fight."

The Darkest One smiled and gave him a mocking bow as he side-stepped me. "A Player against a God. A Keeper against the Destroyer of Bonds. A doomed one against the Invincible One. Come on now, show me once again that it's not the sword that makes the warrior."

Hunter didn't reply; he simply began walking towards him. At that moment, the hope was born in me that we just might defeat this scumbag.

Chapter 28

AS EVERYBODY KNOWS, it's great watching professionals at work. Still I think that this notion only applies to peaceful professions. Like watching a cobbler making a pair of shoes, a woman clicking her knitting needles or a baker kneading a new batch of dough.

Because watching these two expert fighters going at it was anything but pleasing to the eye. If anything, it filled me with primordial fear, making my heart pound in my chest.

Judging by Hunter's initial onslaught, I really thought he would get the upper hand. His movements were far from graceful or eye-pleasing: rather, they were perfectly calculated. He went for Janus like a tank not giving his opponent any possibility to recover and launch a counterattack.

Still, Janus kept either parrying or fending off his every blow, dodging my mentor's charmed sword just before it could meet its mark. And then...

Then Hunter began to get worn out. His movements grew slower, his every lunge taking longer than the one before it. At a certain moment, Janus simply stepped back and struck out. Miraculously, Hunter managed to raise his hand, parrying the blow with the hilt of his sword. With a resounding clink, his enemy's blade slid against the crossguard.

Hunter took a few steps back, trying to evade a potential attack. Still, Janus didn't look as if he was going to follow it up. He was playing with my mentor like a well-fed, obese cat that watches the throes of a tiny wounded mouse trapped in a jug of milk.

Hunter then cast a spell. A dark vine entwined itself around his opponent's leg. How strange. Hadn't Harph cast anti-magic?

Only then did I realize that Harph must have already been dead, therefore his spells didn't work anymore.

Which meant that everyone standing on the hill could now use their magic. The problem was, my mentor and I were the only ones still conscious in my little group. Granted, I could hear Litius groaning but he didn't count, anyway. My own powerful spells weren't even worth mentioning, especially seeing as Hunter was having a hard time.

As soon as the vine touched Janus' leg, it crumbled to dust. Of course. This was the Destroyer Avatar's universal protection at work. Hunter must have realized it too because he switched from damage spells to diversions.

He threw his hand high in the air. The ground in Janus' path rose up like a landmine exploding, throwing clods of earth in all directions. Immediately Hunter moved forward.

The Darkest One wasn't going to be caught out.

He twirled into the air like a dustdevil, avoiding the attack without as much as using his sword.

Hunter then tried a few more spells, including Blindness which I already knew (and which affected me this time as well), but Janus just grinned, dodging his every attempt. He seemed to be testing my mentor, trying to find the limits of his technical ability.

That was awful.

It's awful when you consider your mentor an expert and he turns out to be a common fighter compared to an invincible god incapable of either mercy or pity. A god who could afford being disdainful of common people.

Another awful thing was that by then, Hunter was completely exhausted. After only a few minutes of combat, he was already panting heavily. He was sweating like a pig, his damp clothes clinging to his body. Now I could see that he was in fact an old man: a retired Player who'd been round the block a few times. He had enjoyed a quiet life away from the Game and its problems until one of them had turned up on his doorstep — literally. And now he was forced to remember his old glory.

"Not bad," Janus said, outflanking him. "You're a much better fighter than Jisra used to be. He was writhing on the ground like a worm in the hope that I might spare his life."

Hunter gnashed his teeth and attacked. His sword swept through the air as he dealt a broad slashing blow. Janus promptly stepped to one side, dodging it, then tried to strike back. Hunter recoiled just in time. Janus' sword sliced through his sleeve. Blood, as red as the moon above us, dripped to the ground from Hunter's wounded shoulder.

The Darkest One shook his head. "Only human. Only a Player. You might be older than me but I am still stronger. A god is always stronger than a human being."

At this point, I realized that the tables had turned. The ugly grin came off Janus' face which was now furrowed with a fine web of lines. He stopped retreating — which earlier had made one believe he wasn't sure of the fight's outcome. His eyes turned cold, harsh and prickly, filled with his resolve to finish this drawn-out comedy.

He raised his sword and moved resolutely forward. Hunter managed to block his first blow with the flat of his sword, then dodged the second one at the very last moment. But Janus followed up with a powerful kick, throwing Hunter off balance and sending him head over heels.

He didn't get the chance to get back to his feet because Janus already towered over him. The Dark god raised his sword and with both hands brought it crashing down onto the empty ground.

"You're not serious, are you?" he said, his gaze following the flitting shadow. "Are you gonna keep on running away from me?"

He tore his attention away from the shadow and turned to me. The look in his eyes made my blood run cold. Suddenly I wished I was as far from here as possible.

He took a step toward me. And another one. And again.

Hunter unstealthed behind Janus' back and gave him an almighty blow. Lazily Janus turned and crossed swords with him. He then ducked to one side, dodging the attack, and sliced through my mentor's sword arm.

Gramr dropped to the ground. Hunter bent down to pick it back up but in this, too, Janus was faster.

"The Dark god with a Destroyer Avatar and the Light one with that of the Savior. The god who owns the great Gramr," Janus spoke in singsong. "You've fulfilled your destiny, old man. Now you can die in peace."

The sword which Hunter had had in his safekeeping for so long had now betrayed its keeper. Its impartial blade went halfway deep into his chest, slicing through his flesh. Gramr didn't care who it would serve, whether a Player or a God, a force of Dark or Light.

Hunter grabbed at the blade, trying to take a breath. His disheveled hair covered his face. I couldn't see his eyes, only the thin strip of his pursed lips and his figure frozen against his death throes — the figure of the man who'd tried to save me.

I remembered the Oracle's prophesy. *You'll die in your student's arms.* That was exactly what had happened. He was dead, and it was all my fault.

A wave of inexplicable all-consuming fury flooded over me. As long as I was alive, I could still turn this round.

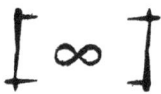

"...die in peace," the Darkest One said, lowering his sword.

He was too busy relishing his victory to notice

the most important thing. He didn't see me dart for dear life, cursing those wretched boots and my low Athletics stats. He didn't see me take an almighty leap, shielding Hunter with my own body.

I'd made my choice. Good or bad, it was mine alone.

Janus' sword softly slid down my belly, slicing through skin, ripping through my guts and exiting my back. As I dropped to the ground, so did Gramr which was now firmly stuck in my body.

Caught by surprise, Janus let go of the sword — which was so firmly lodged in my belly that it immediately changed its owner. Even though I wouldn't say that retrieving it would affect the outcome of the fight: the only way I could get it out would be by pulling my own guts out with it.

You've saved a Player who is neutral to you.

+100 karma points. Current level: +580. You gravitate to the Light Side.

You've sacrificed your life in order to save a Player who is neutral to you.

+500 karma points. Current level: +1080. You gravitate to the Light Side

New characteristic available: Hero of Light
Health: 23/60
Health: 21/60
Health: 20/60

I forced a crooked grin. I'd finally hit the 1000-point mark. You never know, it might come in handy after I die. They might let me through the pearly gates after all.

Then I remembered. Shit. There are no pearly gates. All there is, is Elisium with its wretched Archali and Firoll with its equally stupid Kabirids. The world has no place for Jewish fairy tales. I'll die now, and my ashes will be scattered all over Purgator. Then the Two Face will finish off the others, so that no one will ever find out what happened here. After which he'd move on to destroying all the nearest worlds because he'd now have the two strongest Divine Avatars which he can use at once.

"What a very commendable but silly thing to do," the Darkest One leaned over me. "The funny thing is, it's not gonna change anything. So you're a time master, are you? A boy who shot right to the top thanks to a chain of lucky coincidences. Who therefore believed himself to be above destiny. But in the end, everything fell back into place."

I struggled to peer at him but the world swam before my eyes. I could only make out a blurred spot where the Darkest One stood. There was no sky; no earth; just darkness which hugged me in its tightening embrace.

Oh well. At least it would give me a chance to look at death from the other side, so to say.

The darkness enveloped me completely; all I could still see was a thin strip of light right in front of me. I stood there waiting but nothing seemed to change.

Finally, I got bored and started walking toward it. Strangely enough, the light seemed to grow brighter. Even stranger, I felt no pain as I walked. I touched my stomach but found neither sword nor wound. Which meant I hadn't been teleported here. What was it, then?

Suddenly I realized what it reminded me of. My dream. It had been just like this. A path filled with darkness and desperation. The black mouth of a portal.

The realization made my whole body shudder as if electrocuted. So that's what it looked like? Until now, I'd had no idea what this black portal was. Was it like a tunnel which a Player could pass through? What was the problem, then, and why was I so uncomfortable here?

Never mind. It would have to wait. If this was the portal, then I was about to face the Choruls. Wasn't it ironic that I would only see them just before I died? You never know, I might even find out their true nature. Because for some reason, it looked like my life had been closely connected to them.

I started running. And this was the strangest thing I'd ever experienced in my life. My feet felt as if they were being sucked into something spongy while my body was still moving. It made me think of the Red Queen's race on the spot from Lewis Carroll's *Through the Looking-Glass.*

And still the light was getting brighter, the figures far in front more tangible with my every step. There were three of them, just like in my dream. But I'd hoped for too much: I couldn't make out their faces from under their broad hoods. I wasn't destined to discern their race.

"Am I dead now?" I asked the one in the middle.

"No. And I hope you're gonna do everything you can to avoid it."

The speaker's voice sounded human, even though I couldn't be sure of anything anymore. It also seemed calm and leveled, giving me the impression that we were mundanely discussing the best water temperature for making green tea.

"In that case, how is it I'm able to talk to you?" I asked, feeling the anxiety disappear from my voice. It would be weird to scream and freak out with such imperturbable company.

"Let's put it this way: we can control time, to a degree. So now we've paused it in order to speak to you."

"Does that mean that I'm still over there, dying?"

"If you're talking about your physical body, then yes, it's critically close to shutting down. Humans usually call that death."

"You could have just as easily said 'yes'."

"All right, then. Yes."

"But in that case-"

"You have to survive," he went on.

"Why?"

"Because too much has been put at stake for you. You're the one who can either plunge reality into the kind of chaos it has never seen before, or bring all the worlds back into equilibrium. We tend to err on the latter. The Chorul you killed went willingly to his death in order that you inherit his power. Once that happened, the worlds came back into balance."

"It's too complicated," I grabbed at my head in a gesture all the more comical because I couldn't possibly have a headache here. Or any other kinds of aches and pains, for that matter. "What's in it for you? You seem to keep yourselves to yourselves."

"Any planet — or a world, as you call them — makes up part of a single Multiverse. The disappearance of a stone in Cesspit might change the direction of a trade route in Elisium. The murder of a Queen in Purgator does affect the distribution of royal court positions in Noggle. And something as petty as a mechanoid's rusty joint might-"

"I got it, I got it. The flap of a butterfly's wing can cause a tsunami on the other side of the world."

"You could say that," he agreed eagerly. "In any case, with time you'll understand everything. Some things you'll find out yourself, and some we'll tell you. But not yet."

"Okay, okay. Now I need to survive despite being disemboweled by a Divine sword. I have less than 30% Health left. Do you really think it's possible?"

'When you finally become a wise and experienced Seeker, you'll know that even the most improbable things are in fact quite doable. Depending on the angle from which you look at them."

"All this is great but please let's leave all these expensive notions for some other time. Let's focus on the problems at hand. Like how can I survive."

"Use that which Two-Face is after. It's not for nothing he's been waiting for it to resurface all this time."

I didn't get the chance to reply. I still had a gazillion questions to ask them, dammit! Still, they must have decided they'd done their bit for today. Their figures started to blur. The darkness began to fall apart, revealing patches of light. I was going back, that little was perfectly clear.

The far-off white noise turned into the mocking voice of Jan. My belly was almost exploding with pain.

Two-Face was leaning over me, holding the

sword by the hilt, and whispered something jeeringly into my face. Still, I had neither the strength nor the time to listen to him.

Instead, I checked my interface, desperately scrolling through my stats, until I finally saw it.

The Avatar. In fact, it looked like a white wax mask like those used on theater logos. Nothing too fancy; it was mesmerizing in its simplicity.

It hung suspended in the air. The one worn by the Savior. The one that had made him what he was. The one that had allowed him to work miracles.

The one which, if the Chorul were to be believed, might save me.

I had only one choice. I had only one chance.

I reached out for the white mask and put it on.

Interlude

A Good Day to Die

THE CHORUL TOOK in a chestful of freezing cold air and closed his eyes. Suddenly he saw himself as a little boy all those years ago. A three-year-old child, staring in surprise at the white sheet covering the ground, catching large slow snowflakes with his mouth.

"You don't have to do what the Ephet says," a woman's voice snatched him back from his reverie.

She stood right in front of him: anxious, freezing and in a foul mood.

"The Ephet's words reveal the will of all the others," the Chorul replied calmly. "And they're right. The council is unanimous in regards of this matter."

"But don't you understand? It means you're gonna die!"

"We're all gonna die someday. Even gods are mortal. Whether you live for a year, or ten years, or

435

even a thousand, the outcome is always the same. The question is, how our death can affect the lives of others."

"But why do you have to leave me?" she flew at him with clenched fists.

He patiently restrained her, but she showed no intention of attacking him any further. Instead, she burst into tears on his chest. "What am I supposed to do?"

"You? You'll only become the greatest and most powerful of all the Choruls. One day, you're gonna replace one of the Ephets. Or you might go to some other worlds where we're needed."

They stood there for a long time — if you could use such a term with creatures for whom time is just a notion. Finally, the Chorul eased himself away.

"I'll see you by the Gates in half an hour," he said.

"I'm already there," she replied sadly.

"I can see that," he gave her a hint of a smile, then headed off.

DeKhat whom they'd snatched from the clutches of the civil war and brought here to the safe haven of Archaeth, was busy whirring his gear wheels. Six steel spidery legs carried him around the room with a seemingly instantaneous ease while his perfectly human hands carried out any task with the utmost dexterity. Now DeKhat was busy with the charmed cube from the ruins of the Fortress of Hamerito which had been destroyed four thousand years ago in the world of Lotver.

"Oh hi," the mechanoid cheered up at the sight of a visitor. "Did you see what they brought me? It's just as powerful as a quarter of an ounce of tartum from the central world. If it goes up, it'll be curtains."

"DeKhat, I've come to get my order."

"Sure, sure. I'll go get it straight away. If only I had more time! Then again, what do you care, hehe! But not everyone can afford to lead such unlinear *lives* as you do..." his voice trailed away as he realized the significance of the visit. "Wait a sec. Are you... are you *leaving*?"

"I am indeed."

"By the holy crocuses of Velchoir, is it that time already? I didn't expect it to happen so soon. No, please don't get me wrong. Every Chorul must be ready to leave on their last voyage. You guys seem to take it for granted, so I-"

"Sorry, DeKhat, but I need my order."

"Yes, yes, of course," the mechanoid dashed into a room next door on his spidery legs. The Chorul heard the crashing of things falling to the ground.

Soon the mechanoid reemerged with a small cloth bundle in his hands. "Here's what you asked for. Perfectly adaptable to the wearer's level. For a middle-class mage. I could have made it stronger, you know, that way you'd have had God-class clothes. You know that our facilities are good enough for that now."

"That's a bit over the top," the Chorul said. "It's good as it is. Thanks a lot, DeKhat."

"Wait," the mechanoid jerked toward him and proffered his hand. "Good luck."

The Chorul shook his hand and walked out. He could sense dozens of pairs of eyes upon him. He even knew who was looking at him. Still, he didn't look back. Calmly he continued toward the far Gatehouse where the girl was already waiting for him.

The Gatehouse was always deserted as the portal led only to a few underdeveloped worlds. Cesspit was one of them.

The Chorul removed his clothes unhurriedly, exposing his strong muscular body. He neatly folded his things and lay them down beside him, shuddering as his bare feet touched the stone beneath. Unpleasant.

"Can you cast some clothes for me?" he asked the girl. "You know I'm not big on magic."

She was almost crying, the tears threatening to drip from her long eyelashes. Still, she did as he'd bidden her, handing him an ordinary long hooded cloak and a pair of high boots.

The naked man got dressed, hid a blade in his sleeve and picked up the bundle and a small mirror.

"No pants, but a great cloak," he joked.

"What am I gonna do now?" the girl stopped trying to conceal the tears which rolled down her cheeks.

The Chorul walked over to her and gave her a warm sympathetic hug, gentle but brotherly. Then he eased himself away. "Please go now. It'll be better that way."

She looked at him one last time, turned round and walked away in an unstable, almost drunken gait, sniffing her nose. Her shoulders heaved.

With a heavy sigh, the Chorul turned to the Gatekeeper. "I need to go to Cesspit, to a place called Threshold."

"You know that this Gate doesn't have a return option, do you?"

"I know. Security measure. But I don't intend to come back."

"Your last voyage?" the Gatekeeper asked.

For a moment, the Chorul got the impression that the Gatekeeper's voice betrayed a hint of sympathy. He nodded. "I have traveled a lot between worlds and I often wondered who Gatekeepers really were. But I couldn't find the answer anywhere. Maybe you can tell me? Now. Just before my last voyage. Who are you?"

"We are the spawn of the Game. We are those who brought it into being. We are the ones it needs."

"That's too generic, I'm afraid. Are you Players?"

"We used to be. And then... we just became Gatekeepers. We're a bit like you, to an extent."

"Only we find ourselves at opposite poles."

"No," the Gatekeeper slowly shook his head. "If anything, our understanding of reality is on a different plane. You believe that the worlds need equilibrium. We place our hopes on the connectivity within the interworld network, whatever it might bring. That's the difference between us."

"No good me trying to compete with your rhetoric."

The armor-clad giant nodded. "That would be rather imprudent."

"Let's leave it till later, then. It's time for me to leave."

"As you wish, Chorul."

The Gatekeeper reached under his armor, produced a pinch of dust and threw it onto the stone. Instead of dropping, the dust hung suspended in the air and started moving, gradually gaining momentum.

The Chorul touched the altar, as did the armor-clad creature opposite him. The next moment, the silence of the constantly overcast Archaeth was shattered by the pandemonium of Cesspit.

The Gate was different. The exit the Chorul used wasn't one of those in the Community, either. He stepped out into a deserted little lane and paused to find his bearings, then strode confidently toward the Order.

Prague met him with a wave of chilly air. Still, he didn't feel the cold, his mind focused on other things. He had to think what to say to the Grand Master. He was neither worried nor anxious about their conversation because he already knew how it was going to turn out. He'd already seen it. As the Choruls say, he'd "already finished the conversation without saying a word".

The Order occupied an age-old three-story building guarded by regular humans — trained professionals sworn to secrecy. The fencing master Oliverio — one of the Magister's closest confidants — stood with them too. The group reacted to his arrival with suppressed anxiety. Although no one had said a word, he could see they were awaiting explanations.

"I need to see the Grand Master."

"Who are you?" Oliverio sized him up.

"I'm a Chorul. I am the voice of Ephet 76, from Archaeth."

That seemed to be sufficient. Oliverio nodded and disappeared inside. He hadn't stood the guards at ease though, so they continued to stare at the strange man in the hooded cloak.

The Chorul waited patiently, staring at the large cobblestones, until Oliverio re-emerged.

"The Grand Master will see you now."

Oliverio showed him inside the lavishly decorated building, past dozens of Seers who stared at the Chorul in surprised curiosity. They walked through two rooms and into a third where the head of the Order was sitting.

"Chorul," the man said in surprise. He was fit and tanned. "Fancy seeing you here! Have you come to tell me something?"

"There're lots of things I'd like to tell you. For example, that in order to confuse me, you decided to see me here and not upstairs as usual. I could also tell you that the Magister is now listening into our every word in the secret room next door. Or I could tell you that I've arrived with an important proposition, next to which all your little tricks would pale into insignificance. So what do you want me to tell you, Numa?"

On hearing his name, the Grand Master jumped. His real name, which had been lost through the millennia and buried within these ancient city walls destroyed by the Visigoths. Even his closest entourage who'd been with him during the fall of the Empire and had followed him through all the Crusades and hundred-year wars didn't know it, either.

"Leave us!" the Grand Master shouted. "You too, Oliverio!"

The Chorul heard rustling coming from behind the wall, then the fading sound of footsteps. Apparently, Oliverio didn't dare contradict his boss.

"I knew that Choruls were powerful. But this..."

"Yes, we're powerful enough not to be affected

by flattery. Now we should get down to business."

The Chorul spoke unhurriedly for a long time. The Grand Master who had once been called Numa listened patiently, occasionally trying to butt in. Every time he did so, the man in the cloak raised a commanding finger and continued elaborating on his plan: step by step, word by word.

When he finally stopped, the Grand Master of the Order of Seers couldn't speak for a long time.

"This is... atrocious," he finally whispered.

"It's a necessary sacrifice."

"Half of my Order a necessary sacrifice?!"

"Not half. Only a few dozen. It's either them or the whole of Cesspit. The moment the Time Master manifests himself here, so will the Darkest One."

"Well, then we need to make sure this snotnose doesn't turn up!"

"Too late. It's already been destined, so it can't happen any other way. All we can do now is try to alleviate the consequences."

"But many of them are just stupid young boys!"

"it's a few dozen lives in exchange for millions. I'm afraid the ratio isn't in their favor. Just try to convince Oliverio not to hinder the murderer. He shouldn't predict anything."

The Grand Master hung his head. "What a terrible sacrifice..."

"I'm sacrificing myself," the Chorul replied.

He rose and walked out, considering their conversation over. Because it really was over. He knew that the Grand Master was going to make the right choice. If he didn't, his life would lose all meaning. Who would need Seers without Players? And who would need Players without commoners?

Now the Chorul headed for the local Community, one of the oldest in Europe. Shop signs flitted before his eyes, advertising wizards, battle mages, alchemists, summoners, sorcerers, journeymen and master blacksmiths, precision jewelers and archeologists. Every nook and cranny were packed with cages containing all kinds of fantastical beasts. Flying ports circled the sky: the airfield was just down the road from the city.

But above all, the streets were crowded with every race imaginable from Noggle to Lemstein, including mechanoids from the wretched Dump and even crocodile men, the most cunning and merciless among their kind.

The Chorul walked indifferently past all this, hiding his face deeper under his hood. He wasn't interested in the wondrous beasts nor in the powerful spells. The rare races didn't catch his eye; the worlds they inhabited didn't attract him. The aromas escaping the doors of the many bars and eateries didn't tempt him, either.

The Chorul stopped by a building so wide and shapeless that it resembled a blob of dough. He checked the sign of Gatekeepers over the door: the circle lined with a fine weave of runes and crisscrossed with a complex pattern of straight lines.

The Chorul pulled the door open.

"*Sorrow*," he said to the Gatekeeper as he placed some dust into the bowl.

As usual, the moment of the teleporting happened so fast that he couldn't tell whether he was here or there. Still, he had no doubts he'd arrived. He wrapped his cloak tighter around himself and walked outside.

He could hear the clinking of bottles in the house two doors down, accompanied by a rough male voice whose owner could only have come from Noggle. The Chorul shook his head, then headed toward the Community gate.

He boarded a bus and perched himself on a seat by the window. He wasn't afraid of arousing anybody's curiosity. To the untrained eye, he was just a skinny college student in drab gray clothes. The conductor herself just walked past without even noticing him.

The Chorul stared out of the window at the wintry city, apprehensively huddling itself against the cold. A yet-unknown wave of peaceful sadness swept over him, so untypical for creatures whose fate had already been decided.

Consumed by it, he very nearly missed his stop. The street was almost deserted, which was probably a good thing. The Chorul walked past the car factory, studying the area. The industrial zone, then the woodland park and the faint trail that snaked through it.

The Chorul produced the bundle and laid it onto the trail. He then stepped off it and hid behind a tree.

He didn't have long to wait. A little demon came skipping and hopping on all fours along the trail, apparently heading for his lair. Suddenly he stopped and started sniffing the air until he detected the bundle.

The demon walked over to it on his hoofed hind legs in a very human-like manner, then dropped back to all fours. He touched the bundle gingerly with a finger and promptly snatched it away, as if afraid of the object hurting him. After some deliberation, the demon scooped up the bundle and pressed it to his chest.

The Chorul emerged from behind the tree and gave a short whistle. The demon pricked up his ears and swung toward his unseen enemy, clinging to the ground as if deliberating what to do next.

The Chorul produced his moon-steel knife and gave another whistle, sharp and loud. The demon darted off with his trophy.

The Chorul walked back to the bus stop, certain that the trench coat would now end up in the demons' lair.

After a while, a shiny brand-new bus arrived. Its doors swung open in silent welcome. Once again no one noticed him, except for an old lady who swore at him for no particular reason. Just a nasty old hag — then again, she might have indeed been a witch. There was no way of telling.

In any case, he reached his destination without any further problems. To the right of the bridge, the traffic wasn't moving but here, the road was still more or less free. Just as he'd been told.

He got off the bus and spent some time looking around trying to find his bearings. He wasn't sure whether this was the right place. A corner shop, a shawarma joint, then a street heading off to the dormitory highrises. He'd arrived.

The Chorul walked unhurriedly. He still had plenty of time.

The night had descended too quickly, as always at the start of winter. Slowly the drab glow of the streetlights grew brighter. The temperature dropped.

The Time Master

The passersby's breath misted as they shuddered in their thin autumn jackets. Even the dog that fearlessly ran past him kept his tail firmly between his legs, focusing only on finding a nice warm shelter for the night.

The cold practically didn't bother the Chorul: his charmed clothes, the work of a powerful wizard, did their job well. He walked confidently until he came to a five-story apartment block which loomed in front of him. He walked around it, peered in one of the windows and smiled at something known only to him.

Then he headed confidently to one of the front doors.

A frail old man in a funny knitted cap was shuffling his feet against the cold next to the entry system by the front door. He nodded to the Chorul, forcing him to nod back.

The Chorul walked over to the door and punched in the code required by its security system. He then climbed to the right floor and rang the bell by the door he needed. But first, he'd shrugged off his hood.

"Hello, Hunter," he said when the door had opened.

"Who are you? And how do you know me?" asked the fit albeit middle-aged man who'd answered the door.

"I'm a Chorul. I need to talk to you."

"A Chorul. I see," the man drawled sarcastically. "Now listen to me, *Chorul*. If you ever as much as come here again, I'll kick you down the stairs. If you need me, leave a note at the Community. I'll make sure I get it. Bye now."

The man attempted to shut the door but the Chorul jammed his foot in it. "I really need to speak to you, Kefal."

The man's face erupted in dark spots. "So you *are* a Chorul, are you? Wait a sec," he grabbed a jacket off the coat rack and hurried to change out of his house slippers into a pair of winter boots. "I'll just pop out to the shop," he shouted to someone in the apartment.

They walked downstairs in silence and left the building, bypassing the funny old boy. Then they headed down into the maze of the city's dormitory tower blocks with their worn-out roads and shattered curbstones.

Finally, Hunter spoke,

"You couldn't find out my name from anyone. Everybody that ever knew it is already dead."

"We Choruls have access to all kinds of strange information. If we focus and want it hard enough, we can find out everything about any Player."

"What do you want from me?"

"Your life."

"You gonna kill me?"

"No, no. You read too much into what I said. I don't need your death. I need your life. What keeps you here?"

"You know everything, you tell me."

The Chorul nodded. "Your wife. But she's only a pale shadow of your Procris. As were all the other women before her. Nothing but failed attempts to replace Thespius' daughter."

"So what do you propose?"

"I'd like you to become a mentor for a very young man who's about to face lots of tribulations."

"I stopped doing that sort of thing a long time ago."

"I know. Ever since your sons died. How old were they in Earth time?"

"In Earth time? Haesper was six hundred and eighteen. Adumnis, just over a thousand. They didn't want to become Players. They were very angry about my decision."

"And still they lived such long lives. Not by your standards, of course, but still. Now a lot hangs on your decision. I'm not going to force you to take the right step, I'm just gonna tell you its potential consequences. Both what will happen if everything goes to plan, as well as if it doesn't..."

The Chorul spoke for a long time. Hunter listened attentively. His wizened face frowned as he looked at the intruder who was trying to turn his well-ordered life upside down.

"So the Oracle was right," he finally said.

"It all depends on you. Everything always depends on one's choice."

"But not in your case."

"Why not?" the Chorul sounded surprised. "I too have made my choice. Which is to die today. This is the only way to save our worlds and bring about some kind of order to them instead of the all-consuming chaos."

"How much can I tell him?"

"Everything you think necessary. I should feed him information in small doses, if I were you. That would allow Sergei to work things out in his own head. That way, he might get smarter quicker. And it's high time he got a bit smarter."

"You might be right. It actually might be the reason for my existence, you never know. I've lost all purpose a long time ago."

"You're no different from any other Player who's lived to be over a thousand. Same applies to quite a few *gods*," the Chorul stressed the last word but Hunter didn't seem to notice. Or at least pretended not to.

"Very well. I agree."

"Take this," the Chorul offered him the small mirror and the knife. "I want you to give these to him."

They parted company in silence. No words were necessary. They just shook hands and went their own ways. Hunter took the road back home while the Chorul headed for a small supermarket on the outskirts.

He came across little Boris just in time. Which couldn't have been otherwise, of course. The boy was just about to head home because his time outdoors was coming to an end.

"Hi, Boris," the Chorul said, investing every ounce of friendliness into his voice.

"Hi," the boy said hesitatingly.

"On your way home?"

"Yeah."

"For sure you don't know where I know you from?"

Uncertain, the boy shook his head.

"I'm your guardian wizard. I've been watching you for a long time. I know that you go to that school over there. You Mom's called Lydia, and your Dad's name is Victor. You've got a little brother but he's still very young. He's only just been born. And I also know," the Chorul dropped his voice to a conspiratorial whisper, "last winter you and other boys went rafting.

And you fell in the water. The other boys started a bonfire to warm you up and dry your stuff out. Your Mom never even found out."

The boy's eyes opened wide. "How do you know?"

"I already told you I'm your guardian wizard. I know everything about you."

"Wizard, yeah right! Pull the other one!"

The Chorul raised his hand by way of reply. His fingers sparkled as if ablaze. This was only a cheap trick in his vast arsenal of spells but it worked wonders with the boy.

"Would you like to become a wizard?" the Chorul asked.

The boy nodded vigorously. "You bet!"

"Come with me, then."

"My Mom's waiting for me," the boy said uncertainly.

"It's all right. Your neighbor will come and get you in a moment. Uncle Sergei."

He tugged the boy's hand. Obediently Boris trotted along.

The Chorul had no idea what was on the boy's mind. He wasn't a mind reader, after all. But everything went according to plan. The Chorul knew exactly what to say because he knew it all. He'd already said all this before. It felt now as if he'd just remembered it. Easy.

They crossed the road and walked over to the foundation pit. The boy cast a scared look behind him as if doubting his decision. Once again the Chorul had to resort to magic and show him another trick in order to distract him from his current train of thought.

"There down below is a great place for magic,"

the Chorul lied. "Come on, let's go. There's nothing to be afraid of."

They climbed down into the foundations. The boy kept looking back. You didn't have to be a Seer to feel his fear. To a certain extent, the Chorul couldn't help blaming himself for inflicting such an unpleasant feeling onto such a tiny defenseless creature. But there was nothing he could do about it. He'd made his choice.

Until Sergei's arrival, the Chorul whiled away the time casting spells for the boy: from the simplest ones that any newbie wizard could do to some quite serious Destruction magic, as effective as it was spectacular. The boy had almost lost his nervousness when the Chorul froze.

The time had come.

"Whatever happens, don't be afraid. Take this," he shoved something into the boy's pocket.

"Boris! Boris!" a voice came from above.

"That's Uncle Sergei," the Chorul whispered. "Answer him."

"I'm down here!"

"Boris, where are you?"

The Chorul heard the sound of falling clumps of frozen earth. The winter had only just begun so there wasn't much snow around.

Finally he could make out the approaching figure: a stocky half-blood Korl in an unbuttoned jacket, holding a flimsy plastic shopping bag. Although the Chorul had "seen" the man before, he couldn't suppress a smile.

"Hey, what's going on, dude?" the Korl paused, then headed toward them. "Don't make me do something I'll regret."

The half-Korl laid his shopping bag on the ground, still reluctant to attack him. The Chorul already knew that the man wasn't the bravest of souls and he would need some encouragement.

"Man, get away from the kid."

Now was really the time. The Chorul reached out his hand, casting Telekinesis.

His opponent flew several yards away and landed on his shopping bag and its meager food supply. Or rather, his alcohol supply, judging by all the clinking.

Grunting, the Korl was struggling on the ground, trying to get back to his feet. For a moment, the Chorul thought it had been a bad idea. Still, he immediately shook off every doubt. This half-blood Player was capable of making his journey. He had to. The weight of responsibility was entirely on his shoulders.

The hardest thing was to offer himself to the blow. The Chorul closed his eyes the second before the fiery jet from the aerosol can burned his face. The edges of his cloak caught fire, singing his skin. He had to use his hands to smother the flames a little.

That's when he felt the blow.

It was actually very weak — a joke really. Still, the Chorul had taken up exactly the right position. The one he was meant to do. There was a large rock right under his feet, over which he was supposed to stumble. And a bit further on lay a sharp stone which his head was meant to hit.

The Chorul knew. He'd already seen it.

Everything happened quickly. His skull cracked against the rock's sharp edge. The Chorul was still alive but his mind was gradually fading, merging with the black sky.

It was a good day to die. A good day to fulfil a plan. A good day to make your own choice.

The Chorul closed his eyes and died.

End of Book One

Want to be the first to know about our latest LitRPG, sci fi and fantasy titles from your favorite authors?

Subscribe to our *New Releases* newsletter:
http://eepurl.com/b7niIL

Thank you for reading *The Time Master!*
If you like what you've read, check out other LitRPG,
fantasy and science fiction novels published by Magic
Dome Books:

Level Up LitRPG series by Dan Sugralinov:
Re-Start
Hero
The Final Trial
Level Up: The Knockout (with Max Lagno)

The Way of the Shaman LitRPG series
by Vasily Mahanenko:
Survival Quest
The Kartoss Gambit
The Secret of the Dark Forest
The Phantom Castle
The Karmadont Chess Set
Shaman's Revenge
Clans War

Dark Paladin LitRPG series by Vasily Mahanenko:
The Beginning
The Quest
Restart

Galactogon LitRPG series by Vasily Mahanenko:
Start the Game!
In Search of the Uldans

The Bard from Barliona LitRPG series
by Eugenia Dmitrieva and Vasily Mahanenko:
The Renegades
A Song of Shadow

The Neuro LitRPG series by Andrei Livadny:
The Crystal Sphere
The Curse of Rion Castle
The Reapers

Point Apocalypse (a near-future action thriller)
by Alex Bobl

The Game Master series by A. Bobl and A. Levitsky:
The Lag

AlterGame LitRPG series by Andrew Novak:
The First Player
On the Lost Continent
God Mode

Citadel World series by Kir Lukovkin:
The URANUS Code
The Secret of Atlantis

The Expansion (The History of the Galaxy) series by A.
Livadny:
Blind Punch
The Shadow of Earth
Servobattalion

The Sublime Electricity series by Pavel Kornev
The Illustrious
The Heartless
The Fallen
The Dormant

You're in Game! Books 1 and 2
(LitRPG Stories from Bestselling Authors)

Captive of the Shadows (Tne Fairy Code Book #1)
by Kaitlyn Weiss

Moskau by G. Zotov
(a dystopian thriller)

El Diablo by G.Zotov
(a supernatural thriller)

[1] The history of the Communist Party of the Soviet Union: an obligatory subject in all Russian colleges and universities from 1938 to 1991.

[2] "Symposium" is a play on words: the Latin word "symposium", which these days stands for a scientific conference, used to mean "a drunken party" in Roman days.

[3] These are names of Russian TV shows. Vremya (Time), Vesti (Tidings), and Novosti (News) are news programs; Comedy Club is an entertainment show.

[4] During shortages in the Soviet Union, furniture from Czechoslovakia was valued. Anyone who had any was considered rather well-off.

[5] When people reach military age in Russia, sometimes they illegally purchase a military card to avoid serving in the army.

[6] Alexei Leonov, a Soviet cosmonaut who completed the first spacewalk on March 18, 1965.

[7] Shawarma is a Middle Eastern dish that is popular in Russia. It contains pieces of chopped meat and vegetables rolled in lavash bread.

[8] Leave the Twilight! — a reference to the bestselling Night Watch urban fantasy series by Russian author Sergei Lukyanenko. This is a phrase uttered by the Night Watch members to challenge and expel the forces of the Dark from the city streets.

[9] FSB: Federal Security Service, the Russian counter-intelligence office

[10] Employment record book: in Russia, a small notebook the size of a passport used to keep record of the person's professional activities throughout their life. All legal employers are under obligation to enter relevant records in their workers' employment books, including any pay raises, promotions, professional achievements, incidents of professional misconduct, etc. It serves several purposes, like allowing their next employer to see their entire career at a glance or helping to calculate their pension once they retire. Currently, the Russian government is planning to abolish traditional employment books, creating a single electronic database instead.

[11] Gorokhovets (pronounced goh-roh-hoh-VETS): one

of the oldest towns in Russia dating back to the 6th century A.D.

[12] In Russia, the low intellectual level and bad taste of most TV shows have led to a situation where many progressive Russians don't watch TV at all. Many don't even own a TV set, preferring to use the Internet instead.

[13] "Wanna do a three-way split?" — traditionally in Russia, three alcoholics would club together to buy a half-liter bottle of vodka (about 0.5 quart) which was considered enough to go round for three people. So it's quite common for one or two drunkards to approach strangers looking for a third person willing to share both the expense and the drink.

[14] Sweetened condensed milk is very popular in Russia, making the base for a multitude of delicious desserts.

[15] STS: a Russian entertainment channel specializing in sitcoms.

[16] REN-TV is a Russian entertainment channel known for its many programs on conspiracy theories and UFOs.

[17] TNT is an entertainment channel specializing in comedy programs, usually of the slapstick variety.

[18] Channel One and Rossiya (Russia) broadcast many political and analysis programs.

[19] Two thousand Russian rubles is about $30

[20] In Greek mythology, King Acrisius was warned by the Oracle at Delphi that he would one day be killed by his own grandson. Acrisius then locked his daughter Danaë up in a bronze chamber for fear of the prophesy coming true. Still, Danaë got pregnant from Zeus and had a hero son called Perseus who, many valorous feats later, took part in sports games where he accidentally killed his grandfather by hitting him on the head with a badly-aimed discus, thus fulfilling the prophesy.

[21] Samy Naceri: French actor known for his performance in four of the *Taxi* films.

[22] Chelyabinsk (Russia): a major industrial center in the Ural Mountains suffering from pollution and heavy smog

[23] RPG: a Rocket Propelled Grenade

In order to have new books of the series translated faster, we need your help and support! Please consider leaving a review or spread the word by recommending *The Time Master* to your friends and posting the link on social media. The more people buy the book, the sooner we'll be able to make new translations available.

Thank you!

Till next time!

www.ingramcontent.com/pod-product-compliance
Lightning Source LLC
Chambersburg PA
CBHW060759030726
47503CB00002B/311